A Duke Changes Everything

Nick looked at the dark drop of honey on her skin and his mouth watered. He licked his lips and looked into her eyes. The heat there made him want more. More moments like this with her. When there was no Enderley boxing them in, no duties that needed their attention. Just Mina and the odd, undeniable spark he'd felt between them from the day he arrived.

"I'd like a taste," he told her quietly.

Mina bit her lip, and her brows dipped in concentration. She locked her gaze on his mouth and seemed to hold her breath as she slid a honeyed finger across his lower lip.

Nick swept his tongue out to taste and reached for her hand. Flavor burst inside his mouth in a shock of floral sweetness.

"Delicious," he whispered before leaning closer, flicking his tongue out, and tasting the tip of her finger once more. "But I honestly can't tell whether it's you or the honey."

By Christy Carlyle

A DUKE CHANGES EVERYTHING

The Duke's Den

CHRISTY CARLYLE

AVONBOOKS

An Imprint of HarperCollinsPublishers

A DUKE CHANGES EVERYTHING. Copyright © 2018 by Christy Carlyle. All rights reserved. Printed in the United States of America. No part of this book may be used or reproduced in any manner whatsoever without written permission except in the case of brief quotations embodied in critical articles and reviews. For information, address HarperCollins Publishers, 195 Broadway, New York, NY 10007.

First Avon Books mass market printing: December 2018

Print Edition ISBN: 978-0-06-285395-0
Digital Edition ISBN: 978-0-06-285396-7

Cover illustration by Jon Paul Ferrara

Avon, Avon & logo, and Avon Books & logo are registered trademarks of HarperCollins Publishers in the United States of America and other countries.

HarperCollins is a registered trademark of HarperCollins Publishers in the United States of America and other countries.

FIRST EDITION

18 19 20 21 22 QGM 10 9 8 7 6 5 4 3 2 1

To my husband, John. In my life, your love and support have truly changed everything. And to my editor, Elle, for brilliant insight and support and for giving me so many amazing opportunities.

Acknowledgments

Love, appreciation, and a thousand thanks go out to Darcy, Lana, Erica, Christina, Megan, Jan, Karen, Charis, Cynthia, and my agent, Jill, for feedback about this book from the earliest kernel of an idea through the writing process. The faults in execution are, of course, only my own, but your insights were never faulty. And your thoughtfulness was always appreciated. Thanks too to Monique for amazing insights.

Heartfelt thanks too to everyone at Avon who touched this book as it moved from proposal through to production.

Most of all, enormous gratitude to my readers, whether this is the first book of mine you've ever given a chance or if you've followed me for story after story. Thank you.

A DUKE CHANGES EVERYTHING

Chapter One

London, August 1844
Lyon's Gentlemen's Club, downstairs

*Y*ou know why I've come, Lyon."

"I know you're wasting your time." Nicholas Lyon waited, hoping the man would accept his fate and retreat. "My answer hasn't changed."

"Monster."

The man spat the word under his breath, but Nick heard the whispered curse. He'd been called as much before, and far worse.

"There are advantages to being a monster," he told his visitor.

Nick had come to think of his villainous reputation as a unique brand of freedom. He did as he pleased, and no matter how badly he behaved, no one could ever claim surprise or disappointment.

Of course, the gasps of horror and curious stares when strangers caught sight of his mismatched eyes—

one green, one blue—and the jagged scar bisecting the left half of his face were vexing.

Strangers assumed his deeds would match his mien.

But down here in the darkness, in the bowels of the gambling emporium he'd built, his looks weren't what men feared. They feared how much they needed him. They feared his refusal. Yet they still came. Impulse drove gamblers downstairs again and again, an endless march of loss-prone noblemen petitioning for cash.

In the belly of Lyon's Gentlemen's Club, Nick discovered the bliss of being master of his own domain. To exert control, he simply replied with an unbending *no*.

Two letters. A single breath. So much power.

Let those he refused think him cruel. Once he made a decision, he never yielded, no matter how much they bellowed.

The aristocrat currently hovering at the front of Nick's desk looked as if he might combust.

Cheeks flaming a splotchy red, Lord Calvert clenched pudgy bejeweled fingers into fists until his knuckles cracked. He didn't argue or demand, as others did. Instead, he stood in grim silence. Until a noise burst free. A whine that built to a roar, like the unholy wail of a dying beast.

Nick recognized the sound. He'd felt the same bellow of agony claw its way up his own throat a time or two.

Loss. Disappointment. Devastation.

He understood misery, but his determination didn't falter. When it came to business, Nick's instincts rarely failed him.

"A hundred pounds," the nobleman wheezed, barely able to speak past clenched teeth. "Seventy-five?"

"We aren't negotiating."

"You've ruined me, Lyon." Balding head bowed, Calvert sucked in a ragged breath and exhaled as if the effort hurt. "Give me a chance to win back what I've lost."

"You've ruined yourself." Nick pulled out a drawer, gesturing at the row of neatly arranged documents inside. "I hold an alphabet of your vowels. What else could you possibly have to barter?"

He didn't intend for Calvert to answer. Whatever the nobleman offered, he wouldn't extend more credit.

Here, in an unadorned room next to his private quarters, Nick acquired true wealth. Players called it the Lyon's Den.

When gamblers needed ready cash, he offered loans at moderate interest with a requirement for collateral. That was where real bounty was to be found—in artwork, antiquities, and the unentailed pieces of property that aristocrats wagered and lost. Like a pirate hoarding his loot, Nick had assembled a sizable portfolio of assets in five years.

He couldn't say which he relished more. Owning rambling country estates he'd never visit or ruining arrogant noblemen.

"Take this." Calvert wrenched a ruby ring from his index finger. "No loan. Just pay me what it's worth."

Nick never shifted his gaze from the man's desperate eyes. "I don't want your baubles." Who did the nobleman think he was? Some pawnbroker from the East End stews?

As the viscount's bloodshot gaze registered a flicker of shock, his demeanor shifted. He stretched tall, settling back on his heels. Whiskered chin notched high above drooping jowls, Calvert sneered. "How dare you turn your nose up at my family's history? This ring was given to my ancestor by Queen Elizabeth herself." Sniffing in that haughty way every aristocrat had perfected, he added, "I know where you come from, Lyon. Your own father thought you were a by-blow. What would you know of honor and nobility?"

"Not a damn thing." Nick shot the man a tight grin and shrugged off the slight. "I don't care about your history, or mine." Rising from the chair behind his desk, he faced the viscount, feet planted wide. "In this room, in *my* club, your title means nothing. And my answer remains the same. No more loans."

"You bloody bastard."

Nick's smile stoked Calvert's anger. The paunchy man lumbered forward as if to strike.

"Anything amiss here, gentlemen?" As usual, Aidan Iverson possessed impeccable timing.

Nick's business partner and one-quarter owner of Lyon's pushed the door open and stepped into the room. He stood several heads above most men, and when the bulky redhead planted himself next to Calvert, the aristocrat's bluster withered.

"You're banned." No one could be allowed to threaten the only possession that truly mattered to Nick.

"May I call you a hansom, my lord?" Iverson's deep voice was so smooth, his accent so polished, none would guess he'd grown up in London's worst slum.

"The matter doesn't end here, Lyon." Calvert's glare

narrowed his eyes to menacing slits. "You may hold my vowels, but never doubt that I shall find a way to make you pay."

Threats were as plentiful in Nick's life as the gold coins stacked in Lyon's vault. Desperate, defeated men like Calvert had no power. "No. You won't."

Nick nudged his chin at Iverson, who stepped forward to guide the nobleman from the room.

When they'd gone, Nick worked to steady his breathing, shaking out the tension in fists he'd clenched during the entire encounter. *Bastard. By-blow.* Those epithets—those lies—had defined him for too long.

Not anymore. His bloodline didn't matter at Lyon's. What he had, he'd earned. He held the purse strings and managed every gilded inch of the club. Proud aristocrats like Calvert who came and lost everything only made him richer.

Climbing the hidden staircase that led from his den to a private upper balcony circling the club, Nick swept his gaze around Lyon's glittering marble-faced walls and took in the assembly of black-suited men crowding gaming tables.

Tonight, for the first time—perhaps ever—he wanted to stop and appreciate the moment. Not look ahead to where ambition always drove him or back on his wretched past. Tonight marked a milestone. Five years since Lyon's opened its doors. Five years of unimagined success.

"I packed him off to his townhouse." Iverson climbed the stairs to join Nick. "Has he truly lost everything you loaned him a month ago?"

"The club only makes money when members lose theirs."

"Have a care, Lyon. A man like Calvert could cause trouble. What if he convinces his cronies to withdraw their membership or makes claims about dishonest play at Lyon's?"

"Our tables are fair." Nick had fought and struggled and occasionally told fictions to achieve success, but he insisted that Lyon's run without fakery. The house did take a cut of every bet placed, but that was sensible business practice. One that provided healthy dividends for those who'd invested in the enterprise.

"Gamblers return no matter how often they lose. Men hope their luck might turn. There's no need to twist the terms."

"It needn't be true if a man like Calvert repeats the claim often enough. He's the son of a duke."

"So am I."

"You're acknowledging it now?" Iverson shot Nick a bemused glance.

"Every mirror serves as a reminder." There was no denying his damned black hair and pale blue eye. He was branded with his father's likeness, but Nick rarely shared his history with anyone. Only Iverson knew. Many club members had no notion of his parentage. Or the juicier gossip that his father's jealous delusions had convinced the old man that his second son was a bastard. He'd loathed Nick with white-hot malice.

"However much you enjoy watching these aristocrats destroy themselves, it doesn't affect your father."

"I enjoy filling the club's coffers. Watching noblemen fritter away their fortunes is secondary." Only when they were associates of his father did Nick take perverse enjoyment in their downfall. "You disagree with my methods?"

"I never disagree with fattening the club's accounts, but I like to turn my eyes toward the future and keep the past behind me, where it belongs."

"As do I." Nick would merrily banish most of his history from memory if he could.

He'd earned his bitterness fairly, but he hated admitting to it. At times he feared everything—all his ambitions, struggles, even his victories—led to Talbot Lyon, the late Duke of Tremayne.

Iverson approached a cart laden with drinks and delicacies. "Tonight of all nights, let us think more about the club's prestige than its profits."

Iverson was right. He usually was. Like Nick, he'd turned the miserable hand he'd been dealt into unimaginable success. After a childhood scrabbling for every farthing, the man had earned a reputation as one of London's cleverest investors.

"Neither of you need fret." Rhys Forester, Marquess of Huntley, bounded up the stairs and beelined for the drinks cart, completing the trio of Lyon's Club owners. "Our books are flush. As Nick well knows, since his nose is never out of them." He gestured with a dismissive wave toward the pile of ledgers Nick had been working on earlier. "Good God, man, do you never cease working?"

"I discovered a miscalculation and needed to track down the error." Nick loathed grit in the seamless workings of the life he'd constructed. His business matters were carefully regimented. Pleasures, when he sought them, were discreetly arranged. The club ran like clockwork because he took care with every decision and detail.

"Hire someone to keep the books." Huntley frowned and shoved a hand through his already hopelessly mussed blond hair. "Save your energies for other pursuits," he insisted with a suggestive smirk.

"And let someone else have all the fun?" Nick wouldn't forfeit control of the club's finances. He didn't dole out faith in others freely. "Besides, I like numbers. I trust them. They're uncomplicated and reliable." And they never gave a damn if he looked or behaved like a beast.

"Suit yourself." Huntley's carefree expression turned mischievous. "I prefer music hall dancers and midnight soirees. And you're in luck, gentlemen, because this evening I've arranged for us to partake of both." He scooped up a glass of champagne, downed a bit, and raised the half-empty glass. "First a toast. Take some champagne."

Iverson crooked one auburn brow and claimed a glass of sparkling wine. "I've never liked this stuff. It's too bubbly."

Huntley scoffed. "You could use a bit of effervescence in your life. You too, Lyon. You've both grown insufferably stodgy over the years."

"Because we don't dangle from chandeliers like madmen?"

"I *fell* from the chandelier, as you both well know. Personally, I blame the absinthe." Huntley tipped back his glass and drained its fizzy contents. "Besides, I paid my price. I was abed for weeks nursing my injuries."

"Doesn't seem to have slowed you down." Nick

spent more time scanning *The Times* for news about commerce than attending to London's gossip mill, but Huntley was on the tongue of every scandalmonger in town. Every story confirmed what Nick knew of Huntley's recklessness.

"Where a man has a sturdy will, there's always a way." Huntley lifted a fresh glass of champagne. "Now a toast, to two of the most willful bastards I've ever known."

Nick grinned at the men who, despite his vow never to trust anyone, had managed to become his friends.

He didn't like to think on his days of picking pockets and scrounging for coin to provide shelter each night. Somehow, he'd managed to befriend the two men in London who didn't care. Iverson understood deprivation, and Huntley judged others by their character, rather than the color of their blood.

"To many more years of success." He raised his glass high and Iverson and Huntley followed suit.

"What shall we do next?" Huntley's question was precisely the one Nick wished to address.

"More," he said with a grin. "A larger club. Perhaps a new enterprise. What do you think of a luxury hotel in the heart of London?"

"You're thinking too small." Iverson leaned in, a glint in his eye. "You mustn't be afraid to dream a little bigger."

"Bridges? Steamships?" With great effort, Nick managed not to roll his eyes. "You're going to try to lure me into backing one of your industrial projects."

"The future belongs to creators, my friend." Iverson's voice deepened an octave and he began gesticulating as he warmed to the topic. "Not just any bridge. The longest bridge ever built in England. Not another steamship. The fastest to ever cross the Atlantic."

"How does one earn a profit from a bridge?" Unlike Nick, Huntley fully claimed his aristocratic heritage, but his father's dukedom was land rich and cash poor. He'd acquired his wealth through clever investment, much of it guided by Iverson.

"Trust me. There's money to be made." Iverson tipped back the remaining champagne in his glass and winced. "Though one could also argue for the legacy a man wishes to leave behind over a profit he can't enjoy in a single lifetime."

"You mean they'd name a steamship after me?" Huntley's dark eyes lit with interest. "I rather like that notion."

Iverson chuckled. Nick laughed too, amusement and pride fizzing inside him like the bubbling wine he'd just downed. He'd achieved a milestone that had nothing to do with his name or his father's legacy.

He pushed away the gnawing hunger that persisted underneath the joy. The constant craving for more. More wealth. More power.

A shout echoed up from the gaming floor below. Not the usual exclamation after a win or defeat. A man's voice, high-pitched and angry. A moment later footfalls thundered up the stairs.

"We have a problem, boss," Spencer, the club's factotum, called to Nick as he reached the upper balcony. His bulk caused his every step to reverberate with a resounding thud.

"Who?" Nick shed his tailcoat, approached the balcony's edge, and folded the garment over the balustrade.

Between them, he and Spencer had developed code words, euphemisms for those vexations that arose now and then in the running of a gentlemen's club. A *problem* meant a member had lost control, whether from drunken excess or the madness that came on when luck frowned again.

Together they'd always dealt with dilemmas quietly, with delicacy. Men might admit to ruination in Nick's private den, but aristocrats guarded their reputation among other members. A nobleman's good name was every bit as valuable a currency as coin.

"A visitor insists on speaking to you, sir." Before Spencer could say more, another shout echoed from the gaming floor. "He's not a member."

"Then tell him to call at another time." Before Calvert, Nick had been petitioned by three other gentlemen seeking funds. He'd had enough for one evening, and he'd promised to join Iverson and Huntley to celebrate the club's anniversary.

"Two of my men have him restrained, but I suspect you'll wish to see him." Despite how his polished accent lent every syllable elegance, Spencer never wasted words.

"Why?"

"Sir." Spencer hesitated. "He says he's come about your father—"

"My father is dead."

"About your father's estate, Mr. Lyon."

Nick's eyesight blurred. He heard his breath, rapid and wheezing in his chest like a rusty squeezebox.

He hadn't thought of the estate in years. He did everything in his power to never think on the blighted place.

"He insists on seeing you, sir," Spencer continued. "Says his name is Granville."

Nick's head shot up. He knew that name. A crony of his father's who'd become a mentor to Nick's older brother.

"Sir Malcolm Granville?" Huntley asked. "I went to school with his son. Shall I go and speak to him?"

Nick's throat filled with bile, and he didn't protest when Iverson nodded at Huntley, who headed downstairs to deal with their belligerent visitor.

"Do you think Granville's come to say your brother is after money again?" Iverson asked quietly.

"He won't find any here." Nick swigged down another glass of bubbly wine to clear the bitter taste in his throat. "Knowing Eustace, he could spend more in one evening than most of the men downstairs wager in a week."

In the sixteen years since his older brother had inherited the dukedom, he'd spent enough to nearly empty the ducal coffers. Nick wanted nothing to do his wastrel brother or the bloody estate that was the Tremayne legacy.

A few minutes later, Huntley returned and approached the cart of drinks, just as he had when he'd first arrived. His expression was the same mask of jovial nonchalance he always wore, but for the telltale tightness in his jaw.

"What did he say, Huntley?" Nick dreaded the answer. Any news of his brother wouldn't be good.

"He said two letters were sent from your brother's solicitor with no response from you."

Nick drew in a sharp breath and let it out slowly, trying to temper his agitation. "I no longer bother with opening any correspondence from him. Is that all he wanted? To complain on Eustace's behalf that I haven't opened my post?"

Huntley shoved a shaky hand through his hair. "I'm sorry, Nick. Recall that I'm only the messenger, will you?"

Every muscle in Nick's body tensed. "Go on."

When Huntley merely swallowed hard and stood gaping at them, Iverson stepped forward.

"What is it, man? Just tell us."

Nick saw Huntley's shoulders sag and his lips begin to move. Far off, he could hear the man's voice, but it took long minutes for the words to register. For the horror of it to sink in—the past he loathed had come back with a vengeance.

"Your brother, Eustace, is dead. As of a week ago, you're the Duke of Tremayne."

Chapter Two

*M*ina Thorne held the letter in her hand so tightly, the foolscap began to crumple. She'd been gripping the envelope for half an hour, unable to let it go, because everything else she cared about seemed to be slipping away.

In three days' time, she might lose her position. Her home. Friends at Enderley Castle who'd become as dear as family.

Concealing the letter and her trembling hands below the level of her desk was easy enough. Willing away the flutter in her stomach was proving harder, but Mina had become rather good at pretending.

Over the years she'd mastered half smiles, grown proficient at blank expressions, and she would've earned high marks in tongue biting if anyone was offering a grade.

Her father taught her that others' opinions mattered. Along with mathematics and estate management, lessons in good manners were the ones he repeated most.

She'd striven for propriety, always eager to please him.

But inside, in a secret place, rooted so deep as to never be wholly weeded out, she hid a terrible truth. Every single day she yearned to buck the ladylike nature to which she'd been taught to aspire.

Impulsive, Papa had called her, and that was true. She had a tendency to throw herself headlong—into work, problems, and emotions she had no business feeling.

For five and twenty years she'd done her best to act as if wearing a corset and skirt pleased her as much as a practical shirt and comfortable trousers. Even as a child, what her father expected of her never quite fit who she truly was inside. There wasn't a day she wouldn't have thrown over her flawless porcelain-faced doll for a gallop across the Sussex downs on one of the ponies in Enderley's stable.

When her father died two years past, she'd acted as if picking up his duties wasn't terrifying and overwhelming and not at all the path she'd imagined her life would take.

But doing what one must, getting on with one's duties, was what he taught her. *Never let your struggles be known*, he'd often say.

As a child, Mina had endlessly failed to live up to his expectations. Whether her cheeks flamed, or her voice wobbled, or her tongue tripped over words, hiding her feelings had been a constant struggle.

But she kept on trying to be ladylike. To speak gently. To mask her feelings.

This morning those skills were being put to the test. She needed to convince her uninvited visitors that nothing was amiss. Though, truth was, she dreaded the pending arrival of the new Duke of Tremayne.

As soon as Mina spotted the letter from Nicholas Lyon's solicitor, she couldn't shake the sense of foreboding that nothing would ever be solid or steady again. She hoped he'd be different than his father and brother. The list of what required repair and refurbishing at the estate grew each year, and Mina longed to see the estate improved. But it was a goal the previous duke had not shared. His preference had been to spend as little time as possible at Enderley.

Pressing a palm to her middle, she willed her stomach to settle.

"What a drastic change the new duke's arrival will bring for your circumstances, Miss Thorne. We sympathize, of course." Vicar Pribble led the trio who'd come to call shortly after sunrise, hoping to discover all they could about the new duke and demanding to know when he'd finally deign to show his face at Enderley.

They were the unofficial leaders of Barrowmere village—the eldest farmer, the magistrate, and the resident man of God.

"How could we not pity you?" the vicar went on. "A motherless, fatherless girl, without a single prospect ahead of her?"

Good grief. Mina would be sure to never seek out the vicar for encouragement when she was feeling downtrodden.

"We wish to see you living your life as a young woman should," Magistrate Hardbrook barked in his usual gruff manner.

"And how should I live, gentlemen?" She *almost* managed to keep any trace of irritation from her tone.

"As a wife. A mother." Farmer Thurston drew the words out slowly, as if she must be addlepated to even ask such a question.

"I'm afraid that will not be my fate." She drew in a sharp breath, filling her lungs to say more. Retorts surged up and died. She could tie a bow with the knot of yearnings she'd pushed aside.

Of course she wanted to be a wife and mother, to share her life with someone who'd give her loyalty and love. A man to whom she could entrust her heart. But she'd tripped down that road before and ended face-down in a puddle, figuratively speaking. She was done chasing a fairy-tale ending that would never come.

"My father prepared me for this work, and I shall do my duties as long as I'm able."

"Or until the new master dismisses you." The vicar spoke bluntly, but he tempered his words with a furrowed brow and sad gaze. "You must anticipate that he will wish to choose his own steward. One who's—"

"Not a woman?"

"It is unusual, Miss Thorne. That you must allow."

"I woke up on the morning of Father's passing"— her throat ached at mention of that hideous day—"and did what needed to be done." Everyone at Enderley had looked to him for guidance, and when he'd gone, they'd looked to her. "I couldn't leave his role empty. The work needed doing, so I did it."

"Still isn't right or proper," Hardbrook grumbled.

Mina stood and stepped out from behind her desk. Between the three seated men and stacks of account ledgers and estate documents, there wasn't much room. But squeezing close to a bookcase was preferable to enduring the scrutiny of her visitors' disapproving gazes. She ran a finger along the shelf where she maintained a collection of items she'd gathered from around Enderley—a shard of colored glass from the original castle's windows, a bit of polished flint, a Tudor coin dug up near the estate's old tower.

Staring at the items eased her nerves. Nicholas Lyon might be inheriting every inch of the place, but he hadn't visited in years. She could help him understand Enderley, if he let her.

After drawing in a deep breath, she turned to face her visitors once more.

"Gentlemen, this isn't a matter of propriety but of necessity. The previous duke did not concern himself with Enderley, and the estate required management while the 'absent duke' chose to ignore it."

"You did your duty well, Miss Thorne. I'm sure your father would be proud. But it's been two years," Robert Thurston spoke. "Couldn't you have found a new steward in all that time?"

"Not a suitable one."

There'd been a young solicitor who recited the law as if it had been tattooed on his eyelids, but he'd known nothing of animals and jumped in fright when she'd taken him on a tour of the stables. Another young buck had gone cross-eyed when she showed him the pile of estate ledger books. A third had stared so intently at her bosom, she'd cut off the interview before asking the ogler a single question.

Beyond their individual faults, no applicant had

possessed one essential qualification. They didn't know Enderley and Barrowmere village. They didn't care for the inhabitants. Mina had lived in this quiet corner of England her whole life and been raised on the estate. Her cousin, Colin, lived nearby, and he was her only family now.

The villagers and staff were all she had left. They needed her, and she couldn't imagine any other steward appreciating Enderley Castle and its needs as her father had. As she'd been taught to do.

Mina fixed her gaze on two paintings on the wall of his office. One was of her mother, a woman of gossamer delicacy with pale blue eyes, dewy skin, and hair like rays of sunlight. The other was of a stag. A work by Landseer, her father once told her. A print of a famous painting by one of Queen Victoria's favorite artists.

The stag wasn't particularly pretty, but he had a fierceness in his eye, determination in his stance. He knew where he belonged. He knew his purpose in the world.

Mina yearned to possess fairy-tale beauty like the mother she'd never known instead of her father's dark hair and muddy-brown eyes. But, little by little, she'd begun to accept that she was more like the stag. A creature of the land she'd been born to, ready to fight, if necessary, to protect every acre.

"Gentlemen, shall we return to the reason for your call this morning?"

The three men glanced at each other as if trying to remind themselves of just what their purpose had been.

"The new Duke of Tremayne," she said, ignoring how her stomach dived at mention of the man. Before she could explain that his arrival was imminent, Pribble cut her off.

"Indeed." Vicar Pribble leaned forward, his voice pitching higher. "Why hasn't he come to Enderley yet?"

It was a question oft repeated by the house's staff and every villager Mina encountered. *Where's the duke?*

"The old duke died months ago. The new duke didn't even see fit to attend his brother's funeral." Hardbrook shook his balding head in disgust. "This cannot stand."

Mina clenched her teeth and did her best to quell the glare she wanted to shoot in Hardbrook's direction. He was a perennial troublemaker. A first-class grumbler. She had no idea how her father had borne his complaints with such long-suffering patience.

Mina hadn't inherited that virtue.

"We must get the remainder of the harvesting completed and there's not the men to do it." Farmer Thurston always spoke of practical matters, keeping his eye on the estate's bottom line. Her father had appreciated that about the old man.

"I expect the new duke to take matters in hand." Hardbrook nodded, heartily offering support for his own pronouncement.

Mina wasn't so certain.

The previous duke had been dead for three months, and the only contact she'd had with the new one was through his solicitor. The man seemed as disinterested in the duties and dilemmas of the estate as his brother had.

Until this morning.

A letter had awaited her in the center of her desk blotter. Not another demand like the others that had come from his solicitor, asking that she produce inventories of the silver, antiquities, and art at Enderley. This morning's letter contained a pronouncement. Seven simple words that nearly made her toss her breakfast.

The Duke of Tremayne arrives on Friday.

"What we need is a bit of the firm hand of the father," Hardbrook insisted. "The old duke was a strong man."

"He was cruel." Mina failed to stifle the comment before it slipped out.

Hardbrook sniffed and shifted his gaze, no longer able to stare at her with his usual boldness. "Daresay *he* wouldn't stand for a lady steward."

And there it was again. On Friday, all she'd worked for would be lost.

Hardbrook was right. The new duke would probably dismiss her, not simply because she was a woman, but because in all her interactions with the man's solicitor, she'd failed to mention the fact.

She'd not planned some master deception. But when the time had come to tell the truth, she'd kept mum.

"You wish to know when the duke will come, gentlemen? He arrives in three days." The words escaped. She'd been holding them in all morning. The plan had been to tell the household staff first. But the village leadership trio had arrived too early.

"Well, that's excellent news!" Vicar Pribble found a reason to smile.

Mina's stomach lurched.

What would Nicholas Lyon do at Enderley? A man who had a life and a business to attend to in London? Eustace, the previous duke, had preferred London too. But he'd spent his days there in drunken revelry while his brother built his own wealth.

Hardbrook leaned forward, planting a fist on Mina's desktop. "I have a bone or twenty to pick with the next Tremayne."

"The queue is a long one." He'd need to get in line behind tenants, creditors, and villagers who'd waited years for a reasonable man to take the helm of the dukedom. Mina had patched and problem-solved where she could, but nothing compared to a competent lord and master to do his duty by his tenants.

"What will *you* do, Miss Thorne?" Pribble's voice softened.

"I will assist the new duke."

"And if he sacks you?" Hardbrook's forehead buckled, as if he might actually care about her fate, despite his gruff demeanor.

"There are other posts." Not that she could truly imagine herself anywhere else, doing anything else. But she'd tried. Her gaze lit on a square of newsprint at the corner of her desk.

"A position as governess?" Pribble tipped his head to examine the advert she'd cut from a newspaper.

The doubt written in a dozen creased lines across his face matched Mina's own. She'd never had lessons in decorum or music or painting pretty watercolors. Her only hope was to find a family who wished for their offspring to learn household management, animal husbandry, and how to balance sums.

"What about marriage?" Hardbrook asked, latching his beefy hands around the lapels of his frock coat.

Mina tried to conceal a shiver. Young women married old men all the time, but she couldn't fathom such a fate.

A low rumble, like approaching thunder, echoed in the room as Hardbrook shook with the power of his own guffaw. "Have no fear, girl. I did not mean for you to wed me. I'm offering you my son. He's a good lad. Not too daft. Not too daring. He'll be a steady sort you can rely on."

"Your boy is sixteen, Mr. Hardbrook. Friendly, to be sure, but not a marital prospect, even if I were seeking one."

"Give him a few years, and he'll be a fine young man."

"In a few years, I'll be older too, Mr. Hardbrook, and even more of a spinster."

The three men shifted in their chairs, as if the old worn cushions were as uncomfortable as their attempts to talk sense into an unnatural woman.

When Emma rushed into the room, she saved them all from further misery.

The young maid bobbed a curtsy before turning her panicked gaze on Mina. "You're needed, miss. Tobias says you're to come to the stable as soon as you're able."

Mina stood and instantly breathed easier. Work. Problems. That was what she knew. Much simpler than juggling the expectations of grumpy old men.

"Gentlemen, if you'll excuse me."

Hardbrook, Thurston, and Vicar Pribble stood too.

"When the duke arrives, I'll inform him of your visit." Hardbrook opened his mouth as if he'd add another grumble, so Mina added, "And let him know you wish to speak to him."

Mina understood the villagers' concerns all too well. In her desk, she kept a running list of what needed to be done and for whom, and all of it required funds that the estate had long stopped producing.

"Thank you, Em," Mina told the maid after the men had gone. "I thought they'd never leave."

The girl grinned. "If I'd known I would have come in sooner. But I meant what I said. You must come quick. Tobias needs you."

Fear chased goose pebbles across Mina's skin. "What is it? Is someone injured?"

"Not unless you count a few scratches." Emma smiled again. "It's Lady Millicent. She's up a tree and clawed Tobias when he tried to get her down."

The barn cat. Fat and furry and feisty as a mongoose. Especially now that she was in a delicate way.

"Where is she?"

"Up the tall oak at the edge of the copse. He's gone out twice and she's put him off. The poor thing can't jump down in the state she's in." Emma wore a fretful frown. "How will you get her, miss? Tobias is bleeding something fierce."

"She just needs a bit of patience." The stable master was an enormous man of good humor, but his brusque style didn't help when a bit of delicacy was needed.

Mina glanced toward the doorway to make sure none of the other servants were in view, quickly unfastened her belt and skirt, and slipped the fabric down her trouser-clad legs.

Emma, who was used to Mina's preferred fashion, didn't blink an eye. In fact, she lifted her arms to take the skirt. "I'll put it away for you."

"Thanks, Em." Mina squared her shoulders and started toward the stable yard. She thought of Milly and of retrieving the ladder they kept in the kitchen. The awkward meeting with the village elders began to fade from her mind.

Solving Enderley's problems was where she excelled. It was her purpose, at least for a little while longer.

Chapter Three

$\mathcal{S}$top!" Nick banged the wall of the carriage hard with the flat of his hand before the coachman heard his shout over the rattle of the traces.

Admittedly, it was an odd place to ask the driver to stop. A mile, maybe two, from their destination. But he'd had enough.

Enough of being trapped in the dark, cramped space. Enough of being jostled on unforgiving squabs as the coach navigated Sussex's rutted country roads. Enough of the agonizing wait to be delivered to the hellish place he would have been content to never see again.

The closer they drew to Enderley, the more determined he became not to arrive confined within the walls of a carriage. Whatever demons of his past lay ahead, he'd damn well face them on his own two feet.

"Here, my lord?" the coachman shouted.

"Here." Nick jumped out before the driver could climb down. "Deliver my luggage to the estate. Someone will take the bags when you arrive."

At least, he hoped the staff would do their duty. He suspected some would dread his arrival. The longtime staff who'd served his father would recall him as nothing more than the duke's despised second son.

Now he'd proved himself negligent by ignoring his inheritance for months. His early arrival would earn him ire too, by upending the daily routine of Enderley's staff. But it would be nothing to how much they'd soon come to loathe him.

He hoped his plan would take no longer than a fortnight. A neat entry and exit. Clear out the furnishings, see to a thorough cleaning, and dismiss some of the staff so that a future tenant could hire whom he wished. Nick had asked his solicitor to look into every possible means of abdicating a dukedom or breaking an entail. All to no avail. With no means of achieving either prospect, he'd settled on what was possible—putting the estate in a trust and leasing the property in the meantime.

The carriage rolled on toward Enderley, and Nick yanked up the collar of his overcoat against a brisk wind. The air carried a bone-chilling bite and the salty tang of the sea. He drew in a deep breath, savoring the scent.

Shock jolted through him. He hadn't expected to find anything about Sussex appealing.

Even now, he glanced over his shoulder, pondering the fork in the road. Behind him lay London and Lyon's and the life he'd made for himself. Ahead lay only pain. All the ugliness of his past and all of the fresh misery he was about to inflict.

He started forward, abandoning the muck of the road

and trudging through tall field grass in a straight path toward the estate. With every step, his chest tightened a bit more, as if he was being slowly flattened beneath a millstone. Steeling himself, he ignored the pain. This place had tried to kill him once and failed. It wouldn't break him now. He wasn't a child anymore.

Lord help him, he was the bloody Duke of Tremayne.

By the time the battlements of Enderley's towers came into view, he looked more like a muddy marauder. If not for a letter from the estate steward, Thomas Thorne, tucked in his waistcoat pocket, he doubted few would believe he was heir to any estate. Unless some of the old staff remained and recognized him.

He was looking forward to facing down every single one of them who'd abetted his father's villainy.

As he started up the carriage drive, the lane turned drier, coated with pebbles that crunched under his boots. There were so many damn windows in the house, all glinting proudly in the sunlight. The entire house glowed, its gray bricks lit by the steady gleam of the November sun.

He could almost convince himself the sunny-faced facade wasn't Enderley's at all.

Every memory he possessed of the place was shrouded in murk and gloom. And always with one blot of darkness that colored every recollection. The old ruined tower. The structure still stood, more decrepit but still menacing, at the house's western edge.

He cast his gaze ahead as he strode toward the house, refusing to give the vile old tower his attention. Instead, he focused on the cluttered front steps.

The coachman had arrived, departed, and left his luggage lying in an unceremonious heap at the front doors.

Bloody hell.

"What brings you to Enderley, sir?" A gruff voice sounded at Nick's back, and a figure cast a giant's shadow across the path at his feet.

"Duty." Nick turned to find an individual as large as his silhouette. A tall, broad, bearded beast of a man who was too young to have been in service when Nick was a child. A groundskeeper, Nick guessed, or perhaps the stable master. "And you are?"

"Tobias, sir. I tend the horses and carriages at Enderley." The man scrutinized him from his rumpled clothes to his dirt-smeared boots. "Who are you seeking?"

"Wilder." The name came unbidden. "Is he still in service?" He was old and gray-haired in Nick's memories. He'd be ancient now.

"Who may I say's come to call?"

"Nicholas Lyon." He still couldn't bring himself to use his blasted title aloud. He didn't know if he'd ever be able to embrace that inheritance.

"Lyon? Heavens, you're the man himself." Tobias scraped his cap from his head and offered Nick a stiff bow. "Forgive me, Your Grace."

"Is he still alive?" Nick asked, brushing off the man's obsequiousness.

"He is. Shall I take you to him?"

"I'll find him." Nick nodded at Tobias before starting toward the front door. The stable master noticed his bags and heaved a trunk onto his massive shoulders.

Inside the entry hall, the house was eerily quiet, but Nick heard sounds belowstairs.

He descended to find a busy staff, everyone occupied at cleaning some part of the enormous, high-ceilinged kitchen. One girl stood atop a rickety lean-to ladder, swiping at invisible dust on the ceiling. Another had her head buried inside a great blackened oven. A young man swept so fiercely, bits of twig flew up to join a cloud of dust above his head.

"And who might you be, then?" A familiar voice, roughened by the passing of time, called from the kitchen corner. "If you're one of those men coming around to politic or sell your wares, you'll have to talk to the steward."

"Scribb, isn't it?" The moment Nick turned to face her, the old woman feinted back. Her face drained of blood, except for two crimson stains high on her cheeks.

"Mercy, take me." The housekeeper gaped at him.

Nick wasn't sure if she recognized him or was reacting as others did to his eyes and scarred face.

"We didn't expect you today, Your Grace."

"But here I am. Don't let me disturb your work." The anger Nick expected to feel for whatever part she'd played in assisting his father's machinations didn't come. Now he saw only that she was an old woman, one who'd had the grit to stay in this godforsaken place after he'd gone. "I came down to find Mr. Wilder."

She pointed, and Nick noticed that her hands were shaking.

He didn't have to go far in the direction she indicated. The shuffle of footsteps sounded from inside the butler's pantry and Wilder emerged, his gray hair now snow white.

"Master Nicholas." Rather than bow as the others had, he came forward and stood stiffly, his hands behind him. "You've come back."

There was a question in the old man's gravelly voice. Nick was still wondering too. Why had he returned? "If there was any other way, I would have taken it."

"You must be tired after your journey." Mrs. Scribb moved like an agitated bird, fluttering in his periphery. "We'll see to your bags and finish preparing the ducal suite for you, Your Grace."

"No." Nick's bark was loud enough to make the old woman jump. "Prepare a guest chamber for me." The notion of setting foot in any room used by his father or brother turned his stomach.

After exchanging confused glances, all the other servants filed out of the kitchen.

"There will be much to do." Wilder remained in his stolid butler stance. Chest puffed out. Eyes straight ahead. The stiffness of his posture didn't match the emotion in his voice. "You may rely on me, Your Grace, as long as I am able to serve you."

"I know that much." For the briefest moment, Nick considered what job he might offer the old man at Lyon's, and then immediately rejected the notion. What Wilder deserved for his long years of service was a nice cottage in the country. A bit of rest in his dotage. He would reward the man in that small way, at least. "You may start by never calling me *Your Grace* again. Of all the staff, you must understand how I loathe those words."

Wilder responded with one dip of his square chin. "But you are Tremayne now. Others will call you such."

"And my father would rise from the grave to stop them if he could."

"But he cannot." The old man's eyes flicked to his. "He is powerless now."

Powerless. The word loosened some of the tension that had ridden his shoulders since he'd left London.

"I suppose this is his worst nightmare." A little grin pulled the edges of Nick's mouth upward. "I survived him and the heir he groomed for the dukedom."

"And you're here at Enderley." Wilder spoke softly, tentatively, like one attempting to gentle a dangerous beast.

"Direct me to Thorne." Nick cleared his throat to shed the gruffness from his tone. "There's much to do, and I want to make a start."

"You were not expected until tomorrow."

"I presume the estate steward does his job every day. Now where is he?"

"Sir—"

"Just direct me to him, Wilder."

The butler pointed toward the kitchen's service door, where milk and food were delivered. The door exited onto a yard that contained all of the work buildings on the estate—the granary, bake house, and stables.

"Out back, sir. Most likely in the stables."

Nick wasn't sure why the steward would be wasting time in the stables, but it wasn't nearly as important as getting out into the fresh air. He yanked open the kitchen door and immediately breathed easier. Even a few minutes in the house felt tight and confining.

On the threshold, something held him back. A task left undone for decades.

"Wilder? There's a great deal I don't remember. Much I've forced myself to forget." He should face the man, but he couldn't. The memories would come back too sharply. "If I didn't say it then, I owe it to you now."

A hand. A key. Bursting through the door. Running for his life. He couldn't hold them back. Memories washed over him, a flood of vivid images.

"Thank you. The sentiment is long overdue."

"WHERE IS SHE?" Mina stood with a hand on each hip, narrowing one eye at Gleason, the senior stable hand. The man usually did his job well, but he tended to attack trouble with a maul, never considering that a less blunt tool might do the job.

"The copse," he said churlishly, swiping at an ugly bleeding scratch on his chin. "Quite a ways up the tallest oak. Tobias sent me out and I couldn't get her either."

"And how did she get up there?"

Gleason cast Mina a beseeching look. "The wee devil was into the feed bags, miss. Shooed her off. A bit o' shouting. Flapping me arms. Didn't mean the Ole Scratch any harm."

"She's not the devil, Henry. She's a cat, and she needs to eat now more than ever."

"I'll go and try again." He started for a roughhewn ladder they used to reach the storage level of the barn.

It was a rickety old thing, and Mina doubted it would ever hold his weight.

"You'll only make it worse. I'll go. Give me the ladder."

"Let me carry that for you, miss." Gleason viewed her as Hardbrook did. A feminine flower to be protected and treated with delicacy. "It's not work for a lady."

"I'm not a lady, and I don't need help. Surely you have enough to keep you busy before the new duke arrives."

"Will he be as rotten as the last two?" Gleason called as she started out of the stable yard.

"There's every reason to think he'll be worse." Mina turned back to face the young man. "But if we show him we can be relied upon to run Enderley efficiently, perhaps he'll spend as much time in London as his brother did."

"Leaves a good deal on your shoulders," Gleason retorted.

Mina lifted the ladder and hefted a rung over her shoulder before starting off toward the tree line.

She knew Gleason meant well, but she bristled at the implication she was too fragile to be a proper steward. She hadn't chosen her post, but she couldn't imagine giving it up. If she could gain the trust of the new Duke of Tremayne, Mina prayed she wouldn't have to.

Near the rise where oak trees stood, she stopped for a moment and took in the view. She'd never been to London, never set foot out of Sussex in her entire life.

But she doubted she'd ever see anything as stunning as the way Barrowmere's ribbons of fields stretched out to meet the horizon.

She heard Milly mewing miserably from a high branch. A summer ago, the feline was a fleet-footed hellion. Now her belly swelled with kittens that Mina had expected to arrive last week.

"I'm coming for you, Millicent. Don't do anything daring." Mina braced the ladder against the trunk and started up the first rung. The wood and rusted nails protested, but she continued up. "Did you have to go quite so far?"

Milly's meow grew less desperate. A bit high-pitched, almost defensive.

"I suppose Tobias and Gleason can be fearsome when they shout."

The cat was so high, Mina realized she'd need to abandon the ladder and scramble up a few of the branches. They were low, not as thick as those higher up, and she prayed they'd hold.

"If we both come out of this unscathed"—she gritted her teeth and heaved up, wrapping an arm around a branch—"I want a promise that you'll never do this again."

Millicent responded with a slow blink.

"And that you won't teach your babies this trick either." She pushed up toward a higher branch and crooked a knee against the one below to keep steady while she reached for the cat. "When I grab you, it's to help. I mean you no harm."

The cat was already shifting in a less than helpful

direction, retreating an inch on her branch. Below Mina, the ladder clattered to the ground, and Milly's eyes bulged before she scooted back another inch.

"You're not going to make this easy, are you?"

The cat narrowed her eyes to little jeweled slits, but her swishing tail announced how irritated she'd become.

Mina reached out and just brushed the scruff of the cat's neck. "Got you, girl."

Chapter Four

The place was so bloody vast. In London, a square mile cost a small fortune. Here in Sussex, a hundred acres could be gobbled up by the railway and few would raise a brow.

Where would a steward hide on Enderley's endless acres? The man wasn't in the stables, and the two irritable servants Nick encountered there directed him toward a clump of trees on the highest patch of ground on the estate.

Oaks and maples heavy with autumn leaves—gold and orange and patches of crimson—made a spectacle at the top of the hill. The sound floating down from the rise wasn't nearly as appealing. A growl carried on the breeze, like the warning cry a tomcat offered before scratching your eyes out.

Nick detected a woman's voice too. A gentle, cajoling murmur. Almost seductive. "Come closer, darling. Stop being such a stubborn creature."

A jolt of awareness rippled across his skin. He couldn't recall the last time a lover had spoken to him in such an arousing purr. Hell, he'd been so focused on Lyon's of late, he could barely recall his last lover at all.

Scanning the horizon, he expected to spot a trysting couple. Perhaps a lusty tenant farmer and his bride. What he saw instead was a flurry of leaves and twigs floating down from a single tree.

Narrowing his gaze, he noticed something *up* the tree. A small figure with feminine curves but garbed as a man—black vest, white shirt, and dark breeches. Exceedingly snug breeches, Nick couldn't help but notice, made more so from her odd position.

"Hello?" he called as he approached.

The role of hero had never suited him, but he couldn't imagine the young woman getting down from the height she'd reached without aid.

She didn't seem to agree. He received no acknowledgment of his greeting.

A bit louder, he called, "You look as if you're in need of rescue." He swung a discarded ladder up, locked it against a notch of bark, and started up one rickety slat.

That caught her notice. The lady tipped her head to glare at him, and that odd sizzle of awareness skittered across his skin once more. Her eyes were arresting, a unique whiskey shade that caught the light like amber. He felt a twinge under his breastbone, as if one of his sparring partners had got in an unexpected blow.

Her eyes widened, and he braced himself for the usual feminine reaction to his features. But she didn't scream or blanch as if his visage repulsed her. Which was as odd as the unexpected pleasure of looking up a tree at her trouser-wrapped legs and lush derriere.

"Kindly cease talking," she whispered angrily. "You'll frighten her."

"Her?" Nick spotted the lady in question. A fat orange feline with a glare as ferocious as the woman protectively cradling the cat in one arm. Nick lowered his voice. "Let me help you." He wasn't sure if he was attempting to reason with the cat or her mistress.

"I got up on my own." The lady huffed out an irritated sigh. "I can get down on my own."

"I'm sure that's what your cat thought too."

More glares. A cool jade glower from the cat. Gold fury from the tree-climbing female. "I. Can. Manage."

She couldn't. Not unless she possessed the power of flight or suddenly sprouted much longer legs than the shapely limbs above his head. He climbed another step on the ladder.

A little growl echoed down when he lifted a hand. But it wasn't the cat. The creature now assessed him with bland indifference from the crook of her mistress's arm.

"You are," the tree climber grumbled as she planted her free hand in his, "a decidedly stubborn man."

Yet even as she made the declaration, she gave him her weight and made no further protest when he placed his hands around the very soft, very warm curve of her waist.

Nick held tight until she planted a boot on the top ladder rung.

She looked back at him. He expected more chastisement or revulsion at glimpsing his freakish eyes and broken face. Instead, she stared, cheeks flushed, as he slid his hands down her legs to steady her.

"Here. Take Millicent." As gently as if the cat were made of spun glass, the young woman adjusted the creature in her arms and aimed the feline toward Nick's head.

"If I take her and you fall, I won't be able to catch you." Of course, he'd do his damnedest. For a moment, he let himself imagine how the lady's heat and softness would feel on top of him. But he did as she bid and retrieved the feline.

"It's all right," he murmured to the cat, giving her soft orange-and-white fur a few strokes.

"Now move down," the lady commanded, "so I can descend."

Nick took a single long step off the ladder, attempting not to jostle the cat too much. As insurance, she'd sunk ten tiny needle-sharp claws into his arm. But even that agony didn't distract him from appreciating the plump swell of the young lady's backside as she climbed down. He also noted that her hair was a wild tangle, her shirt was littered with bits of bark, and her boots were sorely in need of a polish.

She dusted her hands on her breeches before turning to face him. "I'll take Millic—" Her voice cut off on a strangled gurgle.

Ah, finally. The horror. He wondered which sort she'd be. Would she faint dead away, dash off, or simply do her best to pretend the sight of him didn't turn her stomach?

"I'm sorry, Your Grace. I didn't recognize you."

"You must have known my father." Nick didn't think he was acquainted with the tree-climbing woman, so it was the similarity to Talbot Lyon she must have seen in his face.

Yet when she swept a strand of hair behind her ear, a memory danced at the edge of his mind. There had been a girl on the estate when he was a boy. A servant's daughter he'd never been allowed to speak to. The child had possessed unruly chestnut hair and a giggle that carried all the way up to where he spent hours suffering lessons with his tutor in the nursery.

When he moved close to get a better look, Miss Thorne's eyes widened. She swallowed hard, muscles working along the pale stretch of her throat.

"Yes, Your Grace. I knew your father."

God, that honorific grated on him. "I'm looking for Mr. Thomas Thorne. Do you know where I can find him?"

Her expression changed instantly, from unease to wide-eyed panic. But she reined her emotions in quickly and squared her shoulders.

"I suspect you're looking for me. My name is Thomasina Thorne. My father has been dead for two years."

Nick frowned.

The lady bit her lower lip and fixed her gaze on a spot over his shoulder, suddenly unable to look him in the eyes.

"My condolences, Miss Thorne. But that makes this letter rather curious." He retrieved the missive from his pocket, unfolding the note with the Tremayne crest and *Thomas Thorne, Estate Steward* engraved at the top.

Her blush deepened from pink to scarlet. "I used my father's stationery."

She'd done more than that. "You signed his name."

Miss Thorne came closer and pried the cat from his arms. The beast took some cajoling, and Nick felt each pinprick sting as her claws detached from his skin. He also felt the sweep of Miss Thorne's hands as she petted the creature, inadvertently stroking his arm.

"Look again, Your Grace," she insisted, glancing at the letter.

Nick narrowed an eye at her and then scanned the document once more. *T. Thorne* stared up at him from the signature line.

"There's a dot after *T*," she said pertly.

"A dot."

"It's the initial letter of my name."

"Clever." Or exceedingly foolish. If she'd truly taken on her father's duties, it was quite a burden for a young woman to concern herself with. Especially at a gloomy place like Enderley.

Color still stained Miss Thorne's cheeks, but he couldn't detect any true remorse for her deception.

"Which came first? Adopting your father's name or wearing his clothes?"

"These are *my* clothes."

That Nick believed. They hugged every inch of her body possessively. He could even acknowledge she was sensible for not binding herself inside oceans of fabric. He liked practical solutions, especially those that made life simpler. But he hated nothing so much as being deceived.

"You lied to my solicitor, Miss Thorne."

"I did not lie. I always try to tell the truth." She pursed her mouth, tilted up her chin a fraction, and shot him a look of pure defiance. Except for the tell-tale quiver in her jaw. "I simply didn't fully explain."

"Everyone lies. You'd be the most extraordinary woman in England if you didn't." Looking at her— wild hair, lush legs encased in buckskin, and a hostile cat clutched at her hip—Nick acknowledged that she *was* the most unusual woman he'd met in a long while.

"I did say I try." She dipped her head before looking at him again, and an errant curl slipped down to curve around her chin. "I have been a trustworthy steward, Your Grace."

"We'll see, Miss Thorne."

She'd already proven herself skilled at deceit. Not a good start for the one person he was relying on to tell him the truth about Enderley's finances before he divested himself of every asset the entail would allow.

As they assessed each other, clouds rolled in. Angry black-gray billows that perfectly matched his mood. In the distance, thunder shook the sky.

"We should get inside, Your Grace." Without waiting for him, she started toward the stable yard.

Nick stared at Miss Thorne's backside as she stalked away and cursed under his breath. He'd been back an hour and already Enderley was turning him into a beast.

The lady's appeal was nothing more than an irritating distraction. And a surprise. He hadn't anticipated finding beauty in this blighted place.

He wasn't sure he could trust the woman, and he certainly couldn't bed her.

As if she sensed his wayward thoughts, Miss Thorne turned back, gazing across the distance at him expectantly. "Your Grace?"

"Can you arrange for a meal to be brought to me?" His stomach growled as fiercely as the storm clouds.

"Of course." She turned away again as if he'd formally dismissed her.

"Come and find me in an hour, Miss Thorne."

She stopped but didn't turn back.

"I want to review the inventories my solicitor requested." Business. Practical matters. That's why he was here.

Looking out over the field they'd just trudged through, Miss Thorne said over her shoulder, "Very good, Your Grace. I shall meet you in your study."

He hated the prospect of entering his father's space, but he focused instead on how much closer every task brought him to leaving this place forever. If she had the inventories prepared, Miss Thomasina Thorne was efficient, and that would serve him well.

"An hour then, Miss Thorne." He heard an odd thread of hope in his voice.

He was counting on her, feisty, curvaceous, deceptive woman that she was.

"COME NOW AND tell us what he's like?" Mrs. Scribb quizzed as she dug inside Mina's bedchamber wardrobe of serviceable and rarely worn gowns. Nearby, Emma sorted ribbons and pins Mina hadn't glanced at in years.

"Not what I expected."

Good heavens, what a fool she'd been to assume

Nicholas Lyon would be like his brother. Eustace had been too occupied with vices to care that Mina had taken her father's place. But this new duke was a man of business, creating enterprises and success with his own force of will. He wasn't the sort to let anything slip his notice.

She'd underestimated. Badly. Now she had to find some way to fix it.

"I can't be late, Mrs. Scribb." Mina tugged at the skirt and bodice the housekeeper had chosen for her to don after she'd washed. Fighting the vise grip of her corset, Mina fumbled with the fastenings. There were too many panels and buttons and hidden hooks, and she had no time for any of them. "Why is this so complicated?"

She cast a longing gaze at the breeches she could slip on quickly and the soft cotton shirt she'd tossed over her head this morning.

"Let me." Mrs. Scribb shooed Mina's fingers aside and had her laced and buttoned before she took her next breath. "Perhaps you need a bit of practice with ladylike clothing."

Mina would have laughed if her insides weren't churning and the corset she'd imprisoned herself in wasn't cutting off her air.

Behind her, Emma, the closest Enderley had to a lady's maid, steered her to a chair. "Sit, miss, and I'll fix your hair."

"Just something simple." She never did more with her hair than tie it back in a plain knot, even when the previous duke was in residence. Mina wasn't certain they should be making such a fuss over the new duke.

He was going to be trouble. Tall, broad-shouldered, unexpectedly appealing trouble who now held their fates in his hands.

Mrs. Scribb stuck her head out of the wardrobe long enough to plant her hands on her hips and give Mina an assessing look. "He's unsettled you. What did he say?"

"I'm perfectly settled." Except that she couldn't keep her heel from tapping, and her heartbeat hadn't steadied since he'd put his hands on her waist.

The man's scent still clung to her skin, and his eyes haunted her. They marked him as his father's son, whatever the rumors might be. Only one was the same cool blue as the old duke's eyes, but the unique almond shape of them made the men mirror images. The jagged scar lancing Nicholas Lyon's cheek did nothing to diminish the chiseled symmetry of his features or the striking beauty of his eyes.

There was life behind his gaze, intelligence and flickers of fiery emotion, though she'd detected little in the way of compassion. Except when she'd caught him scratching Millicent's chin, attempting to soothe the feisty cat. Millicent hadn't taken much notice, but Mina had.

"He didn't seem pleased to learn that I'd taken on my father's role." Her deception had displeased him, as she'd feared, though he'd seemed more irritated than furious. "There's every chance he'll sack me."

"Then we shall all go." Mrs. Scribb sealed the declaration with a fervent nod. The wholly unrealistic plan had been proposed in the months they'd fretted over the new duke's arrival. If he attempted to dismiss one of them, Mrs. Scribb insisted they should all give their notice in a show of unity.

"I can't lose this post," Emma said softly as she swept her fingers through Mina's hair.

"We'll find you another, girl." Mrs. Scribb was quick to dismiss the maid's distress. "Mr. Wilder and I will write you a good character."

"No one is losing their post because of me." Mina turned in her chair and clasped Emma's hands. The girl didn't only fear for her own future. Mina knew she sent wages to her parents in Dorset, who struggled to support her six siblings. "I'll apologize to His Grace the moment I see him again."

She wouldn't let the new duke take his anger at her out on the rest of them. They hadn't chosen her as steward any more than she'd chosen to lose her father.

"Besides, he's likely to keep all of us in our posts. A duke can't run an estate without a staff, and why wouldn't he prefer servants who know Enderley well?"

Emma seemed satisfied with that logic. She nodded and reached up to finish arranging Mina's hair. "Tell us more about him, miss."

"He's a gentleman, like most others." Now, that *was* less than the whole truth. He didn't look like any man she'd ever met, and so far he hadn't behaved like most men of her acquaintance either. She struggled to focus on what was mundane about him. "He's tall like his brother. Well-dressed. Arrogant." *Confident* might be a better word. His self-assured air was every inch what a duke's should be. "He has his father's eyes."

"Odd eyes, Tobias tells me. One dark and one light. Some say he wasn't his father's son at all." The young maid mumbled the words just above a whisper.

"Bite your tongue." Mrs. Scribb stepped close, wagging a finger of chastisement. "Those rumors were never true. The duchess was faithful as they come, but the old duke's jealousy blinded him to the truth. Anyone can see the new duke is the very image of his father, and the man's our master now, come what may."

"But will he be a good one?" Mina wondered aloud.

Masculine beauty didn't matter. Eustace had possessed the cool Tremayne eyes and an occasional charm too. All that counted was what the new duke intended to do with Enderley and those who depended on the estate for their survival.

"Can't be worse than his father and brother," Mrs. Scribb declared before clapping a hand over her mouth. "Forgive me. 'Tisn't kind to speak ill of the dead."

Mina noticed she didn't take a single word of it back. She couldn't. The old duke had been a tight-fisted bully, and his son a spendthrift dilettante who'd merrily bled the Tremayne coffers dry.

"Sometimes we must tell the truth, even if it's not kind," Mina put in. "My father always did."

Mrs. Scribb cast her a sympathetic look. "Aye, he was a good man."

The best Mina had ever known.

"We know the new duke is good at business," Emma said as she returned Mina's brush to a bedside drawer. "That's already an improvement over his brother."

A vast improvement. And he *had* helped her down from the tree and refrained from dismissing her on the spot when he'd learned of her deception. Maybe she'd judged Nicholas Lyon too quickly.

Frantic footsteps sounded in the hall outside her bedchamber. A moment later, Hildy, the youngest maid, burst through.

"Come quick," she said, clutching her chest to catch her breath. "The new duke's gone mad."

"That was fast," Mina said drily. Hildy did have a tendency to exaggerate. "Where is he?"

"The study. He's behaving very strangely, miss."

Mina followed Hildy and tried to match her frantic sprint. Halfway down the hall, the young maid failed to notice a bucket left in the hallway.

"Watch out," Mina called, catching the girl by the elbow before she hit the freshly mopped floor. "You take care of the bucket. I'll see to the duke."

What Mina couldn't see were the steps as she descended the stairs. *Blasted skirts.* They did nothing but keep her from maneuvering as she wished. Wrenching her hem up, she strode quickly toward the duke's study. Mrs. Darley, the estate's cook, stood outside the door, knotting her apron in her hands.

A man's voice emerged through the half-open door. A deep rumble. *Wilder.*

Mina pushed into the room, and her breath tangled in her throat. Wilder shot her a look of desperate uncertainty.

Nicholas Lyon loomed above both of them, standing atop a Chippendale cherrywood table pushed up against the unlit fireplace. Polished black boots planted wide, he stared down at her, skin glistening with perspiration, eyes aglow. Then he turned his back on her.

He'd shed clothing since she'd last seen him.

Don't stare, she told herself. But her mind cataloged broad thighs, a tight, muscled backside, and a wide back encased in a scarlet waistcoat straining at the seams as he reached above his head.

"Your Grace?"

"There will be new rules in my dukedom, Thorne." He unbuttoned the cuffs of his white shirt, rolling up his sleeves to reveal a dusting of black hair over muscled forearms. "First rule. Don't call me that."

"What shall I call you?" Mina cleared her throat. "And what, if I may ask, are you doing?" She glanced at Wilder, who merely shook his head in the same miserable manner he employed when Mrs. Scribb was on a rampage or Mrs. Darley burned his favorite apple tarts.

"This"—he pointed at the painting above his head—"needs to come down."

The duke lifted off his boot heels and grasped the edges of an elaborate gilt-framed portrait of his mother. Without a moment's hesitation, he plucked the painting from the hook that had kept it affixed to the wall for decades.

"We could," Wilder began in his slow, steady drone, "get a ladder."

Whether the duke failed to hear him or was giving in to the stubbornness Mina had already encountered at the oak tree, he ignored Wilder's suggestion. The portrait came down at a precarious tilt, but his arms were long, his shoulders broad, and he managed to gently maneuver the enormous canvas to the floor.

"Wilder, see to preparing this for transport back to

London." The duke jumped down with a bone-shaking thud and placed the painting in the old man's hands. "Take good care of her."

Wilder nodded solemnly and then shuffled out, maneuvering the tall frame through the doorway.

Mina closed the door behind him, shooing off the gaping gaggle of staff who'd assembled in the hall.

"Your Gra—"

"Try *Mr. Lyon* or *sir* or whatever you damn well please. I could even live with *my lord*." Tremayne moved toward his father's desk, an enormous bulk of dark walnut that Mina always thought looked as if it had been carved from the hull of a Viking ship.

She expected him to sit and savor the first moment of reclining on the worn leather throne from which his father had ruled Tremayne lands with a merciless fist. Instead, he perched his backside against the front edge, crossed his arms, and watched her expectantly.

"Mr. Lyon." She dutifully tested the name on her lips. "I wish to apologize for not being clear in my correspondence with your solicitor."

"I hate deception, Thorne." He drew in a deep breath and let it out slowly. "But I can understand seeing an opportunity and seizing it."

"You *don't* understand." He made her sound like one of the card sharps who played at his gambling tables. Mina's hands balled at her sides. "I view my father's post as a duty, not an opportunity."

"None of the staff here owe me or my family a lifetime of employment. There are always others seeking work."

"Others without loyalty to Enderley." Mina gritted her teeth. Emma had been wrong to hope the new duke would be better. She was beginning to think he was worse.

"Ah, loyalty." The man had the audacity to chuckle, a low, resonant sound that echoed in the spacious room.

Was he laughing at her? For caring about his family home. For trying her best to step into her father's shoes and keep his brother from bankrupting Enderley. But it was clear he wasn't. His gaze took on a faraway look, and any mirth he felt was quickly replaced with a creased-brow frown of unease.

"My only loyalty, Miss Thorne, is to my business."

"Is Enderley not your business now?" Her father thought of the estate that way, not as some collection of ancestral acres but as a living, breathing enterprise that took in the work of the staff and tenants and, in return, gave back a good living for everyone, including the Lyon family.

"Enderley is my burden." He shifted his shoulders like he felt the weight of his inheritance clinging to his back. "So they're a loyal lot." He waved toward the doorway, as if fully aware there were half a dozen ears pressed to the other side of the wood. "I know Wilder and have memories of Mrs. Squibb, but I'm unfamiliar with the new staff." With one sweeping glance, he took her in from the hem of her skirt to the fringe of hair across her forehead. "Like you."

"I hardly consider myself new. I've lived here my whole life."

"Why did you stay?" He studied her intently, as if her answer mattered.

"I never seriously considered leaving." It was what she knew she should say, but her cheeks began to warm the moment the words were out. She had considered leaving but never taken a single step toward independence. Mostly childish fancies, and that one single moment of romantic folly that had ended in disaster. "I never wish to leave Enderley."

He tilted his head, narrowing his eyes. "I don't believe you."

"You still distrust me, Mr. Lyon?" Mina huffed out a sigh. She needed to earn his trust. "As long as my father was here, I couldn't truly imagine living anywhere else."

He looked around, lifting his arms to encompass the room, the whole estate. "He's not here anymore, and yet you are."

"Enderley is my home. Wilder and Mrs. Scribb are like family to me." Mina felt heat creeping up her neck.

She'd revealed too much. Duty was only part of why she stayed. The rest of what rooted her at Enderley was a tangle of sentiment and what she hated admitting most. Where would she go? What would she be if she left Enderley? There was guilt too, for even thinking of abandoning the estate her father loved so much.

"I don't consider staying a burden." She winced, knowing she shouldn't have thrown the word back at him. "But if you feel you cannot trust me or wish for another steward"—Mina fought to keep her chin up, back straight, as all the morning's anxiety rushed in— "that is, of course, your prerogative."

"Keep your post, Thorne." He pushed off the edge of the desk and stepped closer. "I do consider this estate a burden, and I'd like your help managing it."

"I would be pleased to, Your Grace. Er, Mr. Lyon. There is much to be done." Mina swallowed against a knot in her throat.

His eyes widened a bit, as if her enthusiasm surprised him.

Relief. A sweet, heady balm rushed through her veins. She could keep her position. "And the other staff? None will be dismissed?"

"I didn't say that." The hint of a smile that flickered near the duke's mouth faded. "I have other plans for the estate."

Chapter Five

*A*h, the gold sparks again.

Miss Thorne's eyes flared with irritation. The lady went from the thin edge of insolence to absolute fury faster than any woman Nick had ever known.

But he didn't mind. He had some experience with beautiful women. With claiming a dukedom, he had none. Looking at her, focusing on her flushed cheeks and clenched jaw, Nick could almost forget where he was. He could almost keep all he loathed about Enderley at bay.

Not just the title he never wanted and duties he had no idea how to embrace, but being in the room where he'd withstood his father's cruelty for years. The man's vicious condemnations had thundered to the ceiling, and the sting of his lash had drawn Nick's blood countless times. Glancing down at the carpet, Nick traced the familiar vine pattern. His father always bid him to avert his gaze, unable to bear his cursed eyes.

Nick lifted his head, pushed the ugly memories away, and focused on his very unexpected steward.

Though she looked as angry as she had at the oak tree, everything else had changed. He tried, and failed, not to notice what her dress accentuated that her men's clothing hid. Oddly, he rather missed the sight of her in trousers and a waistcoat. Not to mention the tangled waves of chestnut hair that were now imprisoned under pins.

Yet even in the plainest drab brown dress he'd ever seen, Miss Thorne was unaccountably appealing. Especially her fierce amber gaze and cheeks that heated whenever he irked her.

"Whatever your plans, Your Grace, the staff need to know." She inhaled sharply. "Should they begin seeking new posts? Many were dismissed over the last few years. I understand the need to economize, but I assure you all of those remaining are essential." She lifted a hand and fussed with her collar, waiting for him to respond. When he didn't, she added, "I could forgo my own wages for a time, if—"

"That won't be necessary, Miss Thorne." Nick swallowed down a chuckle.

She was earnest and determined. Demanding, for one supposedly in his employ. Why the hell did he find her tenacity so bloody amusing? The lady had installed herself as estate steward and deceived his solicitor, aided and abetted by a staff who she claimed were loyal to him.

The worst part was that he couldn't blame her. Claim a bit of power for oneself? That he understood. And untruths? He'd lost count of the lies he'd told to save himself from hunger.

"May I have your assurance, then?"

He snapped his head up. "My assurance?"

"That the other staff won't be dismissed and that I may keep my post as steward. Most dukes wouldn't approve of a woman serving in such a role."

"My brother did, apparently."

She bowed her head. "The late duke was absent from the estate a good deal and resided mostly at Tremayne House in Belgrave Square."

"Ah, yes." A property that, blessedly, was not entailed. Nick had already hired a crew to clean and refurbish the elegant townhouse to go on the market. "He must have returned now and then. When he did, he couldn't have failed to notice that you weren't your father."

Everything about the woman was noticeable. She had a vivid bristling energy about her that filled up his father's dimly lit study.

"I'm not sure he thought about who ran the estate, as long as the work got done."

Nick remembered his brother's laziness well. Eustace had never been interested in duty. Only play, diversion, and avoiding the responsibilities their father heaped on him. Poor, useless sod.

"How did he die?" He wasn't sure why he was asking. Wasn't sure if he truly cared about any Tremayne history that had passed since he'd departed.

But this woman cared enough for both of them. He could hear devotion in her voice when she spoke of Enderley. He could see the pride in her eyes when she swiped a bit of dust off the edge of a lampshade as she passed.

For whatever reason, she loved this accursed place.

"An injury, my lord. He fell and never recovered." Miss Thorne swallowed like she was parched, as if the memory disturbed her.

"Fell?" The solicitor's letter had been vague, but Nick had always imagined Eustace's end involved women or drink or some argument over one of his vices.

"From his horse."

"Here at Enderley?"

She bobbed her head, and Nick kept his gaze on her as long as he could while he crossed to the cart on the far side of the room. He poured her a finger of what smelled like sherry and approached to hand her the tiny cut crystal glass.

"No, thank you." She wouldn't look at him. Wouldn't even turn her head an inch, though he stood less than a foot away.

"You're shivering, Miss Thorne." Nick got a few inches closer and caught her scent. Flowers, peonies, and hyacinth, sweet and fresh, blotted out the room's old smells and dark memories.

"There's always a chill in this room." She gestured toward the fireplace. "I can ring for a maid to light a fire."

"I don't plan to spend any more time in here than I must." He positioned himself in front of her, giving her space to breathe, and offered the glass again. "This will warm you."

Her eyes flickered closed. From the tension in her jaw, he guessed she was biting her tongue. Eventually she took the glass, tipped it back, and swallowed the contents in a single gulp.

"Thank you," she said hoarsely.

"So, Miss Thorne, it seems I inherited a dukedom, and you inherited your father's post as steward."

He'd meant to state facts, simple truths, and yet the lady bristled.

"I have a knack for organizing and ensuring tasks get done." She straightened her back, rising half an inch. "My father taught me all he knew about the duties of an estate steward, and he always said I possessed a natural talent for numbers."

"Did he? And yet I've already discovered a flaw in your calculations."

"What flaw?"

Nick slid one of the massive account ledger books he'd found on his father's desk toward the edge, flipping the pages open to a grosgrain marker that had been placed near a row of recent entries. He planted his finger in the middle of the column. "There."

She came closer. Her heels clipped hard against the wood floor, and Nick wondered if she was still wearing Hessians under her skirt. Bending at the waist, she peered at the page, tilting her head this way and that. Then her eyes slid closed, as his did when calculating a large sum in his head.

A sharp little intake of breath sounded in the room before she opened her eyes. "You're right. I made an error."

She sounded so bereft, Nick had a momentary impulse to comfort her. He hated making mistakes in his calculations too.

"We all make errors, Miss Thorne." He leaned closer. "As you see, it was easily corrected."

"But if I made one, perhaps there are others."

"There aren't. I checked."

"All the entries? That's impossible. There are months' worth of transactions."

"You needn't sound so impressed. I've been stuck in this blasted house for an hour." Nick noted that her brows leaned toward each other, two pretty arches, as she frowned at him. Something about her scrutiny unsettled him, and he felt that odd little charge of awareness she seemed to spark.

He was surprised to find they had anything in common.

"I like numbers," he told her. "One might even say I have a *natural talent*. And I'm a *very* thorough man."

Miss Thorne gasped in shock.

Nick cursed himself for infusing the words with more seductive intent than he should have. And for being far too intrigued with the woman.

She approached the fireplace mantel and nervously rearranged the knickknacks on top so that the porcelain milkmaid and a little marble goddess were equidistant from a hideous ormolu clock. Nick mentally calculated how much each item might fetch at auction.

"The wall looks bare without the duchess's portrait," she said, glancing up at the empty patch of plaster. "The room feels far colder now."

"It's always been frigid. But you're right. The space is empty without her." The wall was still cluttered with small paintings, landscapes mostly, and the single dominating portrait of the man Nick would always think of as the Duke of Tremayne.

"She had kind eyes." Miss Thorne spoke softly and then turned back to face him.

No one needed to tell Nick his eyes weren't kind. Most saw them as an outward sign of his blighted nature. But his mother pointed to their shape as proof of his parentage. She'd often led him to a looking glass as a child, pointing out how much he resembled his father.

She'd done her best to reassure him he wasn't a bastard, but Nick only noticed his own strange unmatched eyes looking back at him and, after one of his father's attacks, the scar marring his face.

"What else do you remember about her?" Nick pushed the past away with such ferocity, he sometimes feared he was losing every memory of his mother. He couldn't bear to recall the time they'd spent together after leaving Enderley, a time of poverty and fear in France. They'd been free of his father's cruelty, but illness had taken her from Nick too soon. He wanted to remember the best of her.

"Not much, I'm afraid. I only met the duchess a few times when I was a child. My father did not like me to disturb them."

"And my father? What do you remember of him?" He forced himself to ask the question, pretending that speaking of the man didn't cause his stomach to burn with bile.

"He . . . did not like me." Miss Thorne shivered, clearly recalling some unpleasant encounter.

"What did you do to provoke him?" He quite liked imagining her snapping back at the ogre. But what would his father have done in response? The duke had never tolerated any inkling of rebellion.

"A music lesson." She lowered her gaze to the ground and her forehead tightened into grooves of worry. "Your mother caught me plucking at one of the harps in her music room. She wasn't angry. She encouraged me to learn and arranged for the governess to give me lessons, but the duke was livid when he found out. I was only the steward's girl, and the governess was hired to teach your brother. The duke shouted at me and banished me from his sight." She shook her head as if attempting to erase the memory. "I don't think he approved of me being underfoot around the estate."

"Then we have something else in common, Miss Thorne."

She exhaled sharply, as if she'd been holding a breath, and offered him the slightest hint of a grin.

That one little sliver of kindness and Nick's body tightened. He resisted the instinct to lean closer. He hated how much he wanted her grin to bloom. For some inexplicable reason, he craved approval from this woman.

But her grin faded and Miss Thorne gazed at him with the same mix of wariness and loathing as when she'd stepped down from the old oak. As if she'd never forget what he tried so hard to forget—that he would always be his father's son.

In that moment, he wanted nothing more than to send the woman and every other staff member at Enderley packing. He could hire new servants and sweep away everything from this wretched place's past.

But it wasn't efficient. Securing new employees would take time. He wanted to flee these stones, not lengthen his stay.

"You needn't worry." Nick stepped back and settled against his father's desk, arms braced across his chest. "I have no intention of dismissing you."

The tightness in her jaw softened. "And the rest of the staff?"

"They can stay too. For now." What the hell was wrong with him? A quarter hour's resistance from Miss Thorne and he was already conceding. "Though the young maid may have to go."

"Hildy?"

"She screamed when she got a look at me. I don't blame her, of course, but she might be happier somewhere else." He didn't relish the child's shrieks every time he encountered her in the hall.

"She's just a girl." Miss Thorne scanned his face. Nick assumed she sympathized with the young housemaid's response to him, at least until her gaze fell to his lips and her breath seemed to catch in her throat.

It was almost as if the odd creature found something to admire in the shape of his mouth.

"A skittish girl," he said.

Miss Thorne blinked and squared her shoulders. "One who relies on her position at Enderley. Allow me to speak to her before you dismiss her?"

"What will you tell her? That I'm not the ogre I seem to be?"

She began to speak and then pressed her lips together, as if thinking better of whatever retort sat on the tip of her tongue.

"Say it," he urged quietly, because apparently the one thing that had been missing from his life was a woman who couldn't decide whether or not she loathed him.

"Whether you're an ogre or not remains to be seen, Mr. Lyon."

Nick grimaced. "Keep the jittery little housemaid, Miss Thorne. I'm sure she'll get used to this." He gestured vaguely at his face.

"Thank you." Her voice went breathy, uncertain. The first real crack he'd seen in her no-nonsense manner.

Nick swallowed against a lump of unease. He moved behind his father's desk. After a moment's hesitation, he pulled out the old devil's chair and sat on the cold, stiff leather.

She stood in front of him, tense and expectant, as if awaiting her first instructions as his steward.

"The fact is, I need you, Thorne." To get out in a fortnight, he'd need her efficiency most of all. "I'll be relying on your knowledge of the estate and leadership with the staff."

"I'll serve you as diligently as my father served yours."

Nick narrowed his gaze. "Our relationship will be different than theirs." He leaned forward, flattening his palms on top of his father's desk. Now *his* desk. "You're going to help me get the estate in order."

"Yes, of course." Her eyes lit as if he'd just offered her the moon. "I have a list. I can't tell you how glad the staff are to have you in residence, to direct them and see to all that needs doing."

"Good." A little muscle under Nick's eye twitched. She wouldn't like the rest. "I've begun reviewing the inventories you prepared and noted that some are not finished."

"No, but you did arrive early. I'll ensure all of them are updated by end of day tomorrow."

"Excellent." Nick stared at the beaten leather blotter of his father's desk rather than into the amber gaze he sensed tracking his every movement. "I need a notation of everything of value with detailed descriptions so I can send the inventories off to the auctioneer."

"Auctioneer?" The syllables came out slowly, as if she'd never heard the word before. As if she couldn't fathom its meaning. At least not in relation to Enderley.

"This house is cluttered with possessions that benefit no one. Much of it, thankfully, is not part of the entail. I intend to sell what I can." He wasn't sure why he was detailing his plans and rushing through his words as if he were forcing out a confession. With a gesture around the room, he indicated the ridiculous suit of armor standing sentry in the corner and an old sword collection hanging on the far wall. "Once we clear these out, the room can be thoroughly cleaned."

"I . . . don't understand." Her voice came in a raspy whisper. "You wish to sell off your history?"

"I don't give a toss about my history, Miss Thorne." Nick approached the cart and poured himself whiskey, a rich old brew, the same honeyed brown as the eyes shooting daggers at his back.

"Perhaps you should, *Your Grace*. Tremaynes have owned this land for centuries."

Nick downed the whole finger of liquor in one searing swallow. "It's time for a change."

"Your father—"

"Don't mention him again."

The little growl of frustration she emitted under her breath wasn't quite low enough for Nick not to hear.

"May I mention your brother then?"

"If you must."

"As you see from the account ledgers, the previous duke left little behind." She took two steps closer.

Nick turned to refill his glass, but he sensed her nearness, breathed in a lungful of her fresh, sweet scent as she came to stand just over his shoulder. When he turned, she was too close. Dangerously so. An arm's reach away.

She gazed up at him, emotions raw, her desperation palpable.

"Even he did not think of selling Tremayne heirlooms," she said stiffly.

"Despite appearances, I am not my father. And I sure as hell am nothing like my brother."

She began shaking her head, as if she didn't believe him, or didn't want his denial. Nick reached out and slipped a finger under her chin, urging her to look into his eyes. To hear him. To understand the man she was dealing with.

But her skin was warm and so damn soft. He found himself stroking his thumb against the silken edge of her chin.

She tensed but didn't pull away.

"I'm not a nice man, Miss Thorne. Not even a particularly good one. He saw to that." Nick tipped his head to indicate the portrait looming over them. "Inheriting this estate proves I'm not a lucky man either. But I am fair."

Hope flared in her eyes, and Nick clenched his jaw against the urge to give her something, anything, to be hopeful for. But he couldn't. He'd only come to Enderley to settle matters and leave the pile behind him once and for all.

He let her go, clenched his fist to hold on to her warmth, the only heat in this arctic room. "I'll give you and the staff a fortnight to get Enderley in order. I can bring in help to remove the items we wish to sell."

Hope sputtered in her gaze, like a snuffed candle. "You truly mean to gut the house."

He hated the emptiness in her voice, the telltale quiver in her chin.

Nick put on his business mien. The one he used with aristocrats in the den. The one that said he would brook no argument.

"Don't cling to any other possibility, Miss Thorne." He needed her to understand what he was and that he hadn't come to give any of them hope. "I mean to gut Enderley, lease it, and never think on these cold stone walls again."

Chapter Six

Nick punched the pillow, angling the lumpy thing to find a bit of comfort, but Enderley wouldn't give him any relief. Scents and sounds were too eerily familiar. When he closed his eyes, the past rushed in, ghost fingers reaching out from every corner and crevice of the damnable house.

Sitting upright in the creaking guest bed, he scraped at the stubble on his chin and longed for his own room at Lyon's—the thick double mattress, the lush velvet bedcovers, the soft silken sheets. If anyone wondered why he insisted on such luxuries, let them suffer a night in this grim place.

But it wasn't truly luxury he craved. He'd happily return to the smoke-filled rooms at Lyon's or wander the soot-filled streets of London. Anything was preferable to spending the night in this damp, musty tomb. The place stoked memories he'd long kept at bay and he sensed his father's presence everywhere.

Especially in his portrait in the study.

Thankfully, there were no portraits staring out at Nick from the guest chamber's walls, just bland landscapes of pallid men hunting outnumbered foxes.

Still, his father's specter hovered over the house, eyes burning from that damned portrait. The one Nick couldn't stomach seeing next to his mother's.

When they'd escaped together in the dark of night from Enderley, from one who'd become more monster than man, neither of them had ever dreamed of returning. His mother wouldn't have wanted her portrait hanging next to his father's.

Giving up on any possibility of sleep, Nick donned a shirt and trousers and set off toward the study like he was striding into a brawl—chin up, chest out, hands flexing into fists. But deep inside, in places he stomped down, a part of him was still that damned skittish boy he'd once been.

Nick's hand shook as he pushed open the door. Memories rushed back in a torrent of images.

Even at nine years old, he shivered so fiercely his teeth rattled whenever his father summoned him.

The old man glared from the moment Nick stepped into the room. Eyes pinched under the weight of his glower, nostrils flaring, he flicked his hand, urging Nick closer.

"Come, creature, and look at me when I speak to you." He snatched a tumbler from his desk, tipped the glass back, and drained every last drop before scowling at Nick again. "Bastard child. Why didn't you perish in your cradle? Would've saved me the trouble of feeding and clothing you."

He grimaced as if Nick's existence turned his stomach. Then he reeled back and swung, the back of his hand cracking against Nick's cheek.

The thud in his ears made him dizzy. He'd learned to keep himself still. A flinch, a cry, any sign of weakness stoked his father's rage.

"Don't look at me, boy! Turn those devil eyes away."

Nick flicked his gaze down and focused on the carpet, the carved wood of his father's desk, anything but the man himself. The duke's commands never made sense. Look. Don't look. Speak. Don't speak. Kneel. Stand. Nick obeyed, hoping to end their encounters quickly. But they never ended after one blow or lash. Teeth clenched, body shaking, he waited for the next.

"What do you have to say for yourself, evil imp?"

"Nothing, sir." Nick tried swallowing, but his mouth had gone dust-dry.

"And *what* are you?"

"Nothing, sir." Nick rasped the words his father made him repeat every time.

The duke shifted. Nick winced, anticipating the next strike. Fire came instead, lancing across his cheek, gouging into his skin. Pain spread until his whole face burned. Hot blood trickled onto his chin. Nick lifted a trembling hand to his face. His fingers came away sticky and red. Daring a glance at his father, he found the man smiling as he flipped a penknife in his hand.

"Your mother won't remark on our resemblance anymore, will she? Now you look like the monster you are."

Nick shoved the memory back, gripped the cold metal knob of the study door, and sucked in deep breaths until he was here, now, not shivering like the pathetic child he'd once been. Inside the room, a shaft of moonlight slanted through the draperies. Its glow found his father's portrait, lighting the devil's glare with a silvery gleam.

Those pale blue eyes, so like his own, jabbed at Nick. Poking at old wounds that should have healed years before. Two glowing shards, perfect windows onto his father's glacial soul. Not even a paid portraitist had managed to hide the viciousness in the old man's gaze.

"You're dead," he told the creature on the wall, but no satisfaction came. Nick imagined his father, in his own twisted way, enjoying Nick's misery at being back at the estate. Shackled to all its responsibilities. Imprisoned in the place his father had once turned into Nick's prison.

No. That was one memory he would never revisit. The tower. The lock. The months of fear and hopelessness. He wasn't imprisoned here anymore. A fortnight and he'd never see this damned house again.

Nick approached the man's hulking desk and lifted the penknife that had once dripped with his own blood. The scar on his cheek twinged in recognition.

What a weakling he'd been. Sensitive and fragile. His father had loathed him for that weakness as much as his deluded certainty that Nick was not his true born son.

The shock of his father's loathing had been the worst part. He'd been so innocent. Eager for Papa's approval. Desperate to please. Never dreaming just how far the man would go to make him suffer.

"There's no victory for you here," he told the man who'd never get a chance to strike at him again. "Now that this pile is mine, I'll tear it all down. Everything you've built. Every Tremayne family heirloom will be sold, and I'll rent this hellish place to the highest bidder. A stranger will sleep in your bed and eat at your table."

Nick flipped the knife in his hand, raised his arm, and launched the blade straight between his father's eyes. For one delicious moment, the tip impaled its mark. Then the hilt's weight pulled the penknife down.

Failure. Again. He'd known it every time he faced his father.

He strode to the window, wrenched up the glass, and stuck out his head to drag in long, chilling breaths. A smoky haze filled the air. The smoldering scent of burning leaves. A whisper of memory came. Huge piles of leaves gathered by the groundskeeper. Jumping in with all the glee of a seven-year-old. Being whipped afterward.

At his back, he still felt the man's empty eyes on him. *You're dead.* Nick refused to allot the man another thought. He sure as hell wasn't going to stare at his image for however long he remained in this bloody house.

He turned to face his father's portrait, strode to a delicate wood table, kicked the edge with his boot, and sent it slamming into the wall. After climbing atop, he knocked the portrait from the wall. The frame split with a satisfying crack when it hit the floor.

Nick jumped down and poured himself a finger of whiskey, contemplating how best to rid himself of the thing. The frame would never fit into the fireplace, or even the kitchen hearth, which was crowded with pots and racks.

Through the open window, smoke curled up into the clear night sky.

Nick smiled.

MINA BOLTED AWAKE as if she'd been shaken from a dream, yet her chamber was empty and quiet. She held her breath, straining to hear an errant sound or some portent of trouble.

A man's voice filtered up from downstairs. Not Wilder. Not Tobias.

Deeper. Richer. *Angrier.*

She pulled on her dressing gown and stepped into her tall boots. A terrible scraping noise made the hairs on her nape quiver, and she rushed toward the stairs without lighting the candle she kept by her bed.

As she descended, she heard the duke shout once more.

"Get out!"

Good grief, had the cat crossed his path?

Mina broke into a run. The ruckus seemed to be coming from the ducal study. She burst into the room and found chaos. Glass lay in broken shards on the carpet, the cherry table sat dusty and scratched against the wall, and the window sash had been thrown up as wide as it would go. Drapery swept past the sill and fluttered in the breeze.

Mina glimpsed movement through the open window. The Duke of Tremayne strode across the grass. His white shirt stood out in the moonglow and an object trailed behind him in the grass.

Scanning the room, Mina noted another empty patch of plaster. He'd ripped down the old duke's portrait.

But where on earth was he going with it?

Mina climbed over the low sill as the duke continued on, dragging the enormous portrait behind him. Her nose burned at the smell of smoke in the air and she knew. The burn pile of leaves the groundskeeper had assembled midday still flickered with a few hot embers. He was going to banish his father to the flames.

She didn't blame him. That portrait had always sent shivers down her spine. But the duke couldn't take to wandering the fields at night, burning whatever displeased him. What piece of the estate would he choose to destroy next?

She strode quickly through the grass, stepping close enough to hear him grunt as he heaved the massive frame, nearly as tall as his considerable height, into the smoldering pile of leaves. He planted one hand on his hip and watched, unmoving, as a few sparks leaped into flame. Then he let out a bitter, deep-throated chuckle.

Had the man gone mad?

"Your Grace?"

He whipped around to face her, his expression bemused but not shocked. As if he fully expected her to find him burning furnishings at the witching hour. "It's quite late. You should go back to bed."

Mina's reply got stuck in her throat.

The man looked dangerous. Wild. Tangled waves of black hair framed his face. A few messy strands crisscrossed his forehead. His shirt, unbuttoned low on his chest, revealed hard planes and shadowed muscles.

She tried not to gawk but wasn't quite sure where to fix her gaze.

The painting. She pointed past him toward the spot where flames licked up into the night sky. "It is indeed late, Your Grace. Why are you stomping around the grounds half-dressed, burning art in the leaf pile?"

The duke stared at her finger a moment, crossed his arms, and arched one dark brow. "It's my painting. My grounds. My bloody leaf pile."

Mina gritted her teeth. "We don't generally spend our evenings at Enderley tossing portraits into the flames. The staff will think you've gone dotty."

"The staff are all tucked in their beds. Why aren't you, Miss Thorne?"

"Because I'm too worried about which piece of Enderley you plan to burn next."

He let out a startled laugh, not the bitter chuckle of watching his father burn, but a warmer sound. "I'm done burning furnishings for the night. Does that satisfy, Thorne?" He glanced over his shoulder at the smoking portrait. "You knew the man. Can you blame me?"

Mina understood disliking Talbot Lyon. The man had been a tyrant, brutal in his treatment of the staff, irrational and unhinged in his later years, but she couldn't encourage the new duke's destructive bent.

"Did you know the artist who painted your father was quite famous? If you disapproved of the portrait, we might have sold it for at least a hundred pounds."

He narrowed his eyes and approached until he was close enough for her to smell his woodsy cologne. The scent of lavender wafted off him too. An Enderley scent. Mrs. Scribb always put a bit on the linens before placing them on the beds.

"I would have paid two hundred pounds for the pleasure of burning it."

"That two hundred would have allowed us to hire new staff, refill the larder."

"I hate to tell you this, Miss Thorne, but I don't give a damn about Enderley."

Mina's chest burned as if he'd speared her with a fragment of the burning picture frame.

"If I had the time, I'd wrench it apart stone by stone." He cast his gaze past her shoulder, to the far edge of the estate, where the old Tudor tower stood.

"You won't do your duty then?" Mina understood having responsibilities thrust upon one's shoulders and finding one's life veering in an unexpected direction. But she couldn't imagine shirking one's duty, especially not when so many relied on him for their livelihood.

"I'm here, aren't I?"

"But it seems you do not wish to be duke."

"I can't tell if you have a dry sense of humor, Thorne, or an extraordinary talent for understatement." A single long stride and he was too close. So near that her body began to warm. He radiated heat, even in the cool night air. "Surely, you know the rumors. Most say I have no right to the Tremayne title. Or haven't you heard that my father believed I was a bastard?"

"You're not. That portrait proves it." The old duke's face was nearly obscured now, in a wash of melting paint and burning canvas.

"Resemble him, don't I?" He bent his head so that they were eye to eye. "Same cold eyes."

"The likeness is undeniable." Mina could hardly tell the man he was more attractive in every way than his father. "Not to mention that you seem to share the same temper."

He smirked, but his eyes flashed with pain, as if the accusation stung.

"Of course, I've only known you for a handful of hours, Your Grace. But if you truly mean to abandon the estate, then you're more like Eustace than your father."

"I'm nothing like them." He moved in close, as if to emphasize his words. His chin trembled. A muscle flickered in his jaw. "Eustace? You speak of my brother familiarly. Were you close?"

"I knew him all my life."

A grimace twisted his full lips. "Ah, yes, because he was here and I was not. As you said, Miss Thorne, you don't know me." He began to turn away, and Mina suddenly wanted to know why he'd left the estate as a child and never returned. Had the rumors about his parentage been the cause?

"I did see you once, the day you left. I was watching from an upstairs window. I liked to look out on the countryside, until the maids chased me away."

"And what did you see?" He cast his gaze across the field, taking in much the same view she loved, though obscured now by nightfall.

"A dark-haired boy waiting at the carriage circle. A huge black brougham that came to collect you. I remember being grateful my father refused to send me to boarding school. Was it awful?"

"Where I went that day? You can't imagine." His voice dipped low and raw. Even in the dim wash of moonlight, Mina saw bleakness shadow his features. "I saw you too, Miss Thorne. More than once. You were always giggling or dancing or moving about."

He assessed her, as if retrieving the memories and comparing them to the woman who stood before him.

Mina wasn't used to being looked at. Not like this. Not with curiosity by a handsome man. Especially not when she was wearing nothing but Hessian boots and a dressing gown and his bare chest was inches from her own.

"You seemed a strange creature to me with your carefree happiness." He took one step closer. They were toe to toe. His breath warmed her face as he gazed at her. "Do you still enjoy dancing?"

"I've no need to. There's very little cause for an estate steward's daughter to dance."

"That's very bleak, and yet you persist in caring for this place? Not just as your father's successor, but because you think this pile of stones means something."

"I do." The two words came out breathy and earnest. Like a plea.

He simply watched her, but it seemed a small victory that he didn't offer a scathing retort about Enderley in reply.

"Go back inside, Miss Thorne. Dawn will be here soon."

"You won't burn anything else?"

"Not tonight." He almost smiled. The edge of his lush upper lip edged upward a smidge.

Mina felt the urge to say more, to extend this fledgling bit of goodwill between them. "Do you not possess any fond memories of Enderley?"

"My mother," he said immediately. "She's my only happy memory of this place."

"We put flowers on her grave every season."

"What grave?" All the openness in his gaze vanished, replaced by wariness. Anger. "My mother is buried . . . elsewhere."

For a moment, Mina stood in stunned silence. "But there was a funeral. There's a plaque next to your father's in the family crypt. Why would he tell everyone she's buried there?"

"Because he was mad." He shook his head and stepped away. "I'll never tell that story. To anyone." He waved toward the house. "Go to bed, Miss Thorne. There's much to do tomorrow, and I need to leave this godforsaken place as soon as I can."

He stormed off, long legs stretching into an enormous stride as he headed back toward the house.

Mina remained rooted in place. His anger came on quick as a summer storm. It seemed to pass quickly too. Yet there were also hints of charm and humor.

Whatever his emotions—rage or irritation or amusement—the new Duke of Tremayne was dreadful at hiding his emotions. They seeped out, glowing as fierce as a furnace fire in his eyes.

A sound drew her gaze to the field beyond the stable

yard. The tree she'd climbed earlier in the day stood out against the indigo sky. And then another outline appeared. A horse approached, its reins dragging on the ground.

It wasn't like Tobias to let an animal get out of the stables at night.

Mina started forward, slowing her pace when the creature began to shy. The stallion was lithe and sleek, not one of the Tremayne workhorses. She knew them all by heart.

"Where did you come from?"

The creature stalled, dipping its head to munch grass. Mina tiptoed the rest of the way, holding her breath until her fingers brushed one strip of its leather rein.

She held her hand low, allowing the horse to take in her scent, giving him time to determine that she intended no harm.

Then she glimpsed the sheen of his flank in the moonlight. Long dark wounds had been cut into his flesh, and blood trickled down his coat. The stripes were the length and shape of a whip.

"Who did this to you?" Her throat burned as she ran her fingers into his mane, stroking his velvety neck. "Doesn't matter. We have a place for you."

"Miss?" Tobias came out to meet her when she led the horse into the stable yard.

"He's injured. We need to clean him up, give him some supper, and let him know he's safe."

Tobias reached out to stroke the horse's forelock, but he cast Mina a dubious look. "Who's he belong to?"

"We can worry about that tomorrow."

"But he belongs to someone, Miss Thorne. Fine piece of horseflesh like this, I'd suspect Lord Lyle."

Mina suspected the same, but she wanted nothing to do with Lyles.

"If he's Lord Lyle's, then the viscount or his horse trainer is an ogre." She couldn't bear cruelty, especially toward those who were weak and trusting.

"He'll want his stallion back."

"So he can beat him bloody?"

Tobias grimaced, nudging his shoulders up in a shrug. "Some take a firm hand to break."

"Just help him," Mina said softly. "We'll deal with Lord Lyle later. I'll mix up one of those poultices we used on Mercury when he caught his ankle in the blackberry bramble."

The young man nodded grimly. Tobias would do as she asked. He always had. They were nearly the same age and had always got on like siblings. Now her position as steward required him to do as she requested.

"Mina?" he called when she headed toward the kitchen door. "The duke say anything about us staff keeping our posts?"

"We can stay. He's brought no staff with him, so he needs us for now." She couldn't bear to tell him the man planned to empty the house down to its bare walls. "I'll find out more tomorrow and do what I can to secure employment for all of us."

Whether it was at Enderley or elsewhere. She wouldn't let any of them worry about where they'd find their next wages.

"Is he a good sort?" Tobias gestured with his elbow to the house. "Better than the other two?"

Mina stared up at the windows of the second floor windows where the guest bedrooms were located, then glanced at the smoldering burn pile. She thought of Nicholas Lyon's mercurial eyes, the misery whenever he spoke of his father, the pain at mention of his mother, the loathing whenever he referred to Enderley.

"I'm not sure. What sort of duke he'll be or how he'll change Enderley remains to be seen."

"Bit of a mystery, then, is he?"

He was indeed, but for all their sakes, he was a mystery Mina needed to solve.

Chapter Seven

There's no hope for the new master." Hildy kneeled on a cracked kitchen tile while she blacked the grates. "He's worse than the others." The girl swiped a corn silk curl from her forehead with the back of her arm. "What shall we do about him, Miss Thorne?"

That was the trouble. There was nothing to be done about him. Enderley was his, and beyond the near impossibility of his solicitor finding a means to break the entail, he could do with the estate as he pleased. She couldn't stop him if he wanted to pull it apart, as he claimed.

But she was going to try.

Late in the night, she'd formulated a plan. The wounded horse was a reminder that loathing Nicholas Lyon would get them nowhere. There was no use fighting his anger with more of the same. Some creatures required a bit of coaxing and kindness to make them trust. Perhaps the duke simply needed a dose of kindness too.

What if they could show him that Enderley could be a haven from all the muck and bustle of London life?

"He's caused nothing but wreckage since he arrived," Mrs. Scribb complained, all respect due their new master apparently forgotten. "Goodness, how he carries on. Such beastly manners for a gentleman. Climbing on furniture and removing paintings. If he goes on this way, he'll have the house down around our ears before long."

"A slight exaggeration," Mina said, praying she sounded the least bit convincing.

"We could give him a bit o' bad mutton," Mrs. Darley suggested. "That's what a cook friend of mine did until her master could bear it no more and took himself off to London."

Mina narrowed her gaze on the cook. She'd never imagined such schemes might be running around the sweet old lady's head.

"I fear he'll return to London soon enough," Mina told them, though she still hadn't divulged his plan.

There was much to do before the house could be rented, and in that time she hoped to convince him of the estate's value. She had to make him see it differently, not as a burden but as an opportunity.

Poisoning the man with mutton was not among the tactics she intended to employ.

"Good riddance to him if he only means to hate us and make our lives miserable." Tobias popped a hunk of fresh bread in his mouth.

"Bad mutton could kill a man," Emma said in a worried version of her usual soft tone. "Old Mr. McKintrick died of bad stew just last summer."

"Word is *Mrs.* McKintrick helped that along." Tobias smirked around his next bite and lowered his voice to a whisper. "Ever wonder why she kept nightshade growing in her garden?"

Emma's cornflower-blue eyes went round as saucers. "Cor, do you think it's true?"

"We're not poisoning him!" Mina's shout startled her as much as everyone else, and she worked to calm the nervous energy born from too little sleep and too much fretting. "Not with food or anything else. We should be treating him better than he expects."

From what she could tell, Nicholas Lyon was a man who anticipated the worst. Of Enderley, and perhaps of people too. Why not defy his expectations? Surely he could be brought around to seeing value in the estate, its staff, and the tenants.

"We should welcome him." Mina sought out Hildy's wide-eyed gaze. "Which will mean not shrieking when we encounter him in the halls."

The girl tipped her head down and gave a sheepish nod.

"'Tis not her fault he looks a fright," Tobias said defensively.

"Looks all right to me," Emma murmured. "Striking, I'd say, with that dark hair and pale eyes."

"The broadest shoulders I've ever seen. Never known a man to fill a suit as he does," Mrs. Scribb admitted with a sniff. "Cuts an imposing figure, our master."

"I could sharpen my knife on the edge of his cheekbones." Mrs. Darley's voice carried from across the room.

"His mouth—" Mina caught herself. Some instinct kept her from complete mortification, because none of her thoughts about Nicholas Lyon's mouth were lady-like or proper. "It's quite well made."

Hildy giggled. "I do think he has pretty lips, that I'll admit."

"My hair's dark." Tobias planted his chin on his fist and glanced miserably at Emma.

Mina tried steering them back to the topic at hand. "If the man has a dim view of Enderley, let's show him otherwise."

"How?" Mrs. Darley called from the table where she stood peeling vegetables. "Repairs are needed, more staff, and a good deal more in the kitchen budget if we're to fill the larders and feed him as a duke ought to be fed."

Adding more funds to the household budget was on the list of all Mina intended to ask of the new duke, but first she had to earn the man's trust. "I intend to speak to him about our concerns, Mrs. Darley."

"Whether we treat him like a king or a foe, he's master now." Mrs. Scribb adjusted the collection of keys at her hip and nodded as if she'd decided on a course of action. "We'll endure him as we have all the others. I've outlived two dukes. Wonder how long this one will last."

"Hope he goes quicker than his brother," Tobias grumbled. When Emma gasped, he managed a brief expression of contrition. "I only meant to London. 'Spect he wants to go back to his gambling club. Word is it's quite grand."

"We shouldn't wish him away just yet," Mina insisted. When he went back to the city, he'd be even less inclined to consider Enderley. "We need to keep him here as long as we can. We need him to invest in the estate if it's to survive."

"Not to mention the list of villagers who'll want to see him and come with their complaints," Mrs. Scribb said knowingly. Despite how much time she spent doing her duties as housekeeper with diligence, she seemed to know everyone in Barrowmere and every bit of gossip that festered in the village.

"Perhaps we should hold them off awhile." Wilder, who'd sat listening quietly, stood, gnarled hands gripping the back of his chair. "Let him get used to the place again before we heap on other troubles."

"A very good idea." Mina nodded in agreement.

There were so many troubles. She knew each one as if the list in her office had been etched in her mind. And more always came. That was the one certainty about her work as steward. Trouble might be as small as a broken tile or as large as a wounded horse, but dilemmas popped up at the estate every day.

"In that case," Emma said, picking up a tray filled with covered dishes, "I should take his breakfast up to him."

Mina glanced at the watch pinned to the gown she'd donned instead of her comfortable well-worn shirt. "Did we not send it up yet?"

"Told her to wait," Mrs. Scribb said as she headed toward the small anteroom she used as an office. "Expected him to ring like his father used to do."

"I don't think we can expect him to behave like his father. Or his brother. He may have been born here, but he's been away for two decades."

"He was never reared to take the title." Wilder squared his tall, thin frame and cleared his throat. "Perhaps it's up to us to show him the way."

Mina smiled at the older man who'd become as dear to her as her own father. He was a voice of reason when she sorely needed one. "He respects you, Wilder. Will you help me?"

"Of course I will." He cast a bemused glance around at the other staff members. "And help ensure that none of the others poison him." He shot a knowing wink at Mrs. Darley. "The duchess, God rest her, once charged me with protecting that young man as if he were my own. I've no quibble with seeing to what's best for him now."

Mina looked at Wilder, wondering what he knew about the child who'd become a seemingly intractable man. If Wilder was convinced the new duke could grow into his role, then she felt hopeful too. She'd have to ask him more about Nicholas Lyon's short history at Enderley.

A few minutes later, the clatter of metal and porcelain drew Mina's gaze. Emma nearly lost her grip on the full breakfast tray before setting it on the kitchen table.

"He didn't want his breakfast?"

"It's not that he didn't want it, miss. The duke has left."

Mina glanced at Wilder again.

"He must be here," he said with reassuring certainty. "Tobias would have been called to equip the carriage.

We would have heard him depart. Are his clothes still in his room?"

Emma blushed as if the notion of examining a man's wardrobe was nothing short of scandalous. "Didn't check, Mr. Wilder, but the bed's made. Perhaps he rose very early or went out last evening."

Mina frowned. When she'd last seen him, he'd been striding back toward the house. Where might he have detoured? "Perhaps he's in the breakfast room. Emma, you look about upstairs, and I'll head to the dining room. Tobias, check the stables."

Mina's heartbeat hitched as she searched.

He wasn't in the dining room, or the morning room, or any of the sitting rooms nearby. She poked her head into the library, one of her favorite rooms, but it was empty too.

"Mr. Lyon? Your Grace?" She still wasn't sure exactly what to call the man.

She'd never met anyone who hated a place as he hated her home. He seemed to reserve a special wrath for the study, and some instinct led her there. But the room was just as it had been last night. A mess. The window sash still stood open and she crossed the room to close it.

Where would a miserable duke go?

She noted that the door across the hall was crooked open. The door that led to the estate steward's office. Her office.

Surely he wouldn't go there.

She nudged the door with the toe of her boot, holding on to the frame to avoid the squeak in the hinges, and found a sleeping giant sprawled on the sofa where she'd once played and read and done her lessons while her father worked.

The duke overwhelmed the lumpy piece of furniture, his body weighing down the cushions, long legs stretched out in front of him. His clothes weren't the same he'd worn the day before. Apparently he'd risen, washed, and dressed on his own before coming down to speak to her. And then dozed off.

With his head tilted back against the cushions, the unscarred side of his face was turned toward the window. A shaft of morning light gilded his skin, highlighting the high cut of his cheeks, the broad swell of his mouth.

He was a beautiful man. Achingly so. The kind of face she would have drawn if she possessed an ounce of talent.

She took one step closer and studied him. Of all the paintings and sculptures of Roman generals and Greek gods she'd seen in books, none had this man's appeal. Perhaps because his face was imperfect and the rest of him seemed to push past the bounds of what one expected. He was taller, broader, longer-limbed. A man of contrasts and excesses.

"You've found him, miss," Emma whispered over Mina's shoulder.

"Perhaps you should bring that breakfast tray here. Or at least some tea." She made her way quietly into the room, though she wasn't sure why she took such care. She had to wake him, yet part of her envied him. She'd gotten only an hour or so of sleep herself and would have loved to curl up on the sofa for a doze.

"Your Grace." A little louder, she tried, "Mr. Lyon."

Ink-black lashes flickered up, and she found herself staring into his blue and green gaze. He blinked. For a moment he looked frightened. Young. Vulnerable. "What the hell are you doing here?"

"This," Mina told him softly, "is my office."

"Pardon me." Wilder's deep voice sounded from just outside the door. "Visitors to see you, Your Grace."

Nicholas Lyon swept his right hand across his head, which only made his ebony hair settle in tumbled waves. "I'm not entertaining guests today. Miss Thorne and I have much to do."

"What reason shall I give, sir?"

"*The duke is indisposed.* Isn't that the excuse you gave on my father's behalf when he was in one of his rages?" the duke said in an irritated huff.

"Very good, Your Grace."

"Wilder, who is it?" Mina imagined the triumvirate of magistrate, vicar, and Farmer Thurston descending on the front drawing room.

"Lady Claxton and her granddaughter."

Even worse.

"You should consider meeting them," she told the duke, trying for a tone of suggestion rather than command.

"Did you hear nothing I said? We have work to do. I've no interest in small talk with village wag tongues. Go, Wilder."

"But if you refuse them, it will cause grave offense. That village wag tongue, as you call her, will speak ill of you to all her friends—"

"Do you think I care what some country squire's wife has to say about me?"

"You will if she turns the whole village against Enderley. They'll all march on our doorstep." Mina stepped closer, lowering her voice to a conspiratorial tone. "Charm her with this single visit and she'll go away happy and never trouble you again. Snub her and she'll find a way to make you pay."

He pinched the bridge of his nose between his fingers, then glowered at her.

"Did you expect to come here and never once have to play duke?"

"All right," he said on an irritated huff and shot up from the sofa to stand toe to toe with her.

Mina offered him a smile, the way she would a recalcitrant child who'd finally consented to eat his beets. "Show her to the green drawing room, Wilder. I'll ring for tea."

The duke started toward the door but turned back when she stepped behind her desk. "Oh no, you don't, Miss Thorne. You're coming too."

"That's nonsensical. No duke requires his steward to accompany him while entertaining guests."

He smirked, clearly unmoved by her argument. "I did say there would be new rules. You know these women. I don't. I take your point about kindness paid to them. Perhaps it will serve to salve the villagers when the estate is let to a stranger." He held out his hand to her. "Now, since I'm taking your advice, you will accompany me."

Mina hesitated as she stared at his outstretched hand.

In a lower voice, through clenched teeth, he added, "Please."

Chapter Eight

The two female visitors in their pastel gowns—one pale pink and the other paler blue—blended perfectly with the faded decor of the drawing room. The once hunter-green wallpaper had been leeched of color over time and was now a wan pea shade.

Miss Thorne receded to the back of the room after introductions.

Nick wished he could be so lucky.

"Lady Claxton, Lady Lillian, so good of you to call." Nick heard the stiffness in his tone and felt tension echo in every muscle of his body. He had no experience making polite conversation with ladies.

Formidably statuesque, the marchioness stood only a few inches shorter than his six and some feet. She lifted a pair of spectacles hanging on a beaded chain around her neck to inspect him. Beginning with his boots, she inched up until her magnified gaze snagged on his face. The scar always drew women's notice eventually, like a freakish magnet.

Most recoiled. Lady Claxton did not.

"But for that single green eye, you're the very image of your father."

"So I've been told." Nick didn't smile.

No compliment had been intended. The lady's thin lips puckered in a disapproving frown, as if she'd taken too much lemon in her tea. Apparently, he'd failed whatever test she meant to put him to.

He spared a glance at Miss Thorne, who'd seated herself on a stiff-backed settee in a shadowy corner, clever enough to avoid the old dragon's further notice. Apparently, she wasn't at all interested in saving him from the unpleasantness of the noble ladies' visit.

"What can I do for you, Lady Claxton?" Some quick, meaningless favor, Nick hoped. He wasn't interested in passing anyone's test.

"For me, Your Grace? No, no, I've come to assist you. First, let me say how good it is to find you at home. Enderley Castle is too grand, too essential to the good of the village to stand empty long."

"I promise I'll do my best to never leave Enderley unoccupied." He glanced again at Miss Thorne, but she was studying her hands as if a particularly intriguing novel had been tattooed on her skin.

"We shall hold you to that promise, Duke." The granddaughter, Lady Lillian Portman, spoke with such a smoky huskiness to her voice that a shiver of dread worked its way up Nick's spine.

She was a fetching feminine specimen. Auburn haired, blue eyed, and amply curved in all the best places. Even his scarred face didn't seem to put her off. When he glanced at her, she licked her lips. Slowly.

Pretty but not at all subtle.

Lady Claxton gestured at the young woman. "My granddaughter has just come out, Your Grace." The steel-haired woman enunciated carefully so there'd be no mistake. The girl was on the hunt for a husband, and he was her intended prey. "I understand you've been awhile in London, Your Grace."

"Indeed." *And will soon be returning.* "I've lived there most of my life."

"We are all eager to return to London once the Season commences," Lady Lillian enthused. "It's so diverting." When she giggled, her entire body quivered. "Usually," she purred, spearing him with a hungry glance, "there is little to entertain a young lady in the countryside."

"We'd like to aid you in remedying that." Lady Claxton finally lowered her lens, ceasing her appraisal of every item in the room, and turned her disconcerting gaze his way. "As the lodestar of Barrowmere society, it is your duty to entertain."

Nick's head had already begun to ache. Aid him, indeed. "What did you have in mind, Lady Claxton?"

"A ball." The noblewoman's wrinkled face lifted in a beaming smile.

"Oh, say you will." Lillian's voice lost a bit of its seductive quality when she whined. "I've not danced in ages." She cast her grandmother a pouty moue, plumping out her perfect Cupid's bow lips. "Have I, Grandmama?"

Lady Claxton raised her spectacle glass toward his steward. "I'm sure even Miss Thorne would agree. A ball will lift all our spirits."

"Dancing does tend to make people merrier." Miss Thorne sounded so intrigued with the notion that a muscle in Nick's jaw began to twitch. If she thought she could finagle him into playing host to a country house ball or any other frivolous entertainment, she was gravely mistaken.

"I can't provide the remedy you require, Lady Claxton," he said as decidedly as he turned down noblemen in the den.

"But you must. You're the Duke of Tremayne. Your father may have grumbled and groused, but he did his duty by the village and always hosted at least one ball each year."

A hammer began pounding inside Nick's head. He longed to reach in, pull it out, and smash the whole drawing room to rubble.

"Sometimes the duchess encouraged him to host two in one year," Miss Thorne put in unhelpfully. "What date would you suggest for the ball, my lady? And what would you require?"

"Soon. Very soon, indeed." Lady Claxton's eyes bulged. "As to what's needed, only what every such event requires. Food. Drink. Musicians. A ballroom. Surely the servants at Enderley know. The duke and duchess were such gracious hosts."

Nick couldn't hold back a bitter chuckle at that. His mother was friendly, warm, gracious—all that a duchess should be—but his chief memories were of his father sulking in corners and stoking meaningless arguments with guests.

"We could provide food and drink for a ball . . ." Miss Thorne started blithely, as if he wasn't even in the room.

Lady Claxton beamed. Lady Lillian clapped her

gloved hands in quick little pats of excitement. Nick clenched his jaw so hard he heard a click and feared he'd cracked a tooth. When he caught Miss Thorne's eyes, he shot her a glare, which seemed to dull her enthusiasm.

"But if you intend for the event to take place soon, I'm afraid the ballroom at Enderley is not available," she said resignedly, shooting him a *happy now?* glare.

Nick returned a tiny nod of satisfaction.

"I'm afraid," she continued, "the room is in need of repairs."

All the sweet relief fizzled. Repairs? There'd been no mention of repairs in her inventories or her communications with his solicitor.

Lady Claxton let out a long-suffering sigh. "We could offer the ballroom at Claxton Hall, I suppose. Of course, it's smaller than Enderley's." The elderly noblewoman tapped her bottom lip with a gloved finger. "Will we have your support, Your Grace, and a promise to attend?"

Nick didn't like making promises, especially those he didn't intend to keep. "I'll assist in whatever manner I'm able," he hedged.

His halfhearted commitment seemed to please the noblewoman. "I thought you would be a different sort of Tremayne, Your Grace." She arched a thin gray brow. "Perhaps it's a boon that you are." She stood, apparently ready to depart.

Nick took a deep breath and felt the tightness in his chest loosening a smidge. That had been easy. Quick. As well as any task he dreaded could have possibly concluded.

When Miss Thorne stood, he rose too.

"I shall save you a spot on my dance card," Lady Lillian whispered as he steered her toward the entrance hall.

Miss Thorne shot him an inscrutable glance over her shoulder.

"Do you ride, Your Grace?" Lady Lillian pressed a gloved hand to his forearm as if they were strolling through Hyde Park.

"Only in carriages."

"Pity. I find nothing so invigorating as a dash across the fields on a sunlit morning." As she stepped outdoors, the young woman looked around the estate. Her eyes lit when she spotted Tobias's brawny figure leading a horse out of the stable yard.

"Now that's a fine specimen."

Nick swallowed a guffaw when he realized the debutante was referring to the horse, not his servant.

"In fact . . ." She held a hand over her brow to block the sun and peer through narrowed eyes. "That raven coat and mane puts me in mind of Hades from the Lyle stables. Has the viscount sold you one of his stallions?"

Before Nick could explain that he had no interest in or knowledge of Enderley's stables, Miss Thorne appeared at his elbow. She wedged herself between his body and Lady Lillian's to approach Lady Claxton, who was making her way toward the stairs.

"Send any details you have regarding provisions for the ball, my lady."

"Yes, of course," the older woman said. "We shall prepare a list of all that's required. Come along, Lillian. Don't dawdle."

Nick helped each lady into the Claxton carriage, even offering one palm up gesture in return for Lady Lillian's frantic waves as the vehicle rolled away. Their departure loosened more knots of tension. Somehow he'd lost nothing in the bargain, except the cost of food and drink. A small outlay of funds to finance the ball? Nick considered that a worthwhile expense if he could be back in London before the dancing began.

He turned to find his steward hovering nervously on the threshold. "Was that true, Miss Thorne? About the ballroom?"

"Yes, unfortunately. The plaster is peeling and there was a good deal of water damage last winter. May I show you?"

"Lead the way."

He didn't truly need her to guide him. He remembered the ballroom with perfect clarity. Once, he'd stolen down while his parents hosted a ball and spied his mother dancing with one of the local noblemen. He'd never forget the sight of his father seething in the shadows.

Thomasina Thorne used a key to unlock the double doors, then gripped each handle and pushed them open, giving Nick his first glimpse of the room in decades. Dust bellowed out and he pressed a finger to his nose to keep from sneezing.

A musty scent hit him, and he noted a scar on the far wall. Water had trickled down, warping and discoloring the wallpaper. A matching dark splotch stained the ceiling.

"We try to keep the damp from the rest of the house. Rain comes in from an opening in the outer wall, or possibly the roof. We've had a mason out to look, but he couldn't find the source." She bit her lip before turning to say, "He said he'd need to take part of the wall down to find the problem, and it was a cost the previous duke refused to bear."

Not a cost Nick wished for either, but he could hardly lease a country house with a rotting ballroom.

"Isn't it beautiful? Magical, even." Miss Thorne stepped toward the middle of the room, lifted her arms, and spun around as if the sconces were lit and the walls glittered as they had that night Nick snuck out of bed as a child.

She swept the toe of her boot through the grit and dust to reveal the curving pattern in the parquet floor. "I love how the pieces of wood are arranged to suggest movement. Perfect for a ballroom. And the chandeliers." She pointed skyward. The crystal-heavy light fixtures had been covered with white cloth and looked like enormous beehives ready to crush them both. "When they're lit, it's as if every star had been pulled down from the firmaments."

She was the only beauty Nick could see in the room. Her vibrance trumped all the ruin and rot. He could even admire her sense of loyalty to Enderley, but he could never feel the same. "This place doesn't deserve your lyrical praise."

She deflated before his eyes, and Nick hated himself for snuffing out her joy. Her chin went down, tucked toward her chest, and the fingers she'd used to point to all the beauty she saw in the room curled into fists. "Perhaps it doesn't deserve your loathing either."

"Perhaps it does." She didn't know its secrets. If she did, Miss Thorne would have fled years ago.

"You think me naive, Your Grace?"

Nick gripped the back of his neck and stifled what he most wanted to tell her. That her faith in these walls was misplaced. That her belief that he'd come to cure all of Enderley's ills was mistaken.

"Just look around you," she urged. "Do you not see what this ballroom could be with repairs and a bit of cleaning?"

"I see unexpected expenses." Hundreds of pounds to fix the wall. Hours of work to paint and scrub and polish the place back into a proper ballroom.

"But if you invested in repairs, you could host a ball next year and impress Lady Claxton and everyone else in Barrowmere society." She smiled at him. An open, warm grin that made something in his gut flutter in ways that set him on edge.

The smile wasn't for him, he told himself. She was simply imagining the ballroom alight, thronged with bejeweled ladies and gentlemen in their finery.

"I have no intention of hosting a ball, Miss Thorne."

She flinched as if he'd burst whatever vision she had in her mind's eye.

"I'm a dreadful dancer." He didn't know why he was admitting to his faults. Especially when he loathed the flicker of sympathy in her gaze.

"You could hire a dance instructor."

"I don't give a damn about balls. I have no interest in mixing with Barrowmere society. Gambling club owners, like lady stewards, have little cause for dancing."

He'd touched a nerve. She bit her lip, tapped her fingers against her thigh in an angry tattoo. She opened her mouth, and he wondered if she might curse him to Hades. Instead, she snapped her jaw shut and strode past him, kicking up a cloud of dust in her wake.

Nick glared at the damaged wall, calculating the cost of repairs, trying not to think of the disappointment in her eyes.

A few minutes later, Wilder's deep voice echoed to the high ceiling. "You've upset Miss Thorne."

"I'm the one who should be upset." Nick glanced back as the old man approached. "No one told me this place was falling to ruin."

"Not as bad as all that, Master Nicholas. A few broken bits. Easily remedied." Wilder matched Nick in height and stood shoulder to shoulder with him, hands clasped behind him. "'Tis your duty to see to improving the place now."

"I will never reside here, Wilder. Nothing could compel me to think of this place as my home."

The butler dipped his head, a semblance of a bow. "Your prerogative, of course. But the damage must be dealt with or it will fester. And repairs do take time."

Nick side-eyed the butler. The man stared ahead, chest puffed, chin up, hands laced in that dutiful, obsequious way behind his back.

"You could do better than either of them, Your Grace." Wilder's voice was infused with the sort of rock-solid assurance Nick only ever felt about business matters. "Better than your brother or your father. You could be a good duke. Perhaps a great one. Succeed where they both failed." The butler cast him a raised-brow glance. "Would that not be the very best revenge?"

Wilder's opinion mattered to Nick, but he wanted none of what the old man described. Not the title, or the house, or all the troubles that came with them. But he understood the need to see an enterprise to its end.

"Three weeks, Wilder. That's all I'll give this place." Nick pivoted on his heel and strode from the ballroom. He looked down both ends of the hall but detected no sign of Miss Thorne, just a few lingering whiffs of her floral scent. Ten long strides took him to her half-open office door.

She looked up as he approached, swiping at her cheek and then rising from her chair.

Before she could get out a word, Nick stepped inside. "The wall needs to be repaired. See to it, Miss Thorne. Whatever the cost."

She blinked at him in shock. "I will. Immediately."

Nick walked away, but her face lingered in his mind's eye. Along with a shocked gaze, she'd offered him the hint of a smile.

He liked her smiles. Far too much.

Chapter Nine

$\mathcal{T}$he duke's missing." Hildy slipped on the patch of polished wood in front of Mina's office door in her haste to reach the threshold.

"Again?" Mina laid down her nib pen and tucked away the ledger book she'd been working on.

The man had a habit of wandering off. Usually out of doors, traversing the fields for hours, as if he couldn't bear to remain inside Enderley's walls.

"Vicar Pribble came to call, and when Emma went to the duke's chambers, the man was gone."

"The vicar's not waiting, is he?" Mina silently prayed no one told the man they'd misplaced the Duke of Tremayne.

"Emma sent him on his way, but what shall we do about the duke?"

"I'll find him. He has to be somewhere." Never mind that there were fifty-eight rooms in which to hide. Based on the rain-drenched turn of the weather, she guessed he hadn't ventured out of doors. "Let me have a look."

His disappearance gave her an excuse to explore parts of the estate she usually had little cause to visit. After sticking her head into the conservatory and each bedchamber, sitting room, and drawing room, she headed for the library.

Instantly she knew she'd found him.

There was a new energy in the somber, high-ceilinged space. Stepping inside quietly, she stopped and listened for movement. From the far corner, behind an enormous table covered with maps, she heard the distinctive sound of someone flipping the page of a book.

Mina tiptoed over. A few inches from the table, she spotted two polished black boots sticking out.

In a room filled with overstuffed furniture, he'd chosen to sit on the floor?

She cleared her throat, and the duke immediately got to his feet, rising from behind the table. He wore the same expression she imagined on her own face when Mrs. Darley caught her filching fresh scones from the baking tray.

"Miss Thorne." He glanced down at the book in his hands and cast the slim volume onto the table, as if it held no interest at all. "I was just—"

"Hiding?"

"Reading."

"You chose a good spot."

He cast her a hesitant gaze, as if assessing whether she intended to taunt.

"This room is always kept a bit too dark, if you ask me." She hadn't meant to tease him. She approved of anyone longing for peace and quiet and the solace of a book, though meeting the vicar was a duty he could only avoid for so long. "I always thought the maids should open the curtains a bit wider."

"My father forbade it. He insisted his books' leather must never fade." His voice roughened whenever he spoke of the late duke.

"But the room was created to diminish that possibility. The window is there and the bookshelves—"

"—are all arranged so they don't receive direct sunlight," he said, completing her thought. "An ingenious design."

"Yes." In her enthusiasm to point out the window's location, Mina stepped close to him. Close enough to notice how his clean scent contrasted with the mustiness of the room.

He gestured behind him. "When I was young, I'd dive beneath the table and read, squinting in the dim light, straining to see the words. But I don't seem to fit underneath anymore."

No, he wouldn't. Every part of him was fashioned on a generous scale. The top of Mina's head barely aligned with his chin.

Pointing toward the tall drape-covered window, she confessed, "I used to sit in the bay window, behind the curtain."

"Whom were you hiding from?"

"My father, and yours, I suppose, though the old duke rarely visited the library."

"Why were you hiding from your father?"

"Because of the kinds of books I liked to read. He didn't approve of them."

Nicholas Lyon's dark brows twitched up on his forehead. "What exactly were you reading?"

"Nothing awful." When Mina hesitated to say more, he approached and began a slow circular prowl around her. Mina turned rather than have him at her back.

"Come, confess it. Your father isn't here to chastise you." He scratched his chin and twisted his mouth thoughtfully. "Adventure stories by Sir Walter Scott?"

"No."

"Something sentimental then. Dickens?"

Mina nodded reluctantly. "I do enjoy Mr. Dickens, but his stories can be rather—"

"Maudlin?"

"Exactly."

"I know." He stuck a finger in the air. "With your fondness for ballrooms, no doubt you admire Miss Austen's novels."

"Have *you* read Jane Austen?" The only copies in Enderley's library were delicate little octavo editions that would disappear in the man's enormous hands.

He shrugged, but Mina detected a slight flush of color in the regal cut of his cheeks. "My mother enjoyed her books."

"My father approved of Miss Austen." Mina gestured toward the wall where the author's novels were shelved. "But you should tell me which book was your favorite."

"Don't try to put me off." He took a step closer and Mina held her ground, even when she had to crane her neck to meet his gaze. "I asked first."

"Fine." Mina let out a sigh, preparing herself for his reaction. "The Brothers Grimm, if you must know. I like fairy tales."

"Of course." He crossed his arms and smirked, somehow managing to look both simultaneously appealing and maddeningly smug. "Raised in a decrepit old castle, how could you help but love goblins and fairy-tale monsters?"

Now *he* was making fun of her. Mina hadn't searched him out to discuss literature. "The vicar came to call, and you should prepare yourself because he'll be back. Also, the inventories are complete. We can review them now, if you like."

Mina shifted on her feet, took one step toward the door, eager to escape his inspection. She'd already shared too much. But the duke drew closer.

"Why did your father object to fairy tales?" He lowered his voice to a damnably enticing timbre. "They seem just the sort of thing a young girl should wish to read."

Mina frowned. "Have you read the Brothers Grimm?"

"Probably. At some point."

"The stories are quite violent and complex. Not childish and as simple as many imagine. People misunderstand fairy tales."

"Like your father?"

"He thought they were impractical." Mina stared at the toes of her boots. "He said if I wished to read, I should take up biographies or the books in his office." She looked up to find the duke wearing an unexpectedly sympathetic expression. "Fanciful nonsense, he called them."

"But you persisted in climbing into the window nook?" He approached the spot and reached up to yank back the heavy gray drapery. Bending, he placed one knee on the upholstery that had faded from crimson to a lighter rose after years in the sun.

It was strangely transfixing to watch him settle onto the spot where she'd reclined a thousand times. He glanced out the window, inspecting the view she'd studied during an endless march of lonely days. Then he reached down to where the cushion met the wall.

"Wait," she said too late.

He turned back and smiled, lifting a handful of ribbons she'd kept on hand to mark her place in books. A far better use than tying the silly things in her hair. Her father urged her to be practical, and ribbons made entirely fitting bookmarks.

"Did any of these actually make their way onto your head?" he asked, his mouth curving in amusement.

"Not if I could help it."

In two long strides, he came to face her toe to toe. He took her hand gently into his, and Mina forgot to breathe. Or rather, she breathed too much. A strange thrashing in her chest caused every breath to come quick and sharp.

He lifted her hand, and she had the wild notion that he meant to place a kiss against the back of her fingers. Instead, he turned her palm up, held his closed fist out, and opened his hand to let the ribbons cascade down.

Every inch of satin and grosgrain was warm after being locked against his skin. She shoved the pile into the pocket of her skirt.

"You're not what you seem, are you?" The smile he gave her was the first true and unambiguous expression of amusement she'd seen from him. The wonder of it made her breath bottle up in her throat.

"You've known me all of four days, Your Grace. I doubt you have a clear grasp of who I am or what I seem."

But he did know. This man who'd come to Enderley to loathe every inch of it and tear down everything she'd been working to hold together. Even he could detect that she wasn't the agreeable, ladylike young woman her father had taught her to be.

She tried stuffing her impulses and rogue yearnings down like the ribbons beside the cushion, but it had never worked.

"Believe it or not," he said with shocking gentleness, "I'm a rather good judge of character." He stepped back, settled his backside against the edge of the map table, and crossed his arms. "Comes in handy in my line of business. Gamblers always wear a mask of confidence, no matter what cards they hold. Assessing people and their motives is how I survived."

"You're the son of a duke. Was surviving truly such a challenge?" Mina knew men who fretted about where they would obtain their next meal and young women like Emma, who felt the burden to provide for their siblings.

"I never benefited from being my father's son. It's only ever been a curse." He assessed her a moment, tipping his head to the side. "When I left Enderley, I had nothing. My mother and I . . ." The duke's voice faded as if he'd lost the next words or was too distracted by his memories to speak of them. After a moment, he cleared his throat and went on, his voice raspier, thick with emotion. "We resided in France for a time. I came back to England after she died."

France? Mina wanted to ask questions. So many questions. "The Enderley servants were told that the duchess was ailing in a sanatorium by the seaside."

"My father was a liar." The duke's chest rose and fell quickly, and his eyes lit with anger. Anger and pain.

"But why did you go to France? And when?" Mina thought back to the day she'd seen him depart as a child. The duchess's illness came on months later, along with her removal to the seaside. Or at least, that's what they'd all been led to believe.

"That history is long past. Nearly two decades ago." He looked away from her, crossed his arms, then took a breath to say more. "She died when I was sixteen, just two years after our arrival. She was ill, but he never sent her to a sanitarium. The man was deluded, but it sounds as though he spun lies to hide a truth he could not stomach. Or perhaps he just wished to protect the precious Tremayne dukedom."

Mina's throat ached for the pain she heard in his voice. "I'm sorry about your mother."

The duke didn't look at her or acknowledge her words, but he drew in a deep breath and fell momentarily silent.

"I returned to London soon after her death and built a new life for myself. My father's name gained me nothing. Everything I earned, I worked for. Fought for." He glanced out of the long library window before swinging his gaze back to hers. "Being a duke's son is only a benefit when your father doesn't resent your very existence."

"He was cruel to you." Even as a child, Mina had sensed the old man's menace and she'd never forget how his shouts had reverberated through the house's walls.

He scoffed. "He was vicious to everyone, wasn't he?"

Mina noticed the muscles in his neck jump as he swallowed hard.

"My memories of this place are mostly nightmares, Miss Thorne."

Mina bit her tongue, stifling all the questions whirling in her mind. She suspected he wouldn't answer any of them and wasn't certain she could bring herself to ask. The answers, the memories, only seemed to make him miserable.

She didn't know all that had passed between him and his father, but she was beginning to understand why he hated returning to Enderley. Her memories of the house were colored by her father's presence, his sensible nature and wise guidance. She struggled with his expectations, but he'd never been cruel.

When Mina got lost in her thoughts, the duke turned away and moved toward a bookcase near the windows. He ran his finger along the shelves, diligently searching for a book.

"Are you searching for your favorite?"

"No," he mumbled. "Ah, here we are." He pulled the old, well-worn copy of Grimm's tales from the shelf. "Is this the one?"

"That's the one." She watched as he shuffled through the pages, letting them cascade against the pad of his thumb. "What are you doing?"

"Looking for ribbons." He shot her one mischievous glance before replacing the book on its shelf. "I thought I might find notes you scribbled at the edges that would help me decipher your contradictory nature."

She was contradictory? Was the man unaware of the dramatic sea changes in his own behavior?

"You needn't scrunch your face like that, Miss Thorne." He stepped closer, dipped his head, and gazed at her through needlessly thick lashes. "I meant no offense. I rather like that you're a contradiction."

"I am not."

"You *seem* dutiful." He leaned forward. "Loyal enough to remain in this hopeless place when it must bore you to the bone." He inhaled sharply, tilted his head. "But deep down, you want more, don't you? To have adventures like the characters in this book. To leave Enderley and see the world. To choose your own future."

"You don't know me or what I want, Your Grace." Pain shot across her jaw when Mina bit down to keep from saying more. Words she'd regret.

"No." His tone dipped low. "But I find that I'd very much like to."

Mina didn't know if the hoarse pitch of his voice was a figment of her own wayward imagination. She only knew that his words caused an odd tremor to ripple across her skin.

She felt everything more sharply—the blood rushing in her ears, the fluttering pulse in her neck. He was too close. The mad thought came that she should reach out and touch him.

To shock him. To prove she was as adventurous as she yearned to be.

His words struck deep because they were true. With ruthless accuracy, he'd somehow seen what she tried so hard to hide. Longings. Kernels of wanderlust. A desire to do more, see more, than her commitments at Enderley would ever allow.

In childhood, she'd fed her daydreams with fairy tales and fables. Now she simply kept busy and told herself that solving the estate's problems and doing her duty as her father would have wished equaled contentment.

And then the new duke had arrived.

She couldn't bear the smug tilt of his mouth, the way his height made her feel small, the way his too-perceptive gaze flitted from her eyes to her mouth and back again.

Never mind that the house she managed was his. Even the library that had become her haven on lonely days. None of that gave him the right to be so ridiculously unnerving.

Breath by slower breath, the frantic pace of her pulse settled. Her skin stopped tingling. Her mind stopped spinning with scandalous possibilities.

She rescued herself from the brink.

"You needn't know me any better than you do, Your Grace." She wielded the honorific as a shield, feeling a little thrill of satisfaction when he flinched every time she said the words. "Especially since you only intend to remain for a fortnight."

"Three weeks. I've changed my mind."

Her pulse kicked up again, hesitation tangling with the thrill of victory.

This was what she wanted. They needed him to stay. She was supposed to be convincing him of Enderley's merits. Getting him to see the estate as she saw it—the romance of its long history, the way the house reflected the work of every servant who kept it going.

Instead, he saw her too clearly, sussing out truths she rarely even admitted to herself. Suddenly, keeping him at Enderley seemed as dangerous as allowing him to depart and never return again.

"Three weeks is a short time for what you wish to accomplish." Mina tried for an even, businesslike manner. "I've left the inventories in your study. Should we get started going over them?" Turning away from him was easy enough. Walking toward the door was harder. The toe of her boot caught in her skirt, and she yanked to set herself free.

She heard the thud of footsteps, and then a large hand settled at her elbow.

His skin was warm, his touch surprisingly gentle. And tantalizing. That one point of heat made her want to lean closer. Instead, he stepped near. His boots brushed the hem of her skirt. A single step, a handful of inches, separated his body from hers.

Mina leaned away from the duke's touch. She couldn't let herself give in to what he made her feel and want, or waste time entertaining the fanciful view he had of her.

The only thing she needed from him was that he do his duty. Then she would continue doing her duty, and everyone at Enderley would benefit.

She'd put away her fairy tales and daydreams.

NICK KNEW HE shouldn't enjoy sparking a reaction in Mina Thorne quite so much. But he loved discovering that the lady wasn't quite what she seemed.

Of course, she was right. He needed to focus on why he'd come.

But something in him couldn't let the fragile truce between them break. He didn't like the fresh wariness in her gaze.

"Have I upset you, Miss Thorne?" Nick worked his jaw, trying to find the words one used when making amends. "I was a bit of an arse. I often am." He wasn't a man used to curbing his urges. When one ruled a gambling empire, there was rarely a need to admit one's faults. He sure as hell never asked for forgiveness.

"You are very confident in your assessment of others."

"I am."

"Though smug and insensitive."

"I did acknowledge being an arse. That should encompass everything."

She leaned an inch closer, eyes flashing, one hand settled on the curve of her hip. "You're actually proud of being boorish."

"*Boorish* seems harsh."

"Do others find you charming?"

Nick grinned. Miss Not What She Seems had a waspish sting. If he didn't admire her for it, his ego might have mustered an ounce of indignation.

"Many do. Or at least, they say they do. When you're wealthy, it's difficult to know if anything others say to you is true."

"That implies you're a man who can be swayed if people appeal to your vanity."

"No. It only means that they try."

"I won't." She squared her shoulders, stiffened her spine, and nudged up her chin. A terribly pretty chin. Smooth and softly curved and notched by an enticing cleft in the center. He wanted to touch the spot. Press his mouth to it.

Nick never dreamed he'd find defiance so arousing.

"I'll keep that in mind, Miss Thorne." He pointed toward the doorway, then started toward the threshold. If she kept looking at him as she was, he was liable to do things they'd both regret. "Shall we go and take a look at the inventories?"

He told himself that no matter how much he enjoyed sparring with her, he'd enjoy returning to Lyon's more.

"Wait." She uttered the word with the same tone of authority Wilder employed with the footmen.

Nick turned back to find her framed in the glow from the window.

A few shafts of sunlight had fought their way through the clouds to caress her skin and gild her hair, showing off hidden strands of gold, a darker burnished shade than the color that sparked in her eyes.

"What is it, Thorne?" He risked a teasing tone. "Did you squirrel away more treasures to be found in the window cushions?"

How could a young woman who'd spent her life sequestered in the countryside fascinate him?

"You haven't answered my question."

He had every right to walk away from her. His father barely tolerated a staff member raising their voice, let alone speaking with an ounce of insouciance.

He was beginning to wonder if allowing her to stay

on as steward had been a mistake. She occupied far too many of his thoughts and stoked far too powerful a reaction every time she was near.

"What question is that?"

"Which book was your favorite?"

"It's not here." He winced, recalling the old flat he'd shared with his mother in Paris. Their rooms on the Rue de Vignon contained no luxuries. Purchasing the book had cost her weeks of saving.

"Did you lose it?"

"I left the volumes behind when I returned to England."

She scuffed her boot on the floor and bit her lip, assessing him. He could see the questions burning in her mind.

"You left when you were sixteen?"

Nick nodded. That much wasn't hard to admit.

"I don't understand why your father lied so thoroughly. To everyone."

"And yet he did. Especially to himself. My father couldn't bear the notion of scandal ever marring the Tremayne legacy." Nick's throat reverberated with a bitter chuckle.

"And now that reputation is yours to protect."

Nick flicked back the edges of his frock coat and braced his hands on his hips to keep from clenching them into fists. "None of my feelings about the Tremayne legacy are appropriate for your ears."

She laughed, and the light sweetness of the sound chilled his rising rage. "Have you heard Mr. Wilder when he's in his cups? I promise, my ears aren't as delicate as you think."

Her words caused him to focus on her ears. They

were indeed delicate, perfectly curved shells that he had the urge to trace with his tongue.

Miss Thorne cleared her throat. "So what is the book? Even if you don't have it anymore, you must remember the title or author."

"I do. There's an English translation, but the copy my mother bought me was in French. The author's language."

"You speak French?" She sounded so impressed Nick was tempted to tell her he spoke a bit of Italian and Spanish too.

"I do, but *Notre-Dame de Paris* by Victor Hugo is the first book I read in the language." He rubbed his fingers together, recalling the texture of the two red leather volumes.

"What's the story about?"

"A beautiful gypsy."

Her eyes glowed with interest and she took a step toward him. "And?"

"She captures the heart of many men, including one the townspeople consider a monster. He's deformed. A hunchback. Probably not much to look at."

She lifted a hand, toying absently with the button at the top of her gown. "What happens?"

"His love goes unrequited. No one loves a monster. It all ends in tragedy. Not like a fairy tale, Miss Thorne."

Her forehead pinched as she frowned at him. "You clearly haven't read many fairy tales, Your Grace. There's plenty of tragedy, and sometimes the creature is actually an enchanted prince." She blushed fiercely, as if she'd revealed some secret she hadn't meant to.

Nick's heart did a strange little stumbling dance behind his ribs.

Her eyes widened, and she did that thing he'd come to dread. Her expression became serene, drained of emotion, and she flattened her tone. "I'll be in my office if you need to discuss the inventories."

Nick didn't stop her from leaving.

He struggled to bring his thoughts back to the present. To push away memories of Paris and the book about a gypsy and the monster who loved her. Pressing a hand to the back of his neck, he squeezed at the knot of muscles there.

That's when he noticed the ribbon. A pale pink length of satin that young Mina Thorne had thought better suited to marking pages than adorning her hair.

Nick retrieved the length of fabric, stroked his finger along its satiny length, and tucked it carefully into his pocket.

Chapter Ten

$\mathcal{M}$ina had managed only a few winks of sleep and her nerves jangled like the set of household keys hanging from her belt. Especially now, with Nicholas Lyon's heated bulk at her back.

He followed, two steps behind, as she led him along the wind-whipped path of Enderley's parapet, an old stone walkway above the house's rear facade.

He'd surprised her by arriving in her office early, wishing to have a look at the roof and exterior wall of the ballroom. Mina intended to take the opportunity to lead him on a tour of the estate's gardens and most interesting features. If her plan was to get him to appreciate Enderley, showing him its beauty seemed a good strategy.

Unfortunately, it also meant he'd spy all the signs of dilapidation. She was prepared to address those too. Notes tucked in her pocket contained estimates of how much the most urgent repairs would cost.

Under their feet, the stones were weathered, the

mortar worn away, but the walk had endured for hundreds of years. Surely it would hold for one more day.

Mina told herself the path was safe, but *down, down, down,* the edge seemed to urge. Being so high had always unnerved her. She had the constant sense of tipping over the edge, as if she possessed some rogue avian instinct to jump off and take flight.

Glancing back at the duke only worsened her sense of vertigo, and she stumbled.

His hand locked at her waist. "Have a care, Miss Thorne," he barked, his breath a heated gust against her cheek. "Are you steady now?"

"Yes, thank you." Mina nodded, and he released her instantly. She kept her eyes averted from the edge as they continued toward the west side of the house.

The duke didn't acknowledge her expression of gratitude.

After five days' acquaintance, she'd learned the man was exceedingly surly in the morning. She wondered if he slept as poorly as she had since his arrival. The skin under his eyes had taken on a darker pallor, but the color only served to highlight the cool shade of his eyes.

Glancing back, she caught him staring at the hem of her skirt. When he looked up, his eyes were shadowed, his sensuous lips pressed in a grim line.

"Are you not fond of heights either?" she asked, wondering if he was feeling the same dizziness that plagued her.

"I don't mind heights," he said with mock cheerfulness. "I just prefer them to be in London, where the sea air doesn't chill you to the bone."

"Just a bit farther." Mina infused her tone with as much sunniness as she could manage. Her stomach quivered, not because she was afraid of tipping over the side, but because she was about to give the new duke a good deal more to be grumpy about.

"I know the way." His voice dipped low and raw. "I was born in this godforsaken house."

"Of course." She let out a sigh and hoped he didn't hear.

Mercy, the man was taciturn. Too unpredictable. If he'd been this moody as a boy, perhaps it was why he'd been sent away. She'd resolved to be kind, to show him Enderley's charms, yet the two of them seemed to begin each day at odds.

"The maze has been maintained, I see."

Mina followed the direction of his gaze toward the enormous hedge maze that had been laid out by his ancestor nearly a century before.

"I'm afraid it's rarely used." With no master in residence and no parties or social events at Enderley, the winding avenues of neatly trimmed shrubs stood empty, unless Mina or a servant decided to take a stroll.

"Why not cut it down?" the duke asked emotionlessly. "Seems to do nothing but create work for the gardener."

Mina bit her tongue, but she couldn't keep silent. "I believe the maze was quite beloved by your mother." And by Mina too. She'd spent many a day wandering its paths, enjoying its shade. When her father became irritable because the duke was in one of his black moods, the hedge maze had been a safe, quiet place to retreat to. "Of course, it's yours now to do with as you wish, Your Grace."

When she glanced back, the man had the audacity to smirk.

"Is that the game now? I set off your short temper and you call me *Your Grace* as punishment?"

"I'm not short-tempered," she said as blithely as one could past clenched teeth. Then she began thinking of far worse punishments than using his honorific. Maybe mucking out the stables. The image of him stripped to his shirtsleeves, his skin glistening with sweat as he worked, distracted her for several minutes.

Mina stopped and turned to face him. "Is there nothing about Enderley you approve of?"

The duke studied her intensely, searching her face as if she held the answer. "Why do *you* love it so much?" he finally asked.

Not at all the question she expected, and one she didn't anticipate being so difficult to answer. "I've known Mr. Wilder and Mrs. Scribb since I was a child. My father loved Enderley."

"I asked about you. Not them."

"Enderley is what I know." Mina looked out across the fields rather than into his watchful eyes. His gaze followed her movements, steady and curious.

"You're young, Miss Thorne. I suspect you could set your mind toward any number of pursuits."

Mina glanced back at him, shocked by the sincerity in his tone.

No, not today. She couldn't let him fill her head with fanciful nonsense about her adventurous spirit. She was supposed to be convincing him to do his duty, not allowing him to persuade her to abandon hers.

"Enderley is all I have, Your Grace. Not good breeding or a title, nor a proper education. And I've no plans to marry." *No prospects either.*

Her cheeks heated despite the chilling breeze. He was the last man with whom she should be discussing anything as personal as a lack of marriage prospects.

"My father taught me that devoting oneself to Enderley is a worthy endeavor."

In fact, he'd been so devoted that at times Mina feared he cared for the estate more than her. But that wasn't why she and the new duke were standing atop three stories of old stones as a brisk wind whined across the parapet.

"Also," she added, remembering her purpose, "the house's architecture is beautiful."

He quirked his lips and crossed his arms. "There are far finer country estates in England."

"Well, I've never seen them."

That earned her another twitch of his broad mouth. Not quite a smile. "Have you ever been outside of Sussex?" The question amused him far too much.

"No. I've rarely had any reason to leave." He didn't need to know that the old atlas in the library had been one of her favorite books or that she'd occasionally entertained childhood fantasies of running away to the city. Now a London man of business turned miserable duke thought her a simple country miss, and she told herself not to care. But his opinion did matter.

Stupidly, she blurted, "I went to Brighton once."

That earned her a smile, but it was such a brief flash of white Mina wondered if she'd imagined it. "Still in Sussex, but lovely seaside. No doubt you went to enhance your freckles."

The dusting of spots along her nose and cheeks snagged his attention, and the longer he stared, the more potent the heat that spread from her face to her neck.

"How did you find the seaside, Miss Thorne?" He looked her up and down, one brow peaked in curiosity. "Was the sand warm under your feet? Were you daring enough to venture out into the icy water? Somehow I suspect you were."

Two dimples appeared when he smiled, one on either side of his mouth. Mina couldn't look away. She could barely recall the question he'd asked while she'd gotten stuck staring at his mouth.

"I don't remember. It was a long time ago."

"Too long, I imagine. You should go back. I'm overdue for a visit to the seaside myself." He sounded wistful and so intrigued by the prospect that Mina half expected him to suggest they hitch a carriage and head off directly.

But, of course, he didn't.

The gulf between them and their desires was an enormous one. He was a duke and could hie off to Bath or Brighton or anywhere he pleased. Mina's life didn't work that way.

"My place is here, Mr. Lyon." Unless he or whoever leased the estate dismissed her. "At least for now."

He worked his lower jaw like he was chewing on a retort but said nothing more. Clearing his throat, he scanned the fields beyond the maze. "Is that Eustace's horse, the one involved in the accident?"

Mina bit her lip when she spotted the ebony stallion. The wounded racehorse was healing quickly. Mina visited every morning, taking him apples and checking his wounds, but she'd yet to decide what to do with him.

"Not my father's either," he said decisively. "His favorite was white and bulky as a prize fighter."

The odd sense of falling while she was standing perfectly still swept over Mina, and she took a quick step back from the ledge. She struggled to slow her breathing.

"You truly hate heights." The duke reached for her upper arm to hold her steady.

Mina looked up to find him close, the flaps of his overcoat brushing her skirt, his eyes locked on hers.

"Is he yours?" he asked softly.

"None of the horses in the stable are mine." One deep breath for courage and she confessed, "He's not a Tremayne horse."

Just as Mina expected, the duke's glower deepened. He tensed his grip on her arm. "I don't understand."

"I found him wandering the field near the copse on the night you arrived."

"But where does he belong?"

"Here," Mina said emphatically. "For now."

"Miss Thorne, who does he belong to?"

Mina chewed the inside of her cheek. "Lord Lyle of Stebbing Hall. His estate's just outside the village."

"I know the man. Or my father did." He waved toward the field. "Have Tobias return Lyle's property to him immediately. His lordship is not an even-tempered sort." The duke started past her on the walkway, carefully sheltering her from the edge.

When Mina didn't follow, he glanced over his shoulder. "Are you coming?"

"I won't return the stallion to Lord Lyle."

Shock made Nicholas Lyon look younger, softening the striking aspects of his sharp-angled face. The lines of worry between his brows melted. The grim tension in his full lips eased. Shadows faded from his dark-lashed eyes. Then one black brow shot up and clashed with the wave of hair that had dipped down to dangle over his forehead.

Mina pushed away the notion that she should aim to surprise him more often.

"Are you defying me?" His voice rasped low. Little more than a whisper.

"I suppose I am." A gust swept a lock of her hair from its pins, and Mina pushed the strand back behind her ear. "Lord Lyle, or someone in his stables, beat that horse bloody. There were deep stripes on his haunches when I found him."

She steeled herself. He'd tell her what she already knew. Lyle's cruelty didn't matter. Property mattered. Ownership. Especially here in the countryside. Lyle was known for his interest in horseflesh and betting on races. He'd want his fine stallion back.

The duke said nothing. One narrowed blue eye, a tightening of his jaw, and he seemed to come to a decision he didn't plan to share with her.

Another burst of wind swept the tail of his coat out behind him and pulled more of her hair loose.

"Let's have a look at the damage and get off this bloody roof." He waved his arm to urge her over. His manner had gone as gruff and cool as the wild weather.

"There." He pointed to a spot in the sloping roof tiles, a bit darker than its neighbors. "The depression runs down toward the wall." He lowered himself, balancing on his haunches.

Mina approached but didn't dare get near the wall's edge.

He noticed her wobble and glanced up, all the earlier warmth in his gaze gone. "Go back inside. I can do this on my own."

"I prefer to stay with you."

He turned back slowly, then stood to face her, their bodies inches apart on the narrow walkway. "Are you worried I loathe this place so much I'll fling myself off the side?" He stared down at the multistory drop between them and the ground. "Or are you hoping I will?"

"Of course not." Mina risked a glance and immediately regretted it. A wave of nausea hit and she reached out, her fingers grabbing his coat lapel.

The duke gripped her arm. A comforting heat, sheltering her from the parapet's edge. "You're all right," he said softly, as gently as she'd murmured to the shying stallion. "I'll have a quick look and we can get back on solid ground."

Mina nodded, and he let her go to examine the damaged tiles again.

If they ever got off the roof, she wanted to show him the gardens and the folly near the pond. Enderley's groundskeeper had created topiaries that hadn't existed when the duke was a child.

"I'm not sure what good we can do up here. Wouldn't a mason have far better knowledge of the structural integrity of a centuries-old wall?"

He turned back to her, a smirk softening the sharp peaks of his upper lip. "You underestimate me, Miss Thorne. I do know a bit about old walls."

Mina squinted skeptically. "Don't tell me you're a bricklayer *and* a gambling club owner."

His chuckle was deep and appealing, and far too brief. "When I found the site of my club, it was a shambles. I learned more about masonry and plaster-work and the fine art of window glazing than you could ever imagine."

"You did all the work yourself?"

"No." He snorted and the left side of his mouth slashed upward. "I hired the best I could afford. But I insisted on knowing everything. Overseeing the work closely. Lyon's is the only thing I've owned, and I wanted to understand every part."

"You really don't trust anyone, do you?"

"There are a few people I trust." He narrowed an eye at her, and she was uncomfortably reminded that she'd already proven herself faithless in his eyes. More than once. "I can count them on three fingers."

"They must be extraordinary." It irked Mina that she'd never be counted among those Nicholas Lyon trusted. "Why did you choose a shambles as the site for your club?"

He shrugged. "Good location."

Mina waited. There had to be more.

The duke let out a sigh. "I saw something others hadn't. What it could become. I saw potential."

Mina felt a strange fluttering inside, as if a cage of sparrows had been freed inside her. "So you *are* capable of hope."

Shock softened his features again. A bit of warmth lit his eyes. "Only very occasionally." He pulled back the lapels of his overcoat and shrugged the garment from his shoulders. "Would you hold this? Or, better yet, put it on and keep yourself warm."

Mina gathered the woolen coat in her arms, sinking her hands into the warmth he'd left behind. His scent wafted up, bergamot and something darker.

Down on one knee, he braced his hands on the sloping roof tiles to get a closer look, and the crisscross pattern of bricks beneath him shifted.

"Careful." Mina hadn't imagined the movement. The bricks beneath her feet shifted too. The slightest of movements.

"Speaking of hope, I suspect that's all that's holding these bricks together. The mortar's gone," he said tightly. The bricks beneath him began to bow out toward the parapet edge, and a piece of the limestone facade emitted a terrible scratching groan as it moved.

The duke got to his feet slowly, widening his stance for balance. Mina started forward and reached out a hand.

"Don't come closer," he hissed. "Back away. Quickly."

Mina took one tentative step back but couldn't make herself retreat any farther. She couldn't leave him balanced on the edge of a crumbling stretch of stones.

"Take my hand." She bundled his overcoat under one arm and leaned forward, trying to find an extra inch of length in her arm. A vertigo swirl of dizziness pulled at her, but she kept her eyes fixed on the duke.

"Stubborn woman," he grumbled. Taking one long stride, he placed his boot closer to hers. "This patch is solid beneath my feet. Now turn around and head back to the stairs."

Mina looked down at the dark grooves between the stones where mortar should have been. She wasn't at all certain the pathway wouldn't crumble. "Just take my hand," she insisted.

If he fell, at least she'd have a hold of him. She stretched again, lifting off her boot heel, and lost her balance. Her body responded like metal to a magnet's pull and she tipped toward the ledge. A scream burst from her throat.

Her body went weightless, unbearably heavy, as her foot slid off the edge.

Then Nicholas Lyon was there, leaning over, his hand latched onto her arm in a vise grip. "Hold on to me. And drop the bloody coat."

She let the overcoat fall and reached to grasp his shoulder. He immediately wrapped a hand around her waist and heaved her up.

They landed in an awkward, half sitting, half reclining pile far too close to the edge of the three-story drop. Mina didn't want to let go of him. He was warm and solid, and it was far preferable than focusing on the way her heart thrashed painfully.

"I've got you," he said, his breath coming fast. He settled his chin on the top of her head a moment, then cupped her cheek, tilting her face toward his. "Are you all right?"

His gaze settled on her mouth, and he slid his thumb gently against her cheek.

Mina watched as he studied her. For a man who seemed to know exactly what he wanted, he moved hesitantly, taking such care as he lowered his thumb to her mouth and traced the outline of her lips.

She felt delicate under his tender exploration. Desirable. And she recognized the look in his eyes. The hunger and need. She felt it too. And she desperately wanted to touch him, to trace his mouth as he had hers and then replace her fingers with her lips.

Mina's pulse rushed in her ears as she held her breath, waiting, hoping. Yearning for what she couldn't have.

Then he shocked her. Lowering his head, he pressed his mouth to hers. One too-brief taste and he pulled back, then kissed her forehead. "Let's get inside," he whispered against her skin.

He untangled himself and stood, keeping hold of her hand. "I'll go first. You stay close behind." A single long step and they both stood on a solid part of the walkway. "You go ahead of me, Miss Thorne, so I can make sure you don't try to heave yourself over the edge again."

"Mina."

"What?"

"Call me Mina." The man had just kissed her, saved her, and she knew he hated the formality of titles and honorifics.

He said nothing and released her. Mina feared she'd made an error in judgment. Or the duke had. Problem was, she'd enjoyed the feel of his lips against hers too much to count the experience as anything but pleasure.

She followed him toward the doorway that led to an interior set of stairs. He encouraged her to go down first, but after descending only two steps, she turned back.

"Never mind the name. Such familiarity would be improper." Mercy, she was a ninny. She'd embarrassed him and herself. He was a duke. She was a steward. His steward. Perhaps throwing herself off the parapet walk would have been the better course.

Do try to be proper, Mina. Her father's voice echoed in her mind.

"Sometimes propriety isn't my first instinct," she confessed.

A rich, infectious sound reverberated against the stone walls. "I've noticed that about you. I rather admire it." He dipped his head so they were eye to eye. "In addition to your stubbornness, and, of course, your short temper."

Did he truly like her for her failings? Her inability to behave as she ought, to be ladylike when she should. She still took umbrage at the bit about her temper.

But Mina found she liked hearing him laugh. And the smile that accompanied his amusement? Devastating. Somehow, his toothy grin, framed by deep dimples on both cheeks, managed to make him both more enticing and infinitely more dangerous.

"I fear we'd scandalize Scribb and Wilder if I call you Mina." His forehead creased as if he was working out a thorny problem. "Of course, I'd insist you call me by my name too." His gaze dropped to her mouth, as if daring her to say it.

Nicholas. Mina couldn't bring herself to speak his name, but it echoed in her mind.

"Let's get inside where it's warm."

That sounded good. She longed for a cup of Mrs. Scribb's oversteeped black tea and a blanket, and for her heart to beat at a normal rhythm. But she hadn't accomplished anything she'd wished to.

"I wanted to show you around the estate." To showcase the beautiful parts, not the crumbling bits.

"I've seen every inch of Enderley."

"But the garden—"

"—has been cut back for the winter, I suspect." He descended to the stair step just above her.

Mina reached out to stop him going farther. Her palm landed on his chest, pressed against the buttons of his waistcoat and his firm muscles beneath. Mina dropped her hand, but she needed to stall him.

"I'm sorry I didn't tell you about Lord Lyle's horse." She'd planned to confess all to him eventually, but the guilt of her deception weighed on her mind now more than ever.

"You should have told me. Trusted me, as I must trust you. If you remain at Enderley when I leave, I'll be relying on you to represent my interests, not engage in horse stealing."

"You *can* trust me." The reminder that he would soon depart made her heart squeeze if as a fist had been wrapped around her middle.

"No matter what I decide?" He pressed his hand against the wall next to her head. "What if I send the stallion back to Lyle? What if I told you to dismiss every member of the staff?"

Mina's throat tightened until she could barely breathe. "Why would you?"

"To start anew and be done with the past."

"Emma's nineteen. Hildy is sixteen. They have nothing to do with the estate's past. They never knew the father you hate so much." Mina pressed her lips together. She hadn't meant to speak so bluntly.

"I see." He huffed out a breath of frustration. "So you'll do my bidding, and resent me for it every single day?"

"Most dukes don't bother with what their employees think of them."

Chuckling, he pushed off the wall, crossing his arms over his chest. "What have I done to make you think I'll be like most dukes?" He pinched the bridge of his nose. "To be perfectly honest, I'd pass the title to Tobias if I could."

"Tobias would be an awful duke."

"Worse than me?" His voice had gone quiet, vulnerable. As if it mattered to him whether she thought he could embrace a role he loathed.

"Definitely."

He lifted a shoulder. "That's something, I guess."

"If you wish to be a good duke, I could help you." Mina's father had once described a steward's work that way.

"What would you suggest?" His gaze was wary, as if he'd agreed to a spoonful of medicine but was dreading the taste.

Enderley came to the fore of Mina's mind, as it so often did. If he planned to do better than his father and brother, taking care of his birthright was where he needed to start.

Reaching into her pocket, she closed her hand around the list she'd prepared earlier in the morning.

"This would be a good place to start."

Staring into her eyes, he reached for the folded list. Their fingers brushed and heat shot down Mina's arm, then lower, to her middle, then her thighs. Like swallowing that bit of sherry he'd given her. One touch and her insides were warm.

"You need to let go," he said in a voice so low it made her shiver.

Mina opened her fingers and took a step back. She was acting like a fool. Like that impetuous infatuated girl she'd once been. Such lovesick nonsense couldn't happen this time. Her wayward heart would obey her.

The first man she'd set her sights on had been a bad choice, but the Duke of Tremayne was an impossibility.

As he examined her notations, both brows edged up his forehead. "This is a substantial list." He flipped the page and found the rest. A muscle began pulsing in his cheek. "Might have been easier to note what did not require repair."

She couldn't blame him for hating the burden of what his brother allowed to founder. Sympathy for the man kindled on a bone-deep level. It wasn't his fault the estate had been ignored. She yearned to show him some part of Enderley that deserved saving.

"There are things that aren't on the list."

"What else? Another rotting room? A wall on the verge of collapse?"

"Down here." She descended the stairs and stopped at a small circular window set into the stones.

He joined her, sharing the same step so that their bodies were pressed side by side. Hunching his shoulders, he peered through the old bubble-dotted glass.

"Do you remember the tower? It's the oldest standing piece of Enderley's history." Mina studied his profile and noticed his mouth tighten. "Some things here don't need to be repaired. But they're part of what makes the estate special." Mina leaned in to peer over his shoulder.

He turned so abruptly, she slammed her back against the wall to avoid a collision. "I want it pulled down."

"But—"

"Burn the wooden structure inside and have the stones removed from the estate. Every one of them." The ice in his voice matched the glacial blue of his eye. There was no warmth left between them. Not a shred of the man who'd saved her, kissed her, smiled and laughed with her. "Do it, Miss Thorne. I never want to see that tower again."

Chapter Eleven

*M*ina rubbed at her sleepy eyes and tried to focus on finishing off the morning's correspondence. The previous duke's creditors were losing patience, and bills kept arriving for debts he owed dozens of London businesses. She paid those she could and delayed those she couldn't, but overdue accounts were the last topic she wished to broach with Nicholas this morning.

The duke. She mustn't think of him familiarly.

Never mind that she knew how it felt to be wrapped in his arms and had spent a sleepless night thinking of the soft, heated press of his mouth. He'd kissed her to offer comfort. Nothing more.

She did not need the complication of anything more. Even if she wanted it.

A knock at her office door caused her muddled thoughts to scatter, and a moment later Wilder stepped through.

She swallowed down her disappointment.

"Mrs. Scribb says you didn't take your breakfast this morning." He carried a small tray bearing a cup of tea and a slice of Mrs. Darley's glazed orange cake.

Mina hadn't slept well and had no appetite, but she smiled at the old butler, grateful for his thoughtfulness. "Thank you, Wilder."

"The duke only took tea this morning too. Something ailing the pair of you?"

"I'm not ill. Just busy." Mina fought the heat she sensed crawling up her cheeks.

The older man nudged up one brow. "Emma tells me you suffered a mishap on the parapet walk yesterday. I trust you weren't injured."

"It was nothing. Though I suspect the duke is now convinced of the need for immediate repairs." Mina's heartbeat sped at the memory of her near fall. The too potent thought of Nicholas came, his hands reaching for her, his arms lending warmth and safety. Then a less pleasant memory. His face contorted in anger. His shouts echoing in the stairwell and his demand that she tear down the old tower.

"The ballroom is an excellent place to start," Wilder said. "I'm sure the master will soon see the merit of restoring Enderley as it should be."

"Tell me about the tower." The man Mina wanted to ask wouldn't wish to speak of it, and she had no desire to stoke his anger. But surely Wilder would know. He'd been at Enderley longer than all of them.

The butler's forehead buckled in a frown. His pale cheeks took on a bit of color. "Surely your father told you its history."

"Why would the duke wish to have it demolished?"

"Demolished?" The old butler was shocked by the news. His lips fell open and he drew in a sharp breath before composing himself. "Dilapidation *has* set in. The structure is unsafe. Perhaps removal would be for the best."

"I thought our goal was to get the duke to appreciate the estate's history, not destroy it." Mina let out a sigh of frustration. Her plan to highlight Enderley's assets and show Nicholas its merits had gotten off to a disastrous start. "Is there anything he'll like here?"

"He's a man of business who appreciates turning a profit, I imagine. I understand he's quite keen on investing in enterprises such as the railroad. Might the Wilcox farm interest him?"

The Wilcoxes maintained the most successful of the many tenant farms on the estate, and thanks to Mina's cousin, Colin, and his inventions, it was by far the most efficient.

"Yes, of course." Mina grinned and rose from her chair, excitement and anticipation sweeping away all remnants of fatigue. "A brilliant idea, Wilder." She took a quick sip of the tea he'd delivered and broke off a bit of orange cake. "Is he in his study?"

"Should be. Unless he's gone for a wander."

Mina swept her fingers through her hair and straightened her bodice as she made her way across the hall. After how they'd parted the previous day, she'd dreaded approaching him. But now she had purpose, a plan to show him something about Enderley he couldn't help but admire.

She knocked softly and received no reply, then tested the handle and stepped inside.

"Mercy," she breathed at the sight before her.

A tall vase lay shattered in half a dozen pieces on the carpet and the duke stood over the wreckage gripping one of his father's ornamental swords.

"It's not what it looks like," he said in a defensive tone. "I did not attack the pottery."

"Certainly not." Mina glanced from the sword to the broken antiquity to the irritation on the duke's face. "You're just standing over it with a weapon drawn."

"I removed the sword from the wall to have a closer look and . . . collided with the bauble." He stared down at the scattered shards. "Was it worth a lot of money?"

"Who knows. It was a piece Eustace installed after one of his jaunts to Europe." Mina shrugged, strangely less concerned with the broken vase than with the outing she hoped the duke would agree to. "Would you care to accompany me on a short journey?"

At her words, the duke snapped his gaze up from his perusal of the broken shards at his feet. "Yes."

Mina couldn't hold back a smile at hearing the single word spoken so eagerly. "You don't even know where we're going."

"You're right. Perhaps I should know more." The duke's mouth twitched as he laid his father's sword on his desk, sidestepping the pieces of porcelain on the carpet. "Does it involve heights or crumbling masonry?"

"Neither, I'm happy to say. Just a bit of fresh country air and a well-run farm."

"A farm?" He braced his arms across his chest and frowned. "Not the seaside?"

He sounded so disappointed that for a moment Mina imagined venturing with him to a place that had nothing to do with duty and Enderley. But it wasn't why she'd sought him out.

She had a plan and much she wished to show him.

"I think you'll find much to interest you at the Wilcox farm."

He cast her a dubious look, then the edge of his mouth quirked in an inscrutable smile. "We'll see, Miss Thorne."

NICK LET OUT a grunt when a rut in the country road they were traveling pushed Mina's body closer to his. Their thighs had been locked against each other for a quarter of an hour, and her arm brushed his every time she shifted the reins.

She'd opted to take the pony cart, with its very narrow seat and Nick was beginning to wonder if she'd meant the conveyance to be quicker to prepare or simply a means of torturing him with her sweet-scented nearness.

"Isn't it lovely?" she asked for the third time about some feature on the estate.

First, it was the glittering arched roof of the conservatory his mother had loved so well, then the topiaries a groundskeeper had carved with unexpected whimsy, and now she pointed at an old flint stone wall that Barrowmere's villagers had constructed ages before either of them were born.

Nick turned to look at her—the strands of hair fluttering against her cheek, the sharp line of her upturned nose, the soft curve of her chin.

"Yes, lovely indeed," he agreed, as he had every time.

This time she seemed to take his meaning, to realize he was watching her and not the passing scenery. She turned to look at him, her gaze soft and searching.

"Mina—"

"The farm is just ahead," she said breathily, then turned the cart onto a narrow path girded by a low stone wall.

There was much he wanted to say to her, and so much he couldn't explain. He'd kissed her and then barked at her. She'd have questions. She always did. But he couldn't give her answers. He'd never told anyone about his time inside the tower's dank walls.

When she pulled the carriage to a stop, Nick jumped down and offered a hand to help her down. Neither of them wore gloves, and the slide of her bare skin sent warmth dancing up his arm and shot a flare of heat straight to his groin.

"The threshing barn and granary first?" she asked blithely, as if their brief touch didn't affect her at all.

"Lead the way, Miss Thorne." Nick was almost grateful one of them could still manage to be sensible.

"As you see," she said as they entered a long, high-ceilinged barnlike structure, "it's used for both processing and storage."

"Most impressive." Nick's gaze widened as he took in the scene. He'd once visited one of the cotton mills he'd invested in and the Wilcox barn had the same air of productivity and organized efficiency.

Mina waved to two young gentlemen working machines, and they tipped their hats as if seeing his steward wander around the farm didn't surprise them in the least.

"This used to be a horse gin." She pointed to a series of pulleys and flywheels with a wide shaft attached. Inside lay grain that had been threshed and ground. A spout of steam nearby indicated why horses were no longer required. "As you can see, it's been adapted to run on steam power."

Another machine arranged along the wall of the barn took canvas sacks strung on hooks attached to a conveyer belt down to where one of the farmworkers tipped a shoot of grain to fill each bag. The grain itself was carried by another long belt above. All of it powered by steaming boilers.

"How much does this single farm produce?" Nick had no great knowledge of farms, but the speed with which they were filling bags and threshing wheat seemed far quicker than what a few men and horses could do.

"Enough to provide for Enderley's livestock year-round and take feed to markets throughout the county. They're among the best tenants on the estate."

She smiled at him so proudly that Nick felt an answering smile tugging the corners of his mouth.

"And nothing's broken or in need of repair," she added with a mischievous glint in her eye.

"What a refreshing change."

"Are you ready to see more? I'd like to show you the apiary next." She was already striding toward the entrance of the barn, as if she knew full well he was prepared to follow her all day.

"Be on the lookout, Miss Thorne. One of the cottage hive lids is damaged." The young farmhand made the admission almost sheepishly, as if loath to contradict her declaration that everything on the farm was in good order. "I mean to fix it right away."

"Thank you, Billy. We'll be cautious."

"Hive?" Nick asked as they walked side by side. "As in bees?"

Mina didn't answer but suddenly stopped short and stuck out an arm to keep him from going any further. Her hand landed on his stomach. Even through his layers of shirt and waistcoat, he could feel the warmth of her skin.

"We should approach slowly, just to be sure. If the damage has disturbed the cottage hives, the workers may be restless."

Nick heard the insects first, a steady rustling hum that carried on the breeze. He'd never much liked bees, but when she started forward, he followed close behind.

"Take care, Mina."

"It's not as bad as I imagined," she said on a relieved sigh. "Let's have a closer look."

The woman was either fearless or foolish or a bit of both. She strode straight toward several tall multi-story wooden structures and approached one capped by a broken wooden lid.

When she bent to examine the damage, Nick stepped closer and laid a hand on her arm.

"You are aware they sting, aren't you?"

"They're busy right now," she told him, reaching down to take his hand and guide him closer. "See for yourself."

Nick took one wary step forward and winced when

Mina gingerly removed the broken lid to look inside at the hive.

"When the temperature dips, they work harder to keep warm."

Nick was amazed to find she was right. The little creatures were assembled tightly on honeycomb-lined frames and took little notice of their curious inspection. Only two flew out when the lid came off.

"This farm supplies some of the best honey in Sussex." She swept her finger along the edge of the frame and held it out for his inspection. "See how dark it is? Something about the flowers they grow makes for a richer flavor."

Nick looked at the dark drop of honey on her skin and his mouth watered. Not because he was longing for a taste of the county's finest sweetener, but because he longed to take her finger into his mouth.

He licked his lips and looked into her eyes. The heat there made him want more. More moments like this with her. When there was no Enderley boxing them in, no duties that needed their attention. Just Mina and the odd, undeniable spark he'd felt between them from the day he arrived.

"I'd like a taste," he told her quietly.

Mina bit her lip, and her brows dipped in concentration. She locked her gaze on his mouth and seemed to hold her breath as she slid a honeyed finger across his lower lip.

Nick swept his tongue out to taste and reached for her hand. Flavor burst inside his mouth in a shock of floral sweetness.

"Delicious," he whispered before leaning closer, flicking his tongue out, and tasting the tip of her finger once more. "But I honestly can't tell whether it's you or the honey."

He half expected her to chastise him for his boldness. Instead she swallowed hard and took one step closer.

"We should . . ." she began on a husky whisper.

"Kiss," Nick said decidedly.

"That's not what I was going to say." She let out a breath of laughter, and her mouth tipped in the hint of a smile. Then she looked around them as if recalling where they were.

"I came to show you the farm. I wanted you to see that something about the estate is worthwhile and productive."

Nick released her hand and clenched his fingers against the spot that was still warm from her skin. He was a damned fool. Of course, her intentions were about Enderley and had nothing to do with spending time in each other's company.

"We should probably go back." The Wilcox farm was indeed admirable, but he'd seen enough and desperately needed a drink of anything that would wash the flavor of honey off his tongue.

"Yes," she finally agreed, her tone full of the same sense of disappointment Nick felt like a heavy stone in the pit of his stomach.

He wanted the moment five minutes earlier back. And, damn it all, he still wanted to kiss her. But when Mina took a step away, he knew the chance was gone.

His head, where he'd convinced himself to value a life unencumbered by personal entanglements, knew she was right to draw a boundary line between them.

But his heart, that rarely used thing that thrashed every time Mina was near, didn't seem to agree.

Chapter Twelve

$\mathcal{N}$ick stood on Enderley's front steps, let out a yawn, and watched his breath dissolve into the morning fog.

Sleep had eluded him since arriving at Enderley, but he was more restless since the visit to Wilcox farm with Mina.

Every time he closed his eyes, he saw her face. Or worse, he remembered how it felt to hold her and taste her lips for a far too fleeting moment.

They hadn't spoken in days.

She avoided him but continued to do her duty diligently. She left documents on the desk in his study before he could ask for them, brought in masons to begin work on the ballroom, and had arranged the removal of several pieces of furniture to the auction house.

He needed to make peace with her, regardless of all the other things he wanted to do with her but never could.

For days, he'd stewed over his errant desires, but

this morning a peculiar impulse had begun jabbing at him like a persistent finger. It was no mystery what Mina wanted from him. She longed for him to do some good for Enderley before he departed forever.

For her sake, he'd decided to do it. Not because he'd made peace with the place. Among all their other sins, Tremaynes were stubborn to their cores.

But for the first time his thoughts weren't of the past nor of his loathing for Enderley, but for Mina. She had done something to him. Altered him, so that her expectations mattered more than his desire to blot out his past.

He couldn't imagine ever loving Enderley, but he walked the halls now and no longer wished to burn it all to the ground. He entered the library and focused first on the window cushion where she'd daydreamed and shoved ribbons in books. Even his father's study was now a place of fresh memories with Mina rather than ugly nightmares of the past.

Nick patted his upper coat pocket where he kept her list of repairs. There was much to do before he could return to London, but being a businessman had taught him to see a project through to its end.

Rehabilitating Enderley made good business sense. Refurbished, it would fetch a renter more quickly. And overseeing repairs would be a welcome distraction. A funnel for energy, a diversion from the chief distraction in residence at his ancestral estate.

As if on cue, Mina approached from behind.

Nick was already becoming ridiculously attuned to the woman. Blindfolded, he would have recognized her scent and the insistent clip of her boot heels.

"Shall we depart?" she asked with what sounded suspiciously like forced exuberance.

Of course, she didn't mention the awkwardness of how they'd parted at Wilcox farm. Miss Thorne, it seemed, understood how to be businesslike too.

She'd convinced him to hold court in the village, as a means of preventing every member of Barrowmere society knocking down Enderley's doors. They'd been calling in a steady stream since his arrival, and he'd put off every one of them, except for Lady Claxton and her granddaughter.

"I've asked Tobias to bring the carriage around." There was a tautness to her tone that disturbed him.

Turning, Nick braced himself for his first sight of her. He felt the same disconcerting tingle across his skin that came whenever she was close. She'd done something different with her hair. The tight bun at her nape had been transformed into an artful arrangement of curls and waves. The same cold misty morning air that had him clenching his fists to warm his fingers, painted her cheeks in pink and her lips a riper shade.

She wouldn't return his gaze.

Horse hooves crunching gravel drew his attention toward the carriage approaching from the stables. Like a nightmare come to life, the black brougham crawled through the fog, its ebony sides scuffed and unpolished.

Just as it had on that day he tried so hard not to think about, the carriage stopped before him, looming at the bottom of the stairs.

Mina started down, but Nick called her back.

"We could walk to the village."

"We could," she admitted hesitantly, "but it would take thrice as long. The carriage is warmer." She returned to stand beside him. Pulling a knitted shawl tighter around her shoulders, she cast him a questioning glance. "Do you take umbrage with Enderley's carriages too?" Her breath billowed when she spoke, and her teeth chattered as soon as she fell silent.

One look into her irritated gold-brown eyes persuaded him.

"Fine. We'll take the brougham." His throat closed and every muscle in his body seized, but he could endure it. He'd endured much worse, and the village wasn't far.

She ignored his offered hand and climbed into the carriage on her own. Nick held his breath and launched himself onto the opposite bench.

The interior was the same. The sapphire velvet squabs he'd sat on the day he'd been sent away had been faded by time, but the memory remained sharp. He'd been so small. When he'd settled all the way back on the seat, his feet hadn't touched the carriage floor.

"You see. The carriage is quite accommodating." She pushed the foot warmer his way with the toe of her boot. "And infinitely warmer than walking into the village."

Nick nodded. It was all he could manage. His mind spun for any thought that didn't make him want to hurl himself out the vehicle's window.

"I do admit," she said with a sigh, "this carriage is probably the oldest at Enderley. Your brother sold the others."

"I remember it."

Realization seemed to hit her all at once. Her forehead buckled, then her brows winged up and she lifted her hand as if she'd reach for him.

Nick was disappointed when she didn't.

"Is this the carriage you departed in that day? It must bring back unpleasant memories."

She couldn't imagine. He didn't want her to know how ugly the truth could be.

Nick focused on Mina. Her quiet voice and lovely face. "Tell me about your father." *Tell me anything to make me forget.*

Her eyes softened, but her tone turned wary. "Why do you want to know about him?"

"Because he's the reason you're here, pretending to tolerate a man you dislike."

"I don't dislike you, and he's not the only reason I'm here." She bit her lip and then added, "I'm not sure what to tell you about him. He was a good man."

Nick couldn't help hearing what she left unsaid. The oblique contrast between him and her father. Thomas Thorne had been a good man. Nick was not.

She dropped her gaze to her gloved hands, then looked out the carriage window, scanning the passing countryside. Perhaps she was uncomfortable being near him. Or unused to talking about herself. Nick suddenly had the sense her desire to escape the vehicle matched his own.

"I disappointed my father a great deal," she finally said with a gusty sigh.

"That's impossible." A daughter so earnest, so loyal, so willing to take on her father's duties could never be a disappointment.

"I assure you, it's true."

"Why?" Nick leaned closer, balancing his elbows on his knees. "Because you liked to read fairy tales?"

She faced him, bit her lip again, and Nick couldn't help staring at her mouth. He told himself to fight the urge building inside him. The urge to touch her again. To kiss her properly. To discover whether she truly tasted as sweet as the honey he'd licked from her finger.

"He wished me to be more ladylike. To behave properly."

"And propriety isn't your first instinct." Nick grinned. "Is that why you stayed at Enderley? To make amends to your father?"

Mina shook her head, notched up her chin an inch. "He would never ask that of me."

She was magnificent when she was declaring her loyalty, whether for Enderley or her father. The quality seemed an inherent part of her nature, and Nick admired it. Hell, he was beginning to adore it.

"Everyone thinks I must regret the life I have, that I should be pitied." She leaned forward, until they were inches apart. "Don't pity me. I'm perfectly content."

Her clenched jaw made her claim far less believable.

"If you'd ever left Enderley, you might have made a different sort of life. One with dancing in ballrooms and strolls on parapet walks that aren't crumbling."

Throaty laughter burst from her. Nick liked seeing her smile almost as much as discovering the single dimple at the corner of her mouth.

"Is that the choice you think I made? Dancing at balls or the drudgery of managing an estate." She lifted a finger, like a governess scolding him. "Mind you, I'm not saying it is drudgery."

"Was there never a suitor?" The question was brazen. Entirely inappropriate. He wouldn't have dreamed of asking Spencer or Iverson about affairs of the heart. He dearly wished Huntley would brag less about his conquests.

But she was different.

That was the trouble with Miss Mina Thorne. She was unlike anyone he'd ever met, and his feelings for her were a disturbing ferment of conflicting impulses. He swung between wanting to avoid the woman and aching to kiss her.

Both of which were ridiculous, inappropriate, and not at all what he'd come to Enderley to do.

Her fingers worked the fringe of her shawl, winding and unwinding the strands of yarn. She hadn't looked his way since he'd asked his impertinent question.

"There was someone."

"He must have been terribly smitten." Nick regretted asking the question. He didn't want to know some other man had wooed her, loved her.

"No, I don't think he was." She shifted uncomfortably on the seat and swallowed. "I was a fool."

"He hurt you?" He saw the answer in the way she tensed, the way she averted her gaze out the window. Nick wanted to find the man and pummel him.

"It doesn't matter." She gazed at him a moment, and then shook her head as if pushing away old memories. Then she lifted a folded piece of paper from her coat pocket. "We'll be meeting in the public hall," she said, straightening her skirt and employing her no-nonsense tone. "The vicar has arranged for some refreshments, and I've prepared a list of villagers I know will wish to speak with you."

Nick reached out to retrieve her folded list. She let go too quickly and the paper fluttered down between them. Mina reached out to catch it and her bare hand closed over his thigh.

She jerked her hand back, curling her gloved palm into a fist. Her breaths came fast and her eyes widened. But it wasn't horror or regret he saw in her gaze.

Nick saw the same spark of desire he felt sizzling in his blood. The brand of five small gloved fingers and a heated palm warmed the top of his thigh.

He wanted her, and it took every ounce of self-control not to reach for her before the carriage stopped in front of the vicarage.

This was madness, and he was already in far too deep.

As soon as the duke took his seat at a long table the vicar had set out, Mina positioned herself off to the side where she could watch his interactions but go largely unnoticed.

The duke appeared wary, almost as if he had something to fear from the villagers. The truth was that all of them were coming weighed down with their own fears. He possessed the power to reject their petitions. Many probably worried he'd be like his brother, or worse, his father.

Rowena Belknap approached first. An elderly widow with four grown children and two still at home, she boasted half a dozen grandchildren too. Her late husband had been a longtime tenant on Tremayne lands, but she was struggling to pay her rent and produce enough to feed her family.

The duke listened intently as she made her plea, asking for mercy, for aid if it could be had. With more care than he'd treated Lady Claxton, he nodded and smiled at the older woman, even standing to take her hand as they spoke quietly to one another.

Mina leaned closer to hear.

"It will be done," she heard him say in his low baritone.

Mrs. Belknap beamed, her face transformed. She looked half her age and as if her burdens had been lifted.

The duke turned back to look for Mina, his brow pinched and jaw tense. The moment their gazes locked, his expression eased, as if he was relieved to find her close. But there was more. An energy passed between them, somehow soothing and disturbing at the same time. The others in the room faded, and for a moment, he was all Mina could see.

When Magistrate Hardbrook stepped up to meet Nicholas, his arrival broke the spell between them.

Mina dipped her head to make a notation in the notebook she'd brought along, a reminder to ask Nick what he'd promised Widow Belknap. But it was a long while before her heart beat steadily again. Something in the way Nick looked at her stripped all pretense away.

"Finally come to take up your birthright. 'Tis good to see a Tremayne at Enderley, Your Grace." The magistrate didn't bow, but he removed his hat and clutched the weathered headgear to his chest. "Might I have a word about some tasks that need doing around Barrowmere?"

"Do you have a list, Hardbrook?" Nicholas stood, though he didn't reach out to shake the magistrate's hand. "My steward likes lists."

Hardbrook had no trouble finding Mina in the corner of the room. He stared straight at her and told the duke, "Thought you might have found yourself a proper steward, Your Grace. She's naught but a girl." Leaning in, he spoke low, though not quietly enough to be unheard. "Mean to match her to my boy if she'll have him."

The two men gazed at her, and Mina's skin itched. It was disconcerting to have both of them watching her, debating her fate. She realized she was holding her breath, waiting to hear what the duke would say.

"Miss Thorne is an efficient steward. Loyal to the estate. Clever and stubborn."

Mina gulped and swallowed hard.

"I'm not sure I could stomach a *proper* steward now."

Hardbrook's frown was priceless. In fact, the duke had struck him speechless and the grizzle-haired man backed away like a stunned deer.

Mrs. Shepard approached next. Of all the ladies of the village, Mina thought her one of the kindest, and her eldest daughter had become Mina's dearest friend before leaving Sussex to take a position as governess in Hampstead.

"Your Grace." Mrs. Shepard bent a flawless curtsy. "I do not come to petition for anything more than your attendance at our Christmas dance."

The duke cast Mina an over-the-shoulder look again, but this one was full of misery that signaled the lady's request was not one he welcomed. "I'm afraid I'm not skilled at dancing, Mrs. Shepard."

The older woman's face fell. Mina knew she and a group of villagers worked for months planning their country dance. After the death of Eustace Lyon, they'd expressed hope that the new duke might grace them with his presence. It was a precedent his grandfather had started, though his brother had rarely been in Sussex in the winter to carry on the tradition.

Mina approached. "You needn't dance, Your Grace. The tradition is that the Duke of Tremayne visits the dance and supplies a gift of food or drink as a kind of blessing over the festivities."

"The celebration is so large that we must secure the upstairs of the village inn, and festivities spill over into the vicarage. We would be deeply honored by your presence." Mrs. Shepard extended a cream-colored envelope decorated with calligraphic swirls and carefully painted holly leaves and berries. "The dance is the Sunday before Christmas, Your Grace."

Nicholas looked up at Mina. She wasn't sure whether or not he expected her to save him as she had with Lady Claxton.

"Most of the staff members at Enderley will attend," she told him. "Even Mrs. Scribb and Mr. Wilder."

One dark brow inched up. "Will you attend, Miss Thorne?"

"You're invited, of course, Miss Thorne." Mrs. Shepard offered a kindly smile. "I recall how you used to like the Christmas dance."

Mina used to, but that had been shattered two years earlier.

"Thank you, Mrs. Shepard," the duke said warmly. "I would be delighted to attend."

Delighted?

The man hadn't been delighted with anything since his arrival. Except for when she'd saved him from hosting a ball. He gave every indication that he loathed dancing and frivolity, and now he was delighted? About a dance that was to take place long after the three weeks when he vowed to depart Enderley forever.

After bidding Mrs. Shepard farewell, he resumed his seat and waited for the next villager to approach. They came in a ceaseless line, and the duke spoke to each of them with kindness and interest. Some came only to meet the new master of Enderley, but most asked for some favor or repair or consideration that only the Duke of Tremayne might grant.

Mina had filled several pages with notes and had her head bowed when a voice called to her from the rear of the vicarage. "Mina, I didn't know you'd be here."

She stood and barely had time to turn before two thin arms embraced her in a hug. Her cousin, Colin, was five years younger and two heads taller, nearly as towering a figure as Nicholas Lyon. Since her father's death, he was her only family residing in Barrowmere. The rest of her mother's relatives were scattered in the north, while her father's people hailed from a village an hour's drive away.

"The duke asked me to accompany him. I'm taking notes on what he's promised to each villager." Harder to explain was how much the duke's kindness and generosity shocked her.

"What's he like?" Colin pushed a wave of sandy overlong hair off his forehead. Under one arm, he clutched a messy pile of papers, their edges bent and frayed. "Could you get me an introduction? I wish to show him my designs."

"Anyone the vicar invited may approach," she told him. "Go and introduce yourself. He doesn't bite." He snarled once in a while, but Mina was increasingly convinced the man's heart wasn't as black as he wished others to believe.

Mina took a step closer to the duke. Two men were presenting him with the details of an ongoing fight over a disputed hedgerow and apparently expected him to serve as arbiter.

"Aye, but you know him." Colin followed close on her heels. "You could smooth the way." He drew up beside her and offered one of his crooked grins, suddenly every inch the boy she'd taught to climb trees and fish in the mill pond. Pointing to his sheaf of papers, he added quietly, "I intend to ask him for funding. The London papers say he's invested in the railroad."

Mina tried to get a look at the sketches. "Tell me this isn't your sock-removal device. Or the mechanism that turns the pages of a book with a metal arm."

Colin rolled his eyes. "I've grown up since those days." He patted his collection of papers. "This idea has merit. A steam-powered thresher. Better than the one I designed for Wilcox farm. Smaller, faster, and more efficient than any ever conceived. If I can secure funding, this device could aid the entire village."

"Are you ready to depart, Miss Thorne?"

Mina jumped at the sound of the duke's voice. She turned to find him casting a curious stare at Colin. "There's one visitor you've yet to meet, Your Grace. My cousin, Colin Fairchild."

"Mr. Fairchild, you should have come earlier." The duke gave him a firm handshake and then turned his attention her way. "We agreed to two hours." He flicked the chain dangling from his waistcoat and caught his pocket watch in his palm. "It's a quarter past. I fear if I stay longer, I'll be invited to more dances and asked to judge the flower show in the spring."

Behind her, Colin poked gently at her elbow.

Mina turned to whisper, "Call at Enderley tomorrow. I'll get you in to see him."

"Thank you." Colin bent to peck a kiss on her cheek before heading off to speak to the youngest Shepard sister.

"Shall we?" The duke gestured toward the carriage circle and then headed out the door of the vicarage.

Mina was at a loss. The man changed too quickly, zigzagging like the path of Enderley's hedge maze. One minute kind and benevolent, as she'd seen him today with the neediest of Barrowmere's tenants. The next, utterly inscrutable.

Mina found him inside the carriage, dominating his bench, thighs spread, his gaze fixed toward the carriage window. When she climbed inside, he moved his legs aside to give her room.

Another reason she loathed skirts. Too much fabric that took up far too much space.

His silence gave her another opportunity to study him.

He was blessed with an extraordinary profile. Pensive brow, square chin, and a large, sharp nose that dominated his face, but also lent him a strikingly noble air. If only she could see beyond those glossy dark locks, into his head. What thoughts compelled him? What burdens knotted his brow in lines of worry?

"You made many people happy today."

He looked at her, a questioning expression in his gaze, then down at the notebook she held tucked in her lap.

"Mrs. Shepard was beaming, and I think Mrs. Belknap will sleep more soundly tonight. What did you promise her?" Mina lifted her notebook and readied her pencil over a blank page. "I'll make a note and see that it's done."

"A reprieve from rent until the summer and repairs to her cottage by year's end." He shifted on his seat. "Did the day please you, Mina?"

"Yes, of course." Her voice had gone scratchy.

He sat tensely on the bench, shoulders squared and arms crossed, but his eyes were full of longing. The man possessed exquisite eyes, not because they were different colors, but because of what she saw in them. His gaze gave every emotion away.

What she saw now was need, and it took every ounce of self-restraint not to reach for him. When she didn't, he turned to look out onto the passing countryside.

"Tell me about your cousin, Miss Thorne."

Mina swallowed down the irritation of being addressed formally again. She told herself it was better. Proper. Exactly how a duke and his steward should speak to one another.

"He wishes to call on you tomorrow, Your Grace. He fancies himself an inventor and wants to talk to you about a thresher."

"So he wants my money."

"His idea sounds like a useful invention. Do you not invest in new inventions?"

"On occasion. Usually at the behest of my friend Iverson. He's the champion of inventors."

"You helped people today. An invention like Colin's would be another way of doing so. If you've decided to stay longer—"

"I haven't."

His brow was smooth now, but she felt her own pinch in lines of worry. "But you told Mrs. Shepard—"

"I've changed my mind."

"In the last half an hour?"

Before he could answer, the carriage stopped in front of Enderley. The duke jumped out first and began striding away. Then he seemed to remember chivalry and turned back to offer his hand and help her down.

Mina didn't need his assistance, but she wanted the opportunity to press him. "Why have you changed your mind about staying for the Christmas dance?"

He came one step closer, and Mina found the carriage at her back and Nicholas Lyon towering in front of her, his body a few inches away.

"There are good people here. I do see that. But what I feel for Enderley will never change." He swallowed and lifted a hand as if he might touch her face, but instead he rested his palm on the stretch of carriage next to her head. "I've become distracted. I came here with a plan, and I intend to see it through. When the three weeks are over, I need to be able to leave all this behind."

She knew he meant the estate, his duty to the villagers, whatever blighted history he had with his father. But he was looking at her face intently, his gaze shifting from her eyes to her mouth.

He leaned in, until his nose brushed the edge of her face. His breath came fast and hot against her cheek. "I need to be able to leave you behind." The low husky timbre of his voice ignited shivers across skin. "Every day that gets harder to do."

He dipped his head and placed a tender kiss at the corner of her mouth. Then he stepped back, turned on his boot heel, and started away. Not to the house, but toward the field beyond the stable.

"Where are you going?" Mina called after him.

He clenched his fists, increasing his pace as he strode into the distance. "I need a walk."

Chapter Thirteen

*H*ours later, Mina lay in her bed and stared up at the ceiling, tracing the cracks in the plaster and shadowy smoke stains she knew by heart. In the two years she'd slept in this room, she'd identified various geometric shapes—a sphere here, an ellipse there, a hat-shaped trapezoid in the far corner.

Tonight, all her thoughts pulled her toward the man sleeping one floor below. He couldn't know that the guest room Mrs. Scribb had set aside for him was directly under her bedchamber. And, of course, she'd never confess to anyone that she listened to him moving around in the wee hours of the night.

A faint creaking noise sounded in the darkness and she held her breath. She recognized the groan of the bed frame and imagined Nicholas settling onto the guest chamber mattress.

Minutes later another sound echoed up. A moan? A murmur? She couldn't quite make it out.

Then quiet descended again. Mina pressed two fingers against her breastbone. A familiar ache pinched there, a sense of emptiness that always seemed to plague her at night.

She reached for the copy of *Aesop's Fables* she kept on her bedside table. When she opened the familiar pages, words melded into a blur. The outlines of a sharp, straight nose, full lips, and a prominent brow emerged from the blob of ink.

Stop thinking about the man.

He wasn't her problem to solve. Let him keep his mysteries. Soon, he'd return to London and Enderley would be peaceful and quiet. They'd made do between Eustace's death and Nicholas Lyon's arrival, and they'd carry on after he'd gone.

Of course, her mornings would seem oddly empty without the sounds of his murmured curses as he wandered his father's study. In less than a fortnight, she'd gotten used to glancing out her office door and catching a glimpse of him pacing a path in the carpet in front of his father's desk.

She'd grown fond of his scent and the belly-tickling timbre of his voice.

Curse the man. Full of bluster one moment and unexpected charm the next? He'd been downright magnanimous to the villagers. More than his father or brother had ever been.

But could she or any of them count on his new display of generosity when the man changed his mind like the flip of a coin?

One day burning portraits and a week later promising villagers repairs to their cottages.

Mina would never forget the moment they met. The reassuring grip of his hands as he'd held her steady as she descended the oak tree. The tall imposing figure of the man as he stood with Millicent crooked in his elbow. The odd frisson between them when they finally stood face-to-face. Not only was he far more appealing than she'd anticipated, he'd made her feel seen. Noticed. Not just as another servant, but as a woman whose knowledge of the estate he respected.

He was nothing she was expecting in the duke whose arrival she'd so feared. Even now, she struggled to reconcile the man whose anger toward his father shocked her and the one she'd seen show empathy to Barrowmere's villagers today. As she attempted to fit all the pieces of him together in her mind, the memories that burned brightest were the moments when they'd touched.

The slide of his finger against her chin. His warm, solid embrace. The heat of his mouth on hers.

Mina groaned, set her book aside, and closed her eyes. She'd had enough of ruminating on the Duke of Tremayne for one night.

Yet Nicholas persisted in her mind's eye. Strands of black hair dipping over his brow. His surly slouch in the carriage. His awkwardness when admitting he wasn't proficient at ballroom dancing.

A cry sounded below her. Nicholas's voice calling out. She thought she heard her name. Slipping from bed, she crept toward the door and listened. The cry came again, but muffled. Turning, she knelt by her oval rug, peeled back the edge, and pressed her ear to the chilled floorboards.

"Leave," she heard him say distinctly. Then he repeated the phrase with one word added, "Don't leave. Let me out!"

Mina stood, donned her dressing gown, and tiptoed into the hall. She detected no movement in the servants' rooms and walked as carefully as a cat on a ledge as she descended the stairs, trying not to make a sound.

In front of his door, she paused with her hand on the latch.

What she was about to do wasn't proper, or ladylike, or anything else others would expect of her. But she refused to turn back.

Her pulse started a wild, stuttering dance when she stepped into his room.

Lying in bed, he looked still and peaceful, no longer crying out. Then one word came, quiet and anguished, no more than a breathy whisper. "No." He twisted his head on the pillow, then lifted his arm as if grasping for something. "Please don't go."

Mina wasn't certain if he was awake or still lost in a night terror. Drawing close, she struggled to see him clearly as her eyes adjusted to the dim light of the single lamp turned low by his bedside.

He was a breathtaking sight without a frown marring his mouth or lines of worry notched between his brows. Black hair spilled over his forehead and cheek, obscuring part of his face.

Mina crouched beside the bed and pushed the strands back, revealing the jagged line of his scar. The wounded flesh contrasted sharply with his pale unmarred skin. The cut had been deep. Who would dare attack a duke's son, especially one who towered over most men?

She jolted back when his eyelids lifted.

"You shouldn't be here." Despite the warning, he reached out and clasped the hand she held hovering above his face.

"I know."

But he didn't let her go. He stilled for a moment, watching her. There was a glint in his eyes, a hint of a curve at the corner of his mouth. As if he was pleased to see her, relieved to wake and find her beside him.

Then he swept his thumb against her palm, a delicious caress that made her gasp.

She leaned closer, impulsively reaching out to trace the curve of his mouth with her fingertip. His lips trembled under her touch.

"Mina." He whispered her name with a rasp of desperation.

She wanted his mouth on hers again, wanted it so badly that it frightened her. "You're right. I shouldn't be here."

He sat up in bed and swung his legs over the side, all the time stroking ribbons of heat along her wrist with his thumb. "So you're short-tempered *and* impulsive."

"And you're difficult and moody." Mina preferred the heat in his gaze to his teasing tone. She was tired of pretending. "Now that we've identified each other's character flaws, I'll go back to my room."

Mina straightened, and he stood too so that they were toe to toe. This close, she had to arch back to look at him or stare at his bare neck and the patch of chest his open shirt did nothing to hide.

He loosened his hold on her hand, but the bleakness in his eyes called to her, echoing her own loneliness.

"Your sleep was troubled?" she asked softly.

"It always is."

"I heard you call out. I thought you said my name." Mina swallowed hard after the admission. She'd probably misheard him, but some rationale felt necessary to explain her presence in his room.

"Did I? Perhaps you're haunting me in my sleep." He did that thing with his thumb again, a seductive slide against her skin. His touch rippled out to spark goose bumps along her arm and heat between her thighs.

"You don't remember your dreams?" she asked, her voice trembling like her insides.

"I try not to."

"What troubles you?"

"Everything." He let out a low chuckle, like the rusty creak of a door hinge. Lowering his chin, he assessed her. "Especially you."

"I never intended to." She pulled her hand from the duke's, ignoring the shiver that spiked up her spine from the friction of his skin sliding against hers. "I'll leave you so that you can get back to sleep."

"Mina, wait." He reached out, caught the edge of her arm, and a few strands of unpinned hair tangled between his fingers. "There's something I must say before you go."

She moved closer. He was utter temptation, all blazing heat and forest scents, and she felt an odd comfort being near him. She knew she should be scandalized. To be alone with him, a duke of the realm. A gambling club owner. Especially while he wore nothing but trousers and a half-buttoned shirt.

But she found herself longing to hear whatever he wished to tell her. What had happened between him and his father? And why had he never come back home?

He stunned her by simply whispering, "Thank you."

She'd never heard gratitude expressed more earnestly, but she didn't understand why he was offering the sentiment to her.

"Whatever kindness I showed those villagers today, you inspired."

"Me? That's nonsense. We're not well enough acquainted for me to inspire you to do anything." She wasn't used to praise. It made her long to shy away, to hide behind all the rules of etiquette she usually ignored. "Besides, kindness seemed to come quite naturally to you."

"Not like it does to you." His mouth quirked in a thoughtful slant. He studied her face, then tucked a strand of hair behind her ear. "I wish I could tell you I'm a benevolent sort, but let's just say it's not my first instinct."

"Perhaps you should try it more often. From what I saw today, it suits you."

He made a dismissive sound. "As each villager approached, I asked myself what you would have me do."

"You treated the villagers differently than Lady Claxton."

He shrugged. "None of them demanded or assumed I owed them anything. They simply asked." He frowned. "I take great pleasure in saying *no*, in protecting what's mine. But today, with your voice in my head, I found *yes* frighteningly easy."

"My voice in your head?" Her cheeks heated, then her neck and her ears. She suspected every inch of her body had flushed as pink as the carnations that bloomed at the edge of Enderley's carriage drive.

"Not only your voice." His gaze flickered over her face and fixed on her mouth.

"You impressed me this afternoon." She'd already come to the man's room. The least she could do was tell him the truth.

"Unlike all the other days when I've horrified you?"

Mina's heartbeat thundered in her ears when he leaned closer. She lifted a hand tentatively, desperate to keep him at bay. Or to touch him. She wasn't sure anymore. Gently, she rested her palm against his chest and felt the strong, insistent thrum of his heartbeat.

"Forgive me for how I barked at you." He hesitated, drawing in a sharp breath, then added, "There are some parts of this place I can't bear."

"Only some? That seems an improvement over when you arrived." Mina bit her lip when he smiled. To see his face soften into amusement did strange things to her.

He wrapped one large hand around the curve of her waist. "There are some things at Enderley I like quite a lot. And I do regret shouting. I vow never to do so again."

"Are you sure you can make that promise?" Mina found herself smiling.

Nicholas's gaze dropped to her mouth. He studied her lips and leaned closer. "A man can only try."

"Why pretend to be someone you're not?" she asked with the last gasp of air in her lungs. She needed to know. Not just his answer, but hers too.

As he'd done the first night he arrived, he slid a finger against her jaw, notching her chin up. "Don't mistake me, Mina. I am the monster you see. I am my scars and greed and every other curse that's been thrown my way."

"That's not all you are. I see more."

He was more. She'd seen as much today, and she felt the truth on a bone-deep level. His tenderness had worked its way past her doubts and uncertainty. He was quickly becoming the biggest dilemma she'd ever faced, because she found the man irresistible.

"What do you see?" His jaw tensed, eyes narrowing warily.

"Pain. Compassion." Mina fixed her gaze on his. "Temptation."

So much temptation that she folded her fingers into her palms when he was near. So much that she'd taken up her pencil and paper and tried to revive the meager drawing skills she'd learned as a child in an attempt to capture his likeness. So much that she found herself looking forward to her first glimpse of him every single day.

"Ah, but you're a woman who likes fairy tales and fantasy. You see what isn't there." He took one step backward, leaving a gaping emptiness in the stretch of floor between them. "You should go."

Mina moved forward. "And if I stay?"

"Then you'd learn what I truly am. And regret ever wishing to know." He reached for her, bracing a hand against her lower back and dipping his head until their foreheads were pressed together.

The fall of his hair tickled her nose. His breath

gusted against her face, down her neck. Heaven help her, she arched into his warmth. Into him. She wanted to feel his heat everywhere.

Twisting her head, she reached up to touch his cheek, settling her palm gently over his scar. A little tremor rippled through him, but he didn't pull away.

Mina couldn't resist sweeping her thumb out to feel the texture of his mouth. His lips were so full, softer than she could reconcile. How could this be the same man of growls and glowers? The same whose words cut sharp as broken glass.

She lifted onto her toes until her mouth met his.

NICK THOUGHT PERHAPS he'd died and gone to heaven.

She had to be a fool, this lush, lovely woman in his arms. Yet he knew she wasn't. She was clever, hot-tempered, efficient, and single-minded. She was his bloody steward, for God's sake.

What she felt for him was surely nothing more than pity, and he never wanted that from anyone.

Especially from Mina.

But he was hungry, starving for everything she offered. One brush of her soft lips and he was hard and aching as if he hadn't had a woman in years. God, he wanted her. Even if he could never have more than this one kiss to savor.

Yet he held back.

He was so used to taking what he wanted. Claiming what was his. When he craved a woman, he pursued her, bedded her, and left her well satisfied when he departed. But he always departed.

He wasn't cold by choice, but necessity. And only

on the surface. Inside, the fury that fueled him burned hot as the sun.

But here, now, with Mina's plush mouth on his, he found himself hesitating. He'd kissed women before and felt nothing more than arousal. Nothing more than carnal need.

Mina was different. His opposite. Everything he wasn't. Good and loyal and so damn hopeful.

And he knew as well as he knew the odds of every game at Lyon's tables that she was a risk he could not, should not, take.

One taste wouldn't be enough. He already wanted more. He couldn't kiss this woman and walk away unscathed.

When he didn't respond to her kiss, she tensed and began backing away.

Yes, go. Flee. Save yourself. He wasn't sure if the words ringing in his head were for her or him.

"Forgive me. I've been presumptuous and—"

"Mina." He touched her cheek, wrapped an arm around her waist, and took her mouth as he'd ached to from the moment they'd met.

Slow. He reminded himself to go slow, but his body raced from aroused to raging need. Warm, she was so warm. She tasted of cinnamon and jasmine tea, and her lips were a heaven he could never deserve.

After a moment, she pulled away, breathless, her eyes glowing and locked on his.

"Please tell me you'll stay," she said in a soft, husky voice that made him ache.

Part of him wanted to respond to her whispered plea. He wanted to please her, to give her whatever she wished. Except that. Except the misery of remaining in this place that was as close to hell as he'd ever been.

"Go back to your room, Mina." If she stayed a moment longer, continued looking at him with such longing and desire, he'd have no defenses left.

One kiss and this woman nearly had him on his knees.

He pulled her close again, took her mouth harder than he should have, swept his tongue inside to taste her. Then he forced himself to step away.

"Go," he urged her again. *Save yourself.*

All the fire in her gaze dimmed. He told himself that was good. She needed to see him for what he was.

She turned her back on him and slipped from his room without another word.

Nick slammed the closed door with his palm, as much to get out his frustration as to keep the door shut. To keep himself from going after her.

But, God, how he wanted to find her, bring her back, and kiss her again.

Chapter Fourteen

Cold air rushed against Mina's cheeks and she squeezed her knees tighter, savoring the heat and strength pounding the earth beneath her. She bent forward, leaning over the stallion's mane, giving the horse his head. He rewarded her with a burst of speed. Fields and hedgerows and umber-leaved trees flashed by in a blur.

By the time Enderley's stable came into view, both she and Hades were winded and sweaty, but the stallion neighed happily and Mina's head felt clearer. Though she still had absolutely no idea how to face the duke after the events of the previous night.

"Seems the beast's fully recovered now." Tobias took hold of one rein as she walked the stallion into the stable yard. "Time he goes back to his master, don't you think, Miss Thorne?"

Mina avoided Tobias's question and swiped the dust from her trousers. "Any sign of the duke this morning?"

"Why? Have you lost him again?" The stable master guffawed at his own quip.

When Mina didn't join in, he gestured toward the house.

"Only person I've seen other than the stable boys is Emma. She's been creeping around that old tower this morning."

Creeping? Emma never crept. She was tall and lithe, and Mina noticed Tobias's eyes following her more often than not. "What's she doing at the tower?"

"Heaven knows." He yanked at the stallion's saddle straps with frustrated vigor. "Hope she's not sneaking off to meet some knave."

Tobias was a decent sort, if a bit blustery, and he was clearly smitten with Emma.

"Are you attending Mrs. Shepard's Christmas dance? Perhaps you should ask Emma to stand up with you." With that bit of advice, Mina left the brawny stable master blushing and speechless.

Her pulse kicked into a gallop as she approached the house. She had work to do, but what if the duke was in his study?

She couldn't bring herself to regret their kiss. It had been inappropriate. Dangerous, even. A step down a path she'd trodden before. And she knew how it would end.

But the memory of the duke's kiss was fresh. Being in his arms, being desired—had all felt so right.

A flash of movement caught her eye. Emma was indeed near the tower, carrying a bundle of something Mina couldn't quite make out. The girl knew better than to go into the dilapidated pile of stones. Occasionally the old ruin had been used for storage over the years, but the wooden framework inside was severely rotted, and the stones themselves were crumbling.

Curiosity, Papa often warned, would be her undoing. Mina only knew she could never resist the impulse to turn over rocks to discover what was hidden underneath.

She strode across the lawn, keeping her eyes ahead as she passed the window that led to the duke's study, and stopped at the bottom of the tower.

"Emma?" Her voice echoed eerily in the empty stairwell. She scanned the field and gardens near the tower.

"Shhh." Footsteps sounded on the spiral stairs, and Emma appeared steps up. "I'm trying not to frighten her."

Mina didn't have to ask. A plaintive meow echoed down. "Millicent."

"I think the kittens are coming. She's gotten herself into an old trunk and won't come out." Emma kept her voice low and flicked glances over her shoulder. "I got her some blankets, but I'm not sure what else to do."

"She knows what to do, but it's not safe in here. You should come down."

Emma descended until she was a step above Mina. "There must be some way to help her."

"Maybe a bit of water in a dish."

"I'll fetch some right away." Emma bolted past, and Mina gazed up at the top of the tower. Much of the interior had been constructed of wood, and the planks were warped and softened with water damage. Yet even in its ruined state, the structure evoked a certain charm. What history had passed by these rounded walls? And why was Nicholas so adamant about its destruction?

Above her, Milly continued to cry, little mewls of effort and distress. Mina tiptoed up and took a tentative step onto the tower's main chamber. The space was small, the ceiling low. Mina was shocked to see a small cot, a narrow wardrobe, and the trunk Emma mentioned. Almost as if someone had lived in the space.

"You all right, miss?" Mina called to the cat as she approached. Peering over the trunk's side, she found Milly panting, her eyes closed, concentrating on her painful task. When she stroked a finger between the feline's ears, Milly leaned into her touch. "We're getting you some water, but I'm sorry to say there's not much more we can do."

Settling back on her haunches, Mina noticed writing on the trunk and inhaled sharply.

Nicholas Lyon had been engraved below the lock.

She looked again at the small bed and noticed a pair of ragged slippers underneath. Small slippers, the size a child might wear.

A chill crept up her back.

She crossed to the wardrobe and wrenched open the door hanging on rusted hinges. A few pieces of clothing, dirty and mildewed, lay in the bottom. With trembling fingers, she lifted a child's shirt. What stitches remained were neatly sewn, but most of the buttons had been lost, and moth-eaten holes dotted the fabric.

Writing scratched into the backside of the door drew her gaze and she dropped the garment. Tears pricked her eyes. Bile rushed up her throat. She traced the letters with her finger.

LET ME OUT.

She couldn't breathe. Her lungs clogged with the room's musty scent. As she stumbled toward the threshold, pain radiated out from a spot beneath her ribs. A fearsome thrumming in her head made her dizzy.

What had they done to him?

Mina tripped on a rotted slat of stairs and her body bumped against the stairwell's rough stones. Pressing a hand to the hard granite to steady herself, she felt hot tears streaming down her cheeks.

She didn't understand.

Emerging from the tower, she knelt on the ground, swiped at her cheeks, and fought to catch her breath.

"Mina, are you all right?" Emma stood over her, resting a hand gently on her shoulder.

"The duke. Have you seen him?"

"I haven't, but Mrs. Scribb says he's gone out to inspect the hedge maze. Says he wants to destroy the lot of it."

Mina stood, grasping Emma's arm for balance. "Take the water up and then stay out of the tower. It's not safe."

Emma nodded, her brows knitted in a worried frown. "Yes, miss. But what about Milly?"

"As soon as she has her kittens, one of us can find them a safe spot in the kitchen or the stables."

When the girl was out of sight, Mina started for the maze. Her body felt heavy, sluggish. But she had to find him.

The maze walls towered over her, and Mina felt a surge of trepidation when she started inside. The leafy walls that had often been her haven felt ominous now. She trailed her fingers along the leaves, letting the sharp edges of glossy foliage ground her.

"Nicholas," she called out weakly.

The name on the trunk. The boy who'd been sent away. The man she couldn't imagine leaving Enderley in a few days' time.

She called his name again, her voice stronger.

"Mina?"

His reply made her so happy her knees wobbled. But he was too far away, and she had no idea which direction.

"Where are you?" She came to a fork in the maze, a choice of paths, and took the one to the left. "Call out again."

"Stay where you are, and I'll come to you." His voice sounded clearer.

Mina couldn't make herself stop. She kept striding forward, compelled to reach him. "I'll find you."

The rumble of a chuckle carried on the breeze. "Mercy, you are a stubborn woman."

"I prefer *determined*." Another fork came, and she chose the right path. No logic drove her. Just instinct. And the faint scent of his cologne on the air.

"Shall we start a list of your qualities? I know how you like lists."

Mina stopped and turned back. His voice came from behind her. She circled back, stretching her legs, striding faster. The teasing tone of his voice soothed her. "Go on then. Make your list."

"Stubborn," he started. "Impulsive. Determined. I'll add that at your request."

Mina rushed toward the sound of his voice, turned a corner, and slammed into the firm, warm wall of his chest.

"Irresistible," he whispered against her hair.

Everything she wished to say, all the questions she needed to ask, stalled on her tongue. She didn't want words. She just needed to hold him. Slipping her hands inside his overcoat, she stroked up the satiny back of his waistcoat, and tucked her cheek against his body.

He grunted and then melted against her. Arms locked tight, he pulled her closer, resting his chin on the top of her head. Mina was grateful he simply held her, saying nothing.

She didn't want the moment to end. Their heartbeats seemed to synchronize in a comforting rhythm. Then he dipped a hand into the messy bun at her nape. His fingers blazed a trail of sensation extending down her spine, sending ripples of warmth down her legs.

"Mina?" he murmured.

"I don't want to talk." No words for now. She needed his heat and nearness, and to offer her own. Just this small bit of comfort and affection. To push away all the rest. She needed to get as close as she could to this version of him that he showed only to her. Lifting her head, she rose on the toes of her boots and kissed the edge of his jaw.

He groaned and bent to capture her mouth. With one hand he pulled her closer. The other dipped down to cup her bottom. All the hesitation of the night before was gone. He was out for plunder. One kiss became another, each fiercer than the last. He slid his tongue inside to taste her deeply. She learned quickly, nibbling his lower lip as he'd nibbled hers. Darting her tongue out to tangle with his.

Her fingers found the buttons of his waistcoat and she slipped two free, then the buttons of his shirt below. She gasped when she touched his bare chest. He was so warm, every hard plane of muscle, every smooth stretch of skin heated her fingertips.

He unfastened her buttons too, starting at the top of her blouse and working his way down until he reached the edge of her chemise. His fingers danced gently over the bare skin of her throat and neck, then lower to cup her breast.

Mina hissed and arched into his palm. "Nicholas."

He pressed his forehead to hers as he had the night before, then pulled back to look in her eyes. His brow dipped in a frown. "Mina, what's wrong? You've been crying. Tell me why."

So many questions perched on the tip of her tongue, the heartache of what he'd been through weighing her down, yet she couldn't speak. The last time she'd mentioned the tower, he'd stormed off in anger.

Yet she knew this—kissing him, holding him—was a mirage. He would go and she would remain at Enderley, and nothing would change their fates. But she wanted as much as she could have of him first.

"Tell me," he insisted, placing a kiss on her brow.

Another at her temple. A heated brush of his lips on the tip of her nose.

"I can't."

"No one's here but us. Whatever we say, only the hedges will hear." He sighed and pulled her into his arms again. "You're worried about the estate?"

"No." For once, none of her thoughts were of Enderley. Only of him. Of how much she wanted to understand his past.

He stroked a hand down her back. "Come to London with me."

Mina swallowed hard. The offer was tempting. To escape? With him? The prospect of throwing propriety aside and being alone together held enormous appeal. Part of her wanted to say yes with no promise of anything more than knowing she would be where he would be.

But that wasn't practical. That was the same blithe foolishness that had led her to heartache before. And Enderley was where she was meant to be, though discovering the tower put a dark stain on everything she felt for the estate.

"My place is here." She'd said the words to him before, but they'd never felt so shallow and meaningless.

He pulled back, and cupped her cheek tenderly. "You can choose your place. Not your father or a sense of what you owe others. Consider your own wishes for once."

Mina reached up and pushed back a strand of black that obscured his eyes. She was getting used to the silky slide of his hair between her fingers. "I would like to visit London."

His eyes lit and he offered her a blinding smile. "Then I'll take you. A visit to see the city." He looked momentarily abashed. "I'll put you up in a hotel. You can bring Anna if you like."

"Emma?"

"That's the one."

What he was offering was scandalous. Mina didn't need to read the etiquette book her father had bought her on her thirteenth birthday to know that an unmarried nobleman escorting an unmarried commoner around London would ruin her forever in the eyes of those like Lady Claxton. Not that the noblewoman thought much of her now.

He took her hand and kissed the backs of her fingers. "Shall I make the arrangements? We can depart next week."

"I should remain here while the ballroom repairs are underway." Mina nibbled the edge of her fingernail. "I also sent out for a mason to work on the parapet walk, and the library is to get a new rug and repaired window glass."

"I'm not taking you to London as my steward."

Mina's throat burned. In order to take his offer, to embrace the possibility of spending more time with him, she'd have to give up the one thing she had long held on to. The one point of certainty in her life.

Yet now that was tainted too.

"I went to the tower."

He turned to stone. Every warm, pine-scented inch of him. All the light flickered out in his gaze. Then he moved, lifting his hands from her, buttoning up his shirt and waistcoat as he backed away.

She couldn't stop now that she'd started. Whatever was between them, whether it would bloom or turn to pain and rejection, she didn't want to add any more pretending.

"I ordered you to destroy it." His voice was low and deadly calm. One could almost mistake his demeanor for poise, except that he'd clenched his hands into white-knuckled fists.

"Tell me what happened."

"I don't need to explain. Not to you. Not to anyone." His chin quivered and his mouth trembled. "You wish to remain my steward? Then do your job."

He swept past her, and Mina reached out, only managing to grasp a handful of his overcoat. "Please don't go."

NICK JOLTED TO a stop. *Please don't go.* The words might as well have been chiseled on his tongue for all the times he'd screamed them.

He stopped, but he couldn't look at her. When he did, all he wanted was to touch her, kiss her. To lose himself in her sweetness and never think of the past again.

And all she wanted was to be steward of a miserable pile of stones.

"You spent time in the tower." The tentative, broken catch in her voice made his own throat ache. "When you were a child?"

Nick's ears burned, a piercing pain, as if someone was screaming an inch away. Maybe it was an echo of his own voice, screaming in his head.

He should never have come back to Enderley. Except that if he hadn't, he would've never met Mina. Whether she knew it or not, she and the estate she clung to so fiercely were not one and the same.

To hell with Enderley. Every impulse told him to take her, seduce her, use whatever charms he possessed to keep her. He needed to leave Sussex and never look on this gloomy heap again.

He would not tread near the story of how he'd been shoved inside the tower and feared he'd never escape.

"Don't ask me to tell that tale." He turned back to her, but he couldn't look into her eyes. "If any of this is real"—he waved a hand between them and wished he was close enough to touch her one more time—"then never ask me that question again."

She said no more, and a rush of relief loosened the knot in his stomach. Perhaps she understood, or at least accepted that this was a history he could never divulge. Then she looked up at him, a glistening line of tears streaking down her cheek.

"Did he . . . lock you in? Your father?"

He hadn't meant to show her anything, but something in his face, his gaze, must have given the answer away. Whatever masks he'd mastered in business matters, they didn't work with Mina.

"Why would he do such a thing?"

That answer was easy. "Tremayne hated me. He believed rumors that my mother was unfaithful. In his twisted mind, they became true. He said he'd make me pay for her betrayal."

Her hands came up, clutched over her mouth. She looked as if she might wretch. Then her eyes ballooned. "That day I saw you," she whispered. "The day the carriage came to take you away. That's why you never came back."

Nick's throat went dry. His heart burned in his chest. His skin felt as tight and useless as old parchment. One more word and he feared he'd tear in two.

She wouldn't stop. She was too impulsive, too bloody bullheaded. She'd storm straight toward the empty gaping darkness inside him. She wasn't afraid. The lady was unhesitating. She was going to march right in and poke her finger in the bloody, aching wound.

"Nicholas, where did the carriage take you?"

"To hell, where I belonged, according to my father." Nick gritted his teeth and rushed over the words. Despite how much he hated returning to those wretched memories, he found himself telling her. "I cried like the weak little fool I was. Wouldn't even look out the window for fear my mother would notice my tears."

He could see the blasted carriage in his mind's eye, hear the gravel crunch under its wheels. The black hulking beast of a brougham waiting to take him away from Mama. But he'd been happy to leave his father's vitriol behind, and that's what finally propelled him onto the single carriage step.

He'd never admitted to anyone that he'd cried as he settled on those velvet squabs. Half his emotions had been relief. Boarding school, he'd thought, would free him from his father's wrath.

"I don't know who he was, the man who took me. Not the usual coachman. He was a behemoth who reeked of onions and ale." The vehicle had jerked forward and he'd slammed against the bench, praying the journey wouldn't take long. "The carriage stopped minutes after we departed. The man wrenched open the door and snatched me up." Nick swallowed back a rush of bile. "He locked his hand over my face so tightly, I couldn't breathe."

Mina said nothing, but a little cry of distress escaped.

"Did you know that hell is up, not below? Up, up, up we went. The stones cut my knees when he dropped me in the room. I barely had a moment to look around before the door was locked behind me." God, he'd been hungry in the beginning. "No one returned for three days. Then a tray was slid inside. Gruel. Tea."

"How long?"

"Months."

Mina let out an agonized moan. He felt it echo inside him, but he couldn't make a sound. Even when she came to him and wrapped her soft body against his, he couldn't respond as he longed to.

His muscles wouldn't work. His tongue wouldn't work. His heart wouldn't work.

Mina pulled back to look at him, tears brimming in her eyes. "How did you get out? Why did no one know you were there?"

Nick drew the pad of his thumb across her cheek. "My mother thought I was at boarding school. She even visited the headmaster when all her letters to me went unanswered. She confronted my father when she returned. Wilder helped her, helped both of us, to escape."

"I'm sorry." She wept, little hiccuping tears, and held him. Lending him her warmth, her comfort, her goodness. But it was as if a wall separated them. He couldn't feel her. Even as impulses rushed through him—to taste her, to push her against the hedge, strip off her trousers, and sink inside her lush body.

Urges raged, but he couldn't feel the emotions connected to any of them. Suddenly, he was empty. As useless as his father always claimed.

And now Mina pitied him. Now she knew he wasn't the business maven gamblers feared. He was a pathetic wretch who'd been his father's prisoner.

"I don't want your pity."

"What about my sympathy?" She gripped the front of his shirt and lifted onto her toes. "What about this?" Her mouth touched his, an urgent press of need and heat.

Nick willed himself not to respond. To pull away. "You should go, Miss Thorne."

If she stayed, he was going to do something they'd both regret. The anger would come back, and he'd turn it on her. Either that or he'd seduce her. Spend an hour pleasuring her until they both forgot their own names. But she deserved better than a thoughtless tumble in the open air on a cold midwinter morning with a scarred, empty man.

And he didn't deserve her at all.

Her eyes lit with sparks of gold as she backed away, then she snapped her head around at the sound of shouted voices.

Two men's voices. No, three.

She started off to follow the sound. Always charging into trouble, his steward was.

"Do you know the way out?" he called after her.

Back stiff, she halted but didn't look back at him. "I'm not certain. Do you?"

Nick approached until he was directly behind her. Close enough to touch her. Close enough to get a whiff of her floral scent. Close enough to feel frustration vibrating off her.

"Follow me," he said before striding ahead.

Chapter Fifteen

$\mathcal{M}$ina might have spent her whole life trying to be ladylike and biting her tongue and living up to her father's expectations, but no one she'd ever met pretended as well as the Duke of Tremayne.

As long as one didn't get a good look at his eyes.

Striding briskly toward the stables, one would think he'd just left a meeting over upcoming repairs or his plans for leasing the property. No one would guess they'd just spoken of the most painful memories of his childhood. Nor would anyone have an inkling any intimacy had ever passed between them. That he he'd touched her, kissed her. That moments before his body had melded against hers.

Mina, on the other hand, couldn't calm her racing heartbeat or smell anything but his scent on her clothes. She could still taste him on her lips, but she wasn't sure if her lungs were burning from their breathless kisses or her struggle to keep up with his long-legged stride.

Thank heavens she wasn't wearing a skirt.

She nibbled the inside of her cheek and cringed. She'd pushed him too hard. Asked too many questions.

"It's Tobias." She recognized one of the bellowing male voices as they drew closer. "I've never heard him so angry."

As they rounded the corner of the house and started toward the stable yard, Mina's heart dropped into her boots and she let out a gasp.

Gregory.

His bronze hair glinted in the sunlight. He stood behind his father, Lord Lyle, as the older man shouted at Tobias. She'd feared the viscount would come for his horse one day, but she never dreamed he'd bring his son, the man who'd broken her heart.

Their attachment had blossomed quickly. Looking back, she knew it hadn't truly been a courtship and wasn't sure why it had begun. A bit of charm on his part when they met at a village auction, and too much eagerness on her part to be charmed by a handsome viscount's son.

Gregory had seemed a way to change her stars. To be more than the steward's daughter. She cringed now to recall the possibilities she'd imagined. But it had all been as solid as dandelion fluff.

She hadn't seen Gregory Lyle since the day they'd met at the conservatory on his family's estate and he told her they must never see each other again.

A bit of fun he'd called their stunted romance that ended almost as soon as it started.

As with all things, she'd rushed in.

Beyond where Gregory stood near the Enderley stables, two men were scuffling on the ground. One

Mina didn't recognize. The other was the enormous unmistakable outline of Tobias.

"Enough!" Lord Lyle's shout drew their attention, but as the man wrestling Tobias stepped away, the nobleman moved in menacingly.

"Oy! Mind yourself, my lord." Tobias scooted back when Lyle raised a cane as if to strike.

"What the bloody hell is going on?" Nicholas bellowed as he strode into the melee.

Lord Lyle immediately straightened and turned to face him. "Ah, Tremayne."

Even from a distance, Mina made out Lord Lyle's ugly sneer. The man looked down on everyone, but he'd never shown this level of disrespect to Eustace or the old duke.

"Or should I call you Nick Lyon?"

"Call me whatever you damn well please, but get the hell off my property."

"Property is precisely why I'm here. Your lad filched my stallion, and I mean to see justice done."

Nick cast a glance at Mina over his shoulder. She bit her lower lip. He had every reason to be angry at her about the stallion, but all she saw in his eyes was concern.

"Do we have Lord Lyle's horse, Tobias?"

The young man flicked his gaze from the duke to Mina and then Lord Lyle but didn't utter a word.

Mina noticed movement out of the corner of her eye and spied Gregory slinking into the stable. It wouldn't take him long to find Hades. She broke into a run, found him inspecting the stalls with two fingers pinched over his nose, and latched her hand around his arm.

"How dare you?" He elbowed to dislodge her, and then his eyes rounded when he turned and saw her face. "Mina?"

He trailed a glance down her body. His gaze flared with the interest she'd seen many times in his cool gray eyes. "You're wearing trousers."

"Please, Gregory. I'm asking you not to do this."

"Retrieve Lyle property? Of course, I must." He indicated with his chin toward where Nick and his father stood arguing. "Not even a duke's groom can steal another man's horseflesh. Tremayne's stable boy must be made to pay for this."

"I'm the one who brought the stallion into the stables."

"Don't speak nonsense. Your pathetic attempt to protect Tremayne's ragtag staff won't do." He shook his head. "I can't believe you've been fool enough to remain on this wretched estate. Get yourself a husband or a keeper. You need a man to show you your place."

Mina tensed so fiercely, a spike of pain shot across her shoulders and up her neck. She ignored the supreme irony of Gregory Lyle chastising her, when he'd been the one who'd tried convincing her that *her place* was on a stone bench in his family's conservatory under his heaving body.

Thank God she'd been sensible enough not to let matters between them go that far.

"The stallion was bleeding when I found him. Your father beat the horse viciously." Mina waited for a reaction, but the news didn't seem to surprise him.

He leaned in, the shapely lips she'd once kissed peeled back in a hideous smirk. "He's my horse. Father never rides him. The beast's too willful and needs to be broken." He dropped his gaze to her neck, to the swath of skin and peek of cleavage Nicholas had exposed. "Just like you, Mina. We both know I should have been the man to break you."

Her fingers curled instinctively and her fist flew like an arrow straight to its target, the small, perfectly sculpted nose in the center of Gregory Lyle's arrogant face.

"You bitch!" Blood trickled between his fingers. He swiped for her with his free hand and Mina stumbled back.

Her hand stung, but Mina didn't regret striking Gregory's arrogant face. Only the rage in his eyes scared her. And not for her but for Nick, especially if Gregory and his father chose to make trouble. And for Hades too, if the poor creature ever fell back into the Lyles' hands.

A thud against the stable's outer wall made them both jump. It sounded like the chaos of a scuffle. Bodies crashing against wood.

Mina spun away and darted toward the yard. Tobias sat on his backside, fingers pressed against a swollen cut on his lip. The burly man who worked for Lord Lyle loomed over him, smirking with brutal satisfaction.

"Leave him alone." Mina started over, prepared to intervene, but she also scanned the yard for Nick.

A few feet away, he and the viscount stood inches apart, speaking in low, menacing tones. Then, in a flash, Lyle turned violent. Raising his walking cane above his head, he snarled at the duke.

"You bloody bastard."

Mina changed course, rushed over, and squeezed her body between the two men. With her bottom pressed to Nicholas's groin, she reached a hand back to hold him at bay and found her fingers wrapped around the hard, shifting muscles of his thigh. Even in this chaos, the solid feel of his body against hers ignited all Mina's senses.

"I took the horse," she confessed to Lord Lyle.

"You?" The viscount arched back, lowering his cane an inch. "Aren't you the impertinent chit who tried to seduce my son?"

"How dare you?" Nicholas's arm shot out around her, gathering the lapel of Lyle's coat in his fist.

Mina spun to face him, nudging him back, her hands braced on his chest. "Don't do this. You'll regret it."

"I'm at my best when I'm doing things I'll regret."

"Father, leave them," Gregory called as he entered the stable yard. He'd taken a Tremayne saddle and bridle and led Hades by a short rein. "The beast seems to have been well cared for. I'll ride him back." He locked eyes with Mina. "No harm done, I'm sure."

"We shall not leave until this matter is resolved. This man"—Lord Lyle pointed at Tobias—"filched my horseflesh. I won't rest until I see him hang for it."

Mina sighed and pivoted back toward Lord Lyle. "I've already told you. I'm the one who found Hades." She shot Gregory a fearsome glare. "We tended his wounds and gave him time to recover."

"You're a meddler, Miss Thorne. What would Magistrate Hardbrook say of your thievery?" Lord

Lyle grimaced as he took in her rumpled shirt and dirty trousers.

"We've retrieved our property, Father." Gregory cinched the saddle on Hades, put a boot in the stirrup and mounted the horse. "Let us leave the gambling club owner and his trouser-wearing steward to whatever *business* they were conducting before we arrived." He tugged sharply at Hades's reins but the horse shied back, resisting his rider's lead. "Come on, you wretched cur."

NICK COULD BARELY see the man or the horse through the waterfall of red fury clouding his vision.

Lyle's son was the one. The knowing glances between Mina and Gregory Lyle hinted at the tale. Whether love or lust or something in between, the man had hurt her. Now the blighter thought he could cast her dismissive glances across the stable yard.

Rage flooded Nick's senses, firing his blood, pushing every rational thought into the flames. He'd never had any patience for bullies. They were irritating sparks to the dry tinder of his anger.

But it was Mina's gasp of horror at how the younger Lyle treated the horse that sealed the beast's fate.

"How much?" Nick strode past her, wishing he could reach for her, reassure her. Instead, he confronted Lord Lyle's cad of a son.

"Good God, you're a duke now, Tremayne." The young man turned his nose up. "I thought perhaps a title might have cured your fixation on lucre, but everyone at your club says you're a greedy rotter."

Nick remembered the young man vaguely. He was one of those pampered noblemen who expected the world to fall at their feet and whined when fortune frowned instead.

"Lord Calvert says your tables are rigged," he continued in a whine high enough to make the horse's ears flick back.

"Calvert is a poor loser." *Like you.* "How much for the stallion?"

The buffoon cackled, a comical attempt at masculine confidence. "He's not for sale."

Nick couldn't imagine what Mina ever saw in the lordling. Except, of course, that he was pretty, with a delicate, almost girlish face that hadn't been slashed open by his father's penknife.

"Everyone has a price." Nick grabbed the slack line of rein hanging under the horse's snout. "A thousand pounds."

Ah, the fancy-faced nobleman liked that. Younger Lyle gulped visibly, his haughty grin folding like a house of cards. "You're a madman, Tremayne."

"Possibly." Nick cast a glance over his shoulder at Mina.

She wore an unbearably hopeful expression, and Nick didn't want to disappoint her. What he wanted was to kiss her more thoroughly, take whatever she offered, and never let his wretched past intrude again.

"Probably," he admitted when he turned his attention back to Gregory Lyle.

"You cannot buy your way out of this." The elderly Lyle wagged a bony finger at Mina, and Nick barely resisted the urge to break it free from his hand. "What this woman has done is a crime. The law will decide her payment."

"Two thousand pounds," Nick said with the last thread of calm he possessed. It was a very thin, quickly fraying thread. He sighed as he waited, darting his gaze between Lyle, who was flapping his gums like a fish flopping on the shore, and the son who'd been struck dumb, his mouth hanging agape.

"The horse isn't worth half that sum." Lord Lyle's voice had lowered to little more than an astounded squawk.

The man's honesty was a pleasant surprise. It meant the old rotter had stumbled on an offer he couldn't refuse.

"Is that a yes?" Nick had made enough deals in his life, seen enough desperate men, to know when he'd won.

The younger Lyle leaned over in the saddle as his father approached and whispered in the old man's ear. The father grimaced and clasped his hands around the lapels of his frock coat, puffing out his chest and lifting his chin.

The coward couldn't look Nick in the eye. Bested noblemen rarely could.

"I'd heard you were quite the man of business, Tremayne, but you've proven yourself a rather hapless negotiator." The tremor in his voice turned what he intended as a victory speech into a pathetic display. "I demand two thousand pounds *and* the surrender of my son's vowels."

Nicholas inhaled deeply, pretending to give the matter due thought. In truth, he knew Lyle the younger would ask to have his debts forgiven. Spencer, the factotum at his club, would know for certain, but he suspected they were worth a good deal more than two thousand pounds. Drawing out the suspense longer seemed cruel.

So he waited another sixty seconds, rolled back his shoulders, and fixed Lord Lyle with a hard stare. "Done."

Nick dug deep for any impulse to be the *better man*, to let Lyle and his progeny turn tail and strut away as if they'd won the day. But Gregory Lyle still sat on the horse like a king on his throne, sneering at Nick.

"Come down now, boy," Lord Lyle said as if speaking to a child version of his heir.

"Let me help." Nick gripped the younger Lyle's boot, ripped it from the stirrup, and shoved. The man flailed, arms pinwheeling in the air, and then tipped over the horse's side. He landed with a squelching thud in the muddy stable yard.

"How dare you?" Lyle the younger stared up at him in disbelief.

Nick leaned closer, battling the urge to haul the man up by his muck-splashed shirtfront. "I dare because everything you see before you is mine." Out of the corner of his eye, the father crept closer. Nick straightened, ripped the walking stick from the old man's hands, and slammed it against his bony chest. "Go, Lyle. Get off my land and keep your son out of my club."

Nick shot Mina a glance over his shoulder. "Miss Thorne, go inside and prepare a check for Lord Lyle along with a note indicating my agreement to destroy his son's vowels."

She didn't obey his command. Instead, she stood rooted in place, eyes wide, throat working as if she had something to say.

But then younger Lyle got to his feet, wiped himself off, and tucked his head and shoulders as he charged forward like a perturbed bull.

"You're nothing but a by-blow," he screamed. "A charlatan. Go back to London. You don't belong here."

Nick struck an arm out, grabbed a handful of shirt, and dragged the puny nobleman close. "I do belong here, you whinging nob. I'm the bloody Duke of Tremayne." He shoved hard and Gregory Lyle staggered back toward his father.

Tobias immediately came forward to retrieve the stallion. Nick waved him off and took the horse, leading the beast toward Mina.

"Here," he said, surrendering the reins to her. "Now one of the horses in Enderley's stable is yours."

Chapter Sixteen

The next morning Mina paced the small confines of her father's office until her legs ached. She'd never been one to waste time treading a straight line back and forth to nowhere when she had lists upon lists of tasks that needed doing.

Maybe she was picking up the duke's habits.

Nick, Lord Lyle had called him, and the name fit. In less than a fortnight, he'd managed to score himself on her heart.

And now he was gone.

When she looked across the hall through the half-open door, he wasn't there as he'd usually be, matching her pacing with his own. He wasn't in the house at all. She'd risen early, eager to see him, and learned from Mrs. Scribb that he and Wilder had gone into the village to meet with Mr. Thurston about repairs to the tenant cottages.

She'd started the morning by penning a letter to two masons in the village who might have use of the stone from the old tower. If they were willing to demolish the structure, she'd have it done immediately. Part of her wanted to take a maul and hack away at the stones herself.

Enderley would never be the same. She knew its secrets now. Ugly truths she'd never wanted to imagine. This morning, for the first time, the halls felt cold and empty. She sensed a pall over the house, and she began to understand that was how Nick might always see Enderley.

Footsteps sounded from far off down the hall. Mina held her breath, shoved a few stray strands of hair into the bun at her nape, and then swept her palms down the front of her bodice and skirt.

Was it him? The tread sounded lighter, the gait shorter than his long-legged stride.

"Mina?" Colin appeared in the doorway, a smile lighting his face. Then his grin immediately dropped into a frown. He'd always been far too perceptive. "What's wrong?"

"Nothing. Come in. What brings you to Enderley this morning?" She tried for cheerfulness and hid her unease by fussing with the pen and ink pot at the corner of her blotter.

"I was supposed to come by yesterday. Don't you remember? A project delayed me, but I heard there was trouble with Lord Lyle and his son. Are you all right?" He flopped into the chair in front of her desk and regarded her with a knitted brow. "I know you and Gregory Lyle have a bit of a history."

Good grief, had the rumors spread so widely in the

village that even her cousin, who usually kept his head buried in books and experiments, knew of her foolishness?

"Thought I should come check on you, and discover whether you're expecting me to call him out for a duel."

"That won't be necessary." Mina pressed her lips together to stifle an unbidden chuckle. Nick had made sure Gregory got his comeuppance. She'd never forget the sight of him flat on his arse in the mud.

"Word around the village is that the duke was had." Colin regarded her skeptically and lifted a paperweight from her desk, flipping the smooth stone in his fingers. "Heard he paid an enormous sum for an ebony stallion that's barely broken."

"He also forgave Gregory's gambling debts at his club." Mina still mused over Nick's actions, and her heart nearly burst in her chest when she recalled the look in his eyes as he'd handed her Hades's reins.

"Doesn't make sense, though." Colin tipped his head in an admirable impression of a confused pup. "Is the duke truly so fond of horseflesh he'd pay an astronomical sum for a dodgy pony?"

"Hades isn't dodgy. He's a fine horse."

Colin was an insightful young man, forever collecting facts and experiences to piece together into unique inventions. Now he studied Mina as if she were a particle under the lens of his microscope. When his brown eyes widened, she knew any attempt to hide her feelings from him was in vain.

"He bought the horse for you," he said quietly. "Mina, what's between you and the Duke of Tremayne?"

She stared at her cousin so long her eyes began to water.

What was there between them? Attraction. Desire. Nick liked to point out what they had in common, but Mina viewed the list as a rather short one. He was a wealthy, successful businessman. She was simply his steward.

Yet a persistent thought weighed on her mind this morning. For the first time in a long while, she thought perhaps it was time she left Enderley.

Once Nick returned to London, would the place ever feel right again?

Yesterday, he'd declared to Gregory that he belonged at Enderley, but now that she knew what he'd endured at the estate, who could blame him for wishing to leave?

"You're not going to answer, are you?" Colin asked in a gentle tone, curious, but not pressing for more than she could give.

"I'm not sure I can." She didn't have the answers herself.

"Then tell me this. If he can be swayed to purchase a horse for two thousand pounds, do you think he could be convinced to invest in my thresher?"

"He said his friend was the investor."

"Ivanson."

"Iverson." Mina shuffled through a stack of letters that had arrived in the morning post. "Aidan Iverson," she read from one of the envelopes. The man boasted an address in Mayfair.

She stared at the neat, sharp angle of his handwriting and imagined what a life in Mayfair must be like.

What London must be like, with its colors and sounds and all variety of people bustling through its streets. She'd always wanted to visit.

Nick was right. She didn't know much beyond the acres of Enderley. She'd never been out of Barrowmere for more than day trip to Brighton. After her father's death, she'd expected to remain in her role as long as she was needed. To remain at Enderley forever.

Nick's arrival had changed everything.

"Mina?" Colin shifted in his chair. "What's going on in that head of yours?"

An idea came, impulse as much as anything. A need to get away. "Why don't we go to London and see Mr. Iverson about your thresher?"

"We? As in you and I?" He swept a hand around the room. "Don't you have work to do?"

"There's always work to do, but practically speaking, all of it can wait. Besides, I haven't had a holiday since I became steward."

She'd been unable to leave her father's role for even a day. Perhaps Nick was right, and she did feel some kind of debt to him, a need to be the dutiful, proper daughter she'd often felt herself failing to be.

For too long the estate had been the only place Mina felt she belonged. Enderley was home, and the prospect of leaving had been terrifying. Now she wasn't so sure. Everything she thought she knew had altered.

Or perhaps she had.

After years of waking and getting straight to her duties, this morning she'd paced the carpet, anxious to see Nick, anxious for something she couldn't quite name.

"We can go today. The trip is only a couple of hours by train and we can be back before nightfall." Mina stood and went to a shelf behind her desk. In a locked box, she kept a collection of coins and notes she'd saved from her wages over the years.

"What if this Mr. Iverson won't see us?"

"Then we'll treat ourselves to tea at Claridge's and have a stroll around the city." Mina gestured toward the notebook bulging from his top coat pocket. "Do you have some drawings you can show him if he does see us?"

Colin closed a hand over the rectangular outline of his journal. "I never go anywhere without my notes."

"Just let me tell Mrs. Scribb where we're going and we'll be off."

"Mina." Colin reached out and caught her hand before she could get out the door. "You're not running away, are you?" He stood to face her. "You'd tell me if the duke had behaved inappropriately toward you? He's bigger than me, but I'd do my best to thrash him, if necessary."

How could she tell him the truth? That she'd been the one to go to Nick's bedchamber. That she'd been the one to seek him in the hedge maze, kiss him, devastate him by bringing up the ugly truth of his past.

"You needn't worry, cousin. I won't be a fool as I was with Gregory Lyle."

"Mina, he was the fool for treating you as he did."

Colin wasn't entirely correct. Her heart *had* led her astray with Gregory. But with Nick everything felt different. Irresistible and inescapably right.

Yet even if Nick embraced the title, his duties, and refurbished Enderley from floor tile to parapet walk, nothing would change the fact that he was a duke and she was the daughter of a steward who'd never set foot outside the safe, small world in which she'd been raised.

Mina knew she couldn't remain as his steward, yet she couldn't imagine how they could be more to each other. Unlike with Gregory, she had no girlish illusions.

Staying at Enderley and hoping Nick might return once or twice a year would break her heart. Walking away from all she knew, never seeing Nick again, would hurt too.

But giving in to what she felt for Nick? Where could that ever lead?

It would likely end in heartache. Though this time it would be heartache she chose, rather than one she'd been too naive to avoid stumbling into.

NICK SETTLED ONTO the bench of the Tremayne carriage and felt something odd. A strangle fizzing in his chest. A lightness that suffused his whole body, unexpected and unnatural.

He thought, perhaps, it was satisfaction.

Satisfaction acquired not because he'd bested a desperate nobleman or fattened his own coffers. Quite the opposite. He'd spent wildly. Impulsively. He'd promised repairs for a dozen tenant houses, funds to the village smithy to improve his workshop, and to be the chief benefactor when Barrowmere rebuilt its local mill.

He hated the admission, but Iverson was right. There

was enormous reward in investment for the purpose of improvement, rather than simply chasing a profit.

And a single thread wound through all he'd done and agreed to do—the need to tell Mina. The desire for her to look at him with something other than pity. Wilder's praise was heady too, if subdued. He released a satisfied *hum* whenever Nick did something right. He'd craved those sounds as a child, and he'd stacked them to the sky today.

The old butler sat, back straight, gaze fixed out the carriage window. Questions bubbled up that Nick couldn't hold back any longer.

"Why did you stay?" he asked the old man.

Wilder had been the one to free him. In the wee hours of a rain-streaked night, he'd brought Nick's mother, a handful of bank notes, and the keys to set him free. Nick and his mother had run through wet grass and mucky fields until they reached the road and met a coach that carried them to Dover. Then they'd boarded a boat to France, and finally found freedom from Talbot Lyon's cruelty.

"A difficult question, Your Grace."

"Our years in France were difficult too." Nick and his mother had lived meagerly, but they'd been safe. Though fear still crept in. Until her death, his mother worried that his father would find them. Nick was sixteen when she died, and he'd been determined to return to England and seek revenge.

Instead, on his arrival in London, he'd learned that his father was dead and his brother had inherited everything. So he'd made his own way. On the streets, with his wits and sometimes his fists and an unexpected knack for gambling pence into pounds.

"I will always be thankful for your help, Wilder, but I need to know."

The elderly butler stared out the carriage window a moment longer, as if he hadn't heard the question, but Nick saw tension in the old man's jaw. His gnarled fingers stroked again and again at the edge of his coat.

"Your father could never be sure I was responsible," he finally said in his low timbre. He met Nick's gaze, tired eyes burning with some long-remembered emotion. "I lied for the first and only time in my thirty years of service to the duke. He questioned every staff member. Railing at us each in our turn. I put the blame on the creature your father paid to put you there."

"My jailer?" Nick recalled everything about the man. The pace of his gait, the scraping sound his boots made on the stones, the ale and onion stench of his clothes. For months, he was the only face Nick ever saw.

"The scalawag protested his innocence, of course. For a price, I have no doubt the demon would have dispatched you to the grave on your father's behalf." Wilder wiped a gloved hand across his mouth as if speaking of the man left a bad taste on his tongue. "Your father dismissed him. I sent the villain off with fair warning that if he ever darkened Enderley's door again, I should reveal all to Magistrate Hardbrook."

Nick's chest burned like he'd downed a double dram of whiskey. If only. He stuck his hand in the satin-lined pocket of the Enderley carriage, hoping to find a flask, and came up with fingers covered in ancient dust. "Did you ever go to the magistrate?"

"Considered it. The choices I made haunt me to this day." He stared at the carriage wall behind Nick's head. "I should have known. I should have attended to comings and goings more closely. The duke allowed his henchman to live off the estate, you see. The food he brought you was from the village. His visits to the tower were always—"

"In the evening. I remember." But Nick didn't want to remember. "Those were the longest days of my life. I feared I'd go mad."

"Forgive me." The butler's plea came on a low, fervent whisper.

Nick shook his head. "You didn't put me there, Wilder." He'd come to Enderley determined to make them all pay, but now it was clear only one man had been responsible for his misery.

Tucking his chin down, Wilder stared at his gloved hands and mumbled, "I should have known."

The thought haunted Nick too. Someone should have known. In the early days he'd cried and screamed until his lungs were on fire. But no one heard. No one came. Not the other staff. Not the steward who taught his daughter that duty to Enderley was all that mattered.

In the end, it was fitting that his mother had been the one to discover his father's villainy. She'd borne the man's cruelty herself for too many years. She refused to speak of what happened the day she confronted his father. Nick only knew that by that evening, she and Wilder had come to free him.

"Yet you continued in service to my father?" Nick asked with no malice in his heart or tone. He understood that no one could predict what they'd do to survive. There'd been moments when he'd felt safe inside the tower, when the prospect of leaving frightened him. At least there he'd been free from his father's lash.

"I did, Master Nicholas, and have no excuse that will satisfy you, I suspect. Days bleed into one another before we notice they've begun to run out. One looks up to find a year's gone past, then one more, and nothing is simpler than staying the course."

"And at the end?" Nick hated how much he wanted to know. "I suppose he found his conscience on his deathbed and begged for forgiveness."

"He never spoke of the matter." Wilder bowed his head. "Never mentioned you again, at least not to me. He did make a show of memorializing your mother, claiming to others that she was interred in the Tremayne vault. But he was never the same man again. The evil of what he'd done must have weighed on him."

"I doubt the old devil regretted a thing."

"He was weak when he died. I suspect he was nothing but a collection of regret at the end. But, no, he never said as much. That would have shown weakness. He was a petty, violent, unreasonable man, but he could never bear weakness in others. That would have forced him to admit his own." Wilder's chest rose and fell quickly. He was breathless with the effort of saying so much, revealing so much. He fell silent, a wash of pink staining his cheeks. "I often regret giving so many years of service to such a man."

"I suspect you stayed for Enderley."

"For the rest of the staff. They are my responsibility."

"Miss Thorne speaks like you do. She has your sense of loyalty to those in service to the Tremayne dukedom." After Wilder's explanation, Nick felt nothing but sympathy for the old man. But when he thought of Mina, irritation flared. "Why did you let her take on her father's duties? Did no one think to tell her there was more to life than fretting over a crumbling pile of stones?" Once Nick warmed to the topic, he found he couldn't stop. "She's young, beautiful, clever, passionate, and completely wasted in that hellish place."

Wilder's bushy gray brows quirked, but he didn't argue with Nick's assessment. "You have formed strong opinions about our Miss Thorne in a very short time, Your Grace."

"Stop with the honorifics, Wilder." Nick waved the man's assessing gaze away.

Wilder cleared his throat. "May I ask, sir, what are your *intentions* regarding Miss Thorne?"

"My intentions?" Nick tried not to choke on his next breath. He had nothing to say that Wilder would wish to hear.

All of his intentions were selfish. None of them were proper or polite. And no matter how many times he told himself to put the woman out of his mind, she was there. Dominating his thoughts. Stoking an urge that had gone from spark to wildfire—a desire to claim and keep her for his own.

But she wasn't some seaside cottage he could swindle away from a desperate nobleman. She was a lady who deserved to be free of the entanglements of Enderley once and for all.

"Forgive me, sir, for my boldness. I've known Miss Thorne since she was a child."

"Perhaps she would be better off elsewhere." Nick swallowed against the words, because he didn't much like them himself. He didn't care if she cut ties with the Tremayne dukedom. In fact, he wished to see her free of its burdens. But the prospect of never seeing her again when she went off to make her way in the world stuck like a sliver in his heart.

Heart? Good grief, when had he become such a sentimental fool?

"Maybe I should have dismissed her when I arrived, but I asked her to remain and help me prepare the estate for lease."

"I see."

For a long stretch Wilder fell silent, and Nick was relieved to have the conversation behind him. The five-mile trip from Barrowmere to Enderley was quickly becoming the longest of his life.

But the quiet between them left him more time to wallow in thoughts of Mina.

Finally, Wilder spoke again. "Any thoughts on a duchess, sir?"

Bloody hell. Nick would be sure never to be stuck alone in a carriage with Wilder again. "You are aware I don't wish to be duke?"

"Indeed, sir. And equally aware that you are one, whether you wish it or not."

"Let's stick to repairing the house and getting the estate in order. Shall we?"

"Does that mean you'll be staying on longer than expected?"

"Perhaps." For the first time since arriving in Sussex, Nick was torn. Not because he'd grown any fonder of Enderley for its own sake, but it's where Mina was. Remaining longer was suddenly a prospect he could bear.

But the club weighed on his mind too. Nick reminded himself that London was where he belonged. With so much to do at Enderley, he hadn't thought of Lyon's in days. That realization disturbed him.

The carriage began to slow and Nick stared up at the towering columns of Enderley's front facade. Lord, how he'd loathed the his first glimpse of the place the day he'd returned. Now the sight of it had nothing to do with the house itself, and everything to do with Mina.

"Where's the list, Wilder?" Nick reached out impatiently. The butler had been scrupulous about noting all the repairs to be made and every penny Nick had promised for various projects around the village.

"Sharing the details with Miss Thorne, are you, sir?"

"She likes lists."

"This one will make her quite pleased."

Nick hoped so. The minute the carriage stopped, he jumped out and bounded up the stairs, beelining toward her office. After one knock, he pushed inside.

The room stood empty.

"Miss Thorne's gone, Your Grace." Mrs. Scribb approached from the opposite end of the hall.

"Gone?" The word was a punch in the gut that stole his air.

"To London."

"Alone?" Had what she'd discovered about his past and Enderley caused her to seek other employment so soon? Nick imagined her in London, and he found he rather liked the prospect of her being in the city he considered home. But not on her own when she'd never been and knew no one.

"Accompanied by her cousin, Mr. Fairchild. She said they hoped to return by nightfall."

"Very good." Nick entered the study and paced until his heartbeat settled into a steadier rhythm. She'd be back soon enough, but would her intentions have altered? He dreaded the idea of parting from her, despite his eagerness to leave Enderley behind. But would she leave for good? He was no longer sure of what she thought of the estate. And he'd never been certain of what she felt for him.

He lowered himself into his father's chair and noticed a letter from Iverson on the blotter.

The missive was in the man's usual style—short and to the point.

> *Calvert has filed suit against you and the club. Huntley and I suggest a settlement before this matter reaches the courts. Any plans to return to London or are you more enamored with the countryside than you imagined?*

Nick cast the letter aside and scrubbed a hand over his jaw. He glanced up at the mantel clock and considered how long it would take to reach the station and the city by train. Iverson hadn't demanded he come immediately, but Mina was in London.

Not that he'd find her in a city of thousands. But it felt like he could. He had the sense that they were connected. Maybe it had been the first time he'd seen her, the first touch, the first kiss. Maybe it was her stubborn, willful nature that reminded him so much of his own. Just like her loneliness.

Nick rose from his desk and headed down the hall, startling Mrs. Scribb. The older woman clutched at her apron front as if her heart had seized.

"I need to go to the station. Immediately."

"A trip to London, is it, Your Grace?" A knowing grin lifted the edge of the housekeeper's mouth.

Chapter Seventeen

$\mathcal{I}$n the row of elegant townhouses, Mr. Iverson's stood out.

The windows sparkled like cut crystal, the curtains behind the white-washed facade were a cheerful lemon shade, and lanterns on either side of the dark blue front door had been polished until the brass glinted in the sun.

So different from Enderley's weathered gray stones and imposing medieval-style battlements.

Somehow, the appeal of the townhouse's facade made it more intimidating. Who were they to burst into this man's well-ordered world unannounced?

Now that they stood on Aidan Iverson's doorstep, Mina regretted her rash urge to call without an appointment or any prior acquaintance. They didn't even possess calling cards to leave if he happened to be out or refused to receive them.

"Are we going to knock or did we come all this way to admire the architecture?"

Mina didn't have to glance Colin to hear the smirk in his tone.

"This was foolhardy." Because they were foisting themselves on Iverson unceremoniously, he might reject Colin's invention out of hand.

"We're going to knock." He took a step closer to the door. "Coming was a good instinct, Mina. Sometimes in life, we must lead with our hearts instead of our heads. And I say that as a man whose mind never stops whirring like a spinning top."

Mina had never had difficulty following her heart, but it hardly seemed the time to list the ways that instinct had led her to disaster.

"I have an excellent feeling about this." He smiled back at her and stretched out his hand, hovering his fingers over the shiny lion's head knocker in the center of the door. "Ready?"

"We have come a long way to turn back now." Mina nodded and he rapped several times. Echoes bounced off the other whitewashed houses in the square.

They waited. Colin fidgeted with his journal. Mina fretted that Iverson would see their visit as more intrusive than daring.

"Shall we knock again?" he asked, his face beginning to fall.

Before Mina could reply, the door swung open and a striking dark-haired woman started across the threshold. She gasped to find them in front of her, and paused, regarding them with a startled gaze.

"Hello," Colin said immediately. "We're here to see Mr. Iverson."

"Then you've arrived at the right place. I, on the other hand, am just departing." She cast a glance over her shoulder. "Unfortunately, Iverson's staff are currently preoccupied with a minor nuisance." After tugging her gloves tighter on her wrists and examining both of them from boot to brow, the lady stepped back and gestured for them to enter. "I suppose I could show you in. What business do you have with him?"

"We seek his investment for my cousin's invention." Mina wasn't sure of all the details regarding Colin's thresher. She was only certain that if he'd designed the machine, it would be fresh and unique and beyond what anyone had ever imagined.

The lady lifted one dark brow. "What sort of invention?"

Mina hoped Iverson's interest would match that of the woman leading them toward him in clipped quick strides. Colin fumbled with this notebook, pulling forcefully when the edge stuck in the seams of his pocket. With one enormous tug, the sound of tearing fabric set the journal free, but it immediately slipped from his hands. Torn scraps of paper fluttered down like snowflakes as the leather-bound notebook thudded to the marble floor.

The lady turned and bent to help them retrieve the scattered scribblings. "This is interesting," she said, examining a long mathematical equation. "And I quite like this one too." She held up a torn edge of paper featuring a sketch of some strange-looking machine with disks and levers, all of them numbered.

Though Mina shared a love of numbers with her cousin, her skills were best applied to ledger books, and his education and imagination soared toward creating devices sometimes only he understood.

"Are you fond of mathematics, miss?" Mina asked the finely dressed woman.

"Very much." The lady's whole face lifted when she smiled, immediately transforming her from formidable to friendly. "And I realize I failed to introduce myself." She handed the notations to Colin and lifted a gloved hand to Mina. "Lady Lovelace, and you two are?"

Colin shot to his feet, shoved his notes under his arm, and offered the noblewoman a bow. "Colin Fairchild, my lady, and this is my cousin, Miss Mina Thorne."

"What are you building, Mr. Fairchild? Some sort of calculation device?"

Colin took the sketch from Lady Lovelace's fingers and stuffed it into his notebook. "Oh, that's just a glorified abacus, really. The device we're here to speak to Mr. Iverson about is of an agricultural and industrial nature."

"Really?" The lady stood and assessed Colin, tapping a finger against her cheek. "Are you two engaged for supper this evening?"

"Ada?" A tall, handsome, auburn-haired man emerged from a room down the hall. "I thought you'd departed after Charles."

"I found two visitors waiting on your front step, Iverson. A Mr. Fairchild and Miss Thorne from . . . ?"

"Barrowmere. In Sussex," Colin said, sketching a less impressive bow than the one he'd offered Lady Lovelace. "My cousin is the steward of Enderley Castle."

Iverson's face immediately lit with surprise and recognition, then his brows knitted in concern. "You must know Lyon."

"Yes, Mr. Iverson." A scratchy tickling started in the back of Mina's throat. She began to speak and only managed a squeak, which stoked the flames she felt infusing her cheeks. "We're pleased to have the duke in residence."

"What brings you here? Has something happened to Nick?"

"The duke is well." Colin strode two steps forward. "We've come to discuss an invention with you, sir. One that could change British agriculture forever."

Iverson cast an inquisitive look at Lady Lovelace. "Perhaps they should meet Babbage."

"*The* Charles Babbage?" Colin breathed. "I read his *Economy of Machinery and Manufactures* with great interest."

"I was on the verge of inviting them," Lady Lovelace admitted, "but since you're the host, I thought you should do the deed."

"By all means," Iverson put in immediately. "Join us for dinner this evening. I'm intrigued to hear how the new Duke of Tremayne is getting on. Lady Lovelace and Professor Babbage will both be in attendance tonight."

Mina glanced at Colin. "We had intended to catch the next train back to Sussex."

"Perhaps we could take a later train," Colin proposed, a tinge of desperation in his voice.

"We serve dinner at six," Mr. Iverson told them. "Early by most hosts' standards, but I like to leave time for the best part of the evening. The discussions.

We have another agricultural manufacturer attending, a Mr. Munford."

Lady Lovelace added quietly, almost conspiratorially, "If Iverson won't commit funds, perhaps he would."

"Don't count me out yet," Iverson grumbled. "I haven't even heard his ideas."

"Well, then I'll leave you to it." Lady Lovelace stopped to whisper near Mina's ear on her way out. "Competition gets them every time."

Mina smiled at the intriguing noblewoman. It wasn't every day one met a lady who was equally comfortable discussing mathematics and inventions and knew how to pull the strings of wealthy investors like Iverson. Her confidence was infectious, and Mina held her head high as she and Colin followed Iverson into his enormous office.

Dark wood vied with tall garden-facing windows for dominance, and long robin's-egg-blue velvet curtains brought a comforting harmony to the space.

"Please, sit," Iverson directed as he stood behind his desk, arms crossed, subjecting them to an intense perusal. What could he tell from their clothing and demeanor? Enough to satisfy him, apparently. He soon settled into a chair and leaned forward, hands on his desk. "I take it you have designs to show me?"

Colin rushed to untangle his notebook from his torn pocket and laid out a series of sketches as if he were setting a table, every piece in its place.

"Describe this invention that will change British agriculture forever," Iverson said in a low murmur as he bent over the drawings, twisting and turning them, lifting one to get a better look.

"This thresher is smaller yet more powerful than any yet invented. Powered by steam, able to consume less manpower while producing more grain."

"Sounds too good to be true."

"But what if it is true?"

Iverson quirked a brow and grinned. "I do thrive on possibility." He waved toward Colin. "I presume you've come with estimates. Costs, investment capital, profit projections."

While Colin shuffled through his notebook, Iverson turned his gaze on Mina. "Did you help design the thresher, Miss Thorne? As a steward, I imagine agricultural matters interest you a great deal."

"They do, sir, but alas I don't possess my cousin's knack for invention."

"Mina's the reason we're here, Mr. Iverson." Colin had never quite outgrown the habit of thinking he needed to come to her rescue. "She encouraged me to seek you out. The duke mentioned your interest in funding new inventions, and Mina's always looking for ways to improve Enderley."

Iverson lifted one of Colin's drawings. "And how will this piece of machinery assist the estate you manage, Miss Thorne?"

Mina leaned forward in her chair, thinking of Mr. Thurston and the other farmers who struggled to find manpower during the harvest. "Many have left the village over the years. Young men and women seek employment these days in the cities. Anything that can make the work of harvesting more efficient would be a boon to most of the farmers of Barrowmere."

Iverson nodded, interested. He was an impressive

man. Broad-shouldered, with an easy grin and incisive green eyes.

"Tell me about Enderley Castle," he prompted as he continued studying Colin's designs. "Have you served as steward long?"

"A little over two years." If Mina had ever sought employment, she imagined this was how an examination from a potential employer would feel.

"How is Tremayne? Is he getting on well?" Iverson tapped the blotter on his desk. "The title came unexpectedly, but I'm sure you've been able to assist him a great deal."

"I do my best, Mr. Iverson."

The first memory that came to mind was of Nick's hands on her hips, steadying her as she climbed down the oak tree after retrieving Millicent. Then of his hands shooting out to catch her before she fell to her death from the parapet walk.

Now that she thought back on Nick's moments of chivalry, she had to acknowledge that he'd helped her a few times too.

"Have you known the duke long, Mr. Iverson?"

His mouth curved in a bemused smile. "Forgive me. It's odd to think of him as a duke." His eyes twinkled when he added, "I suspect he feels much the same."

"He's expressed as much. Several times." Mina stared at a seam on her glove that was beginning to fray, much like her nerves. She couldn't stop thinking about the man, and now, with a gentleman who knew him far better than she ever would, she wished to do nothing but ask impertinent questions.

When she looked up, she found Colin staring at

her quizzically. As usual, her flushed cheeks were no doubt giving her away.

"I've known him for many years," Iverson said quietly. "Nearly a decade and a half."

"You met in London? He hasn't told me much about his time there." Mina held Iverson's gaze and saw the flicker in his eyes, a tensing of his mouth. She had a gnawing suspicion that he knew what had happened to Nick.

"It's not a story he likes to tell."

"No, I can't imagine it is."

"Lyon's accomplishments are impressive on their own, but more so when one knows his history."

Mina wanted to see his accomplishments, this Lyon's Club that he'd built up from a crumbling building into a famous gentlemen's club.

"You two should attend the dinner party this evening," Iverson said as he took a look at the estimates Colin had scribbled down. "If you wish to remain in London overnight, I'm happy to offer guest rooms to lodge you. There are far more bedrooms in this house than I ever use."

Mina examined the skirt and cuffs of her dark green traveling suit. Colin's tweed jacket and brown trousers weren't the height of fashion either. "I'm afraid we aren't dressed for a dinner party, Mr. Iverson."

At first he didn't answer. His gaze scanned the numbers and whatever else Colin had listed regarding the financial investment he'd need for his thresher. Finally, Iverson looked up, squinted, and seemed to hear what she'd said.

"Clothes? That's easily remedied." He assessed Colin a moment. "I'm sure I could loan you a jacket, Mr. Fairchild." Then he turned his green gaze on Mina. "Believe it or not, I might be able to help with a dress for you too, Miss Thorne." He stood and started out of his office. "Follow me."

He entered a room across the hall and beckoned her over.

Mina had never seen so many pieces of clothing outside a dressing room or wardrobe. It was as if a lady's trousseau had exploded above the sitting room and spilled out a sea of gowns and gloves and hats. Many of them were red. Various shades and textures.

"I've recently purchased a shopping emporium and must decide which of these gowns to offer ready-made." He perched his hands on his hips and stared at the dresses laid out over chairs, tables, and matching settees as if he had no idea where to start. "Any opinion on the matter?"

"I've no great knowledge of fashion, Mr. Iverson." Mina could hardly tell him her favorite clothing consisted of trousers, waistcoats, and plain shirts.

"Well, do have your pick."

"Of these?"

"Only if you wish to wear something else for the dinner party." He glanced at the gowns, then back at her. "Is that terribly inappropriate?"

"Probably," Mina admitted. "Though I'm no great stickler for propriety either, I'm afraid." She couldn't even recall where the book of decorum her father had given her ended up. As a doorstop or gathering dust someplace, no doubt.

He quirked one reddish brow. "Then I suspect you and Lyon get on well."

Mina left that observation unanswered and was soon saved from any other inquiries on the topic when Iverson's housekeeper beckoned from the hallway.

"If you'll excuse me, Miss Thorne." He started out of the room, pausing once on the threshold. "Please do pick a gown, if you like. Or wear your traveling costume. I assure you Lady Lovelace and the others will care far more about your conversation than whether you're garbed in the height of fashion."

After he departed, Mina trailed her fingers across the pile of gowns laid out carefully over the back of the settee. Her fingers slid across satin as slick as the damask on Enderley's dining room chairs, then sank into plush velvet that reminded her of the curtains in the old estate's library.

The velvet gown was a rich, vibrant red, and she couldn't stop touching the fabric. The cut was simple, with few adornments, and for the first time in her life, she found herself eager to put on a dress.

What would they think of her at Lady Lovelace's dinner party if she showed up wearing such a bold shade? In an eye-catching gown, perhaps they wouldn't assume she was the daughter of a land steward who'd never been to the city before today.

Mina lifted her hand from the gown and drew in a shaky breath. Her green traveling suit would do. Tonight wasn't about her. It was a chance to secure funding for Colin's design.

"You should wear that one if you like it," Colin said from the doorway.

"It's too daring."

He chuckled. "This from the girl who raced every boy in the village and usually won, punched Roger Beck because he called me short, and taught me how to fish with a sharpened stick."

"None of that was daring." Mina shrugged, though hearing her exploits in such a succinct list made her regret what she'd put her father through. Perhaps she had been a bit of a hellion. "It was just childhood."

"We dared to venture to London on nothing more than hope and a whim. And look how far we've come. Tonight I'm going to meet Charles Babbage, and Mr. Iverson seems keen on hearing more about the thresher."

"Do you think he'll invest?"

"I think he might." Colin pressed his lips together, but his eyes were twinkling. "I want to see that thresher at work in Barrowmere, Mina."

She imagined getting in the harvest more efficiently, with increased earnings for tenants if they could process grain quickly and get it to market. The rents might finally come in steadily, adding a bit more to Enderley's coffers.

Her first impulse was a desire to tell Nick. But would he care? His life was here in the city, at his gambling club and conducting business with men like Iverson.

Their commitments and cares were worlds apart. Yet more and more, Mina couldn't imagine her life unfolding and not seeing him, speaking to him, being close enough to touch him.

And she couldn't imagine how his duty and hers would ever allow them to be together.

Chapter Eighteen

$\mathcal{N}$ick could breathe again.

Dusk and a thick umbrella of fog had settled over London by the time he arrived, but the metallic, sooty air tasted sweet on his tongue. Familiar.

Every mile they rolled away from Enderley, the lighter Nick felt. Freer. More himself. The city was the only place he'd ever considered home, and he was glad to be back.

But there was more. A niggling sense of anticipation. Mina was here. Somewhere in this vast metropolis, she was rambling aimlessly with her cousin, who was as ill-prepared for London's dangers as she. He hoped they'd taken in some of the sights. Enjoyed themselves away from the grim walls of Enderley.

He wished he could see her here. More, he wished she could see him at home in the city where he'd achieved so much. The place where he was at ease and might at least seem like a man she could admire.

If only she'd spoken to him first, he might have arranged a meeting with Iverson or Huntley or other investors willing to fund her cousin's agricultural design.

Mrs. Scribb insisted the two planned to return to Enderley tonight, and Nick wondered if they were headed back already.

"Lyon's Club," the driver called down as the carriage drew to a stop.

Nick jumped out and headed to a side door. He rarely entered through the front. To do so invited noblemen to approach and complain about their losses or ask to see him belowstairs about a loan. He wished to avoid causing any interruption in play at the tables, and to spend a bit of time checking in with Spencer before heading to Iverson's.

He'd sent a messenger from the train station to let Iverson know he was in the city, asking him to arrange a meeting with Calvert immediately, if the ill-mannered nobleman was amenable.

He sniffed the air's familiar scents when he stepped inside Lyon's. Slow-roasted beef and stewing vegetables from the dining rooms mixed with colognes and hair pomades from the game rooms. What was shockingly unfamiliar was the quiet. A few voices carried from the large lounging rooms, where men dined or drank and conversed for hours. But the gaming tables were usually abuzz after nightfall. Tonight, the hum of chatter was minimal, the clink of dice and betting chips few and far between.

Nick bounded up the stairs and burst through Spencer's office door. "What the hell has happened to my club?"

His factotum looked up slowly from a ledger book

and removed his spectacles. "Good evening, Mr. Lyon. So good to see you again."

He hired Spencer because he was smart, efficient, and unflappable no matter what trouble arose. But it also made the man damned hard to read.

"Tell me what's happened."

"In two words? Lord Calvert." Spencer stood and approached a teapot and cups set on a tray near his desk. He poured as he continued. "He has engaged in a campaign of near military precision. Choosing those noblemen with the most sway, the wealthiest friends, to poison their minds against you and the club."

"I'm here to meet with him, hopefully this evening."

"Are you?" Spencer lifted his teacup and shot Nick a pleased glance over the rim. "You agree with Iverson and Lord Huntley, then?"

No, not really. But Nick would swallow the whole matter like a child took bitter medicine, hating every minute of it. Still, he knew compromise was necessary to resolve a messy legal battle he'd loathe far more.

"Perhaps I'm learning, Spencer. Maybe you have to let them win a skirmish now and then in order to win the battle."

"Being a duke agrees with you then, sir?"

"Not at all." The title itself had taught him nothing. If he'd learned anything it was because of one petite dark-haired lady with sparks in her eyes and a heart for wounded, hopeless creatures. "But I know there are times a man must cut his losses and walk away."

"Excellent." Spencer returned to his desk and handed Nick a folded pile of papers. "I've gathered all of Lord Calvert's vowels."

Nick narrowed an eye at the man as he went on merrily sipping his tea. "You were certain I would agree to forgive the man's debts?"

"I was certain you would do whatever was necessary to restore the success of Lyon's. As would I, sir."

"Thank you, Spencer." When Nick started out toward where he'd asked the coachman to wait, his factotum followed.

"Will you be returning to London as you'd intended? Or will you be remaining at your castle in Sussex?" Spencer's normally calm tone faltered. "While I will do as you bid, sir, there is much here that would benefit from your oversight."

"I plan to wrap up estate matters soon." Nick glanced through a multipaned window that led onto the gaming floor. There were more gentleman at tables than he would have expected from the sounds, but he still felt guilt at leaving his business behind for so long. Would Calvert have succeeded in his campaign against Lyon's if he'd been in town to deal with the man's mischief?

THE MINUTE THE carriage started onto evenly paved streets, Nick knew they were drawing close to Iverson's townhouse. A bit of tension returned to ride the muscles of his shoulders. He didn't relish another confrontation with Lord Calvert, but he was feeling more generous than he had in years. He'd buy the nobleman's compliance, as he had with Lord Lyle.

Every man had his price.

An unusual number of windows in the house were lit at Iverson's for a man who lived alone and often grumbled about possessing so many empty rooms.

The pretty housemaid blushed as she always did when Nick came to call.

"Is he at home?" he asked. "He's expecting me."

"You're not here for the dinner party then, sir?"

"Dinner party?" Nick heard the bouncing voices of conversation as soon as he stepped across the threshold. A woman burst into throaty laughter and several gentlemen's responses came in a cheerful chorus.

"Lyon, you came." Huntley sauntered into the hallway. "Iverson showed me your message. Did you receive mine?"

"No." Nick shot Huntley an accusing glare. "Was it to warn me there'd be a party?"

"I didn't know about the dinner myself." He held up his hands in mock surrender. "But you know I'm always prepared for a party."

"Of course you are."

"I feel confident saying that every party is better with me in attendance." He looked even more pleased with himself than usual. "But business first. I convinced Calvert to come," he explained. "He's waiting for both of us in Aidan's study."

"Good, let's get this over with."

"Indeed." Huntley clapped Nick on the shoulder. "If we can get Calvert to desist with his menace quickly, perhaps we can join the party."

"I'm afraid the meal is finished, my lords." The housemaid looked truly bereft to deliver the news. "But we're serving drinks in the large drawing room."

"I desperately need a drink, but first we must find Mr. Iverson."

"I believe he's in with the guests." The maid led them toward the heart of the partygoers, but before they made it halfway to the room, a male voice stopped them in their tracks.

"You found him." Iverson stepped out of his study. He offered Nick a somber expression. "We're ready to begin."

Inside the room, Nick saw Calvert had come alone.

"You've told him?" Calvert asked, gaze fixed on Iverson. "He understands my terms?"

"Not yet."

The smile that stretched Calvert's wrinkled face made Nick's skin itch. "Then do let me have that pleasure." He finally turned to face Nick. "Your club, Mr. Lyon. Or should I call you Tremayne? That's my price."

"You're insane."

"Nick." Huntley laid a hand on his arm, as if to hold him back from striking the nobleman. Nick shrugged him off.

"The club is not for sale."

Calvert let out a maniacal cackle. "I'm not interested in buying anything from you, Tremayne. You will sign over ownership because if you do not, I shall drag you through the courts until I've beggared you, ruined you, left you with nothing but a title you don't deserve."

Somewhere inside him, Nick knew there were perfectly rational thoughts. Reasonable, even generous impulses. Mina had unearthed them in a fortnight.

But he couldn't find a single ounce of generosity now.

All he saw was black. Ink spots flickered behind his eyes. This pompous, corrupt fool of a man thought he could take everything. One threat and he and Huntley and Iverson would fold like a gambler afraid of losing his first bet.

"No."

Every head in the room pivoted. Every set of eyes locked on his face. Calvert began to tremble as if he had a lit firecracker inside him and its fuse was burning low.

Nick worked to control his anger and speak clearly. "*My* terms are these. I forgive your debt. I burn your vowels, you go on your way, and you never enter Lyon's Club again."

"Have you been to your club of late? A few empty tables, I'd wager."

"I'd rather have fewer members than arseholes like you laying down your bets."

"How dare you!"

The words were familiar. Though Lyle had pronounced them with more dignified horror. Calvert just sounded tremulous. The man wasn't as sure of the cards he held as he pretended to be.

"I have a strong case," he insisted. "Others have also agreed to bring suit against you for unfair play at Lyon's."

"Then they're liars too." Nick sighed deeply. "I've no interest in tangling with the courts." He waited for the twitching grin on Calvert's face to grow. "But I employ the best solicitors and barristers, and justice rarely smiles fondly on gentlemen who refuse to pay their debts."

Calvert shifted on his chair. Nick could see the man was wavering.

"Do you not recall what you offered if your debt went unpaid? What will your wife say when I take possession of the hunting box bequeathed in her uncle's will?" One step closer to the viscount, Nick noticed the sheen of perspiration on his wrinkled brow. "Or the ruby necklace you bought as an engagement gift? Or the diamond ring you gave your mistress?"

Among the pile of Calvert's vowels, Spencer had included a helpful list describing what the viscount had wagered as collateral. Nick had been employing private inquiry agents for years to look into the property he acquired when nobleman failed to pay their loans. He'd learned long ago that a man's greatest weakness had nothing to do with pounds and coin, but what the money represented. And who might be harmed by its loss.

"Take his offer, Calvert," Huntley put in, employing a friendly tone. "Let the man forgive your debts and think no more about the duke and his devilish club."

Calvert began to tremble like a man taken by fever. Rage carved his face in hideous lines of tension, and then his mouth twisted in a grimace of pure loathing. But, rather than spewing more vitriol, he slumped back in his chair.

"I want forgiveness of Lord Webster's debt too," he said on a choked whisper.

"Who?" Iverson had taken the chair behind his desk to write out what Nick assumed was a statement of the agreed terms of their negotiation.

"Lord Calvert's nephew, I believe," Huntley said. "We can do that, can't we, gentlemen? Anything to put this unpleasantness to rest. I for one wish to join the other guests."

"Are we finished here, Calvert?" Nick asked the nobleman.

"I need your signature." Iverson quickly added a few lines to the paper under his wrist and slid the document to the front of his desk. "After the duke signs, we'll ask for yours and then pass the documents on to our solicitor."

"I want the signed document now!" Calvert's cry contained all the fervor of a childlike tantrum. "I won't leave without it."

Nick glanced at Huntley then Iverson and exchanged a nod with each before signing his name. After the scratch of Iverson's pen on the foolscap and the signature of Calvert, Nick breathed a sigh of relief as he watched the man depart.

"Thank God that's done." Huntley strode to gaze at himself in the mirror over the fireplace and swept a hand through his already unruly hair.

"Perhaps," Iverson said, "we should be more particular about who we admit as members at Lyon's."

"Yes." Nick agreed with Iverson, as he often did. The man was a successful investor because he mixed instinct with caution.

"Shall we join the others?" Huntley asked, already halfway to the door.

As they entered the main hall, heavy footsteps sounded at Nick's back. He turned to find Calvert striding toward him from the front entry hall, spittle clinging to his lips, rage darkening his eyes. "Someday you'll lose, Lyon. All you hold dear will be ripped from you. I only hope I'm alive to enjoy your misery."

"You're too late, Calvert. I've already had my share."

HER CHOICE WAS made, and it was too late to turn back now.

Mina rubbed her gloved hands together, though she wasn't cold. Just rattling with nerves.

The two steps from the threshold of Aidan Iverson's enormous drawing room into the fray of gathered guests seemed an enormous chasm. Strangely, the vibrant red dress she'd chosen soothed her nerves. The velvet felt delicious against her skin, and the comfortable cut of the fabric made every movement seem regal and purposeful. For the first time in her life, she understood the power of wearing a beautiful gown.

One deep breath and she took another step toward the laughter and conversation-filled room. All her hesitation dissolved when she spotted Colin. He was standing in a cluster of ladies and gentlemen and waved her over with an encouraging smile. His easy nature always allowed him to endear himself quickly to everyone he met.

"Mina, come and meet Mrs. Elmhurst. She's writing a book on household management."

After introductions, the lady scanned Mina from head to toe through pince-nez spectacles, brows lifted. "So young. Mr. Fairchild tells me you're steward of a ducal estate in Sussex. What a task that must be for one your age."

"My father taught me well, and I quite enjoy keeping busy." Mina liked Mrs. Elmhurst immediately. The lady wasn't shocked by Mina's sex, only her age. A refreshing change from Magistrate Hardbrook and Vicar Pribble.

"We must sit together when the games begin. If you don't mind a few questions about what you do and how you manage such a large staff."

"Of course."

"Perhaps you should consider writing a book, Miss Thorne. No doubt you have some interesting stories to tell."

"Indeed." Though the most interesting stories of late involved a tall, dark, moody gambling club owner who wouldn't wish to be mentioned in print.

A round of applause broke the low murmur of voices in the room, and Mina and Colin joined in when Lady Lovelace and a man who looked to be twice her age entered.

"It's Babbage," Colin said in a reverential tone.

The older man, Colin had informed her, was a famed professor, inventor, and mathematician. But what caught Mina's eye was Lady Lovelace. Mr. Iverson had been wrong about the lady's disinterest in fashion. The noblewoman's dark plum satin gown was by far the most striking in the room.

When guests moved forward to greet the newly arrived pair, Colin stayed back and nudged Mina's shoulder.

"You're clenching your jaw so fiercely," he teased, "I believe you might break it."

"I'm not hiding my nervousness well. Is that what you're saying?"

"Why be nervous? This is the most perfect collection of party guests possible. Noblemen and commoners. Wealthy and poor. With a single purpose that binds them all."

"Which is?" Mina asked, assuming he meant their connection to Mr. Iverson.

"A commitment to progress."

Mina quite liked that thought. "Stop it," she told Colin. "Your enthusiasm is infectious."

"Good, better that than your nervousness." He smiled over at her. "Enjoy yourself, cousin. You're a clever girl in a pretty dress in a city filled with possibility. We should make the most of this visit."

Colin grabbed two glasses of wine from a passing footman and offered her one for a toast. Glass in midair, Mina froze when a new group of guests entered the room. Behind Mr. Iverson and a tall golden-haired man stood the one person she'd wished to see from the moment she'd opened her eyes this morning.

Nick.

"The Marquess of Huntley and the Duke of Tremayne," Iverson announced to the assembled guests.

Nick's gaze zeroed in on her, and for a moment Mina forgot to breathe. Forgot Colin and the wineglass she held.

He started toward her and she gulped down a sip of wine before handing the glass to Colin.

"Breathe," Colin reminded her. "You're turning as red as your dress."

"Fairchild," Nick said when he reached them, though his gaze never left Mina's.

"Your Grace," Colin said jovially, "what a merry coincidence to come all this way and find you here."

"Yes, especially since Mrs. Scribb assured me you'd both be returning to Sussex by nightfall."

"Mr. Iverson invited us to stay," Mina said, feeling a desperate need to explain that she hadn't put herself here so that he might find her. "I would have told you we were departing, but you weren't in your study this morning."

"I returned to tell you of all I'd promised the villagers, but you weren't in your office."

Mina wondered if he'd felt as lost as she had when she'd found his study empty. "I didn't think you'd mind if I took a day away."

Nick said nothing, but he kept his gaze fixed on her. He stared at her hungrily, as if it had been weeks rather than hours since they'd last seen each other.

"Pardon me," Colin said before starting away. "I must introduce myself to Professor Babbage."

Mina's mind spun with what she wished to say to Nick, but all of it remained bottled up inside.

"Red becomes you," he said, his voice rough and low enough that others wouldn't hear.

"It's not too—"

"It's perfect." He swallowed hard as he swept his gaze down her body, but he also frowned. "Why are you here?"

"Colin's thresher."

The furrows of his frown deepened. "Pardon?"

"His thresher. The idea he wished to present to you. You mentioned that Mr. Iverson might be interested in investing, so we came to discover whether he would."

"On a whim? Without a proper introduction or even the knowledge that he'd be at home?" His voice turned irritated, a gruff pitch she was coming to know well. "If Fairchild had brought a proper proposal to me, I might have been willing to invest."

Unfortunately, his ire always sparked her rebellious spirit. "I thought you were only interested in earning a profit. Besides, you weren't there to consult."

He snatched a drink from the same footman who'd passed a moment before, swigging the liquor down in one swallow. "Somehow, I don't think you would have asked my permission."

"Why are you here?" Mina didn't mind the coincidence of finding him at Iverson's, but was it a coincidence? Or had he come to find her?

"I had business with Iverson and a member of the club."

"Something troubling?" Perhaps she wasn't the reason after all, and yet his expression brought back a memory. A moment in the moonlight, when she'd watched him burn his father's portrait. "You have the same look in your eyes as the night you arrived at Enderley."

"What look?"

"A haunted one."

"Some would say I deserve to be haunted." He deposited his glass and swiped another from the footman's tray. "And much worse."

"I disagree."

"Miss Thorne!" Mrs. Elmhurst called. "We're about to begin the parlor games. Won't you come and join us on the settee? You can sit between me and my son." She shoved at a thin young man beside her. "Move over, Percy."

"Do you know that woman?" Nick asked.

"We met a moment ago. I should . . ."

"Stay with me." He reached for her, his fingers gentle and achingly warm against her wrist. "I pushed you away yesterday and I need to apologize. Speaking of that experience brings the memories back too sharply."

"I'm the one who stormed in where I shouldn't have."

"You only asked for the truth." That bleak look shadowed his eyes again. "You spent your whole life at Enderley. You deserve that much after the way I reacted."

"But not if the memories cause you pain . . ." How could they not? How could he be anything but tortured to recall what his father had done? "I never wish to cause you pain."

"Miss Thorne, may I be so bold?" Mrs. Elmhurst's son came to stand at Mina's elbow. "My mother has asked me to retrieve you and she's quite tenacious."

"She'll join you in a moment." Nick cast the young man a fearsome glare that made him stumble backward.

When the boy had gone, Mina whispered, "Don't be boorish."

"As you once pointed out, I rather enjoy being boorish. It may be what I do best."

"That's not true."

"Selfishness, then?" He took one step closer, and Mina found herself leaning toward him.

"Are you trying to play on my sympathy?" she whispered.

"No, that's not at all the emotion I wish to provoke in you." He flicked a gaze toward the Elmhursts and lifted his fingers from her wrist. "Go be dutiful. You're far better at it than I am."

Mina headed toward the mother and son, causing both to brighten with smiles, but she couldn't resist looking back at Nick. She could feel his gaze on her, the pull of it. Of him. Every moment with him bound them closer together and every separation was becoming more difficult.

As she stepped forward, her eyes focused on Nick, her foot snagged in the hem of her gown. She tried to correct but pitched forward. The silly heeled slippers she'd borrowed quivered as she shifted her weight. Then her right foot slid over the edge of the shoe completely.

She cried out as her ankle twisted.

Percy Elmhurst reeled back, lifting his arm to protect himself as she lunged forward.

Two arms wrapped around Mina's middle, catching her before she slammed into the young man. Air whooshed from her lungs as Nick pulled her snug against his body. Then he bent, hooked an elbow behind her knees, and swept her up into his arms.

The incident didn't escape the notice of the other guests. As he strode with her from the room, jaws went slack and eyes bulged. One lady flicked open her fan and began flapping the stretched fabric near her face.

"Where are you taking me?" she asked him. "You're making a scene."

"Wouldn't it have been worse if you'd given what's-his-name a black eye?"

"You can put me down."

"Probably, but let's get you someplace where you can breathe and try that ankle without spectators."

But apparently they did have a spectator.

Colin exited the drawing room too, hurrying after them. "Is she all right?"

"My ankle gave out. I'm sure it's fine," she assured before glaring at Nick. "I'll know more when I'm allowed to walk on my own two feet."

Nick narrowed one eye at her as he kicked wide a half-open door along the hallway. Inside the book-lined room, he headed for a leather sofa and set her gently on the cushions.

The room was everything Enderley's library should have been. Warm, well-lit, and rich with the scents of book leather and old paper and ink.

Mina looked up at two sets of concerned masculine eyes and pushed to the edge of the sofa. Her ankle screamed with pain every time she moved her right leg, but she tried to stand.

Both Colin and Nick offered their assistance. She took her cousin's arm to brace herself and pushed up on her left leg. And soon crumpled back onto the sofa.

"It stings a bit, but I'm sure it's fine."

"We should send for a doctor."

"It's a twisted ankle, for goodness' sakes. You're both overreacting. Give me a minute, and I'll be up and ready to hobble back to the drawing room."

"Maybe one of the guests is a doctor," Colin said worriedly.

"Doubtful," Nick replied. "Iverson prefers investors and inventors. I have a physician on staff at the club. I'll take her to him." He spoke as if the decision had already been made. No debate. No one bothering to ask what she preferred.

"That's ridiculous. Mina can't depart with you to your club on her own. Besides, isn't the club's doctor busy treating ailing gamblers?"

Nick glanced at Colin, who was pacing and gnawing at his thumbnail. "Finding an available physician might take hours. My club is minutes away."

"Take her," Colin finally agreed. "He can wrap her ankle and assess whether anything's broken?"

"I'll see that she's well cared for," Nick assured him.

"Stop talking about me as if I'm not in the room."

"Do you want me to accompany you?" Colin glanced from her to the doorway, and she knew he wished to be nowhere so much as back among the dinner guests speaking of threshers and industrial machinery. "You need a chaperone."

"I'll be fine. Don't worry. I trust the duke." Though when she glanced up at Nick, the tiny smile at the edge of his mouth made her shiver.

Colin hesitated, shot Nick as hard a look as he could manage, and finally departed. Nick helped her get to her feet.

"Give me your arm?" she asked.

He did one better and wrapped his arm around her waist.

"You'll catch me if I fall?"

"Always," he said without meeting her gaze.

Mina gritted her teeth. "It hurts."

"Well, that won't do." He caught her up in his arms again in one easy motion, as if he'd carried many women before.

"You lift me as if I'm as light as one of Mrs. Darley's soufflés." She expected him to chuckle or for the tension in his jaw to ease.

Instead, he looked at her with an intensity that made her stomach flutter.

"You must know," he finally said, "such a comment only invites thoughts of how you might taste."

Somewhere, far in the back of her mind, Mina knew she should take care. With her reputation. With her heart. A small quiet voice inside urged caution.

But it was too late.

She wanted everything the heat in Nick's eyes seemed to offer.

Chapter Nineteen

*H*e'd carried her away, and it was the headiest feeling Nick had ever known.

Mina was a warm, soft, sweet-scented bounty. He loved the feel of her pressed against him, the heated weight of her in his arms. She wasn't some fragile creature that he might break. And she didn't shy away from his touch.

In fact, she slid an arm around his neck and clutched his lapel possessively between her fingers.

So he took her. Past the noisy drawing room, past the skittish housemaid who blushed at the sight of them, and past Colin Fairchild, who waved goodbye to his cousin with something akin to misery writ across his youthful face.

Nick willed his mouth not to curve in a victorious grin. Thankfully, Mina's gown hid the tightening in his groin.

"You shouldn't be enjoying this," she whispered.

"I know. I'm doing my best."

"Excuse me," an all-too-familiar voice called from behind them. "Where exactly do you think you're going with that young lady?"

"He's taking me to the doctor," Mina answered helpfully over his shoulder.

Bugger off, Huntley would have been Nick's preferred reply.

"I'm taking her to the club to see Dr. Stevens."

"Are you, indeed?" Huntley came around and positioned himself between them and the front door. "You are aware that women are not allowed at Lyon's Club."

"Is that true?" Mina looked utterly offended by that news.

"Miss Thorne, may I present Rhys, Earl of Huntley, who is a co-owner of Lyon's, and also known to thwart club rules on a regular basis."

"A true pleasure, Miss Thorne." Huntley twirled his hand in the air, stuck out his leg, and bowed deeply. The man never did the minimum when he could leap past sufficient and crash straight into excess.

Nick stepped closer, until the spot where his hand that was wrapped around Mina's knee came up flush against the man's bright eyesore of a waistcoat. "We'll be going now, Huntley. The lady needs a physician."

"Do forgive me." Huntley stepped back. "I only meant to see to Miss Thorne's well-being, but I see, Lyon, that you have matters well in *hand*." The scoundrel tipped his gaze down to where Nick tightened his hold on Mina. Then he proceeded ahead of them and gestured toward the door. "Take my carriage. The coachman will bring it back after he delivers you."

With great effort, Nick managed to climb into the vehicle while keeping Mina in his arms.

"I can sit on the bench," she said after they were seated.

"What if I prefer you here?" He slid a hand around her lower back to indicate how much he wanted to keep her right where she was.

"You are warmer than the squabs, I suppose." Her tone was teasing.

"Practical as ever, Miss Thorne." Nick could barely see her in the darkened interior, but he heard the hitch of her breath when he tightened his hold around her waist.

Seated like this, the heat of her body warmed every inch of his. Her scent became richer, not just her usual floral perfume, but a deeper scent that was uniquely Mina.

He felt her leaning closer, felt her breath whispering across his skin.

"This reminds me of the night I came to your room."

"Does it?" His mouth watered for a taste of her, just as it had that night.

"Alone with you in the darkness." She inhaled sharply, tensing in his arms. "I don't regret that night." She waited, falling so silent Nick wondered if she was holding her breath. Then she finally said, "I don't regret this moment either."

"Mina," he whispered before leaning in for a kiss.

She slid a hand around his neck. "Is the club much farther?"

"Not far. Are you in much pain?" Nick stroked her

cheek and his body hardened when she leaned into his touch, nuzzling against his fingers.

"No, but I wonder how much time we have."

"Not as much as I'd like." Nick replaced his fingers with his lips, brushing a kiss against her cheek, trailing down to the edge of her mouth.

He had no idea where he found the control to do it, but he held back. He was determined to let her decide this moment. With a gnawing desperation, he wanted her to want him—his touch, his kiss—as much as he wanted her.

"What exactly did you have in mind?" Nick lifted the hand he'd kept wrapped around her hip and traced his fingers along the edge of her breast.

"So many things." She turned her head a quarter of an inch. A tiny, maddening movement. Not enough for their lips to align, but closer, so that he felt her every breath against his mouth.

Nick's thighs trembled when she brushed her lips against his, but she immediately pulled away.

He slid a hand along her jaw, desperate to kiss her again. "Are you torturing me on purpose?"

"Of course not."

He wanted to take the question back. They were no longer a hairsbreadth from kissing. Now she was inches from him.

Then she pressed two fingers to his lips, following the shape of them gently.

"I'm memorizing," she murmured, carefully tracing the seam of his mouth.

Nick felt the stroke all the way to his groin.

"I don't want to forget after you leave."

Nick took her finger into his mouth, stroked the tip with his tongue, and bucked up against her when she moaned in response. "Mina."

She leaned in, fitted her mouth to his, and he was lost.

All the raging need melted into pure pleasure, and the madness was he wanted to go slow, savor every second. Let Mina take the lead. He found a reserve of patience he didn't know he possessed, his hands flexing against the small of her back while she kissed each corner of his mouth, then took his lower lip between her teeth.

When she moved back, staring at him in the dim light of the carriage lantern, he cursed himself for a fool. She tipped her head, assessing him. Nick turned his face, pushing his scarred side into the shadows.

Mina stroked her fingers through his hair, then down across his cheek, bumping along the edge of his scar. When she reached his chin, she nudged until he faced her again. "You're so beautiful."

"The carriage is dark," he told her. She was the beautiful one and incontrovertibly mad. "You can't see clearly."

"I've seen you in full sunlight."

"Exactly. The glare obscured your view. You never got a good look."

"I looked very closely." She leaned in to emphasize her point, and Nick's skin heated everyplace her body brushed against his.

"The pain from your ankle must be making you delirious." He glanced toward the hem of her gown.

"I know what I'm about. Strangely enough, I can hardly feel the pain."

"Good."

She kissed him again. Freely. Eagerly. Her mouth sweet and lush and warm against his. Fingers twined in his hair, she tasted him with her tongue, and he let her take everything. Even if he'd wished to hide or hold back, he wouldn't have been able to. The woman tore down all his defenses.

Too soon, the carriage stopped in front of Lyon's.

Mina peered out the window. "Goodness, it's very grand."

A flare of pride warmed his chest. "Much better on the inside." As he maneuvered out of the carriage with Mina in his arms, she tugged at his coat.

"What will the gentlemen say when they see you carrying me? Won't this cause you some awful scandal?"

"This may surprise you, but no one inside that building believes I'm a saint." Nick didn't dare laugh for risk of offending her, but it amused him mightily that she was more worried about his already awful reputation than her own. "Besides, we're going in a special entrance that leads down to my private chambers."

A little shiver passed between them, and Nick couldn't be sure if it was the rattle of his nerves or hers. Unlike Huntley, he'd never brought a female onto the premises of the club. His every dalliance was conducted elsewhere. Letting someone into Lyon's private spaces was a measure of trust he'd never afforded any other woman.

Now he found himself breathlessly eager to take Mina to the very heart of all he'd built. So eager he fumbled the key against the lock of the iron door on the side of the building. Nick knew that letting Mina inside was a step he could never take back.

"If you put me down, it will be easier," she said in her practical, governess-style tone.

"You do it." He lifted the key between them. The bit of die-cut metal was more than a means of unlocking the thick iron door. It was the means to unlocking parts of his life he shared with no one else.

She took the key, slipped it into the lock as she held him with an arm around his neck, and twisted the latch.

She gasped as soon as he carried her across the threshold. It was one of the evenings when a quartet of violinists and cellists performed in the dining rooms. The music was a beautiful refrain above the din of conversation and the rattle of dice.

Through a slit in a set of dark red curtains, a slice of the main gaming floor was visible. Mina's fixed her gaze on the spot. "Everything sparkles."

"I am fond of gold."

"But it's so bright."

"Not all of it." Nick stepped toward the curtains so Mina could get a wider view. "See that balcony up there? That's where I sometimes work and watch the play below."

"So you linger in the shadows and make sure everyone else is well lit. Because you don't trust them?"

"My trust is hard to win."

"Mr. Lyon. I did not expect you to return so soon." Spencer, sharp-eyed factotum that he was, noticed them immediately and approached.

"Put me down," Mina insisted.

Nick bent to let her down gently, but she kept hold of his arm, teetering so much he suspected she'd balanced all her weight on her good foot.

"Mina, this is Bastian Spencer, manager, advisor, and a man who could run Lyon's single-handedly if I let him." Nick gestured toward the burly dark-haired man. "Spencer, may I present Miss Mina Thorne?"

"Miss Thorne, to have such a lovely visitor is a rare pleasure." He bowed and cast Nick a questioning gaze that held none of the chastisement Nick was expecting. "What can I prepare for you, sir?"

"Send Dr. Stevens, a tea service, whiskey, and bandaging to my chambers."

"To your private chambers, sir?"

Mina winced as she lifted her hand from his arm and attempted to put her weight on both feet.

Nick wrapped his arm around her waist. "Quickly, Spencer."

"I can walk, but do keep holding on to me."

"If I must." As they neared his rooms, Nick's heartbeat kicked into a gallop. "I should warn you."

Mina looked up. "Whatever it is, it can't be worse than a leaking ballroom and a crumbling parapet walk."

He opened the door to his chamber slowly, trying to prepare her. "I chose to decorate my quarters rather—"

"Lavishly," she said on a shocked whisper. "You truly do love red."

He'd chosen the color for how loud and vibrant and alive it was. The complete opposite of the cold, gray walls of Enderley's tower. "There *are* other colors in the room."

Too quick for him to hold her back, she limped away and ran her finger along the gilded wainscoting. "Oh, I do like the gold."

Nick watched her explore his private space, watched where her gaze went, and listened for her little sounds of interest. He realized he was holding his breath, eager for her approval, not unlike her eagerness for him to appreciate Enderley. This room reflected who he was, who he'd become, and her reaction mattered.

"The bed is rather—"

"Oversized."

"Tall." She glanced up where the four posts reached to the ceiling. "Everything you require is here." With a sweeping gaze, she took in the small dining table, desk, and matching gold settees in front of the fireplace. "Though there isn't much room for entertaining." She shot him a curious glance.

"I don't entertain. I've never invited anyone to join me in this room."

She hobbled another step, and Nick rushed over to lend his arm for support. "It's all rather cozy," she said with a sweeping look around.

Safe is how Nick thought of this space. His alone. But now, for the first time, he wasn't alone, and Mina looked right in a room he'd long considered his solitary refuge.

He led her toward the settee, resisting the urge not to haul her back into his arms. A primal part of him now felt quite certain it was where she belonged.

Before he could get her seated, three short raps sounded at the door, and Spencer poked his head in. "Forgive me, Mr. Lyon, but Dr. Stevens has gone home

for the evening. Apparently, one of his daughters is ill."
Spencer waved a hand, and a servant followed him
into the room, bearing the items Nick had requested.
The young man deposited them, strode across the room
to ignite the kindling in the fireplace, and departed
the room quickly.

Spencer hovered at the threshold. "Shall I call for
one of the other doctors or attempt to find someone
with such knowledge on the gaming floor? I believe
Lord Kellyn was once a medical man."

"I don't think that will be necessary, Mr. Spencer."
Mina spoke up before Nick could tell him to seek
whatever doctor they could find. "I'm walking now
and my ankle feels much better. Thank you."

Spencer responded to her as he would to Nick, nod-
ding his assent and backing out of the room.

To prove her claim, she hobbled the rest of the way
to the settee and dropped onto the cushions. The bodice
of her gown dipped, and Nick tried not to gape at the
delicious view.

She lifted the hem of her gown, inch by inch, watching him as if to gauge his reaction.

If he didn't know her better, he'd think Mina Thorne
meant to seduce him.

"Shall we have a look?" she asked softly.

Yes. God, yes. When Nick realized she was speaking
of her ankle, he hunched down in front of her to assist.

Her eyes widened when he lifted her dress higher,
but then she began to help, gathering fabric in her
hands. Her shapely legs, encased in virginal white
stockings, were the most erotic sight he'd ever seen.

"There's no visible swelling. Does it still hurt?" He touched her gingerly, stroking his hand up her calf rather than put pressure near her ankle.

"Perhaps I should remove the stocking." She lifted her gown an inch more. "Will you help?"

MINA BIT HER lip and watched as Nick froze before her, his hand tensing around her calf, his gaze wary.

"Mina?" He spoke her name as a question, but she wasn't certain whether he intended to plead with her to continue or warn her off.

Every part of her body was humming with an energy that wasn't quite nerves and had nothing to do with the pain from her twisted ankle. She didn't hurt at all, but she ached in places she'd never ached before.

Most of all, she wanted. Desperately. Not to see a doctor or even to explore the decadent gambling club over her head. She wanted Nick. Wanted to savor this moment with him, in this private space he shared with no one else.

He'd let her in. Allowed her to get close to him. But it wasn't enough. She wanted to get closer. She wanted more of him. Even if this was the only night they'd ever share.

Here, away from Enderley, there were no titles or duties. Just this. This powerful, undeniable pull between them.

"No one will interrupt us?"

"I promise." He knew what she wanted. He understood why she'd asked. Something in his eyes changed. Heat replaced wariness.

That's how she wanted it between them. Real and true, without an ounce of pretense.

Slowly, he began sliding her stocking over her knee, dragging his fingers against her skin. When he neared her ankle, he cast her a worried look.

"I don't want to hurt you. Ever."

"Go slow."

He did, peeling away the fabric and revealing that her ankle was slightly reddened but barely swollen.

"Now the other," she told him, quietly, lifting her opposite leg.

Bracing her foot on the broad, hard plane of his thigh, Nick held her gaze as he reached under her skirt, rolled down her stocking. When he bent to kiss her exposed knee, Mina grabbed for his lapel.

She knew where she wanted his lips.

He settled onto his knees and pressed in between her legs, forcing her to spread wider to accommodate the width of his body.

"Is this where you want me?"

"It's a start." Mina stroked her fingers through a wave of black hair on his forehead.

"Tell me what you want. Anything, and you'll have it." There was a desperation in his voice that made her body pulse in response. More than her body, some essential part of her. She understood his need. She felt it too.

"Kiss me." She wanted his mouth on hers. To taste him. Desperately.

He studied her lips a moment, took her face in his hands. Mina tugged at his shirt, and was just on the verge of demanding he end the torment of making her wait when his lips came down on hers.

Their previous kisses had been too rushed. Too new and uncertain. This was different. Slower, and yet hungrier. He tilted his head to kiss her more thoroughly, used his tongue to explore more deeply.

This was right. Everything else fell away. Passion flooded in, pleasure and a sense of belonging she'd never felt in her life.

Mina clung to Nick's shoulders. It didn't matter that she was safe in his arms, perched on the firm edge of an expensive settee. Everything was falling away. All the years of pretending. All the miserable loneliness. All the restless yearning she'd tried so hard to curb.

With him, in this moment, in his arms, she wanted and wanted and he gave her more. Exactly what she needed most. To be bare, without a single wall between them or a single defense. And she was unafraid.

Mina held on to his tensing shoulders and then she got to work, moaning into his kisses as she pushed the coat from his shoulders, worked free the knot of his cravat, fumbled with the buttons of his shirt.

"It seems you wish to undress me too." He laid his feverish forehead against hers, watching her fingers work.

"Yes," Mina hissed as she found his lips again. "I need to see you."

Five little words. Awful words that she immediately wanted to take back. She'd had no idea they'd break the spell.

Nick's hands that had been stroking her, gripping her possessively, stilled against her body, and then he pulled away.

"Nick?"

"We should turn the lamps down." He stood and did just that, casting the already dim room into near darkness but for the flicker of flames from the fireplace.

"You insist on hiding yourself from me?" It was the last thing she wanted.

"I insist on sparing you." He returned to her, bending to put his hands on the settee's back, cocooning her between his arms. "Trust me. You don't want to see."

He kissed her, so sweetly and thoroughly that Mina relented, reaching up to twine her arms around his neck. She would have been quite content for the kiss to go on forever.

But he soon pulled away slightly, slid a hand under her knees, and scooped her into his arms. As he walked toward the bed, the fire's glow danced over his face. Mina traced the edge of his jaw, then gently, tentatively, the line of his scar.

"I'm not afraid of seeing your scars."

He settled her with infinite care on the edge of the enormous bed, not quite meeting her gaze. "I am."

The ache in her chest was so piercing it stole her breath, and she forced her hands to remain on the bolster rather than reach for him. He hated sympathy or any sign of pity. She'd learned that lesson well.

Instead, she reached back and unhooked her gown, pulling her arms from the bodice and pushing the fabric down to her waist. Goose bumps danced along her skin. She wore only her practical, unappealing corset and chemise under the beautiful gown.

Nick didn't seem to mind. He stood watching

breathlessly, eyes squinting in the dim light to take in every detail.

"There's a problem with turning the lights so low." Mina lowered the gown over her hips, arching up to free the fabric under her bottom before letting the red velvet pool at her feet. "If I can't see you . . ." Scooting onto the bed, she positioned herself in the enormous shadow he cast with the fire's glow at his back. "How can you see me?"

Leaning forward, she touched his chest. So warm and firm. She loved the way his muscles jumped under her touch. Sliding her hand down, she found the single fastened button of his shirt and slipped it free. Then she went farther, tugging at the opening of his trousers, her fingers colliding with the hot, hard length of him.

"Mina." He released her name on a sound that was both a gasp and a growl. She reveled in how she affected him.

"Please, Nick. You said I could have whatever I wanted." She worked the hooks of his trousers until they fell open, slid her fingers inside, and savored his heat. "I want to see you."

He toed off his boots, helped her remove his trousers and drawers, and stood before her bare, his body outlined in firelight. Mina unhooked her corset, loosened the ribbon tie of her chemise, and pulled at the generous neckline until it slid off her shoulders.

Moving to the edge of the bed, she got to her feet, testing her ankle gingerly.

"Careful," he said, immediately reaching for her. She caught his hand and then pressed her wrist to his palm. Her pulse raced and she wanted him to feel what he did to her.

The last piece of clothing fell to the floor. She'd let go of the final shreds of hesitation. More than anything, this was what she wanted.

Nick stroked his fingers along the edge of her breast, drawing his thumb gently across her taut, aching nipple. Then he bent to kiss her. First her mouth, then her chin, then the sensitive hollow at the base of her throat. He flicked out his tongue to taste her skin, and Mina licked her lips, eager to do the same to him.

His lips closed over her nipple and she felt the gentle stroke of his tongue all the way to the center of her thighs.

"Please." It was the only word that made any sense, and she wasn't sure what she was pleading for, except for more. To get closer, to see him more clearly. "Come into the light."

He lifted his head, searching her face. Mina stepped out of his arms and inched past him. She reached for his hand and urged him forward. He let her lead him and stepped a bit closer to the fireplace.

Mina held her breath to keep from gasping when she got a good view of his body. She willed the burning in her eyes not to turn to tears.

Faded scars crisscrossed his back, buttocks, and upper thighs. Below the stripes, he was an astonishing man. He possessed the broadest shoulders she'd ever seen, made more so by layers of muscles that bunched and tensed as she studied him.

"Enough," he said roughly. "Let me see you now."

Mina didn't give him what he asked. Not yet. She stepped closer, pressing her body against his back. She traced one scar gently, and he shivered in response. Then she pressed her mouth to the spot, trailing kisses along the healed-over wound she'd traced.

He turned and pulled her in roughly, kissing her hard on the mouth, then gentling. He drew his fingers along her neck as if she was fragile and delicate. "Is this what you want, Mina?"

She cupped his scarred cheek, nudged his face down so they were eye to eye. "I will never pretend with you. This is me, doing exactly as I wish."

"Tell me what you wish."

"To love every part of you." Sliding her hand down to explore, she felt the galloping thuds of his heartbeat. It was strong and thrashing for her and this moment. That's the part she truly wished to get to, to burrow in and soothe every torn and tattered piece.

Most of all, she hoped he'd let her.

Chapter Twenty

Love.

The single word jolted through him, every nerve fizzing. His knees felt unsteady. His heart knocked against his ribs.

Nick prided himself on being strong.

He bested men at Gentleman Jackson's boxing club every week. For years, he'd worked to whip the anemic, pigeon-toed boy he'd once been into a man that no one could get the better of in a brawl.

Now this petite, gorgeous stubborn woman had stripped away all his bravado.

Mina didn't make him feel weak. She made him want to surrender. To give her everything and hold nothing back. Even if it meant she'd see the truth of who he was—the ugliness, inside and out. Somehow, she'd unearthed goodness in him, a vein of decency he'd doubted he still possessed.

Hooking one of her fingers around two of his, she led him toward the bed.

Nick followed. He would have followed her anywhere.

When she reached the bedside, she turned before settling on the edge. For a moment, he got lost in looking. At the way a curling strand of hair hung down over one ripe pink nipple, at the gentle dip of her waist and the ample flair of her hips, at the perfect triangle of curls at the center of her thighs.

"Does it still hurt?" He knelt in front of her and stroked a hand down her leg, stopping just above her ankle.

She shook her head, then bit her lip when he nudged her thighs apart. A little tremor rippled across her skin.

"You need only say the word and I'll stop."

"Don't stop." Threading her fingers into his hair, she pulled him nearer. "I want you close."

Nick moved his hand up her thigh, until the tips of his fingers brushed her damp curls. "This close?"

"Yes." She dipped her head to watch as he slid a finger along her sex.

Nick waited, desperate to be inside her heat, worried she'd soon come to her senses and push him away. But she wasn't hesitating. She was impulsive, impatient. She bucked against his finger and gasped when he pressed inside.

He stroked her, watching the play of emotions cross her face. Wonder and pleasure and need that matched his own. When he pushed in deeper, she dropped her head back, closed her eyes, and arched into his touch. Then she looked at him, eyes glazed with desire. "More," she told him huskily. "I want you closer."

Nick scooted nearer, lifting her legs onto his shoulders as he bent his head. He traced his tongue along every inch he'd explored with his fingers.

"Nick," she gasped his name, clutched at his shoulder, nails digging into his skin. "Please."

It was the plea that broke him, that cut loose any thought of taking this slow, of holding back. He laved her deeply, savoring the taste of her, the delicious moans he felt reverberating against his tongue. Then she cried out, fingers digging into his skin, body trembling against his mouth.

Nick licked his lips and got to his feet, never lifting his hands from her body, always staying close, where she'd urged him to be. He placed a knee on the bed and leaned over her. She looked like a well-sated goddess, her body flushed and glistening, hair spilled out around her in shiny waves.

She lifted both arms, reaching for him, and he swallowed hard. The trust in her eyes sent something strangely like joy sliding through his veins.

"Come here," she demanded, her voice husky and low.

Nick settled between Mina's spread thighs, but held himself aloft, hands braced on either side of her. He'd never been with a woman like this before, eyes locked, his body cocooned against hers.

All his couplings were cloaked in darkness, with paramours who kept their backs to him more often than not. Standing, pressed against a wall, bent over a settee. The beast in him wanted Mina in all those ways, but this, the prospect of crushing her under his weight, terrified him.

She stunned him by arching up on one hand and

taking his mouth in an eager, open kiss, nipping at his lower lip, stroking him with her tongue. He groaned against her lips. Then she wrapped both arms around his shoulders and let go, pulling him down with the weight of her body.

"What must I do to make you yield?"

"That was a very good start." Nick let her take a bit more of his weight, pressed his belly to hers, his cock nestling against her sex.

"Yes," she hissed, wriggling against him, as if she knew exactly where she wanted him to be.

When he still held back, the torment of it made his muscles quiver.

Mina smiled up at him, the most seductive grin he'd ever seen in his life. "I'm not afraid."

"There may be pain."

"It can't be worse than waiting."

Nick dipped his head against her neck and chuckled. "My impatient hellion."

She ground her hips against him, his aching length sliding against her sex. Little by little, inch by inch, she drew him in. Nick licked her neck, nipped at her tender skin, then found her mouth. He thrust deeper as he kissed her, losing the fight to hold back and go slow. Every time she gasped or moaned, he stilled for a moment, fearing he'd gone too far. But then she stroked a hand down his back, skimming the ridges of scars, and reached for his arse. Grasping at his muscles, pulling him closer, bucking to get him deeper.

"Don't hold back," she said raggedly, her breath coming in gasps. "I want every part of you."

Nick pushed deeper, giving her all of him. Her eyes widened, then she moved too, leading the rhythm, lifting her legs to get him closer. He took her mouth again and again as he buried himself inside all her heat and warmth, and he knew that she was where he wanted to be.

Always.

"Mina." He called her name because he was lost. No more control. No more holding back. His release built inside him, but he needed her pleasure first. Reaching down between them, he stroked inside her folds, took her nipple into his mouth and suckled until she keened and trembled and melted against him. Only then did he let his climax crash in, a blinding burst of pleasure that left him dizzy and dazed.

Nick realized a moment later that he was still tucked against her, his full weight bearing down. He rolled onto his side, wrapping Mina in his arms to pull her along with him. She draped a leg over his possessively, fitting her belly against his hip.

Nick realized after a moment that his breathing was tight and shallow. He was waiting for it all to burst. For the bliss soaking his soul to fade away. For the odd wholeness he felt to dissipate like morning mist.

This was the moment when he usually departed. Hell, he'd already have been dressed and gone by now. But here, with Mina, he wasn't sure he ever wished to move again. Her arms around him, her fingers sifting his hair, the taste of her still on his tongue—this was more contentment than he'd ever known in one and thirty years.

Far more than he deserved.

NICK WOKE WITH a start, as he always did from his nightmares. But the usual demons weren't fresh in his memory.

Someone was gently rapping at the bedroom door. Normally, he would have shot out of bed or shot whoever dreamed of bothering him at—he squinted at the clock on the fireplace mantel—three in the morning?

He braced an elbow on the mattress to push out of bed and felt Mina. Or rather, the absence of her warmth as soon as he moved away from her. She was curled up, her back to his side, hands tucked under her cheek. He couldn't resist kissing her shoulder, running his fingers through a curling strand of hair lying across his pillow.

He didn't want to leave her. And more than that, he didn't want her to wake and leave him, so he had to stop whoever was on the other side of the door. He pulled on his trousers and padded toward the threshold.

"Spencer?"

He was the only one with enough brass to bother him at such an ungodly hour.

"We have a situation, sir." Trouble, he meant.

Nick slid the bolt and pulled the door open a crack to shield Mina from his factotum's view. "Who is it? Can't you get some of the men to deal with it?" They employed a handful of men to keep the club secure and members safe from themselves and others.

"You have visitors, sir."

"Do you know the hour?"

Spencer bowed his head a moment and said quietly, "The young lady's cousin, Mr. Iverson, and Lord Huntley. They insist on speaking to you. I asked them to wait in your office."

Nick pinched the bridge of his nose and glanced back at Mina, who still slept soundly. He should have expected Fairchild to come after her when he'd failed to return her to Iverson's. What his two business partners had to do with any of this, he hadn't a clue.

Most of all, he didn't want to involve Mina in a scene that would cause her even a flicker of regret for the evening they'd spent together.

"Give me a moment." He closed the door when Spencer nodded and retreated.

Donning his shirt, he approached the bed once more. Just the sight of her made him want her again.

Instead, he left, closing the door quietly, and walked down the hall to face his trio of visitors.

"Gentlemen," he said as he stepped in the room, and only just ducked a punch flying at him from the right.

Fairchild swung and missed and tried to swing again before Iverson restrained him.

"That's enough." Iverson's shout echoed in the low-ceilinged room.

"Not nearly enough, Mr. Iverson. This man has absconded with my cousin with the claim of helping her and now he's . . ." The young man swallowed and glared at Nick. "Ruined her."

Nick sighed heavily and glanced at Iverson, who looked as livid as Fairchild, and then at Huntley, who looked as worried as if Nick had been sentenced to the gallows.

"This is badly done, Lyon." Iverson spoke in that frighteningly calm way he did when he was seething beneath the surface. "Why did you not return Miss Thorne to my home last evening?"

"How's her ankle?" Huntley asked quietly.

"Yes, is it broken?" Fairchild's tone turned more concerned than wrathful.

"Her ankle is fine." Mention of any part of Mina's body brought fresh memories of every part of her body to Nick's mind. He felt his cheeks warm, and saw horror dawn on her cousin's face.

"My God, you have no decency."

"Of course I don't. But I would never harm Mina. I promise you that."

Fairchild let out a little growl and surged forward, fists balled. "But you already have."

"Gentlemen." Huntley came forward, a half smile on his face. "Would you mind if the duke and I have a word alone?" His voice was butter smooth, low and calm. His charming voice. The cajoling one he wielded so well.

Fairchild and Iverson looked at Huntley as if he'd lost his mind.

"Trust me," he said with a sly smile that would inspire anyone with a whit of sense to do nothing of the sort. "Take Mr. Fairchild to the breakfast room, Iverson. The cooks are up early. Surely they can provide some repast or a strong cup of tea. Tea solves all problems, doesn't it?"

"No, it most assuredly does not," Fairchild bellowed. "I want to speak to Mina. I'm taking her home."

Tinder struck the well of anger in Nick, and irritation sparked to life. "Mina decides where she wishes to go and when."

Huntley was done with charm. He put one hand on Iverson's shoulder, the other on Fairchild's, and began shoving the men toward the door. Iverson pushed back. He and Nick and Huntley all fairly matched each other for height and weight, but Fairchild twisted around as if he was prepared to take them all on in a brawl.

"Just go," Huntley snapped. The sound of his usually mellow voice transformed to a fearsome bark stopped everyone in their tracks. "Bollocks, give us ten minutes." He spoke only to Iverson, and finally his words had the desired effect.

"Ten minutes," their business partner warned as he shepherded Mina's still-grousing cousin through the door. "Then we depart with Miss Thorne."

"They're not taking her anywhere," Nick said when he and Huntley were alone.

"What if she wishes to go?"

"You speak as if we're not both returning to the same place." Nick took a deep breath before adding, "I still have matters to attend to at Enderley."

"Indeed, you do." Huntley lowered himself into one of the chairs in the corner of the room, crossed his long legs, and positioned his tented fingers under his chin. "What of this matter, Nick?"

The wave of his hand took in Nick's disheveled state.

"Did you have no thought for the lady's reputation?" Huntley tipped his head. "You're usually so careful with your dalliances."

"This isn't a dalliance."

"No, clearly it's not. So what is it?" Huntley smiled, not his usual smugness, but an expression full of understanding. Perhaps sympathy. "You and I are far too clever to fall into love's snare."

Nick held his breath, working to keep emotion from his face, attempting to perfect that gambler's mien that gave away nothing. Problem was, Mina had torn down all his facades.

Huntley started to grin. Then his mouth fell open and he returned a gaping stare. "My God, you've been struck down. You've fallen."

Nick scrubbed a hand through his hair, scratching at the back of his head. He could not name what this was. Love? Maybe. Though he wasn't sure the word meant to him what it meant to the poets and storytellers. It was nothing he'd ever aspired to. Nothing he'd ever sought. A strange, ephemeral thing he'd rarely felt.

Love.

Could this overwhelming certainty that Mina was his and he could never belong to anyone else be love? It felt titanic. Overwhelming. She was essential. Her smile, her stubbornness, her sweet, impulsive nature—he couldn't live without them anymore. Only this—the fullness he felt with her—mattered. Only going back to bed and keeping her with him mattered.

Love seemed too simple a term. He wasn't certain what he felt for her could fit into the confines of a word he'd never spoken.

"What the hell is love?" he finally asked.

Looking at the horrified expression on Huntley's face, he suspected he'd asked precisely the wrong person.

"How should I know? You tell me. You're in the middle of it." Huntley had leaned forward, elbows on his knees, head hanging as if he felt ill. His skin had gone ashen. "Iverson is determined to find a wife. You've been felled by a fine pair of eyes and a perfect bosom. Will this madness come for me next?"

"First, never mention Mina's breasts again. Second, stop thinking about yourself for a moment, you selfish bastard."

"Yes, of course." Huntley stood, nodded, and inhaled sharply. "I'm here for you, my friend. To help you out of this muddle." He began ticking off items on his fingers. "First, we must find a way to keep Fairchild from murdering you."

"He's just being protective."

"Indeed. The boy's heart is in the right place, but he truly does loathe you at the moment. You'll need to smooth that out. Apologize. Finance his thresher. Whatever it takes."

Nick rolled his hand, urging Huntley to go on. It was almost as if the man was beginning to make a modicum of sense.

"Then we have to begin planning."

"Planning?"

"Because of your title, everyone will expect something lavish, but you can do as you wish. The only requirement is haste. You do know you must marry her?"

If mention of love put Nick in mind of traps, the word *marriage* felt like a noose tightening around his neck. Husband? He'd never imagined himself as such. And he'd known few men who hadn't failed at the task. What if he failed Mina?

He lived in the underbelly of a gambling club, in a room without windows. He was moody and unfriendly to all but three people. And now Mina, though heaven knew he'd behaved like a fool with her more often than not.

"I take it this means you'll reside at Enderley Castle on a more regular basis."

"No. Maybe." His throat went dry. "I don't know."

"What will become of the club?"

"I don't know." Lyon's was a part of him. His creation. His only true success.

"My sister knows more of all this than I do, of course, but I suspect the first question will be whether you want a church wedding or something more private. What do you prefer?"

"I don't bloody know!" Nick hated not knowing. He always knew what his next step would be. It's how he protected himself. How he ensured that no one could catch him off guard.

Huntley bit the corner of his mouth but couldn't keep his lips from twitching up into a grin.

"What's so damn amusing?"

"This is how I know it's true, whatever you feel for this Miss Thorne. You have no strategy." Huntley stepped forward. "You claim you don't have a heart, but I'm fairly certain you've just made a decision with the rusty old organ."

"I want her." Words welled up, like a confession he couldn't hold back any longer. "As I've never wanted anyone—or anything."

"Well, then I'll leave you to it." Huntley gave Nick's shoulder an encouraging pat.

Yes, leave. If everyone would just leave, he could go back to Mina and the indescribable joy of being with her and locking out the world.

"Now go. Your next step is the most daunting of all," Huntley said before he headed toward the door.

"Is it?" Nick frowned. His next step was going to be returning to bed with Mina and making love to her again before the sun came up, if he had anything to say about it.

"You need to go and ask Miss Thorne to marry you."

Nick's frown deepened to a glower.

"Good luck," Huntley said from the threshold, adding a wink. "Ladies are changeable. One never knows what they'll say."

Chapter Twenty-One

Colin, please calm down." Mina emerged from the dressing room she'd found through a low, concealed doorway hidden behind part of the red velvet drapery in Nick's bedchamber.

Her cousin had woken her with a series of knocks loud enough to bring the entire club to attention. She was only grateful that he'd brought the traveling gown she'd worn to London. Taking a few minutes to wash and change into the skirt and bodice had given her an excuse to escape her cousin's tirade.

"How can you be so serene? Your reputation—"

"You keep saying that word as if I'm some debutante. No one in Barrowmere will care how I spent my evening."

He blushed so fiercely, she thought he might catch fire.

"Certainly no one in London cares what I do."

"What of the duke? Will London not care that the Duke of Tremayne kidnapped an innocent from a Mayfair dinner party?"

"That's not at all what happened and you know it." If not for Colin's already riled state, Mina would have laughed. "What's gotten into you? Do you secretly read scandal rags when I'm not looking?"

"No, but if I did, I've no doubt you and Tremayne would get a mention in this morning's edition." He stalked past the fireplace and then dropped onto one of the gold damask settees, lowering his head to his hands. "I should have protected you."

"I'm not a child, Colin. I'm older than you are, for heaven's sake. A spinster, most would say."

"Let's just go home." He glanced at her, and she'd never seen him more forlorn. "The next train leaves in less than an hour."

"I'm not going anywhere until I speak to him." In the last few hours, she'd slept in Nick's arms and been closer to him than to anyone she'd ever known. Even if they'd never have more than those hours, she wouldn't leave without saying goodbye.

She'd hated waking alone in the enormous bed, the sheets still warm where Nick had slept. According to Colin, he'd brought Mr. Iverson and Lord Huntley to confront Nick, and she wondered if he'd hated leaving her as much as she disliked waking without him.

"The man is a scoundrel, Mina." Her cousin stood and faced her, his gaze bleak and beseeching. "Please don't set your heart on him."

"It's too late for that," she admitted quietly. *Far too late*.

"I don't want to see you hurt, as you were before."

"That was infatuation."

"And this? What's different about Tremayne?"

"Everything." She couldn't catalog her feelings or sift them. They were too fresh, and Colin wasn't in any mood to understand.

"Well, then we must hope Mr. Iverson and Lord Huntley can convince him."

Mina ignored her cousin's bluster and busied herself collecting the gown she'd borrowed from Mr. Iverson. She laid the red velvet dress on a side table, smoothed out the wrinkles, then bent to collect Nick's dove-gray waistcoat. A flash of color caught her eye, and she kneeled to examine a long pink ribbon that had fallen from the pocket.

Her ribbon.

A burst of warmth filled her chest. He'd kept her ribbon, tucked it away, right against his chest. That's where she would have happily remained all day if Colin hadn't arrived.

She smiled, picked up the strip of satin, and tucked it back into Nick's waistcoat. As if she'd emerged from a daze, Colin's words finally registered.

"Convince the duke of what?" A twisting queasiness filled her stomach when Colin looked at her as if she'd gone daft.

"To marry you, of course."

Mina shook her head and hugged Nick's waistcoat to her chest. The scent of him gave her a modicum of comfort, but not enough to diminish the horror of Nick's two friends attempting to force him into marriage.

"He must make his own choice, Colin." After what he'd endured as a child, the man deserved to make all of his decisions freely.

Not that the prospect of spending every future day with him, in his arms, in his bed, wasn't what her heart ached for, but how would it work? He was a duke. She wasn't prepared to be a duchess.

Nick might loathe his ducal responsibilities, but he had to know that marrying a blueblooded lady and providing an heir to the Tremayne dukedom was one of them. Perhaps the most important of all.

She'd known last night that the decision to be with him would be irrevocable, and she wouldn't take back a single moment, even if she could.

"He must do what's right by you, Mina." Colin came forward and placed a hand on her arm.

"I need to speak to him."

"Yes." Nick spoke the single word from the threshold. "We need to talk. Alone."

Mina had no notion how long Nick had been standing in the doorway. She only knew that the sound of his voice sent shivers across her skin. Her body responded to him differently now, as if some part of her was more alive when he was near.

"Would you excuse us, Mr. Fairchild? Downstairs, you'll find a ticket purchased for your return to Sussex. There's a hansom waiting out front to deliver you to the station." The entire time Nick spoke to Colin, he kept his gaze fixed on Mina.

She didn't miss how his eyes kept flickering down to her mouth. Each spot where his gaze lit, she felt a gentle pressure, like the brush of his lips against her skin.

"I am not leaving this room without Mina." Colin stepped too close to Nick, a brawl-sparking distance.

But Nick didn't spare him a glance. He kept his gaze on Mina.

"You are, Colin. Please go home," she urged. "I promise to come back by nightfall." She lifted an eyebrow at Nick in question.

He nodded. "Mina and I will return this afternoon."

"Then it's settled?" Colin sounded breathless and utterly relieved. "Lord Huntley convinced you?"

Before Nick could answer, Mina approached her cousin.

"Colin, come and call at Enderley tomorrow. We'll speak then." She kissed him on the cheek and stepped away. She was done with his attempt to *save* her from her own resolve.

Finally, Colin relented. When he'd gone, Nick closed the door and waited.

She could read nothing in his expression but desire, and it set off sparks inside her. Suddenly, she wished she hadn't donned so many clothes.

The moment she started toward him, he began to speak.

"We have much to discuss."

Mina kept on until her chest was pressed against his. He tipped his head down to hold her gaze.

"I'd prefer that you kiss me." She followed the edge of his mouth with her finger. His lips were full and flushed and bee-stung from the countless kisses they'd exchanged in the dark.

Taking her finger between his lips, he suckled her fingertip before releasing it. Then he cupped her face in his hands and lowered his mouth to hers. She thought the kiss might be perfunctory, but the moment their lips met, she knew they could never be that way with each other again.

She loved that the taste of him was familiar now, that she knew how to kiss him to make a moan emerge from deep in the back of his throat.

When they were breathless, he turned with her, bracing her against the door, the hard length of him nudging the spot where she wanted him most.

"You don't have to do it," she said between kisses.

He bit gently at her neck. "At this point, I'm not sure if I can stop." He laved the skin he'd bitten with his tongue and began dragging her skirt up.

"I meant marriage."

His breathing was ragged, and he didn't stop touching her, at least. But he tensed, his shoulder muscles hard as stone under her fingers.

"I know that Lord Huntley spoke to you."

He lifted his head, but he wouldn't look at her. He fixed his gaze on the panel of door next to her head. "You'd say no if I asked?"

"No. Yes. I don't know. You haven't asked."

NICK'S INSIDES WENT from raging need to icy misery in a heartbeat.

All the way back to his chamber, he'd rehearsed ways to broach the topic. Ways to ask Mina to be his wife. He'd done battle with himself. She deserved a far better man than him. But he was enough of a selfish bastard that he could never imagine letting her go.

He didn't live a life suited to matrimony. His days and nights were consumed by Lyon's, and he'd never shared a bed with anyone in his life, aside from the extraordinary peace he'd found beside Mina for a few hours on this too short night.

She was a creature of the countryside, of racing across meadows on horseback and managing an estate where she cared more about others' needs than her own.

She'd be a bird in a cage at Lyon's. He could provide her luxurious surroundings, but not the open air and endless stretch of land she'd been born to. Everything that mattered to her was at Enderley, and the very thought of the place brought back memories he still wanted to forget.

"Nick?"

He hated the worried frown on her face, the pinch between her brows, the uncertain way she pursed her mouth. She deserved to have happiness and the home that she desired.

That, he could do. He might not be a good man, but he was a duke. Duke of the only place in England she loved.

An idea took hold in his mind. A means of securing her happiness while giving him more than he could ever deserve.

He took her hands in his, stroked his thumbs over her knuckles, noted the ink smudges on her fingers, the indentation from where she held her pen.

"Marry me, Mina." His voice quaked, and he was fairly certain the ground was cracking beneath his feet, judging by how steady his legs felt.

"You're asking me." She was blinking, not truly looking at him, or anything. Just blinking as if he'd shocked her. "You're truly saying the words."

"Shall I try again?"

She nibbled her lower lip and lines of hesitation pinched her brow. "You've been forced into this, haven't you?"

"No one forces me into anything." He notched his chin up.

She retreated, slipping her hands from his body and stepping away. Nick reached for her. "Where are you going?"

"I can't think."

"Then don't think. Just say yes."

"I'm confused, Nick. This feels wrong."

He let go of her hand and she took another step away. That's when he knew. He couldn't let her go. Even a few inches between them felt too far.

"I'll give you everything you want." Nick had heard of men dying because their hearts seized while they were engaged in the most mundane tasks. Proposing wasn't mundane for him, but judging by the wrenching pain behind his ribs, he was no longer certain he'd live to hear her answer.

"Do you know what I truly want?" There was such hopefulness in her honeyed brown eyes.

"Yes." This part was easy. Of Mina's desires, he had no doubts. "Marry me and Enderley is yours. Live there. Improve it. Refurbish the estate from head to toe. Whatever funds you need, you'll have them."

She reared back, a look of wonder softening her features. But then the frown came back, more fiercely than before.

"You can hire more staff. Select the best artists to paint fresh murals in the ballroom. Fill the stables, if you like. Order a new carriage." That part he would insist on himself.

Her mouth slackened. Her hands hung motionless at her sides.

Nick didn't know what else to offer. Fine clothes? Jewels? Baubles didn't seem Mina's style.

"Redecorate the library. Purchase whatever books you please. Add new shelves full of them, if you like."

Nick stopped talking because he wanted with all of his soul to hear her speak. Three letters. One little word. A single breath. He'd never wanted to hear *yes* more in his life.

She bowed her head.

Nick's body buzzed with nervous anticipation. He had no doubt she was composing some polite reply, but he dreaded that it would not be the answer he needed to hear.

When she looked up, her eyes were glistening. "And you?"

"Me?"

"Where will you be while I'm at Enderley?"

"Here at Lyon's." He swallowed hard before adding the rest. "I'll visit you when I'm able, and if you'd be willing, I'd like you here." *Always.* "As often as you wish to come to London."

She licked her lips. He could see her pondering, almost hear the clockwork gears of her sharp mind sifting the matter.

"We could purchase a townhouse," he added, the thought that should have been obvious to him coming clearer. A duchess did not live in the bowels of a gentlemen's club. "In Mayfair or Belgravia. You choose."

"So . . ." she started, but didn't finish the thought.

The tenterhooks Nick hung on began to tear at his insides. "So?"

"This is to be a very *practical* arrangement?"

"Absolutely." Nick knew how she loved practical solutions. He would give her the most sensible marriage in the history of wedlock if it would win her.

"You need an heir."

"I don't care about that." He swiped a hand through the air, pushing that obstacle away. She had to know that he didn't want her as a broodmare. The Tremayne lineage could burn in hell as far as he was concerned. Unless . . . "Do you want children?"

"Up until a few hours ago, I believed I'd die a spinster." She gave him a sad little smile that nearly broke him in two. With a longing gaze at the bed, she added, "But we must think rationally. As your duchess, producing a son would be my duty."

His cock twitched to life. Suddenly he wanted nothing so much as to devote himself earnestly to producing an heir. He imagined ways of starting immediately—taking her on the bed, near the bed, against the bedpost.

She approached until they were toe to toe.

"If I'm in Sussex . . ." Her palm came down on his midsection, and Nick let out a tiny gasp of relief to have her touching him again. "And you're here in London." She trailed her fingers down his row of shirt buttons, her nails clicking on each one. "Then that becomes a tricky proposition." With one searching slide of her hand, she found how ready he was for her. She shaped his hardened length boldly, gaze fixed on his.

"Mina." He breathed her name and that was all he could manage before he bent and claimed her lips. Cradling her neck, he pulled her closer, kissed her hungrily. She stroked him until he feared he'd spill. "I need your answer."

She released him, then pressed her palm low on his belly. "I don't know what answer I should give."

Nick kissed her cheek. "Yes." Then the corner of her mouth. "Tell me yes."

She shook her head, moving her lips away from his.

He caught her chin, held her gaze, prayed she could see that he'd laid himself bare before her.

"Please," he said softly. "What more can I give you?"

"You've offered me so much." Her hand came up, caressing his scarred cheek. "More than anyone would say I deserve." She inhaled sharply, as if trying to catch her breath. "But a part of me will always be that girl who loves fairy tales."

"Fill the library with them." Yes, he knew that was part of her and thanked the gods for her childhood love of fanciful stories. Perhaps it was why she might be willing to bind herself to a monster.

"Love." She waited, breathing in short, shallow breaths. "That's the only thing you didn't offer me. I'm afraid I don't wish to marry without it. If we wed, will there be love?"

The pain that clutched at his chest a moment before became a Herculean fist around his heart, smashing the organ to a pulp. Nick's throat wouldn't work. His mind emptied. All he could see was Mina and sense the future he wanted with her slipping through his fingers.

The word was easy enough to speak, but this wasn't a bluff. He refused to put any cards on the table that he didn't truly mean to play. Everything he had, he'd gladly give her, but he knew she was asking for something more. A fairy-tale prince with a noble heart and romantic words flowing easily from his tongue.

He could never be that man.

Love made men weak and turned some into raving madmen. Love brought men to their knees.

He was prepared to give Mina anything she wanted, but all of him? To be utterly defenseless and keep none of the walls he'd built around himself—to protect himself—intact?

That he wouldn't do for anyone.

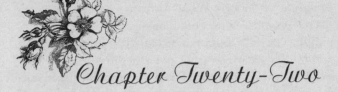

Chapter Twenty-Two

*M*ina hadn't imagined anything could hurt as badly as the loss of her father. But this was worse, because Nick wasn't gone. He was standing right in front of her, and yet he was so far away.

He couldn't tell her that he loved her. In fact, he said nothing at all and only gave a tight twist of his head.

Tears threatened and she turned, desperate to compose herself. Blubbering wouldn't help. *Never let your struggles be known.* Her father's voice rang in her ears.

Then Nick's voice, soft and deep. "I'll give you everything I have, Mina. Please answer."

She sniffed and faced him. "I am honored by your—"

"No. Don't do that. No niceties between us. Tell me to go to hell, but spare me your politely couched rejection."

"It's not a rejection."

"Then you'll marry me?" His head snapped up.

An answer welled up inside her, like a living thing demanding to get out. *Yes, yes.* Marry a duke? Become a duchess when she had no claim to the title through breeding or blood? What woman wouldn't embrace such a proposal with both hands?

But as perfect as the hours had been in Nick's arms, something about this felt terribly wrong. As if he'd offered her a beautiful gilded box with nothing inside. A shell of what she truly wanted, with nothing at its heart. He proposed a marriage of separation. Living as wedded strangers, growing apart rather than getting to know each other better.

She couldn't bear that sort of marriage. Not with Nick.

Her father's voice intruded. *Better one bird in hand than ten in the woods.*

He'd liked aphorisms. Sayings he drilled into her head. All in an attempt to teach qualities he wished her to possess. There were so many lessons he'd hoped she might learn. One had to do with taking what was before you rather than wishing for more.

Now Nick stood in front of her, looking gorgeous in his rumpled, untucked shirt, with stubble shadowing his jaw, hope glowing in his extraordinary eyes. A duke of the realm who deigned to make an estate steward's daughter his duchess. A man who was offering her Enderley, not as a place of duty, but as a home that was the only belonging she'd ever known.

And foolishly, selfishly, she wanted more.

"I don't—"

A knock sounded at the door.

Nick stomped over and nearly ripped the thick slab of wood from its hinges. "What?"

"Your carriage is ready, sir." Mr. Spencer kept his voice low. "Shall I send up a breakfast tray before you depart?"

"No." Mina fought to keep her voice steady. "Thank you, but I'd like to leave as soon as possible."

Nick's jaw worked back and forth. "We'll be up directly." He stared at the floor, speaking to both of them but unwilling to look either of them in the eyes.

When the club manager had gone, Nick slammed the door behind him. He kept his hand flat on the polished wood, his back to her.

"Don't answer now," he said roughly. "This is all very sudden."

He tipped her a glance over his shoulder. A smile curved his mouth but didn't touch his eyes.

"Neither of us planned what happened last evening. I want you to be sure, Mina. Take a couple of days to consider and give me your answer once we're back at Enderley."

"I didn't think you'd go back." The time he'd vowed to spend there was almost over, and Mina knew it was the last place he wished to be. "Why are you returning?"

"Because you are." His lips trembled when he faced her again. There was a wobble in his chin that betrayed the coolness in his gaze. "Also, I've left commitments unfinished. Repair projects in the village and that bloody country dance I promised Mrs. Shepard I'd attend."

"And will you attend Lady Claxton's ball too?"

"I won't go unless you do." An inky brow winged up, and his grin slid into a smirk. He seemed to enjoy issuing the challenge, but he didn't understand Barrowmere society as well as she did.

"I received no invitation to Lady Claxton's ball. Nor would I ever. There's no place for me in her circle."

"There could be." The look of challenge remained a moment longer, and then he approached. "I need to wash and prepare for our trip."

The faded aroma of his cologne and unique scent of his skin made her mouth water. All Mina truly wished to do was reach for him. Feel his arms around her. Forget about words and return to the closeness they'd shared, intimacies she'd never imagined.

"Ring for coffee or tea or whatever you like." He bent and brushed a soft kiss against her cheek. "I'll be quick."

He collected his waistcoat and boots before heading to the dressing room, and Mina rang for tea for both of them.

A short time later a servant brought a tray and departed, almost the same moment Nick emerged clean-shaven from the dressing room. Mina took her first sip of tea and tried not to gape. He'd donned a waistcoat the shade of peacock feathers. The color brought out the green and blue in his eyes.

"I poured you some tea."

"Thank you." His hand was shaking when he palmed the cup, lifted the dainty thing to his lips, and tipped the contents back in one gulp. "Shall we head off?"

There was a buzzing energy about him. Nervousness that heightened her own anxiousness. She didn't know why she was in such a rush to return to the countryside. There'd be no private moments with him once they were back. At Enderley, their roles were defined. But she wasn't quite sure where she belonged anymore.

Going back to just being his steward was unthinkable.

He'd slipped on gloves and extended a hand encased in black leather. "Ready?"

Mina took his hand as she got to her feet. "My ankle doesn't trouble me anymore."

"I'm glad." The merest of smiles flickered across his lips. "We'll depart through the side door," he told her as they made their way down the sconce-lit hall. "Just this way."

"You won't show me the club before we depart?"

She'd been so eager to leave, and now a part of her dreaded going back. What they'd shared here was theirs alone, untouched by any of the memories he had of the estate, or any of the responsibilities she'd long felt to it and its people.

"Just a quick peek around the club?" That single glimpse the night before hadn't been enough. He cared about Lyon's. She wanted to see what he'd built, the enterprise he was so proud of.

"I'll give you more than a peek." Crooking an elbow, he offered his arm as if they were going on a morning promenade. After climbing the stairs they'd descended the night before, he led her toward the velvet draperies, but this time he didn't stop.

"Where are we going?" Mina tightened her grip on his arm. Chatter ebbed, necks craned, dozens of men's faces turned their way.

Mina heard hisses and whispers.

"Has he brought his whore to play?"

Nick made a guttural noise and lunged toward the man who'd made the comment. Mina wrapped both hands around his forearm to pull him closer.

He wielded his gaze like a weapon, freezing men mid-gape. Something in his eyes cut off men as they opened their mouths to comment.

After escorting her into the thick of the gamut, Nick stopped in the center of a dozen green felt-covered gaming tables. He directed her gaze up, pointing to the ceiling. "That may be my favorite part of the club."

A stained-glass dome had been constructed atop the room, its panes constructed in bold, dramatic colors, like the rose window of a cathedral.

"In a few hours, when the club has emptied but for the staff, the sun reflects those colors onto the walls and floor."

Mina realized he was no longer looking up and that his gaze was fixed on her face.

"There are no gray walls at Lyon's."

A month ago she would have defended Enderley from the veiled slight. Now she understood why a boy from a castle that offered him nothing but nightmares would build himself a colorful world far away from Sussex.

"It's beautiful." Some might call the excess of it garish, but Mina could see that every aspect of the club had been designed with care. Not that the gamblers around her seemed to notice. Those who weren't still gawking at the two of them were staring intently as dice rolled or cards were shuffled in front of them. Their desperation was palpable, a wave of tension that seemed to touch every man in the room. Even those laughing or chatting did so at a higher, almost frantic pitch.

Only Nick oozed confidence. Until he looked her way. Then a flash of uncertainty came into his gaze.

"Would you like to tour the upstairs?"

Mina looked up to the balustrade and receded walkway running around the perimeter of Lyon's. "Your private balcony? Yes, please." She understood that he wanted to show her the best aspects of the club, just as she'd hoped to highlight Enderley's assets.

He led her to the stairwell tucked away at the edge of the club and lent her his arm as they made their way up. Once she stepped onto the plush carpet of the concealed balcony, she understood why it was a haven. It wasn't quiet, the noises rose and echoed off the building's glass dome, but the furnishings were comfortable, the chairs plusher, the settee deeper.

And when she stood at the balustrade's edge, staring down at the desperate men below, she understood Nick a bit better. "You have enormous power over them."

"For many years, I had none." He came to stand next to her, so close that his arm and thigh brushed against hers.

"When you returned to London on your own?"

"Yes," he said tightly.

He seemed to sense she wanted more and after a while he swallowed hard and began. "I had nothing. The clothes on my back, a few coins in my pocket." He tugged at his ear and sighed. "I took food off vendor's carts. I fought others for money. I did what I had to in order to survive."

"And how did you get all this?" She stared down at the gilded columns and green baize-covered tables.

He tipped a grin her way. "Gambling. I'd never had any luck as a child, but I made up for it as a young man."

"Do you still gamble?" Mina held her breath. She had meant gaming, but she sensed the depth of her question too. From the moment he'd arrived at Enderley, she'd hoped he would bet on the estate. Invest and refurbish. Now she wanted him to take another risk. With her.

"Never," he said firmly, his gaze steady and determined as he watched the men below. "Gambling gives too much of a man's power to fate. Waiting on the luck of the draw or the fall of the dice." He glanced over at her and said in a low, husky voice, "I'll never be powerless again."

Mina said nothing more as he led her back down and they made their way out.

Mr. Spencer beckoned them toward a set of polished bronze doors. "Your carriage is ready, sir."

Nick's hand at the small of her back soothed Mina's nerves as she headed toward the club's entrance. London's fog had cleared and the morning was so bright, she lifted a hand to shade her eyes.

"Tremayne," a man shouted, not the same from the club. A young man, well into his cups, and tipping precariously toward them. "I have part of what I owe you."

Nick urged Mina forward until they'd reached the carriage, then wrapped his hands around her waist to help her inside.

"Not now."

"You're returning to Sussex? To play duke? I wish to settle my debts, Lyon." The man scuttled forward, tapping on the side of the carriage. "Call on me when you return to London."

Nick positioned himself near the window and leaned out. "Let go of the door or the coachman will pull you under when we depart. Speak to my solicitor about settling your debt."

With that, Nick knocked on the carriage wall and the driver set the horses into motion. The young man stumbled back, and Mina lost sight of him as they pulled into a line of carriages departing various enterprises on St. James Street.

"He gambles at your club?"

"Not anymore." He straightened his perfectly straight necktie, rather than look at her.

"The gentleman seemed quite desperate."

"He's an awful gambler." There was no menace in his tone, nor did he seem to take much pleasure in the fact. Which seemed odd for a gambling club owner who kept the money others lost.

"He behaved as if you hold his fate in your hands?"

"I hold his vowels. Dozens of them." He wrenched his gloves off with a few swift tugs.

"Do you never forgive debts?"

"Why would I?" His gaze was sharp, defensive, then softened the longer he looked at her.

"Why not invest more of your money, as Mr. Iverson does?" Mina could appreciate the idea of a profitable business, but to watch men lose their wealth, their self-respect, their livelihoods. She couldn't see the appeal.

"I do invest. Thanks to Iverson's counsel, I usually do so wisely." He drew in a long breath and let it out. "But I also earn money by lending to gamblers who've lost their funds and want to play on."

"And they continue to lose?"

"Usually."

"And then what?" Mina leaned forward, intrigued by how the process worked.

"Either they quit, which is rare, or they come downstairs and petition for a loan." Nick's jaw tightened and furrowed grooves appeared between his brows. "I require collateral, and often they lose what they promised. Noblemen become desperate when they lose."

Mina sensed his unease. "It sounds miserable for everyone involved."

"I used to enjoy it." He quieted a moment.

"And now?"

"Something in me has altered."

"For the better?" Mina's throat tightened as she waited for his answer. She'd changed too. For the first time, she could imagine a life that had nothing to do with Enderley and duty. But now she also knew she couldn't bear a future without love.

"For the better," he repeated.

Mina smiled and settled back against the squabs as he watched her. An idea came, a wild, half-formed notion, that she couldn't keep inside. "What if no one had to lose?"

In the soft glow of the carriage lamp, Mina saw the flash of his grin.

"A happy ending for all? Like in a fairy tale?"

"A much more practical ending." Mina thought of Colin and the collection of guests at Mr. Iverson's party. "What if the men, or women, for that matter, who came to petition you for funds had something to offer in return? An invention. An idea that could turn a profit?"

"My God, Iverson's gotten to you, hasn't he?" Nick leaned forward, a frown hardening the edge of his jaw. "Exactly how much time did you two spend together?"

"Not much." Mina laughed. "But you've seen fit to assist the tenants in Barrowmere village. Why not the entrepreneurs of London?"

"I don't know. I'll consider it."

Mina could sense his eagerness to be done with the topic. He turned toward the carriage window and watched intently, but there was little to see beyond an endless line of whitewashed townhouses.

The one topic that weighed on her mind was the one she didn't know how to broach with him. They fell silent, so quiet she could hear his breath coming ragged and uneven. She counted the beats of her own heart, slamming heavily in her chest.

His profile was familiar now, but no less breathtaking. She had the urge to run a line with her fingertip from his brow to the tip of his nose to those delicious lips.

He seemed to sense her watching him and shifted on his bench. Turning away from the window, he subjected her to a slow perusal, from her boots to her waist, breasts, lips—all the places he'd kissed so attentively—and then back down her legs again.

"You're sure your ankle is better?"

Mina nodded and bit her lip. She couldn't bear two hours of being cool and polite to each other. "Nick—"

"This isn't right, you know?"

"Tell me why you think so." He felt it too. She didn't know if that made it better or worse.

"You're too far away." He reached out a bare hand. "Last time we were in a carriage together, you were closer."

Her body responded as if she was already there, in his lap.

Mina took his hand, and he pulled her up and across the space between them. Rather than sit across his lap, Mina ruched up her skirt and positioned her knees on either side of his thighs, so that they were face-to-face, chest to chest.

Sentiments bubbled up. Words she wanted to say, but she had no notion where to start. So she held him instead. Resting her head against his chest, she curled her fingers around the edge of his waistcoat and listened to the strong, insistent beat of his heart.

This felt right. This she knew for certain. When he was in her arms, she had no more doubts. Fears faded. Some part of her knew.

This was where she was meant to be.

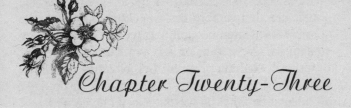

Chapter Twenty-Three

$\mathcal{H}$e was a coward. A spineless fool of a man with more carnal frustration pent up than he'd ever felt in his life.

They'd been back at Enderley for two days, and Nick had tried his best to give Mina time to consider his offer. He'd kept himself busy with village matters and visits from the vicar and magistrate and every other resident of Barrowmere who wished to grouse about his father and brother.

He agreed with every complaint, but none of it improved his mood.

He survived on glimpses of Mina, who was matching him in the pursuit of mindless tasks and busy making. She'd met with masons, painters, men who would remove more of the furniture and antiquities in the coming weeks. Now he wasn't even certain he wished to gut the estate and rent it. He couldn't ask Mina to live in an empty castle.

All he truly wanted was her answer.

Every hour that passed, the terror grew. Was she biding her time before refusing him? The more he asked himself the question, the greater an answering compulsion grew to keep her, win her, convince her. But he still couldn't bring himself to expose the inner workings of his rusty heart as she wished. He couldn't promise to be what he wasn't. Worse, he didn't know if he had the wherewithal to be the sort of man she would find an ounce of happiness with.

He wasn't Huntley, with natural charm and a face like Adonis. He wasn't Iverson, whose instinct unerringly led him to do what was right and good.

He could offer Mina a title, wealth, his devotion. He didn't have more to give.

Each night since they'd returned, he'd started toward her room in the dead of night. Body aching, heart thudding, he'd make it as far as her door, determined to kiss her until she forgot her name and love her so well that she screamed *yes* again and again.

But each night he'd stopped himself on the verge of knocking. As much as he wanted her, he needed this choice to be hers. He couldn't bear a lifetime of doubt. Of thinking he'd seduced her into an answer or pressed for one too soon.

One result of his visits to the village had been a barrage of haranguing to attend Lady Claxton's ball. He'd only agreed when Wilder informed him that half of Enderley's servants would be in service at the event, and that Mina had agreed to help manage them.

He would have far preferred that she was attending as his soon-to-be bride.

But he'd dressed and shaved, and when he descended

the stairs to make his way to the ball, he discovered most of the staff had already gone to the Claxtons'.

Except for Mina.

The light in her office was on, and he heard a crash and curse before he reached the doorway.

She was bent over, her back to him, retrieving a pile of account ledger books from the floor. Nick approached to help her, and she skidded back as if she'd been scalded.

"I thought you would have been on your way to Lady Claxton's," she said, taking in his evening clothes.

"Aren't you attending?" Nick noted that she'd dressed in a prettier gown than her usual dresses. This one had a far more revealing cut that showed off her neck and shoulders.

"I agreed to help Wilder manage the other servants who were sent to assist the Claxton staff."

"But you're still here."

"Mrs. Scribb decided to go, so I won't be needed."

"I need you." The words came out before he could stop them. They were as raw as any truth he'd ever spoken.

He didn't truly want to attend a ball. But he very much wanted an excuse to have Mina in his arms again.

She swallowed hard, but her eyes softened. He liked discovering that whatever she felt for him, masking it was impossible. "I'll be in the kitchen or directing footmen in the refreshment room. It's not as if we'll be together."

"I can manage to find the kitchen."

"You can't go belowstairs at Lord and Lady Claxtons' home. You're the Duke of Tremayne."

"We'll see." Nick offered her his arm. Whatever it took, he was damn well going to dance with her tonight.

He knew the moment she decided to accompany him. Not because she took his arm, but because her shoulders lifted an inch and her back went doorjamb-straight.

"Fine," she said curtly. "If we're to go, we should depart now or we'll be late."

Nick nodded and let her stride past him. He was proud of his self-control when everything in him told him to reach for her.

But as she stomped toward the front door, he couldn't hold back a grin of triumph.

Now the evening had a hope of being bearable.

THIS WAS A mistake.

The minute they'd settled onto opposite benches in the Tremayne carriage, Mina regretted agreeing to accompany Nick to the Claxton ball.

Not that she was truly accompanying him. They weren't attending together. They were simply headed to the same event, at the same time, in the same carriage. Once there, their roles would be entirely different.

He'd be expected to mingle and dance with Lady Lillian and every other young unmarried woman pushed his way. Her job would be to make sure the staff from the two estates didn't step on each other's toes or come to fisticuffs.

But now, in the dark confines of the brougham, all she could smell was his woodsy scent. Every time she glanced his way, she found his gaze was already focused on her. Intently. In the dim carriage lantern, his eyes glowed as they traced the shape of her mouth.

Every nerve in her vibrated when they were this close to each other. She could never be in a carriage with him again and not think of being in his arms or in his lap.

Thankfully the trip to the Claxtons' was short. She willed her nerves to steady and her mind to stop thinking of the scandalous things he could do with his hands as he helped her down from the carriage.

The Claxton footman looked supremely confused as they approached the front door. Especially when Nick moved closer every time she tried to sidestep away. She lengthened her stride to reach the footman first.

"I'm here to assist Mr. Wilder and the other staff from Enderley Castle."

"They are *below*stairs, miss." The Claxton servant arched one thin eyebrow. "Down the hall, first door on your left."

When he glanced past her and got a good view of Nick, both brows shot up. It was a reaction others often had at the first sight of him. Mina still wasn't sure if it was his scar, his unusual eyes, his enormous bulk, or a combination of all his unique physical qualities combined in one singular man.

"That's the Duke of Tremayne," she whispered to the footman as she strode past, forcing herself not to look back as she left Nick.

"I will find you," Nick called after her.

She kept going, despite the ribbon of heat that unfurled inside her.

Downstairs, she found the kitchen in a state of minor

chaos. Two young men were arguing in the corner, an older woman sat fanning herself with a small dinner plate, and Mrs. Scribb looked on the verge of tears. Or outrage. Mina couldn't tell which.

Wilder spotted her and immediately approached. "Miss Thorne. Thought you'd decided to stay back this evening."

"Another pair of hands never goes to waste. What can I do?"

He leaned in to speak quietly. "Mrs. Scribb and the Claxton housekeeper are about to come to blows, and the two footmen have turned against each other to win Emma's affections."

Mina noticed that Emma stood on the other side of the two young men, hands on her hips as she chastised them both in her soft voice.

"Might be worthwhile to take Emma upstairs and see that all is as it should be in the refreshment room." Wilder cast a weary look back at the two young men. "I'll wade into the fray and settle the two young pups down."

Mina found Emma more than happy to leave her newest suitors to their own devices. The girl was far more interested in how Mina had arrived.

"Did you come with the duke?"

"We traveled in the carriage together."

"Alone?" she asked with a knowing pitch in her voice. "As you did from London?"

Mina bit her tongue and willed her cheeks not to burn.

"I only say you should have a care, Miss Thorne. Some are beginning to whisper."

Anger flared like the ember of a hot coal sparking to life. "I spoke to a mason and several delivery men last week. Wilder and I drove alone in the pony cart together. Is anyone whispering about that?"

To catch her breath and get hold of her emotions, Mina fussed with arranging the trays of finger sandwiches and little squares of carved aspic. Dozens of cut crystal glasses were set precariously close to the front edge of the table.

"We should move those farther back," she told Emma. "One swipe from a ball gown and they'll come crashing down."

As she worked, she soon realized Emma wasn't offering any assistance. When she turned back, the girl was watching her with wide eyes.

"You're smitten with him, aren't you?"

The music of stringed instruments filled the air. The dancing would have begun. How many young ladies would be vying to catch Nick's eye? However some might shrink back at the sight of his scar or striking eyes, the man was tall, broad, and sinfully wealthy. Lady Claxton certainly had her sights set on a match with her granddaughter.

"Are you, Mina?" Emma prompted.

"Come with me." Mina led the girl toward the Claxtons' long main hall. She followed the sound of music and stopped a few steps beyond the ballroom threshold.

"There, you see?" Mina indicated Lady Lillian, who was dancing her way around the ballroom in Nick's arms. "She's an earl's granddaughter. I'm a steward's daughter."

At that moment, the couples turned in the quadrille and Mina shrank back from the threshold, determined Nick not see her peeking at the doorway like Cinderella wishing she could join the ball.

"We should refill the punch bowl." Mina pointed to a table set along the back wall of the ballroom. "The guests will be thirsty now that the dancing has begun."

"The Claxton footmen will see to it." Emma stepped toward the ballroom doorway. "Don't you wish you could take just one turn around the floor with a handsome man?"

"Yes." Mina glimpsed Nick and Lady Lillian when the dance brought them toward the corner of the ballroom, and her stomach twisted in knots. She didn't care about taking a turn around the dance floor, but she wanted to be the one in Nick's arms.

He looked miserable. Lines knitted between his browns, he glanced down at his feet more often than at his partner. Lady Lillian seemed determined to get as close to him as possible, pressing her bodice toward his chest every time the dance required them to join hands.

"We should get back downstairs and see what we can do to help." Mina forced her attention away from Nick and noticed Gregory Lyle at the edge of the ballroom. He was watching her intently and immediately started toward them.

"Oh goodness. Do you see who's coming this way?" Emma was the only person to whom Mina had ever confided her foolish feelings for Gregory.

"We should return to the kitchen."

They started back toward the door that led to the downstairs level, but the hard clip of footsteps sounded on the marble floor behind them.

"Miss Thorne, may I have a word?"

"Don't do it," Emma urged.

"Go ahead, Emma." Mina stopped. "I won't be but a moment."

The young woman cast her a doubtful look over her shoulder and a very uncharitable glare in Gregory's direction, but she continued on toward the kitchen.

When Mina turned to face him, he positioned himself near a potted palm. Eager to speak to her, but not eager to be seen, apparently.

"Might we step into the library?"

"No, we can't have much to say to one another. Just speak your piece and then I must get downstairs."

"I think of you quite often." He cast a nervous glance down the hall.

Mina let out a weary sigh and took one step away from him. If he meant to try to charm her after all that had passed between them . . .

"Wait." His hand snaked out, gripping her wrist.

"Let me go." Mina twisted in his grasp.

"They say you've become his lover. But we both know you should be mine." His breath reeked of drink. Not of punch or champagne, but as if he'd been imbibing long before he arrived at the Claxton ball.

She used her other hand to pry his fingers off her wrist. A nail caught his skin and he yelped and released her, but he immediately leaned closer. The fumes of alcohol made her eyes water.

"I always did admire your fiery spirit, Mina."

"Lyle," Nick's voice boomed from the end of the hall. "What does it take to get rid of you once and for all?"

Gregory sneered at Mina before turning to face Nick. "Perhaps you should pay my father another thousand pounds. We have plenty of other horses for you to buy for your whore." He strode toward Nick, weaving unsteadily toward a side table. "Must burn to know I had her first, eh, Tremayne?"

Mina saw guests emerge from the ballroom, gathering in a curious cluster at the threshold. Her stomach pitched up into her throat and nausea swept over her. She shouldn't have come. She shouldn't have let her heart command her instead of using a smidgen of sense.

Nick stood still and motionless, but Mina knew his eyes. She could feel the heat of his fury from three feet away. But he was trying not to lash out. His jaw was a sharp-edged square. She suspected he was gritting his teeth.

"What in heaven's name is going on?" Lady Claxton emerged from the ballroom, tapping her cane on the marble with one hand, lifting a lorgnette to her eyes with the other.

"Go back to the ballroom, Gregory," Mina whispered. "Forget about me."

She'd forgive him all the past ugliness between them if he'd just refrain from creating any more.

But when he turned back toward Nick, he let out a menacing chuckle and took two steps to plant himself in front of the duke. "How does it feel, Tremayne?"

"Let's not do this, Lyle." Nick retreated, removing himself from Gregory's reach. "Don't you want to find a partner for the next set?"

Nick sounded extraordinarily calm, his voice deep and commanding. Mina suspected she was the only one among the dozen or so guests assembled in the hall who could hear the tremor underneath the deep baritone.

He was exhibiting so much control, she had the ferocious urge to kiss him. Privately, of course. Where all that control would come crumbling down. But only for her.

When Gregory said nothing more, a few of the guests started back into the ballroom. Mina found herself breathing a bit easier.

Then Gregory lunged for Nick, an inelegant jut of limbs, so unsteady that Nick reached out a hand and planted it on Gregory's chest to keep their bodies from crashing together.

"How does it feel?" Gregory repeated. "To want a woman as faithless as your own mother?"

Nick moved so quickly, the men's black-clad bodies blurred. In an instant, he had Gregory pinned to the wall, his forearm locked under the man's chin.

"Gentlemen, I forbid violence in my home." Lady Claxton stumped forward and lifted her cane to tap insistently at Nick's shoulder. "I've hosted twenty balls and never had a brawl, Tremayne. I shan't tolerate one tonight."

Gregory squawked out some word. Nick loosened his grip enough to allow him to repeat it.

"Bastard," he rasped, clutching at his neck.

Nick stepped away abruptly and Gregory crumpled to the floor, clawing at his necktie, wheezing in huge gulps of air.

"Good evening, Lady Claxton. You won't mind if I depart early." Nick straightened his cuffs and shoved a hand through the strands of hair that had fallen over his brow.

He shot Mina a glance over his shoulder and her breath quickened. His eyes glowed and ink-black hair tumbled in disheveled waves around his face. His flushed skin highlighted his scar. In his eyes, she saw a fearsome brew of emotions.

He was angry, but with himself or her?

She held her breath, expecting a demand that she depart with him.

Instead, he turned his back on her and strode down the hall. Gentlemen stepped aside. Ladies covered their mouths when he turned a glance their way. One young housemaid squealed when he nearly knocked her over on his way to the front door.

"Everyone back to the ballroom." Lady Claxton hooked her cane around her wrist and clapped loudly, as if every lady and gentleman in attendance was just another servant for her to order as she pleased.

For the most part, everyone did as she bid them.

Except that Mina couldn't seem to make her legs carry her back downstairs, and Gregory still sat slumped against the wall, his unwound cravat balled in his hands.

"You may depart as soon as you decide to get to your feet, Lyle."

When he opened his mouth to protest, Lady Claxton snapped, "Be gone, young man, and be glad I don't inform your father of your tomfoolery here tonight."

Finally, she turned her attention toward Mina.

"You were not invited, Miss Thorne, but you may join the other Enderley staff downstairs, if your assistance is required."

Mina looked at the older woman, but all she could see was Nick's eyes filled with anger and pain. She needed to speak to him.

"Actually, Lady Claxton, I'll be departing too." She bobbed a curtsy, lifted the edge of her skirt to take one long step over Gregory's outstretched legs, and rushed for the front door.

The chilly air stung her cheeks and her eyes watered. Somewhere inside the Claxtons' kitchen, she'd laid aside a wrap she'd worn. It didn't matter. Finding Nick did.

She started down the steps, scanning the line of carriages. Some had been moved toward the Claxton stables, but the Tremayne carriage still stood at the ready, awaiting Nick's departure. Where would he have gone?

Boots crunching on gravel, she rushed down the carriage drive, wondering whether he'd decided to walk the several miles back to Enderley. He was entirely stubborn enough to make such a reckless decision.

Bracing her hands on her hips, she drew in a few drams of cool air and glanced back toward the brightly lit windows of Claxton Hall. She spotted him crossing a terrace along the side of the house, striding quickly toward the open field.

Mina lifted the front of her skirt a few inches and sprinted toward him, slowing to a quick hobble when her ankle began to twinge. "Slow down," she called.

He stopped and swung to face her, but said nothing. They'd reached a patch of grass beyond the house's glowing windows. His face was all shadows and sharp angles in the moonlight.

"Will you speak to me? Or do you wish to continue avoiding me?" Her corset was unbearably tight and she struggled to catch her breath.

"I thought you were avoiding me."

"Not avoiding you." It felt so good to hear his voice, the softer, warmer one he used just with her, that she almost smiled. "I was taking time to think, as you asked me to."

"And what have you decided?" He started toward her, a slow but purposeful prowl that made her pulse thrum.

"You want an answer now? Here? In the cold outside of Lady Claxton's home?"

"Take this." He immediately flicked back the edges of his coat and slipped it from his shoulders. Coming close enough for the buttons of his shirt to brush her bodice, he settled the garment around her. His heat and scent surrounded her. "Warmer?"

"Yes." Unbearably so, and not just where his coat covered her. When he was this close, she couldn't think of the future and practicalities, only that she wanted him closer, to feel his skin against hers, to sink against him and forget everything else.

But as soon as he'd wrapped the coat around her shoulders, he retreated. He pushed his hands behind his back. She felt his gaze on her and the weight of expectation.

He wanted her answer.

She wished desperately that she could simply say yes and trust that the rest would fall into place. But the incident with Gregory only served to heighten the impossible chasm between them. Mina knew what Lady Claxton and her guests thought of her. Perhaps a step above a domestic servant, but nothing more. She couldn't imagine them ever accepting her as a guest at their soirees. Or addressing her as the Duchess of Tremayne.

"I saw you dancing," she told Nick impulsively. "You're wrong. You're a fine dancer."

"I would have tried harder if you'd been in my arms."

He spoke of impossibilities. For that single moment with Lady Lillian, he'd been a part of Barrowmere society. Fitting in seamlessly, doing exactly what everyone expected a duke to do.

And then Gregory, her mistake, intruded to create a scandal Lady Claxton's guests would chew over for weeks.

"Mina, I need an answer."

"Can't you see that I cause you nothing but trouble?" Taking a step so that she could get a view inside a long ballroom window, she watched as ladies in fine gowns and gentlemen in crisp white gloves and black tails danced around the floor in a waltz. If not for her, Nick would still be inside.

"Do you wish you were in there dancing with the rest of them?" he asked.

In two strides, he was in front of her, crowding her back against the cold stones of Claxton Hall. He braced a gloved hand on the wall beside her head.

"Marry me and I'll take you to every bloody ball in London. We'll host our own. One a week, if you like. People will grow sick of the Duchess of Tremayne's balls."

He was close, his mouth inches from hers. His broad, warm body sheltered her from the cold.

"And you think they'll accept me? A spinster? A commoner?"

"Dukes can do what they like. My father proved that."

When she said nothing more, he hooked a hand behind her neck and tipped her head. "I don't care what these people think of me. I don't care about dancing and debutantes. I care about you."

His mouth came down hard, his lips demanding. Mina clutched at his arm, wrapped a hand around his back, reveled in the solid strength of him, in the taste of him and the eagerness of his kisses.

All the rest faded away, and this—his heat, the comfort of him, the need between them—became all that mattered.

"Consider this a new proposal." He kissed her again, softly. "Come to London with me. Leave the past behind in Sussex." Another kiss, longer, lingering. "We'll make a life that has nothing to do with Enderley or Barrowmere or Lady Claxton and her ilk."

Yes. She wanted to make a life with him, and a part of her yearned for a new start. But old habits ran deep. Her thoughts wended their way back to Enderley, as if she hadn't just inherited her father's brown hair and eyes, but his worries too.

"What about Wilder and Emma and Mrs. Scribb? What about the repairs?" She heard herself sounding like his steward, and she wanted to take it all back.

Especially when his body stilled, his breath stuck in his throat, and he took a step away from her.

"I've offered you everything, Mina." His voice was quiet, pleading. Then he squared his shoulders, hardened his jaw. "I'm leaving for London tomorrow. I want you to come with me."

Mina held on to the edge of his coat and watched him let out a frustrated sigh.

"I know you care for the estate, and you've taught me to at least care about those who live on it. But must it come first?" He cupped her cheek. "Tomorrow, I need your answer."

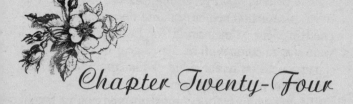

Chapter Twenty-Four

Nick woke with a start and sat up in bed as if he'd heard some crashing noise or been doused with ice water. The fire in the grate had gone out in the night, and the temperature in the room was bone-chilling, despite the sunlight streaming through the curtains.

His insides felt cold.

Mina was gone. He sensed her absence like the quiet after music plays or the darkness of being locked in that bloody tower.

Much of the night, he'd kept vigil, sitting up in a straight-back chair in the corner of his bedchamber. Willing her to come to him. He wasn't a praying man, but he'd become so desperate, he'd fooled himself into believing that he heard her footsteps in the hall. That the wind beating the window panes was a faint knock on his door.

But she hadn't come. From the moment he'd asked her to marry him, some part of him had known the answer.

Who could love him? He was a broken man, the proof of it on his face, even for those who never got a glimpse of his twisted soul.

He stood, ignoring the stiff protest of his muscles, and made his way across the room to yank the bell pull. Moments later the housemaid, Emma, knocked softly at his door before coming through with a tray.

"Where is she?"

The girl gasped. He rarely spoke to her when she came to his room.

He gripped the knot at the back of his neck and tried again in a less demanding tone. "Where is Miss Thorne?"

"Couldn't say, Your Grace." The girl's voice was so soft, Nick strained to hear her. "She departed early. Didn't say when she'd return."

She would come back to Enderley, of course, but would she come with him to London? He had a sickening sense that she wouldn't.

"Will there be anything else, Your Grace?" The girl had backed herself against the door, holding the empty tray like a safeguard in front of her.

"Send a footman up. I want my clothing packed and a carriage prepared. I intend to depart for London today."

The girl's eyes ballooned. "Very good, Your Grace."

Nick couldn't tell whether she was shocked by the news or planned to head straight downstairs and begin a celebration with the other staff. At any rate, she scurried off, leaving him to dress quickly and in peace.

Downstairs, he headed for his father's study. Mina's closed office door felt as wrong as the quiet in the hallway the two rooms shared. She made little noises while she worked, *hmm*'s and *aah*'s and *oh*'s, and he'd learned them all by heart.

What the hell was he going to do when he was back at Lyon's with only himself for company?

After collecting a few notes he'd made at his father's desk, he found himself back at Mina's office door. Standing outside the empty room like a fool, he wished for nothing so much as to twist the knob and find her inside.

But when he pushed the door open, he found nothing but her clean, floral scent to haunt him.

The notebook she often carried with her lay on the edge of the desk. Some of the notes pertained to the repairs he'd agreed to make to tenant houses, the estate, and structures in Barrowmere village. Nick hesitated a moment before lifting the small leather-bound journal, flipping it open to the spot where she'd placed a ribbon as marker.

He let out a sharp breath of disappointment. In front of him was a simple, practical list in a neat but utterly feminine hand. He flipped a page back and found notes from his visit with the villagers, all the promises he'd made in an effort to be benevolent. An effort to let Mina see that he could be better than he seemed.

Turning another page, he found calculations, hurriedly scratched. Numbers tumbling across the paper. Then one more flip and his breath snagged in his throat.

He emerged on the page in dashes of ink. Not the slash on his face or his strange eyes, but his mouth, generously shaped. His jaw, a sharp square below the curve of his chin. His brow, with a sinuous strand of black hair tumbling down.

She drew him in precisely the same way she looked at him. As none other ever had. Not with horror or even perverse curiosity. From the first moment their gazes clashed, Mina saw him and never looked away. As if she wasn't put off by what she saw.

Strange woman.

"Pardon me, sir." Wilder's voice came from the threshold behind him. "I understand you intend to depart Enderley today."

"It's time, Wilder." Nick turned to face the old man. "I've had as much of this place as I can stomach."

"And Miss Thorne?" A mischievous glint came into the butler's gaze. "What will she have to say of your absence?"

Nick laid her notebook aside reluctantly, pondered how much to tell the old man, and scrubbed a hand across the stubble he hadn't bothered shaving from his chin. "I asked her to marry me, Wilder."

"Did you?" The shock on the butler's face was nearly as surprising as the high pitch of his usually deep voice.

Mina hadn't told any of the other Enderley staff, apparently. Nick wasn't sure whether to be grateful or disappointed.

"May I . . ." Wilder cleared his throat and looked at Nick pointedly. "May I be so impertinent as to ask what answer she gave?"

"None." It seemed obvious to Nick. He wouldn't be so damn eager to leave if he knew she would marry him. Or maybe he would. He far preferred the notion of having her all to himself in London. But if she was to be his, even Enderley would be sufferable in the interim until their vows could be made. Or even after, for visits now and then.

That thought hit him like a thunderbolt. Not the notion of returning to Enderley, but the fact that imagining such a thing didn't cause dread to twist his insides.

"No answer at all, sir? Then I see why you wish to depart." The disappointment in Wilder's voice was somehow comforting, though a pale shadow to what Nick felt.

Nick slumped onto the front edge of her desk. "I wished to give her time to consider my offer. She is impulsive by nature."

"Very."

"Which is why three days with no answer from her seems like an answer in itself, does it not?" Nick wanted Wilder to tell him to wait a bit longer.

"An impatient man and an impulsive woman. A match made in heaven or a sure path to doom?" The old butler seemed to be musing to himself, almost mumbling.

"Please don't pick this moment to humor me, Wilder. It's time I stop fooling myself and go back to London. Don't you agree?"

The butler assessed him and drew in a sharp breath. "I have never been a man to give up hope, sir."

"That must be exhausting." Nick quirked a brow, but Wilder seemed in earnest. He wore the stoic expression that Nick would always associate with the man. "Not even with my father?"

A slight shadow of a grin touched the old man's mouth. "Not even with him. I hoped until Talbot Lyon drew his last breath."

"It didn't do you any good."

"I beg to differ, sir. Your father did not bend from his hatred, but I do not regret the hope I held fast to. It anchored me. It always has. Hope does a soul good."

Nick stood and glanced around Mina's office one last time, trailed his finger along the edge of her notebook. "At least until you wake up to harsh reality and all hope is crushed."

"You care for the young lady a great deal?"

"I do."

"And you've told her as much?"

"I've offered her everything I have, Wilder. All that's left is playing on her sympathies or manipulating her into wedlock. I'd prefer not to get a bride that way." Hell, before he arrived at Enderley, he didn't want a wife at all.

"Of course not, Your Grace."

"I need some air." Nick started out of the room. Mina's scent was too tantalizing and her absence was unbearable.

"If I may, sir. The one truth I know about Miss Thorne is that she is forgiving, but her kind heart leads her to put others' cares above her own. She is rather unerringly pointed toward what's good for those around her, while often forgetting what's best for herself."

"Would I be good for her, Wilder?" Nick asked the question with a sarcastic bite, his mouth twisted in a smirk. But inside, he wanted Wilder to dispel his doubts.

"I believe you would care for her, sir. She's never had that. Even with her father. He was a good man, but the estate always came first."

The bloody estate.

Its walls seemed to be closing in on him. Nick patted Wilder on the shoulder and strode from the room. His stride lengthened the closer he got to the front door. He needed to breathe. Needed to be free of this damned castle where his father had nearly killed him. The place that might just come between him and the only woman he'd ever wanted as his bride.

He headed toward the rear of the house and found himself aiming for the stables.

Tobias lifted his head from his work when Nick approached.

"Is her horse still here? Hades."

"She didn't ride this morning, Your Grace." Tobias pointed toward one of the stalls. "She took the pony cart when she left. The stallion is still inside."

Nick's hands were shaking, much like he was quaking inside. He stalked away from the stable master and approached the horse's stable. The creature leaned his enormous head out and Nick patted his warm ebony snout.

"She'll come back for you, and I suspect you'd follow her anywhere." He glanced at the stallion's haunch, where a faint line could still be detected on his coat. "Put you back together, did she? You and I have that in common."

This place had brought them together, and now Nick sensed it tearing them apart.

He glanced over his shoulder, casting his gaze past the house to the outlines of that hideous jagged tower pointing into the sky.

That hellish pile of stones had nearly done him in. Now it felt like the black heart of all he stood to lose. If he was to consider residing at the estate, the tower had to go. Maybe then he could see Enderley differently. As Mina saw it.

Everything in him wanted to tear the tower down and never allow its outline to blight the estate again.

Scanning the stables, he searched for a maul or a pickax or anything that might help him chip away at its stones. He saw nothing but rakes and brooms. And high on a shelf, tucked safely out of the way, a tinderbox.

He snatched the box and marched toward the tower. The place pushed back at him, its evil repelling him the closer he got. Nausea clawed at his insides. A trickle of fear chased up his spine. But he was a grown man now. Not a fool child, too trusting to know that his father wished him dead.

He kept on until he reached the bottom step. The entire tower was naught but a shell, its interior structure built entirely of wood. A fitting metaphor for his father.

A shell with rotting, useless bits inside.

He started up the stairs, not caring that they groaned and threatened to give way. The smell gagged him. A familiar mustiness, mixed now with the scent of moss and rot.

He bit down hard when he reached his prison cell. Bent low to take a single step into the room.

It was too much. He couldn't go any farther. He stepped back, retreating down the stairs. At the bottom, he braced a hand against the stones and fought the gorge rising in his throat. Fumbling with the tinder-box, he struck flint against steel, causing a flame to burst to life.

Nick threw the whole of the lit tinderbox into the tower.

MINA GOT DOWN on her knees and leaned forward to brush dust and a few fallen leaves from her father's headstone. She traced the letters of his name with her fingers.

Rotherhead, where her father's people hailed from, wasn't far from Barrowmere. It was farther south, closer to the sea. The air had a saltiness to it and a stiffer breeze. The church's graveyard was quiet and peaceful, just the sort of place her father deserved to rest after years of hard work and devotion.

She was glad he was buried away from Enderley. The place had consumed him in life. He needed a bit of distance from its problems in death.

"I'm sorry I haven't come more often in the last few weeks, Papa. There's a new duke." Her throat thickened and tears welled in her eyes. "I love him, and I believe he cares for me."

Though she was alone in the graveyard, she lowered her voice to a whisper. "He's asked me to marry him." Mina imagined her father before her, listening. What would he say when she confessed the rest? "If I say yes, that means I'm leaving Enderley behind."

Did her father know what the old duke had done? She couldn't bear to think he'd taken any part in such devilry, even if he only had an inkling of how the old duke had treated his son.

"You gave so many years to the estate. I tried to do as you would have wished, but I'm not sure I belong there anymore." Mina gathered the little bundle of late autumn flowers and placed them atop her father's grave. "I think I belong wherever Nick is." The truth had been there, waiting for her to find it. The rightness of it made her giddy. "He's more like me than you can imagine, Papa, but different too, in the best of ways. Not perfect. Neither of us are, but we suit each other."

Mina stood and dusted off her trousers.

"I won't return as often. We'll live mostly in London, I think." She felt compelled to add, "But we are repairing Enderley. Someone will live there and care for it, even if it's not us."

Leaning forward, she placed a hand on the cold stone slab etched with her father's name and the words *Loving father. Loyal servant.* "Goodbye, Papa."

Each step away from the church got a bit easier. She jumped up into the pony cart and let the horse take the trip back at a leisurely pace. Then anticipation got the best of her and she urged him into a canter. Within quarter of an hour, she spied Enderley's parapet on the horizon.

She squinted when something else drew her gaze. Billowing gray. Not a cloud but puffs of smoke.

Tapping the whip against the side of the cart, she pushed the horse to go faster, until her bones rattled so hard her teeth clicked together. Moments later, she careened into Enderley's stable yard and scrambled down from the cart.

"Tobias!"

The stable master strode out of the granary, a welcoming grin on his face. "There you are, Miss Thorne. The duke was looking for you."

"Don't you see the smoke?" She pointed toward the western edge of the estate as she rushed past the stable.

Tobias's heavy footsteps followed in her wake.

Mina clutched at her chest when she rounded the stables. "It's the tower. Not the house." The structure was far enough away, it was no threat to the house or anyone inside.

"Get help, Miss Thorne. I'll fetch some buckets of water." Tobias started off, but Mina called him back.

"No, don't bother." She stared at the black smoke billowing from that vile structure and felt an odd sense of peace. "Let it burn."

"But what about the cat?"

Mina frowned at him. "She's in the stable. Emma said she brought Milly and the kittens into one of the stalls."

He shrugged and his face crumpled into a panicked grimace. "I've seen her creeping around the tower. She goes back. Maybe she thinks she's left a kitten behind."

"Have you seen her this morning?" Mina sprinted past him toward the stable. "We have to find her, Tobias," she shouted back at him.

Mina skidded down the line of stalls in the stable, peeking inside, trying to spot a clump of white-and-orange fur. She knelt near the straw-filled, blanket-padded box where the kittens were sleeping. Without their mother.

One of the stable boys called down from the loft. "No sign of her up here."

Smoke wafted on the breeze, and Mina ran out of the stable. She passed Emma and Tobias in the yard. "Keep looking for her. I'm going to the tower."

Emma wrapped a hand around her arm. "You can't, Mina. It's too dangerous."

"Check the kitchen. Check anywhere she might hide." Mina twisted out of the girl's grip and dashed toward the tower.

Chapter Twenty-Five

*N*ick stared up at the branch of the old oak and couldn't quite comprehend it had been less than a month since he'd gazed up into Mina's gold brown eyes and been completely lost. Or maybe he'd always been lost and that was the moment he'd been found.

Meeting her had changed everything.

He could take a knife and separate his life between the hours before that meeting and those after. Whether anyone could see it by looking at his mangled face or not, something in him had changed. A great deal, in fact.

For one thing, his feelings about Enderley had changed. The place would forever hold some of his worst memories, but now there were good ones too. Like every moment he'd spent inside its walls with Mina.

He saw now that he could do his duty and not allow the past to destroy any future good he might do for the estate and its people. Mina had done her best to show him why it mattered to do what was right, to be benevolent, and little by little he was beginning to understand.

Since meeting Mina, his heart troubled him every single day. Throbbing and aching and pounding like a gambler's tell every time she was near. He'd deadened the organ so well over the years, he'd rarely noticed its working in over a decade. Now he sensed its pangs and yearnings constantly.

Ever since that damnable day under this tree, with Mina dangling from a branch above his head and her cat glaring down at him.

He turned back toward the estate, settled his arse on the cold ground, and watched as smoke billowed from the tower. Shoving his hands in his pockets for warmth, his fingers tangled with satin. He pulled out Mina's ribbon and stroked his thumb up and down the pink strip of fabric.

Was this truly all he'd have of her when he went back to London? A strip of ribbon and memories that would haunt him the rest of his days?

Burning the tower didn't bring the peace it should have. Oh, the smoke curling up into the sky gave him a measure of satisfaction, but nothing would ever feel right again without Mina.

He watched the burning tower until his eyesight blurred, then swept his gaze across Enderley's rear facade. The window panes glittered in the sunlight, the stones gilded in the early morning glow.

Then he saw a figure rush past the ground-floor windows, slip in the grass, and continue on toward the burning tower.

He made out brown trousers, black boots, and long waves of chestnut hair.

Mina.

Nick scrambled to his feet and flew down the rise, breaking into a run when he hit flat ground. He shouted her name, but she didn't seem to hear. She kept on toward the tower.

He stretched into a longer gait until he was so close he swiped for her arm. "Mina, stop."

She slowed just enough for him to catch up. He stopped behind her and wrapped an arm around her waist. Her hands came up to dislodge him.

"Let me go."

"Stubborn woman." Nick came around to face her, planting himself between her and the tower. "Are you mad?"

"The cat might be in there." She immediately tried to barrel past him, and he caught her again.

"What bloody cat?" But he knew as soon as he asked. The orange ball of fury. They'd come as a pair that first day. "Mina, I promise you she's not in the tower. I went inside. There was nothing, just old rotting furniture."

"But we can't find her." She kept pushing at him, attempting to twist out of his grasp. "Tobias says she goes in sometimes."

Tobias was striding across the grass toward them.

"Did you find her?" Mina called back to him.

Nick glared at the young man, willing him to tell her they'd found the cat merrily slurping milk in the pantry. Anything to stop her from storming into a burning tower.

"No sign of her, miss." Tobias didn't get the intended message.

Mina lunged, nearly breaking free. Nick bent at the waist, swept a hand behind her knees and lifted her in his arms. He walked toward Tobias.

"Take her. Hold on to her. If she makes it anywhere near that tower, you're sacked. Understand?" Nick settled Mina into Tobias's arms gently. "I'll get the bloody cat."

"Nick, no." She stopped struggling and went quiet, eyes wide.

He turned his back on her and strode toward the smoldering structure. Most of the smoke was billowing skyward, but some poured out of a gap in the lower stones. The closer he got, the more he could feel the fire's heat. At the base of the stairs, he lifted his arm to cover his nose and peered inside.

The lower stairs were singed, but still in place. It seemed the fire had rushed upward quickly and focused on consuming the single room where he'd been imprisoned.

If the cat was inside, there was no chance of saving her. The wind shifted, pushing smoke into his eyes. He took one step closer.

"Millicent?" Cats were notorious escape artists, but he couldn't imagine where a feline might hide in this blaze. "Milly?"

An orange flash caught his eye and he leaned in to get a closer look. Only a flame, dancing along the edge of a sizzling wooden beam. Then the beam shifted, split, sparks and fiery fragments raining down. He stepped back, but burning rafters came down too quickly, and a searing pain lit his face on fire. A hot weight struck his shoulder hard, pushing him back against the heated stones. He swiped at his face and staggered back.

"Nick!" Mina's scream filled his ears.

But he couldn't see. Smoke and soot blurred his vision. Arms came around him from behind as he fell. Massive hands locked under his arms and his boot heels bounced on the ground as he was dragged into the grass.

Part of his shirt was wrenched off. He heard fabric tearing. Then a wet cloth came down on his eyes.

Mina's hand slid into his. He recognized the shape of her fingers, the softness of her skin.

Nick reached up to pull the rag away. He could see, but through bleary clouded vision, and his eyes burned. "Mina? The cat wasn't up there."

"I know," she told him through tears. "They found her. She'd snuck into the kitchen. I'm so sorry. Does it hurt?"

Every breath burned. A searing pain raged in his cheek. His arm ached, especially near his shoulder. But most of all he felt relief. He reached for Mina, traced his fingers across her cheek and left a sooty trail.

"I love you." He wasn't sure if he said the words aloud. His throat burned as if he'd swallowed an ember.

Mina leaned forward, swept her fingers through his hair, lowered her mouth to his. "I knew you did," she whispered against his lips.

"We should get him inside," Tobias insisted. "I've sent Emma to fetch the doctor." When the stable master bent as if he meant to scoop Nick off the ground, he pushed at the man's massive shoulder.

"I can walk on my own." He wasn't sure that was true, but he was damn well going to try.

"You're not going anywhere without me." Mina lifted his arm and ducked underneath, wrapping her arm around his waist.

"Promise?"

She nodded as they started toward the house. "You do know how stubborn I am."

Thankfully, they didn't bother with attempting to get him up the stairs. The staff had prepared one of the sitting room settees as a makeshift bed, with sheets and a pillow laid out.

Mina helped him hobble to the edge and he slumped down, trying to ignore the pain, struggling to get air without every breath feeling as if shards of glass were lodged in his chest.

When Mina loosened her hold on his hand, he pulled her back.

"I'm just going for some water and cloths to clean you up." Her gaze kept flickering to his cheek. The one that burned like hell. The one his father hadn't sliced with a penknife.

"Now I'll be a monster on both sides of my face."

She bit her lip. He could tell she was fighting tears. "You'll never be a monster to me." One last squeeze of his hand and she let him go.

When she was gone, Nick laid his head back and closed his eyes. It seemed only a moment, but when he opened them again, the sky was dimmer but for the glow of a fiery orange sunset through the windows.

His face felt tight and constricted, and he reached up to find he'd been bandaged. Not just his cheek, but his arm too. How the hell had he slept through all of it?

"You're awake." A white-haired gentleman stood up from a chair across the room and approached. "I took the liberty of giving you a bit of laudanum for the pain, Your Grace." The man was strangely familiar.

"Where's Mina? Miss Thorne."

"Just there." The doctor pointed to a settee in the corner of the room. "She's been quite insistent about keeping watch over you."

She was half sitting, half leaning on her folded arms, her chin tipped down as she napped. Then, as if sensing his gaze, her eyes fluttered open, and she offered him a beaming smile. "How are you feeling?"

"Better." He was ready to take on the devil himself if he could get her to smile at him that way again.

"Then I shall be off," the doctor said as he turned to collect a leather bag from a table near the settee. "I've left instructions with the staff for treating your wounds."

Nick touched the edge of the bandage on his face. "What's under here, Doctor?"

The old man held two fingers up, one an inch or so from the other. "A burn, about that length. A cinder must have struck you and remained on your skin long enough to leave its mark." The man's eyes assessed Nick's face, tracing the line of his father's blade. "There will be a scar, but it will fade in time."

"Thank you, Dr. Burke." Mina stood and escorted the gentleman to the sitting room threshold. When he was gone, she came back and settled her backside on the edge of the settee near Nick's thigh.

He wrapped a hand around her waist, savoring her nearness. Sliding a hand up her arm, he pulled her closer, leaning in to take her mouth. He wasn't gentle. He couldn't do this with any kind of gentlemanly restraint. Her hair hung down her back, unbound but for a few strands pulled into pins. He sought those pins and worked them free. Dragging his fingers through her hair, he flicked his tongue against her lips, and she opened to him on a delicious moan.

He was hard and ready to have her climb into his lap, let him sink inside her heat.

But someone cleared their throat on the sitting room threshold, and Mina sprang away from him.

"Will you be wishing for a supper tray, Your Grace?" Emma called in her soft voice.

"No," Nick answered immediately. The only thing he wanted to taste was Mina.

"Yes," she protested. "You should eat something."

He arched a brow, failed to hide his smile, and she seemed to take his meaning. Her cheeks bloomed with heat.

"Some soup, perhaps? Thank you, Emma."

The young woman backed out of the room and had the good sense to pull the door shut behind her. But when Nick leaned in to kiss Mina again, she held him back.

"Wilder tells me you planned to depart for London today." She wrapped her fingers around a button on his shirt, not meeting his gaze. "Will you mind staying at Enderley a bit longer? A few weeks?"

"With you?" Nick's throat rasped, but it wasn't the smoke he'd inhaled. It was fear.

"Yes," she said simply. Too simply.

"Yes?"

"That's the answer I should have given you three days ago." She scooted closer, cupping his scarred cheek against her palm. "I'm sorry I made you wait. I'm sorry I made you go in that tower. I'm sorry for ever making you think I cared more about Enderley than you."

"We can stay here if you want." Nick grabbed her hand and kissed her fingers. "My hatred of this house was irrational. My father is dead, and you're right. This estate is the people who live here, the ones who love it."

"But, you see, I'm prepared to go to London." She let out a low seductive chuckle when he pulled her fingertip into his mouth. "If you're in the city, that's where I want to be. If you're here, that's where I'll stay." Her eyebrows dipped, her chin hardened, and her voice went mock stern. "I insist we never live apart."

"Already making demands, Duchess?" Nick leaned in and pressed his forehead to hers. "I agree. Anything you want, tell me."

"Just you." Mina kissed his scarred cheek, the edge of his mouth near his bandaged cheek, and then his lips. A soft, delicious kiss that was over far too quickly. "The house, the club, all of that will fall into place, don't you think?"

"Yes." She made him want a life he wouldn't have imagined a month earlier. Made him believe happiness, contentment, peace was in their grasp. "But honestly, right now I can't think of anything but locking that door, removing every stitch of your clothing, and making love to you on this settee."

"Your wounds."

"Nothing hurts when you're this close to me."

Her hand was balanced on his thigh as she leaned into him. Nick shifted her palm over an inch.

"I promise you, Duchess, I feel quite up to the task."

Chapter Twenty-Six

$\mathcal{M}$ina woke with sunlight warming her face, and Nick's long, hard body warming her everywhere else. She moaned and pressed closer, her back to his chest, his arm wrapped protectively around her.

Then realization crashed in.

She was in an Enderley guest chamber. In Nick's bed. Emma would be up soon to light the fire and bring a breakfast tray.

Nick was still asleep. The gentle rumble of his breath warmed the back of her neck. She lifted his arm and slid as slowly as she could out from beneath his hold.

"Where are you going?"

"The sun's come up. Emma will be here soon."

Nick touched her, dragging his fingers across her skin. Just firmly enough to make heat shimmer down her back and pool between her thighs. "You're still worrying too much about what others think."

"It's more a matter of what they'll feel. Emma will be scandalized if she finds us like this."

"Well, we wouldn't want that." He removed his hand and shifted on the bed.

Mina looked back to find he'd sat up, letting the sheet fall low on his stomach, his hands folded behind his head. Even with the bandages on his arm and face, he looked like a very self-satisfied demigod. Black hair tumbled in tossed curls and tangled waves, almost to his shoulders. The sun lit up his eyes and gilded the chiseled muscles of his chest and arms.

"At least kiss me before you go," he said, reaching out one hand to cover hers.

He was the moon and she was the waves. His magnetic pull was irresistible, but she forced herself to resist offering more than the briefest brush of her mouth against his. "If I kiss you again, I won't want to go."

He leaned in and captured her lips again. "That is rather the idea."

Mina got out of bed, scooped her clothes from the floor, and felt Nick's gaze watching her every move as she dressed.

He surprised her by rising from bed too and bending for a fresh pair of trousers from the trunk he'd brought from London.

Mina gulped at the sight of him. He was sculpted on a different scale from other men, not just his height, but the thickness of his arms, his thighs, his everything.

"You sure you want to go?" He shot her a mischievous grin over his shoulder as he pulled on a shirt.

"Sometimes *want* and *must* are worlds apart."

"Indeed." He came close and refastened the top three buttons on her blouse that she'd misaligned in her haste. "There's some business I must attend to as well before we head back to London."

Mina reached for the buttons of his open shirt, making sure to fasten them correctly. "Please tell me you're not going to confront the Lyles again."

"God, no. Though I can see the sense in mending relations with some of the families in the village."

"Can you?" Mina was quite prepared to leave Enderley and only come back rarely. Late into the night, she and Nick had talked of the future they wanted. He'd agreed that any Enderley staff who wished to could be employed in their future London household, or stay behind and maintain the property for when they were in residence. Nick no longer spoke of emptying or renting the estate out.

"I know this house means a great deal to you."

It had. Always. But it was just a house. Nick was her heart. She could live without Enderley, but she couldn't live without him.

"If we refurbish, rebuild parts, knock down a few walls." He gazed around the guest chamber as if he could see through the wallpaper to the bones of the castle. "Maybe we can chase the ghosts away and make something of our own."

"We needn't decide today." Mina slid her hand up to his face, traced the hard stubbled edge of his jaw. "After all, we have a wedding to plan."

"Lavish."

"Modest."

"I'm thinking Westminster Abbey."

Mina choked on a bubble of laughter. "I'm thinking the village church at Barrowmere with Vicar Pribble officiating." She lifted onto her toes, leaned into him, and kissed his chin. "You did say I could have anything I want."

He sighed dramatically. "As you wish, Duchess."

NICK WAITED A beat after the servant answered the door. The housemaid was waiting for him to offer a calling card, but he had none. He endured her shocked expression a moment longer, musing that it was probably for his bandaged face rather than his scar and odd-colored eyes.

"The Duke of Tremayne." It was the first time he'd announced himself formally in such a manner, and it still felt unspeakably odd. Not as miserable as the day four months ago when his father's friend had come to Lyon's to inform him of his bad luck. But uncomfortable. Ill fitting. He wondered if he'd ever be at ease in his father's shoes.

"Right this way, Your Grace." The maid led him to a prettily decorated sitting room with colorful watercolors dotting the walls and lace doilies under every item on the mantel.

He was surprised to find that nothing screamed wealth or ostentation, but each surface spoke of comfort and family. Small miniatures of children and pets sat in silver and polished bronze frames on various surfaces in the room. He recognized the face of a young girl. She had the same notch in her chin as Lady Lillian.

"She was nine when that was painted," Lady Claxton said as she entered her drawing room. "Wouldn't sit still to save her life. We had to bribe her with the promise of a new toy for the artist to finish his work."

Nick turned to face the old woman and was surprised to see none of the ill will he expected in her eyes.

"I heard of the burning of the Tudor tower. Looks as if you played the hero too well."

"It's nothing." Nick gestured toward his bandage, marveling at how odd it felt to have someone stare at the opposite side of his face.

"Have you come to apologize, Tremayne?" She gestured toward a chair for him before settling onto a well-worn settee. "It's true I don't take kindly to my guests engaging in brawls when I've invited them to a ball, but I noted that you did avoid outright fisticuffs."

"Did I not offer apologies on the evening of the ball, Lady Claxton?" Nick hadn't come about the incident with the younger Lyle, but he was content to take his share of the blame if it would smooth the way for his real purpose in visiting. "If not, accept them now."

The older woman nodded and sniffed, as if that would do.

"The ball isn't why I've come."

"No?" She arched a silvery brow. "Shall I ring for tea while you tell me?"

"Not necessary, my lady. This won't take long." Nick shifted the edge of his chair and thought best how to broach the topic. "I would like your help."

"Beg your pardon?" The lady rose an inch and arched back in surprise. Then she narrowed one eye at him. "You've not visited any of the best families since arriving at Enderley and you've refused two invitations to dine at Claxton Hall. Now you wish for my help?" She lifted her lorgnette to examine him. "What's gotten into you, Tremayne?"

"Would you believe me if I said *love*?" Nick chuckled.

"Love?" A hint of a smile played around her lips, and then she sighed. "You don't mean my Lillian, do you?"

"I do not." Nick tugged on his ear, casting his gaze to the carpet. "I've asked Miss Thorne to be my wife."

She tilted her head, as if she wasn't certain she'd heard him. Nick waited, watching her frown ease and her eyes widen as understanding dawned.

"The steward's daughter? *Your* steward?"

"My future duchess."

"She's not a nobleman's daughter."

"She's perfect."

For a moment she looked forlorn, and she cast her gaze around her drawing room, as if seeking an answer. "You're the Duke of Tremayne," she finally said. "You'll do as you please."

"Nothing will please me more than marrying her, of that I can assure you."

She lifted her spectacle once more. "You do seem in earnest, Your Grace."

Nick smiled. The noblewoman wasn't pleased, but she was taking the news far better than he'd imagined on the carriage ride to Claxton Hall.

"I offer you felicitations and blessings, Tremayne, though I suspect you don't wish or need them. Or anything else from me."

"Actually, I do need something from you, Lady Claxton." Nick swallowed his pride. "I want Barrowmere society to accept Mina with open arms."

The old woman's brows shot up like two silver doves taking flight.

"Miss Thorne is well known within the village, and well liked, Your Grace."

"She'll be a duchess, Lady Claxton, and while I suspect she has a better notion of how to go about being one than I know how to be a duke, I want a promise from you that she will be accepted. Warmly."

"Others will think what they please."

Now it was Nick's time to narrow an eye. The noblewoman knew very well that others in Barrowmere society looked to her to lead the way.

Lady Claxton tapped her cane on the floor and sighed. "Very well. For my part, and my granddaughter's, we shall welcome Miss Tho—" She stopped herself before continuing on. "Your duchess into our circle. Shall we start with a dinner at Claxton Hall next week?"

"Thank you." Nick meant the words. Speaking them seemed to salve over a bundle of worries inside him.

They shook hands as Nick departed, and the old lady hung on for so long that Nick offered her a smile.

"You do know what you're about, Tremayne? London society will be more of a challenge than Barrowmere."

"I'm always up for a challenge, Lady Claxton." Letting go of even the portion of disdain he'd held for aristocrats like Lady Claxton, who'd been cronies of his father, felt extraordinary. Liberating. An echo of that moment he'd finally stepped out of that damnable tower.

The blackened husk of the structure came into view as the carriage drew into Enderley's drive. Nick drew in a sharp breath, expecting the usual wave of revulsion. But it didn't come.

All he truly felt was anticipation, an eagerness to see Mina.

Memories of what he'd endured in the tower didn't matter. They were just a pile of stones. Like the house and the stables and every structure on the estate.

She mattered. Only Mina and the life he wanted to build with her.

He bounded up the steps, burst through the front door, and headed straight for her office. Then he heard her voice and his heartbeat sped. The sound of conversation floated out from the sitting room where she'd tended his wounds.

Inside the room, he found her approaching the threshold with Mrs. Shepard, the lady he'd met at the vicarage. The one who'd harangued him about attending a country dance.

"Mrs. Shepard came to discuss details for the Christmas dance," Mina told him.

He liked that her breath quickened at the sight of him, just as his heart had begun racing the minute he spotted her.

"I do hope to see you there, Your Grace." The older woman skimmed her gaze over his bandaged face, a heartwarming look of concern shadowing her eyes.

"When is it, again?" Nick's chief memory of that day at the vicarage was of Mina, sitting in the corner, watching his every move. He'd spent most of the hours trying not to turn and gaze back at her.

"The Sunday before Christmas, Your Grace."

"What do you think, Miss Thorne?" Nick turned to Mina, and his skin instantly warmed. Would it be this distracting to be near her when they were wed? "Will the ballroom be finished by then?"

"Our ballroom?" She let out a little gasp that made his pulse jump and his groin tighten.

"Yes, our ballroom." He did like the sound of that.

"I believe so." Mina glanced at Mrs. Shepard and then back at him, lips parted, dimples flashing as she broke into a smile. "Would the village planning committee like for us to host the dance here at Enderley, Mrs. Shepard?"

"Why, yes," the older woman sputtered. "Yes, of course."

Nick waited impatiently while Mina saw Mrs. Shepard out. This desperate anxiousness was new. He was a man who'd spent years relishing his solitude, pretending loneliness never touched him.

Mina made him see that he hadn't loved being alone so much as he'd feared allowing anyone close. Now he craved her after five minutes of separation. How had he ever imagined they could live apart?

The sweetest bit was knowing that even when they were apart, she'd return.

When Mina stepped into the sitting room, he swept her into his arms and kissed her.

She didn't hesitate, didn't hold anything back, and that was the best part of all.

"Thank you," she said when he'd set her back on her feet. "For offering the ballroom. It's as if you've given the whole village an early Christmas gift." She ran her hand down his chest, hooking her fingers inside his waistcoat. "Puts me in mind of what manner of gift one gives a duke for Christmas."

"You," he told her without a moment's hesitation. "All I want is you."

"Wherever we are?"

"To tell you the truth, Duchess, when you're this close to me"—he pressed a hand to her lower back, pulling her body flush against his—"I don't notice where I am."

"Me neither." She lifted onto her toes, brushed her cheek against his, and whispered in his ear. "As long as we're together."

Nick tangled his hand in her hair, tipped up her face, and bent to kiss her. But he hesitated, whispering against her lips, "That's the only place I truly want to be."

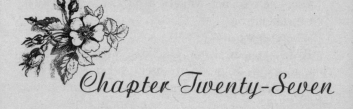

Chapter Twenty-Seven

In the end, Nick and Mina remained at Enderley far longer than expected.

After obtaining a special license, they married just as she'd suggested. A small ceremony was held at the village church with the local vicar presiding. Lady Claxton and her granddaughter attended, as well as Colin, a few villagers, and several members of Enderley's staff, including Wilder and Emma.

Iverson and Huntley arrived in Barrowmere an hour before the ceremony to stand up with him, offering their unwanted advice on marriage.

And it had been perfect. The happiest day of Nick's life. Until the next day. And the next. Each day with her still felt like a gift he didn't quite deserve.

As the holiday approached, it made sense to remain at the estate rather than return to his private quarters at Lyon's. He wished to make their first Christmas one she would never forget.

"Goodness, don't you look wonderful."

The sound of his duchess's voice never failed to fill his chest with warmth, not to mention what it did to other parts of his body.

He turned to watch Mina approach the corner of the Enderley conservatory where he was inspecting a few newly installed panes of glass.

He tracked her gaze as she took in the evening suit he'd ordered from London. None of the interest and admiration waned when she looked at his scarred face and odd eyes.

Strange, wonderful woman.

She bit her lip when her gaze locked on his mouth.

Nick swallowed hard, and then his own gaze widened when he noticed her clothes.

"You're wearing trousers to the dance?" Quite all right with him, of course. He would happily stare at the outline of her legs and backside all day, not to mention how much easier it was to touch her without layers of petticoats between them.

"Of course not." She nudged him playfully when they were standing chest to chest. "But I thought they were more appropriate while I assist with any last-minute arrangements for the dance."

"You needn't worry about such matters. This is a night for you to enjoy yourself, not worry about everyone else." Nick circled her waist with his arm and let his hand settle on the arch of her lower back. "That's why we hired more staff."

"The other staff expect me to assist them. I always have." She bit her lip, not in the seductive way that caused him to haul her into his arms and rush to the nearest bed, but in the way that meant she was fretting. "Besides, I like organizing. I'm good at it."

"You're good at many things." He bent to kiss her, a quick but reassuring taste of her lips. "You probably even have a list."

"Several, if you must know." She beamed proudly, but then her smile faltered. "I hope the staff will come to accept my change in circumstances."

They would. Nick would insist, and he'd seen no evidence that any of Enderley's existing servants were anything but pleased for their happiness.

"Anyone who knows you comes to love you." His voice roughened. He'd fallen under her spell quickly and never wished it to end. "Enderley's staff wish to see you happy. The villagers too. Don't worry about the likes of Magistrate Hardbrook. I suspect he'll come around too."

"And if he doesn't?"

"Then you can content yourself with knowing your husband loves and adores you." Nick pulled her tighter against him, needing her warmth and softness, needing her to feel how much he wanted her. "Alternatively, I'm prepared to pleasure you until you forget the stodgy magistrate."

Her breath hitched. He loved the sound of it and the evidence of how they affected each other.

Mina drew her hand along his waistcoat buttons, down his chest to the edge of his trousers. Nick knew they had a dance to attend within the hour, but part of him prayed she'd continue her explorations.

"This reminds me of the one you wore the first day we met," she said.

"You paid attention to my waistcoat?"

"Mmm." A mischievous grin carved dimples in her cheek. "More the way you looked in your waistcoat."

Talk of clothing made Nick want to remove every thread of hers. He dipped his head to kiss her again, but footsteps just over his shoulder stalled them both.

"A visitor to see you, Your Grace." Wilder stood two feet away.

Nick narrowed one eye at the old man. His footsteps were as quiet as Milly's and her little band of kittens.

"Who is it, Wilder?"

The old man's mouth tightened into a grimace. "Mr. Gregory Lyle, sir."

Mina tensed in his arms, and Nick suddenly wished he'd done more than slam the younger Lyle out of a saddle.

"Let me speak to him," Mina said softly.

Nick held his breath when he saw the determination in her gold-brown gaze.

"Trust me, Nick."

He did. Good grief, there were now four people he trusted. Five if he added Wilder. All things considered, he might even add Lady Claxton to the list.

This love business wasn't quite what he expected. It wasn't a tangle, but more of an unfettering. A feeling that grew and expanded, demanding to multiply and spread. Some sliver of it had begun to encompass the staff, the villagers, even the old stone walls of Enderley that Nick had spent so many years loathing.

"I do trust you," he told her. "But I wouldn't put my faith in him if he was the last man in England."

"Just let me see what he wants." She bounced up and pressed a kiss against his cheek.

Nick waited until she departed and then followed quietly, attempting to be as silent-footed as Wilder. He heard her voice and Lyle's emerge from the sitting room where Nick had rested, and made love to Mina, after his injuries.

"I don't care why you've come. Just go," she told the younger Lyle. "I've found happiness. More than you can imagine."

"If you'd just listen." Gregory Lyle's voice was oddly calm, not the high-pitched whine he'd employed during the business with the stallion. "I've merely come to apologize."

"Why?" Mina's tone was wary and gruff.

Nick grinned with pride.

"Because Lady Claxton insisted, and because you're the Duchess of Tremayne. Our families have resided side by side in this village for centuries. We should not be at war."

Nick bent his head, straining to hear her reply, but there was silence for a long stretch.

"Fine. I accept. Now go. You weren't invited, Mr. Lyle."

The young man had the audacity to chuckle at her.

Nick's hands tightened into fists.

"Goodness, Mina," the younger Lyle finally said. "Perhaps you will make a fierce duchess after all."

"I think I will. Now go before I punch you again."

Nick receded into the shadows of the hall as Lyle departed, then entered the sitting room to find Mina with her back to the door. She was staring out onto Enderley's fields, arms lashed across her chest, the toe of her boot tapping insistently against the carpet.

"Were you listening the entire time?" she asked without turning to look at him.

"Most of it," Nick admitted. "You punched him?"

She swung to face him. "Only the once."

"Well done." Nick approached and took her in his arms.

Mina tensed at first, then melted against him and twined her hands around his neck. "You're not appalled?"

"Why would I be?"

"A duchess shouldn't be throwing fists at viscounts' sons."

Nick stroked her cheek and wished her hair hadn't already been pinned into artful waves and delicate curls. He wanted to take it all down and slide his fingers through every strand.

"My darling hellion." He kissed her, moaning when she took the lead, merrily sinking her fingers into his hair and clutching at his shoulder to pull him closer. "You're my perfect duchess, whether you're organizing the staff or putting irritating noblemen in their places."

She pulled back, breathless. "I should change into my gown for the dance."

"Can I help?" Nick cupped her bottom in his hands. "At least with the undressing part?"

She quirked one brow. "If you did, we'd never make it back downstairs to the dance."

His duchess was being practical again.

Nick let out a long-suffering groan, kissed Mina one last time, and let her go.

MUSIC DRIFTED UP from downstairs and Mina smiled. She hadn't heard music at Enderley in so long. Years. It felt like forever.

Despite what he'd intended when he arrived, Nick's presence had brought more improvement to the estate than they'd seen in a decade.

He'd improved her life too, offering her more passion and joy than she'd ever dared to hope for. Nick held nothing back now, and that was the best gift of all.

Their marriage was still so new, some mornings she woke convinced it was all some fairy tale she'd dreamed. Until she found the warm muscled length of his body pressed against hers.

Nothing compared to the bliss of waking up in his arms.

After checking her gown and hair one last time in the mirror, Mina took a few deep, steadying breaths and started down to the ballroom. In her mind, she checked off the list of everything they'd done to prepare for the dance, hoping nothing had been forgotten.

Then she spotted Nick waiting for her at the bottom of the staircase.

Her breath snagged in her throat. Behind him, every staff member at Enderley had assembled, along with Mrs. Shepard and a few other villagers who'd arrived early.

They were all smiling, looks of encouragement and well wishes lighting their gazes. She feared backlash from the staff or that some in Barrowmere might think her an upstart for having risen from steward to duchess. But she'd underestimated them, and perhaps herself.

She'd certainly underestimated Nick.

Mina stumbled on the skirt of her dress, and Nick bolted up the stairs. He took her arm and stood close enough for his heat to warm her skin.

"I remember this gown fondly," he whispered. "Red becomes you, love."

She'd purchased the gown Mr. Iverson had loaned to her, knowing her sharp-eyed husband would recognize the dress.

"Makes me want to carry you down," he teased. "It's been too long since I had you in my arms."

"I was in your arms less than an hour ago."

"As I said, too long."

"Just let me hold on to you," Mina said as she slid her arm around his.

"Always."

As they descended, Mina noticed how busy the staff had been in the minutes since she'd gone up to dress. Candles were lit throughout the main hall, and rich red poinsettias and glossy holly leaves had been strategically placed on every flat surface. A few pots of flowers even lined the floor on the way to the ballroom.

"Welcome, everyone," she said to those assembled. "Let us be merry and make excellent memories this Christmas season."

"The blessings of the season to you, Your Grace." Wilder spoke in his deep, unwavering voice and offered her a gentle grin before stepping back and taking his place near the threshold to oversee the festivities.

Mina tightened her hold on Nick's arm, but her apprehension melted away.

"There've been a few changes in the ballroom," Nick said as they reached the bottom of the stairs. He'd taken over the project of overseeing the ballroom repairs and cagily kept her out of the room as they finished. "Would you like to see before the rest of the guests arrive?"

"Yes, show me."

Mina felt Nick's muscles tense as they reached the threshold, but he needn't have feared. The changes were spectacular. Her mouth fell open as she gaped at every inch of the glowing room.

"It's extraordinary."

He let out a trapped breath. "You like it?"

"I love every detail." She stepped forward and he let her go. "Thank you."

Not only had the leak been repaired, every wall had been repainted. Not in the original dove gray, but a warm gold. The frescoes had been cleaned, the floor polished until it glittered, and the wall sconces had been regilded so that they shone as bright as the candles flickering inside them.

"The gold reminds me of your eyes," Nick said. He'd come up behind her and placed his hand at the small of her back.

"My eyes are brown."

"Not when you look at me."

Mina looked up to find him smiling. He came around to face her.

"Those gilded sparks in your eyes. They captured me the first time you looked down from the oak tree. Little shards that lodged right here." He pressed a hand over his heart.

"Sounds painful," Mina teased.

"Agonizing." He bent forward and kissed her cheek. "Until you put me out of my misery."

Mina pulled Nick toward the center of the ballroom.

A few guests were milling near the refreshments, some stood taking in the frescoes, and others had drifted off to the drawing rooms to chat and await the start of the dance. When the musicians saw Mina and Nick step to the center of the ballroom, one violinist began to play.

Nick spun with her, and Mina's heart felt as if it might burst in her chest. The joy was almost too much.

As fairy tale endings went, she couldn't have asked for a better one.

"You don't mind dancing with me?" she asked him. "I know you're not fond of balls."

"I told you, Duchess. I'm prepared to give you anything you want."

"And you?" Mina held him closer than was proper, needing to feel his strength and warmth flush against her body. "What have I given you?"

"More than I deserve." He swallowed hard. "A kind of peace I didn't expect to come my way. Ever."

"Even here?" Mina traced the edge of his jaw with her fingers. "At Enderley?" She was still prepared to leave and not return, if that's what he wanted.

"We're together. That's all I need. Wherever we are, I won't even notice the walls. Only us."

"Us." Mina smiled so wide her cheeks ached. "I do like the way that sounds."

Nick smiled, glanced around to see if anyone was watching, and then bent to take her mouth in a searing kiss.

Epilogue

*H*untley frowned as if thoroughly confused, but one blond brow winged up as if he was willing to be intrigued. Iverson was so excited he bounded up from his chair and began beaming, rubbing his hands together as if he'd just won the entire contents of Lyon's vault.

"I take it you like the idea," Nick said drily from one of four chairs he'd set out for their meeting.

Across from him, Mina offered a smile that still caused heat to unfurl inside him.

"Explain it to me again." Huntley crossed one leg over the other and rested his clasped hands on his waistcoat. "No more gambling? No more fun?"

Nick chuckled as Iverson paced excitedly behind him. "I suggest we phase out game play slowly. Shift the purpose of the club and then consider our options."

"We could," Mina started, hesitated, and then continued on when the three of them stared at her expectantly. "Might I suggest that we set aside a few rooms where inventors could wait and prepare their documents and assemble their thoughts before presenting their ideas to you?"

"I like it," Iverson said immediately. "We needn't even see prospective inventors every day. We could set aside one or two days per week to hear their ideas. Bring in five on that day, perhaps."

"How many are we expecting?" Huntley suddenly looked less at ease. "You may love your bridges and railroads, Iverson, but handing out funds to every man in London with a wild idea will soon bankrupt all of us."

"We won't fund them all," Nick put in. "Just as I did not loan to every nobleman who visited me in the den. We listen, assess, and then decide if or how much to invest."

"Not all of them will come with viable ideas like the duchess's cousin." Iverson winked in Mina's direction.

Nick reminded himself the man was one of his dearest friends.

"Fairchild is eager to come with other ideas, so we already have one inventor interested."

Huntley stood too, though he didn't join Iverson in his excited pacing. He assessed the room. "So you're both certain this will continue to make us money? As much as the gaming tables?"

"We won't know until we try," Nick said, feeling extraordinarily hopeful. A sensation he wasn't used to, but he was learning to embrace, along with his wife's impulse to do good.

"And we'll celebrate after every decision to invest?" Huntley asked, then looked around the unadorned space. "This room could do with a drinks cart and more comfortable chairs."

Out of the corner of his eye, Nick saw Iverson shake his head and pinch the bridge of his nose. Mina's laughter carried across the room, making the dimly lit space feel brighter.

"Men don't come down to the den for entertainment and diversions, Huntley." Nick stood up from his chair and approached Mina.

The more he looked at her, the more Nick thought a diversion directly to their private quarters was in order. He'd expanded the space and Mina had made changes to make the rooms her own, but they were still searching for the perfect London townhouse to suit them.

"Are we agreed, gentlemen?" Iverson asked. "Shall we at least try Nick's idea of inviting inventors to the club and selecting a few to present their ideas one day per week?"

"Actually, Iverson." Nick wrapped an arm around Mina's waist and smiled down at her. "It wasn't my idea."

"Well done, Duchess," Iverson said as he shook Nick's hand. "And Duke."

"What shall we call this little investors' club of ours?" Huntley asked as he started toward the door.

Nick shrugged. "The noblemen always called it the den."

"Then it's the Duke's Den now." Huntley waved resignedly as he crossed the threshold. "I shall see you all next week with a pile of pounds to give away to some madman with a clever idea."

"He doesn't seem fully convinced," Mina whispered when he'd departed.

"Huntley is a bit of a pessimist," Iverson told her as he donned his overcoat and straightened the cuffs. "Don't let his n'er-do-well exterior fool you. He'll come around and he's bloody impulsive. The first time a man presents us with an idea he likes, he'll be the first to commit funds."

"What about a woman?" Mina asked.

Iverson frowned and then glanced at Nick with a bemused expression. "Huntley is very fond of the fairer sex."

Mina's laughter echoed off the low ceiling. "I meant what if a woman wishes to present her invention?"

Nick exchanged a raised brow glance with Iverson. They'd followed the custom of most gentlemen's clubs in not allowing women entrance or membership. But this was a new venture, and with Mina by his side, Nick was prepared to consider almost any possibility.

"Isn't that a thought," Iverson said with the hint of a smile. Apparently, he didn't mind the idea either. He turned his assessing gaze on Mina and then Nick. "You two make an excellent pair."

"I think so." Nick shook his friend's hand, one firm grip, as if they were agreeing to a bargain. "Between the two of you, I'm beginning to see the usefulness of progress."

When Iverson had gone, Nick turned to Mina and held her close. Her eyes were shadowed with worry, her brows dipped into a frown.

"What is it, Duchess?"

She stared at his shirtfront, toying with one of his buttons. "When I got word you were coming to Enderley, I was full of apprehension. I thought you'd dismiss me because I hadn't told the entire truth to your solicitor. Then—"

"I came and began burning artwork."

She choked back a burst of laughter. "It was just the one painting. But now I see that your arrival changed everything for the better." She pressed her lips together before looking up at him. "And now I've suggested that you change everything you hold dear. Are you sure it's for the better?"

Nick bent his head and kissed her softly, then whispered against her lips, "Yes."

"No doubts?"

"None." Lifting his head, he gazed around the space where he'd taken such glee in watching other men suffer. He quite liked the notion of undoing that avarice by giving smart inventors like Colin Fairchild a chance. "You have changed my life, Mina, but whether I knew it or not, I was in desperate need of alteration."

She lifted onto her toes and pressed her mouth to his, her fingers tracing the edge of his jaw. "Not entirely, I hope. There's quite a lot about you"—she trailed her hand down his body—"that I like just as it is."

Nick reached down and clasped her hand, then started toward the door.

Mina hesitated only a moment and asked in an amused tone, "Where are we going?"

Over his shoulder, Nick grinned at his wife. "To our chamber. I thought perhaps you could show me all the parts you like."

Iverson's story is next in

Anything But
a Duke

On sale May 2019 from Avon Books!
Pre-order now!